Praise for

The L

Marian Rizzo's *The Leper* is far more than just a simple, uncomplicated Bible story you've come to expect from Sunday School; all fluff and flannel graph with no soul, no danger, no depth. Instead, Rizzo imagines a first-century world where real human beings interact with real human motivations: greed, lust, distain, ambition. She crafts a main character with flaws—major flaws—making readers waffle between feeling sorry for Eleazar and truly disliking him. She paints the backdrop between the cosmopolitan melting-pot of Alexandria and first-century Jerusalem with a broad brush, bringing the City of David to life and populating it with the poor and rich; with pompous religious leaders and disdainful Romans; and with those who follow a popular new teacher reported to have miraculous powers. Ultimately, *The Leper* is a timeless tale of sin and consequences, of damaged people finding faith and redemption.

~Paula K. Parker
Author of the *Sisters of Lazarus* trilogy

One of the most important things I do as a bookstore owner is read a lot. I want the story to not only entertain me, but also to convict me...and *The Leper* does that. It will take you to another place and another time. Yes, the story is fiction, but the lesson is real and relevant for today.

~Marge Forrest
Owner of Gabriel's Christian Book & Supply
Ocala, Florida.

The Leper

Also by Marian Rizzo

Angela's Treasures
Muldovah
In Search of the Beloved
In Search of Felicity
Presence in the Pew
Plague
O Holy Night: A Christmas Gift Book
Silver Springs (with Dr. Robert Knight)

The Leper

a novel

MARIAN RIZZO

WordCrafts Press

The Leper
Copyright © 2021
Marian Rizzo

ISBN: 978-1-952474-96-5

Cover concept and design by David Warren.

Published by WordCrafts Press
Cody, Wyoming 82414
www.wordcrafts.net

To my three grandchildren,
Scarlet, Zelda, and Korbin Jones,
that they may come to know the One True God
and be prepared to serve Him.

And, in memory of baby Rachel,
who is already living with our Savior.

PART ONE
Eleazar, the Boy

"My son, forget not my law; but let thine heart keep my commandments: For length of days, and long life, and peace, shall they add to thee."

Proverbs 3:1–2

CHAPTER ONE
Jerusalem, circa B.C. 4

 $\mathcal{T}$hirteen. His time had come. He'd fulfilled the required recitations and rituals of childhood learning, had sat at the feet of
the rabbi, had obeyed the law—or had pretended to. Now he
could move away from his youth and take his rightful place. Not
yet able to call himself a man, he had approached the threshold
of manhood. And it felt good.

His mother had made a feast. The neighbors had brought gifts.
An embroidered tunic from the widow Minsa. A Torah scroll
presented by Rabbi Heth. A vial of myrrh from his mother's
box of ointments. And from his best friend, Achim, a pouch
of ivory, brought from the coast by the boy's father, a traveling
merchant. There were other gifts, but none could compare with
the one his father had presented to him.

Now he leaned over the pile of presents and lifted the wooden
box with its hand-carved artistry and his name carved into the
handle. He lifted the latch and raised the protective cover. Inside
lay the basic tools of his chosen profession, the one his father
practiced, and his grandfather, and several generations before
them. Like his ancestors, he would be a physician.

There was still much to learn. But hadn't he already helped
his father keep order in their rooftop apothecary? Hadn't he

learned the use of the saw and the blade and the many powders and potions on the shelf? Tomorrow would introduce him to a whole new set of skills during his time on the streets of Jerusalem at his father's side.

His heart fluttered with excitement. A door of adventure had opened up to him. And beyond, the opportunities appeared limitless.

As he sorted through the various tools in the box his father had provided, his joy diminished slightly. Judah had charge over the work they would do. Tomorrow, and every day thereafter. The old man had taken him aside after the guests had left their home.

"I have much to teach you, Eleazar," Judah told him, his voice low but firm. "Under my guidance, you will learn the disciplines of the field of medicine. Disciplines that go beyond the furnishing of herbs and salves and poultices, beyond the binding of wounds and the setting of broken limbs."

Eleazar's momentary joy began to fade.

"Yes," Judah said, nodding. "All those things will serve you well." The old man's furry eyebrows went up. "But, I want to teach you far more, my son. I want you to learn to use your heart. As you minister to our neighbors, you must hurt with them, bleed with them, and even cry with them. The work of medicine can do little good without the sincere compassion of the physician."

He gazed in puzzlement at his father, had tried to look deeper into those steel gray eyes, but had found nothing within their depths except the same unyielding presence that had ruled their home for as long as he could remember. A bitterness rose to his throat and remained there, burning. With only a few sentences his father had smashed his dreams. Where in all of that could he find a word of praise? A promise of fame and fortune? A prediction of a fine home, a family of his own, and freedom to make his own choices?

This was not the kind of lecture that could send a young man into the future with confidence.

Suddenly, the words of the law surfaced. *Honor your father*

*and your mother: that your days may be long upon the land which
the Lord your God gave you.*

He shook his head. While he could easily honor his mother—
the one person who understood him—he was painfully aware
of the barrier that had risen between himself and his father.

His mother had seen it too, and she'd done little to remove
it. Instead, Mara had drawn closer to her son. With whispered
promises she had encouraged him to stray from his father's
plan for his life.

"One day you will be the greatest physician in all Judea," his
mother told him in private, her brown eyes glistening with
pride. "Consider your future, Eleazar. You must move beyond
the impoverished souls your father prefers to heal and set your
eyes on the Upper City. Serve the rich and the powerful. In the
end, a seat on the Great Council may come within your grasp."
Then, with a tilt of her head and a sweet smile she presented
this entreaty: "You will take care of your mother, won't you?"

He grinned back at her. "Of course, Mother. You have
my word."

"Never speak of the Great Council before your father," she
warned him then. "Judah ben Serach does not approve of those
religious leaders or their oral traditions."

He briefly recalled his father's abhorrence of the group he
often referred to as "the Pompous Seventy."

"Those self-righteous hypocrites will try to control you, Eleazar," Judah had cautioned him. "They will promise you a place
of honor. Do not fall into their trap."

Eleazar had shrugged off the warning and preferred to hold
onto the sweet promises his mother had placed before him.

Eleazar's bond with his mother went beyond their plans for
his future. At first glance, few people would doubt he was her
son. Tall and slender, she was a handsome woman with long,
sinewy arms and legs. In the same way, Eleazar had grown a
head taller than most of the boys his age. Like Mara he also had
a crop of thick brown curls, and he'd inherited her regal nose,

long neck, and a natural sweep to the shoulders that implied self-confidence. He was aware that he also walked like her, more of a long-legged stroll that drew admiring gazes from the young females in the city.

In contrast, Judah was two inches shorter than his wife. He had a stocky build, thick, hairy arms, and big hands. The old man often complained of pain in his legs and an ache in his back, most likely due to the odd slant of his spine and the long hours he spent walking the hills of Jerusalem.

Eleazar had inherited only one physical trait from his father—steel gray eyes that seemed to look right into the soul of a person, a valuable asset for someone who planned to make his own way one day. He already knew how to use his father's hard, cold stare when facing down an adversary, like the time he confronted Levi over a desired place before the rabbi. The skinny weasel had scampered off to the back row. What use might such a quality avail in other aspects of life? There seemed no limit to whatever Eleazar wanted to achieve, for he'd acquired the best attributes of both parents.

Meanwhile, Eleazar's younger brother, Simon, was the exact image of their father from his copper-colored, straw-like hair and square jaw to his stocky frame and awkward stance. But a steel-eyed penetrating stare? Hardly. Simon had his mother's eyes, brown and dull. The boy was only six years old. In another year he would make the long walk to the temple and sit at the feet of Rabbi Heth. Then Simon would follow the same path Eleazar had taken, perhaps find his future in the work of medicine as well. But Eleazar could not imagine a strong future in one so meek.

As for Eleazar, he had drifted easily through the early learning stages. He had memorized a large section of the Torah, plus the Psalms and several of Solomon's Proverbs. In a sense, he had earned the right to sit among the elite. But, although he'd reached the threshold of adulthood, it troubled him that his father refused to let him wear the desired tefillin, not even at temple services. Eleazar frowned with bitterness, for he knew the significance of those tiny leather boxes. The men of the city placed verses of scripture inside. They strapped the tefillin to their arms and foreheads and opened them for recitations. Some used the Greek word: *phylacteries*. Eleazar didn't care what they called them. Such were the possessions that would have brought the attention of the Great Council.

But his father had frowned with final authority. "Those who flaunt their faith are not worthy of the Almighty's blessing," the old man had growled. "Look at the Pharisees. They wear long robes with tassels and they display their phylacteries like crowns. They strut through the streets with their noses pointed toward heaven." To Eleazar, this painted a great image. But Judah shook his head with emphasis. "No, Eleazar. You will not join their arrogance. You will recite the scriptures without having to depend on a slip of parchment in a box."

And so, it was no surprise when his first two days of training on the streets of Jerusalem had proven even more disappointing. As his mother had warned him, Judah took him to the Lower City where they entered one mud-brick hovel after another and handed out medicines to the poorest of the poor. In the evening, they returned home with little to show for their labors—a handful of shriveled vegetables and a loaf of moldy bread, but no coins worthy of a physician's hire. His father had smiled graciously and had received the meager payments without complaint. At home he placed the wilting vegetables in the hands of Eleazar's mother who tore them in pieces and fed the scraps to the animals. Though she said nothing, the lines on Mara's forehead gathered in an angry frown, and her dark eyes sent silent daggers at her husband who skillfully ignored them by turning his face away.

On Eleazar's third day of training, he left the house expecting more of the first two days' disappointments. Before he and his father departed, Mara drew close to him and lowered her voice. Judah was in the courtyard loading their donkey with supplies, at that distance unable to hear Mara's whispered warnings.

"Be aware, my son, your father is going to take you to a place where you will not want to go." Her brown eyes darkened even more. "Keep your distance, Eleazar. Protect yourself. This service is your father's choice. It doesn't have to be yours." She shook her head and released a troubled sigh. "Though I implored him to leave you home today, he insisted on including you in this part of his work. The poor man believes it's his duty to minister to those who have no hope." She spat out the next words. "He would sacrifice his own family if necessary."

Without another word, Mara embraced him, the bulge of her abdomen a reminder of the life that was forming within her.

She stepped back and brushed a curl from his forehead. She straightened his shirt and nodded her approval. Then, her eyes filling with moist pride, she released him to his father's charge.

As before, Eleazar and Judah left the house at the break of dawn. This time, instead of carrying a scrip of medicines, his father had piled several bulging sacks on the back of Balaam, their one donkey. With the graying of the awakening sky, they turned onto the stony path that led to the Lower City. Damp walls rose up on either side of them. The stench of human waste began to fill the air along with the odor of yesterday's garbage as they drew closer to the Dung Gate. At the crisp sound of the shofar emanating from the temple, the heavy gate swung open, and Eleazar passed from the stifling city into a blast of fresh air on the ridge. He inhaled deeply of the mountain breeze and caught the welcoming scent of sweet calamus and roses.

Eleazar followed his father along the narrow winding trail from one level to the next. They moved beyond the grassy hillside onto the rocky path, descended to the valley below, then rose to the three rolling peaks of the Mount of Olives. At the crest, a vast wilderness stretched before them, and in the distance the pink-hued mountains of Moab stood majestically against the pale blue sky. With the rising of the sun beyond those hills life came to the desert. Red and yellow wildflowers turned their faces toward the heavens. Patches of myrtle boasted clusters of white blossoms. The sweet scent of purple rockrose and the delicate aroma of white narcissus filled the air.

Eleazar tried to suppress the surge of excitement. He took a deep breath, inhaled the mix of nature, and looked ahead with anticipation. He knew this place, had eyed it from a distance. The miserable ones lived there. His mother's warning came back to him. *He would sacrifice his own family to help the forbidden ones.*

The forbidden ones. A chill ran through him. He looked with trepidation at the row of caves. It was too late to turn back.

CHAPTER TWO

For a while they followed the Jericho Road. In recent years the former footpath had fallen under Roman control. The helmeted invaders had turned many of the able-bodied Jews into slaves, forcing merchants, gardeners, and craftsmen to roll up their sleeves and labor for long hours building up the crumbling roads with layers of mud and clay, then smoothing the surface with a heavy paste of stones and mortar. The finished roadways crossed in a giant web across Judea and beyond, to the far reaches of the Roman Empire.

Eleazar looked at the path before him and marveled at the transformation. He stepped easily along the smooth surface and enjoyed the kiss of sunlight on his brow. Balaam's hooves set off a resounding *clop, clop, clop* in the still morning air. Eleazar could walk forever, if necessary, even as far as the coast by the Great Sea.

"Pay attention, Eleazar," the old man interrupted his thoughts. "During our last two days we ministered to the poor of the city of Jerusalem." Eleazar knew that. He gave his father a sideways glance. "We received meager payment for our labor," Judah went on. Eleazar knew that too and stifled a smirk. "But," Judah said with emphasis. "The Almighty has observed our kindness to the poor. He will reward us in due time."

Judah's words slipped through Eleazar's ears and died within the twitter of a purple-and-green starling perched in a nearby acacia tree. As they drew closer, their footsteps resounded on the path, and the tiny bird spread its iridescent wings and left the branch, drawing Eleazar's gaze with it.

Oblivious to the distraction, Judah went on teaching his son. "Today you will reach yet another level of service," he said, his eyes fixed on the horizon ahead. "You will learn to care for those who have lost all hope of physical healing. They are painfully sick and have great need of kindness, the greatest medicine of all. Rejected by others. Separated from their families. Banned from the city, only to face a slow and agonizing death."

As he had feared, the old man suddenly left the level path and turned onto a rocky trail leading to the limestone ridge. Eleazar froze, his eyes on the row of dark, ominous holes.

Judah began the climb, tugging Balaam behind him. Together, they wove slowly upward along a narrow trail. The bundles shifted on Balaam's back and the animal lost his footing. The flailing hooves kicked up a cloud of pebbles. Dust rained down on Eleazar. He dodged the flying particles.

"Eleazar!" Judah's annoyed call sailed down to him. With a sweep of his arm the old man commanded him to follow.

Eleazar swallowed hard. He looked behind him at the city on the hill. He could go back. But that would be the end of his training. His father would never tolerate such insolence. Reluctantly, he stumbled upward, but he stopped short of the top. Several cloaked figures emerged from the holes in the rock. Silently, he numbered them. Eight forms gathered along the ridge. Though hunched beneath an invisible weight, they appeared to be men. Eight men coming out of hiding to meet with Judah. One of them, a tall man, stood out among the others, like a leader, directing them closer, then holding up one hand to keep them at an approved distance.

Three more forms, slight ones, remained half hidden in the opening of one of the caves. These were women. Eleazar felt a stirring in his heart as he remembered a lesson taught by Rabbi Heth. The disease was not selective. It struck men, women, and even children.

Rabbi Heth's teaching came back with full force. The law was clear. These people had been inspected by the priest and had been condemned to a life of seclusion. They would spend the rest of their days in misery with no possibility of a cure, and no hope of ever seeing their loved ones again. Over time, the agonizing disease would consume their entire bodies, and their only release would be the grave.

He glared at his father. Now he knew where Judah went once a month with Balaam laden with sacks of food and clothing. His mother had mumbled bitterly each time Judah left. Now he was seeing it for himself.

He remained in the shadows and watched with interest. The old man pulled the packs from the donkey's back and dropped them to the ground, stirring up a puff of dust with each *thump* of a sack. He no sooner unloosed the cords and stepped back, than the men moved in and made quick work of the dried meat, cheese, and raisin cakes, the horns of goat's milk, and the wrappings of roast vegetables. Then, one of them, the tallest in the group, lifted a bundle and carried it to the women in the opening of the cave. Like hungry jackals, they tore it open and devoured its contents. When they finished, they tossed the empty sack to the ground and disappeared within the darkness of the cave.

Eleazar's mouth had gone dry. He lifted his goatskin to his lips and swallowed the sweet milk. It soothed the bitterness in his stomach. He kept his eyes on his father. He didn't share the man's compassion for these forsaken ones. Images unexpectedly filled his mind. These people were once active citizens of Jerusalem. They gathered at the city gate and talked about their work and their travels and their families. He blinked and saw what they had become. Broken, withered, soiled by the blood of their own excrement.

Their meal over, the men stepped away and settled in a half circle by the wall. Only one man—the tall one—remained in front of Judah, still keeping a suitable distance. There was no embrace, no customary planting of kisses on each cheek. Yet, there was something familiar about this man, the way he glided across the ridge, the sweep of his arm as he spoke with Judah.

"I have kept you in my prayers, Serus," his father said, his voice unnaturally soft.

Serus. The name sparked a memory. Yes. The robust priest who once strode across the men's court and performed his temple duties with confidence. Now, stripped of his priestly attire, he wore a tattered cloak that hung in limp folds over a body that had all but wasted away. His eyes had taken on the dull and lifeless resolve of the lost.

Eleazar's mind shifted back several months to the day Serus left Jerusalem. That was when Judah began to make these mysterious trips outside the city, always taking along packs of food and clothing and medicines. He'd never thought to question the strange occurrence.

"My wife and my children—are they well?" Serus asked, raising his eyebrows. "Is my son pursuing the priesthood as I requested? And, my daughter? Will her pending marriage take place as planned?"

Judah nodded. "Your fellow priests have provided food for your family. They have encouraged your son to continue in his studies. You need not worry about your family, Serus. Your wife and children obeyed the usual rituals. They burned your clothes and had the walls of your house cleansed. Since your departure, your neighbors have looked after them as they would their own relatives. Take heart, my friend. Your daughter will be wed after the Sabbath. All is well."

Serus' eyes glistened with tears. A lump came to Eleazar's throat. A mix of sadness and fear came over him. If the disease could strike a healthy man like Serus, anyone could fall prey to it. Immediately, he felt an urgency to leave this place.

He caught his breath. Serus had pulled open his cloak and had exposed a patch of broken skin at his neck.

Eleazar watched in horror as Judah leaned closer to examine the wound.

"The lesion seems to have spread," Judah said.

Serus frowned and quickly drew the cloth over the blemish. "I used the medicine you brought last month." He sighed with sadness. "It didn't help, Judah."

The old man reached inside his medical scrip and pulled out a small pouch. He dropped it in Serus' open hand.

"It's a powder I made from the petals of the yellow rue plant that grows in abundance near the Great Sea," Judah said. "A merchant friend sold me a supply of it. Mix it into a paste with the olive oil I am leaving with you. Spread it on your wound. My friend reported having great success with the mixture."

Even before Judah finished speaking, Serus was shaking his head. "I'm afraid it's hopeless."

"Try it, Serus. What harm can it do?"

With a sigh, Judah lifted the empty sacks from the ground and draped them across Balaam's back. The beast brayed and shuffled his feet, eager to leave. A surge of relief ran through Eleazar.

"My prayers are with you," Judah told the priest.

Serus wiped tears from his eyes. Then he turned his attention on Eleazar, who'd been satisfied to remain in the shadows. Now, under Serus' gaze, he squirmed with discomfort.

"So, this is your son?" Serus said.

Judah raised his chin. "Yes, my son has completed his studies at the temple and has begun his training with me."

"Thirteen." Serus shook his head. "Amazing, Judah. I remember when he was this high." He gestured with one hand at the level of his waist. "But, Judah, why did you bring him to this forsaken place? Do you really want this to be part of his training?"

Judah nodded. "The boy has a rebellious streak." His words cut into Eleazar's heart. "He needs to know that our work is not only about medicine. He needs to develop a compassion for the less fortunate." He set his gaze on Eleazar and sighed.

Eleazar pinched his lips together. Rebellious streak? His mother would have described him as independent, courageous, mature beyond his years. He glared at his father.

"I want my son to learn every part of my work," Judah went on. "One day, he will serve the pampered rich in the Upper City, for that seems to be his desire. Those grumblers will pay well for his services. But, while I still have charge of him, I will show him a more righteous path. We spent the first two days of his training in the Lower City. He got to minister to the poorest of the poor. And, yes, I wanted him to see this place, too, Serus. Why shouldn't I introduce him to the most rejected people of all—those who are at death's door—or wish they were?"

Eleazar hadn't moved. Relief swept over him when Judah grabbed the donkey's lead and was about to head down the hill.

Suddenly, a hunched shadow emerged from the cave of women and shuffled to the edge of the ridge. Using a staff for support, the frail creature hobbled into the bright sunlight, her eyes on Eleazar.

"Shemiah!" she cried out. "My boy."

She allowed her cloak to drop from her head. Her face, gray and wrinkled, was framed with a mass of silver strands. She moved past Serus and started down the path toward Eleazar.

He caught his breath and took a step back. The heel of his right foot balanced on the edge of the cliff and his left foot remained frozen to the path.

Serus moved past her and cut between them. "She doesn't know what she's saying. For years she's waited for her son to visit her. He never comes." He held up a hand. "Hilda, this is not Shemiah. Return to the cave."

The old woman pushed past him and took another step toward Eleazar.

"Shemiah," she breathed.

His heart pounding, Eleazar looked from side to side. There was no escape. He tried to turn, but his foot remained fixed.

Serus grabbed for the woman's arm. She evaded his hand and drew closer to Eleazar. Her lips parted, and a foul odor oozed from her mouth. She reached out and pressed bony fingers into his shoulder. The cliff was directly behind him.

"Shemiah?" she pleaded, her eyes filling with tears.

He shook his head, looked to his father for help, then sent a silent plea to Serus. The priest lunged toward them, but the old woman began to cough. A vile-smelling liquid spewed from her mouth and struck Eleazar's cheek.

Serus pulled her back. Eleazar tore off his cloak and used it to wipe the spittle from his cheek. He glared at Serus and the old woman. Then he turned his anger on Judah.

"Look what's happened, Father. I've been defiled."

"Please, forgive this offense," Serus said, his brow lined with concern. "My boy, you must follow the law. When you arrive in Jerusalem, go to the Temple and arrange for a ritual cleansing. And please, do not let what happened here affect your compassion for these unfortunate ones." He gestured toward the bottom of the hill. "There's a spring a short distance from the path. Go there now and wash yourself."

Eleazar turned his back on Serus and lunged down the hill. He stumbled over the rocky terrain until he reached the spring at the bottom. Then he tossed his robe to the ground, and began to bathe away the filth. A few moments later, his father came close with their donkey. He drew up beside Eleazar.

"My son—" The old man began, but Eleazar cut him off with an angry glance.

Bitter words stuck in his throat. Again, the law came to him. *Honor thy father and thy mother.* But how could he honor someone who had so little regard for his safety, someone who had goals in life he could never share?

A bitterness settled in Eleazar's heart. Words wouldn't come, but they weren't necessary, for Judah must have seen the hostility in his son's eyes. The old man backed away and fell silent. Quietly, he pulled a flint from his pack, struck it several times against a rock, and set Eleazar's contaminated cloak ablaze. The fire dwindled, and he tossed sand on the pile of ashes.

"Let's go home," the old man said, and a certain sadness had entered his tone.

They made it to the Jericho Road in silence. Eleazar looked back at the hills only once. The caves seemed less threatening from this distance, just a row of black openings with no sign of life around them. Beyond the ridge stood the mountains of Moab, their mauve peaks streaked with gold created a peaceful background in contrast to the horror that lurked within those caves.

Setting his jaw, he turned toward Jerusalem. He lengthened his stride and quickly moved ahead of his father and the donkey.

"Eleazar!" Judah called after him. "Wait for me."

A smirk crossed Eleazar's lips. Already he had taken the first step toward his independence. Quickening his pace, he set his eyes on the Holy City and left his father and their plodding animal trailing far behind.

CHAPTER THREE

Eleazar's cleansing began with a ritual bath and concluded with a grain offering at the temple. He spent a restless night with images of the old woman swirling around in his head. Like a corpse rising from an open sepulcher, she floated toward him, her lips parted, her eyes aflame. He felt the sting of her vile liquid, flinched away from her outstretched fingers, cowered at the sound of her shriek, "Shemiah."

A cry lodged in his throat. Waking, he sat upright, his body damp and shivering. He raised his knees and hid his face between them. It was only a dream. But so real. He glanced about the room, comforted by the familiarity of the furnishings. There was the kitchen, the smoldering hearth, the scattered cushions, the pottery, the candles and bowls, and beyond hung the veil to his parents' quarters. The rumble of his father's nightly breathing momentarily soothed Eleazar's pounding heart.

He turned his attention to his brother, Simon, slumbering, undisturbed, on the mat beside him. Raising his head he peered through the open window high on the wall. A star-speckled blanket of darkness spread across the sky. A nearly full moon cast a beam on his corner, and he was reminded of the Almighty Creator Rabbi Heth spoke about.

He lay back and rested his head on his pillow. Perhaps a

prayer. But how could he confess the rebellion that lay within his heart? The Almighty wouldn't approve.

Then his mother's words came rushing back to him.

Consider your future, Eleazar. You must move beyond the impoverished souls your father prefers to heal and set your eyes on the Upper City. Serve the rich and the powerful. In the end, a seat on the Great Council may come within your grasp.

He slept easier then with that promise swirling around in his head. He didn't wake again until the sun was fully overhead.

Refreshed, he rose from his bed, eager to resume his training, confident that his mother's desire for him would prevail. For now he would face the days with patience.

He found her in the courtyard pulling herbs from the garden. Her abdomen, heavy with her third child, prevented her from reaching the lower plants. At the sound of Eleazar's footsteps she straightened, and, sighing, she pressed her hand against the small of her back.

"So," she said, arching an eyebrow. "At last, you understand what I've been complaining about all these years." She shook her head and frowned. "Your father spends most of his working hours in the Lower City serving people who can't pay. Then he takes a day away from them to minister to the forbidden ones." She waved the clump of herbs in her hand. "Look around you, my son. Do you see any of the fine things the wife of a physician enjoys? Do you see marble floors, raised tables, cushioned seats? Do you see a cupboard laden with food, expensive Phoenician platters, wine from the vineyards by the Great Sea? No, Eleazar. We have little to show for your father's labors. He serves the poor, yes, and he makes us poor along with them."

Eleazar glanced around at what had been familiar to him, but now he saw his surroundings through his mother's eyes and agreed. Everything appeared to be decaying, from the mended furnishings inside the kitchen to the crack in the laver to the crumbling shelter where the animals stayed.

Mara rested her free hand on her abdomen. "Look at your

mother," she said, drawing his attention away from the house. Her dark eyes filled with tears. "Do you see me clothed in fine silks? Am I adorned with gold and jewels?" She lifted her skirt and shook it. "Rags. Rags. I am ashamed to go to the marketplace, for fear someone will mistake me for a beggar."

He stood speechless. Though he'd heard the muffled arguments on the other side of the veil, his mother had never complained outwardly to him.

She let her skirt drop and gestured toward the house. "Tell me, Eleazar, where are my servants? I am awaiting another child, and I must labor from dawn to dusk, with only one handmaid to lighten my load. The wife of a physician should live like a *queen*, not like a pauper."

He drew close, wrapped his arms around her, and pressed his forehead against her neck. "Don't be anxious Mother. You *will* live like a queen one day. I promise." He drew back and looked her in the eye. "When I am a physician, I'll keep to the Upper City and visit the homes of the lawyers and scribes and merchants. I'll give healing to the Pharisees and the men of the Great Council. They'll pay well for my services." He smiled with encouragement. "One day, you'll have everything you want—a large house, fine clothing, new furniture, and as many servants as you want to do your bidding."

The frown eased from her face, and she returned his smile.

Heartened, he went on. "I'm going to need your help, Mother."

She nodded. "Anything, my son."

"I want to consider a different path for my training. After witnessing my father's work, I no longer wish to learn under him. I would prefer to accompany another physician. Nahum, perhaps. You know him, Mother. He's a highly-respected physician in Judea. I can learn the ways of medicine far quicker under his guidance than with my father."

A sad resolve darkened Mara's face. "That's not possible, Eleazar. The law—"

"Forget the law. We can present our cause before the Council.

We have good reason. Once we have reported my father's faults, how he's misused his position and failed to care for his own, none of the leaders would be able to refuse my request. Think about it, Mother. Nahum is dedicated to his profession. He studied in Egypt. *In Egypt,* Mother. He has established himself among the most important men of Judea. He's a member of the Great Council. He will be flattered when he learns of my request."

Mara's eyebrows went up. A flood of pride filled her steady gaze. "You never cease to amaze me, my son. Such wisdom. Such determination." She grew serious then. "It will be difficult to get the approval from the Council without a word from your father. If Judah had died, we would be able to seek out another teacher. But he's very much alive, and you must not insult him in this way."

"Will you help me convince him? Today? Before we set out? If we approach him together, he can't refuse."

His mother's eyes sparkled with renewed optimism. She placed a hand on his shoulder. "Yes, I will speak to your father." She released a sigh. "But, I'll do so alone."

Eleazar was about to protest. Mara raised her hand and stopped him.

"Judah is a stubborn man," she reminded him. "Your father adheres to the law with an unyielding tenacity. I doubt he will let another physician train you. But, I will do all I can to convince him that it would be best for you and for him."

"And if he refuses?"

A firmness settled the lines on her face. "Then you must continue on as you started. Under your father's instruction you can still become one of the greatest physicians in Judea. Once he is finished with you, like Nahum, you can go to Alexandria. You will learn from the finest physicians and scholars in the world. Then, you will—"

The scraping of footsteps drew their attention to the door of the house. Judah had emerged, shirtless and with a towel tied around his waist. A broad-shouldered man, he stopped walking and rubbed the back of his neck.

"Mara, I'm not sleeping well. Go to the ridge today, gather some branches of hyssop, and make a soft pillow for me."

Mara and Eleazar locked eyes. An unspoken message passed between them. Eleazar shook his head with disgust. Unaware, Judah cleared his throat, spat on the ground, and ambled toward the laver.

"Weave one for yourself as well," he mumbled. Then he splashed water on his face and upper body. He freed the towel at his waist, dried himself, and returned to the house.

Eleazar faced his mother. A sadness had swept the sparkle from her eyes, but she managed a half smile.

"I have sweetbreads warming on the hearth," she said. "And these herbs will make a tasty brew to start your day," she added raising the bundle. "Wash yourself, Eleazar, and allow me a little time to speak with your father."

Eleazar watched her go, then he went to the laver. The cool water refreshed his body and his spirit. While he bathed, he glanced anxiously toward the open door. Then, when he felt enough time had passed, he entered the house and caught his mother's eye. She shook her head, and he knew. His father had refused their request.

Judah was staring at him, his jaw set, his gray eyes piercing Eleazar's. "Today, you will accompany me to the Lower City again," his father said, his tone firm. "A true physician cares for the lowly. Such service requires compassion, kindness, and unselfish generosity." Judah walked toward him and continued speaking. "You cannot learn such qualities under the counsel of a rich and selfish man like Nahum. He has his methods, and I have mine. Until you develop a compassion for the poor, I will not release you to learn under the guidance of another."

Eleazar looked anxiously at his mother. She turned away, went to the hearth, and busied herself there.

"Don't concern yourself with your mother," Judah growled, drawing Eleazar's attention back to him. "She has made your request, and I have denied it. Now gather your cloak and your scrip, and let us be on our way."

Casting an angry glance at the old man, Eleazar snatched his cloak from the hook on the wall. Then he grabbed the leather pouch his mother had packed with food for the day, and he started for the door.

His mother met him there with a cake of sweetbread in one hand and a steaming cup in the other. He accepted the cake, downed it in three bites, and followed with a careful sipping of the herbed liquid. He drained the cup and returned it to his mother. Their eyes met long enough for him to catch her message. *It won't be long, my son. Soon you will make your own way.*

Mara thrust a skin of goat's milk in Eleazar's hand. He flung the strap over his shoulder, then, frowning, he left the dwelling and waited in the courtyard while his father mounted the outer stair to their rooftop apothecary.

A few moments later, the old man descended the stairs with a pack of medicines and ointments dangling from a strap on his shoulder. They left the donkey behind this time and proceeded on foot down the pebbled road toward the Lower City, the most miserable, desolate part of Jerusalem. The entire section lay a short distance from the Dung Gate and within smelling distance of the city's refuse and waste.

The sun rose above the city wall, but its glow was lost among the decaying dwellings on both sides of the street. A cold dampness clung to the limestone walls. Uneven roofs sagged beneath layers of palm branches. Unlike the mansions in the Upper City, there were no courtyards here, just clumsily-made shelters, strung together in an endless wall of poverty. Tattered curtains flapped in the doorways. An old man peered at them from a solitary window. A woman emerged from an opening and flapped a bedcover, sending dusty particles into the gray morning light. An asphyxiating odor rose from puddles of waste beside the road.

"Father, we've already spent two days in this horrible place. Have you no concern for the people in the Upper City?"

Judah stopped walking and stood in front of him, his face grave. "The Upper City?" Judah said with a hint of displeasure.

"All the other physicians in Judea rush to help the wealthy. They don't need us, Eleazar. Look around you." He swept one hand toward the filthy buildings. "The people who really need our care live here, in the midst of poverty. If we don't help them, who will?"

Eleazar shook his head, perplexed. "There's nothing wrong with treating the rich, Father," he said. "Don't you want to buy Mother nice things? Don't you care about our family? Simon? Me? And the new baby?"

He'd spoken with boldness, unsure how his father would respond.

Judah narrowed his eyes. "Beware of the seeking of gold, Eleazar. It will destroy you." He turned sharply away, as though the subject were closed, and picked up his step.

Emboldened, Eleazar drew up beside his father. "Is it wrong to expect payment for our hard work?"

The lines on Judah's face appeared to soften. "No, my son," he said, his voice tender. "It is not wrong to earn a worthy fee. You will have plenty of opportunities to do that. But for now you must trust me. What I am about to show you will change the way you think about medicine. It's a lesson you need to learn before you go running to the rich."

With mounting reluctance, Eleazar followed Judah down the narrow, descending path. They passed a series of crudely built shops and stalls. The sharp scent of roasted fish and the aroma of fresh baked bread mingled with the odor of garbage strewn along the sides of the road.

With the full rising of the sun, the streets of the Lower City came to life. Young girls carrying water jugs hurried past them on their way to a local cistern. Dirty-faced children interrupted their play and held out eager hands. Judah reached into his scrip and released a few coins to them. Eleazar balked. They hadn't yet earned one piece of silver, and his father was giving away what little they had.

Suddenly, a woman bearing a large pan emerged from a doorway and tossed a brackish liquid across their path. Eleazar sidestepped the flow, scowled at the woman, and moved on, more determined than ever to rid himself of this ministry.

They turned a corner where the road grew narrower and damp walls rose up on either side. Judah stopped in front of a small shelter, its frame of rocks and clay barely held together with a poorly mixed mortar of pitch and gravel. The roof consisted of decaying palm branches that had little hope of holding back the rain.

There were no windows, only a small door that led to utter darkness. Judah went inside. Eleazar held back. The opening was half his height. At his father's call he bowed his shoulders and slipped inside the tiny dwelling. He was immediately struck by the smell of urine. From the far wall came the rustle of bedding and a muffled groan. Judah lit an oil lamp, and a burst of light revealed a frail, gray-haired woman lying on a bed of straw. Eleazar caught his breath, certain he was looking into the eyes of death.

He remained close to the door and kept his eyes on his father. Judah pulled a pot from his scrip, turned, and thrust it toward Eleazar.

"Run to the cistern up the hill and get some fresh water. And hurry."

Run? Of course, he would run. He would run away from the stench in that miserable hovel. With the pot in his hand, he fled over the broken pavement to the rock-hewn cistern on the side of the hill. He peered over the rock ledge, glad to discover that a recent rainfall had raised the level of fresh water. He didn't have to descend the inner stair but leaned over the ledge and scooped some of the liquid into the bowl. Though he preferred to stay away a while longer, his father had told him to hurry.

He trudged back along the path, taking care not to spill the precious liquid. He walked into the little house and found the odor of urine was gone, and in its place was the crisp, clean smell of lye and mint. The woman, now dressed in a clean nightshirt, was sitting upright in her bed. A flicker of life had entered her eyes blue as the sky. Her snow-white hair hung in tight ringlets around her face, now flushed with renewed spirit.

Judah stood beside the bed. He was grinding a blend of herbs in a bowl and emitting the scents of myrrh and rose petals. Eleazar held out the pot of water. Judah spilled in the herbs, then he lifted the bowl to the woman's lips.

"Drink, Miriam," he said. "This will give you strength."

Miriam. In an instant the woman became a human being. She had a name. She was someone's mother, someone's grandmother. A seed of compassion stirred within Eleazar. He stared at the old woman. She was taking long, eager gulps of the potion. Then she leaned back against her pillow and let out a contented sigh. She pointed a gnarled finger at Eleazar. He shrank back.

"My son," Judah told her. "He is learning my trade."

He turned toward Eleazar. "Miriam is an old friend—no, she's more than a friend. Long ago, she was a second mother to me." The woman was no longer a poor stranger. She knew his father. Their paths had crossed at one time. Perhaps Eleazar had known her too. A second mother to him? What did that mean?

Judah took a clean cloth from his scrip and began to wipe the vessels clean. "Miriam has no one to care for her," he explained. "Her children moved to distant lands with no concern for their mother." A bitterness had taken over the old man's voice. "I have known Miriam from my youth."

There it was again. A longtime friend, a second mother.

"When she became ill, I began to visit her every week," Judah went on. "I make sure she has food and a change of clothing. I ease her physical needs and her loneliness at once."

Miriam's smile broadened, and a splay of wrinkles spread across her cheeks. Eleazar eyed her with interest. The old woman was lying on the only piece of furniture in that dimly lit hovel. Except for a few dusty cushions piled in a corner, her few possessions filled two small niches carved into the rock wall. He suspected the woman's smile would be all the payment his father would receive in this place.

Judah mopped moisture from Miriam's brow, then he swept a lock of hair back from her cheek. His movements were gentle, even loving, so unlike the awkward man who ruled his home with an iron fist. Miriam turned adoring eyes on the old man.

The two of them spoke softly to each other, as though they were the only people in the room. It was as if Eleazar wasn't there. Puzzled, he turned away from them, arranged a pile of cushions in the corner, and settled on them, content to sit in the shadows. Though he couldn't hear a word they were saying, he submitted to the hum of their voices, and, before he realized what was happening, he didn't hear them anymore.

CHAPTER FOUR

*E*leazar!" His eyes shot open. Judah was standing over him,
a look of impatience on the old man's face. "We must go, son.
Gather our belongings."

Eleazar scrambled to his feet.

Before leaving, Judah promised Miriam another visit in a
few days. "Now," he said, and his voice had turned cold. "I will
speak to your neighbor and scold her for not looking after you
as she had agreed."

Judah departed on heavy footsteps. Stooping close to Miriam's
bed, Eleazar avoided her inquisitive blue eyes as he packed up
his father's scrip. A bony hand reached out and stroked his head.
He lurched backward.

"Will you return with your father?" she said, sweetly pleading.
"I would like that."

He shrugged, then without answering, he grabbed his father's
pack and fled into the street.

He found Judah at the next house, speaking harshly to the
woman in the doorway. She spread her hands in a silent plea.
Judah pulled his money pouch from his breast and dropped
several coins in her open hand. She smiled at him and nodded.

"My husband will repair Miriam's roof," she promised. "And
I'll make sure she's bathed and will take food to her every day."

"See that you do." Judah's tone was firm. "Give her something healthful, not moldy bread made from old barley or crushed locusts." He nodded at the silver in her hand. "You have enough money there to buy fine flour. I will be coming back to see if you have fulfilled my request. Promise me."

The woman shrank under his hard stare. "Yes, yes. When you return, you will see that I have done all you've asked."

Judah grabbed the scrip from Eleazar and beckoned him to follow. To Eleazar's disappointment, instead of heading back up the hill, they moved farther down into the pits of despair. During the remainder of the day, they visited a great number of poor people, though none seemed quite as impoverished as old Miriam. To Eleazar, it was a wasted, fruitless day of work. No one paid, at least not with coins. A hunk of bread, a wedge of cheese, a few potatoes, a handful of raisins, enough to satisfy his hunger pangs. While Eleazar plodded along, Judah had an increasing spring in his step.

As they moved from house to house, Judah gave more instruction, often allowing Eleazar to wrap a wound or mix a potion.

"Remember, my son, boils will heal faster if you first apply a wrapping of figs soaked in olive oil. It's a simple remedy, but very effective."

"Be sure and grind the herbs to a fine powder. You don't want any pieces to catch in people's throats and perhaps choke them."

"Wrap the bandage tighter, Eleazar. A firm wrapping will prevent the blood from oozing through the cloth."

With each instruction Eleazar bobbed his head and followed through. He said nothing. No questions. No arguments. He merely wanted to listen and learn. As they left each dwelling, the teaching continued. For the first time in Eleazar's life, Judah was talking to him without barely taking a breath. The lecture went on and on, while they walked, at every turn of the road, and in and out of every home.

"Be wary of open sores that don't respond to treatment. If they appear suspicious, you must send that person to the priest who will determine if it is an easily treated wound or something much more harmful." His father suddenly stopped walking and faced him.

"Remember what you witnessed on the hills outside the city," he said, a hint of warning in his voice. "Each of those poor souls had gone to the priest. And each of them endured a week of separation. When their time away from home ended, they faced a second examination. Those who showed no sign of disease went through a cleansing ritual and returned to their families. Those who failed the test were condemned to permanent separation. You saw the cursed ones. Let their memory drive you to compassion. This is the lesson I have been wanting to teach you from the beginning. This is the root of all I do as a physician and all I am as a man."

For the first time in hours, Eleazar felt driven to speak. "What about the law?" he said, his voice harsh. "We have broken the command to avoid contact with lepers. That old woman. The soiling of my face and my robe. How can I have compassion for someone who defiled me in such a way? If we had followed the law we would have stayed away from that place."

Judah released a long sigh. "Though I follow the laws of Moses, I cannot turn my back on people who need my help. Sometimes we have to go beyond the law and find the heart of a matter." The old man shook his head and turned sad eyes on his son. "I can see I have not yet broken through your hard shell, Eleazar. That incident the other day has spoiled my teaching." He shrugged. "Someday you will learn. I hope it won't be too late."

Eleazar had already made up his mind to avoid the lepers on the hill. He would never go back to that place, never look those people in the eye, never try to ease their pain. His father could do as he wished, but Eleazar would not join him. And, one day, he also would ignore the cries of the people in the Lower City. Like his mother had said, this was Judah's ministry. It didn't have to be his.

A wall had risen up between him and his father. Whether

Judah was aware of it was of no consequence. Eleazar knew it was there. For now the wall protected him from falling for his father's way of life. It would shield him later when he pursued the path his mother had set before him. He determined to maintain that wall, at any cost.

For now, he would follow his father along the course the old man had chosen. They continued to visit the poor in the Lower City. Near the end of the day, they passed through the outer gate and went down the ravine to the hillside dwelling of Shaul the shepherd. Eleazar had met Shaul a year ago when the man brought a portion of lamb to their home at Passover time. A gift, he'd said, for his physician.

The poor shepherd was employed by one of the wealthy sheep owners in Judea. But he hadn't worked in weeks, not since he suffered a broken leg from falling off his roof while making repairs. They entered the man's house. Eleazar watched as Judah refreshed the bandages and then settled next to Shaul before a table set for the three of them. Shaul's wife served them and repeatedly filled their empty cups with goat's milk.

As the two men fell into lively conversation, Eleazar became aware that his father's service extended more readily to friendship. Here was a man who, because of his status as a physician, could mingle with the powerful and wealthy, but instead, he'd chosen to associate with the poorest of the poor. Miriam. Shaul. And so many others who welcomed Judah's kind words along with his medical care.

Eleazar sat cross-legged on a sheepskin mat, woefully aware of the dwelling's miserable surroundings—crumbling walls of poorly applied mud-brick, a wide opening in the unfinished roof, the meager pieces of furniture patched together with nails and palm fronds.

Shaul's wife offered him a bowl of lamb and vegetables. He savored the tender cuts of meat, the sharp bite of onions and garlic, the sweet juices, certain this meager fare would be payment for his father's services. No coins, no portion of a lamb to take home, not even a slice of that raisin bread that was warming on the hearth.

As they prepared to leave, like he did at too many homes before, Judah dropped a few coins in Shaul's hand.

"To keep you until you're well enough to return to work," Judah said. "Rest your leg for another two weeks, my friend. Then stay with your sheep herding and get one of the village boys to finish repairing your roof."

The next four visits were equally disappointing. Not once did anyone offer even a few coins to Judah. Instead, each visit ended with his father filling their outstretched hands until his own purse was empty.

At the end of the day, they walked home empty-handed. Even Judah's flask of goat's milk was gone, now in the hands of a dirty child who'd approached them on the street. Though he should have been tired, Judah had a spring in his step, a smile on his lips, and a sparkle in his eyes. Eleazar fell behind, frowning. The day had been a waste. They were returning home with nothing to offer his mother. How she would rant. The evening surely would be ruined by her bitter words.

They entered the city through the Dung Gate. Once again, the sharp odor of animal entrails, scraps of rubbish, and human waste struck him, now with more vengeance after having enjoyed the fresh air outside the city. They could have come through any one of the other gates. The Sheep Gate was close to the Temple. They would have passed through the Upper City for a more pleasant walk on their return home. For his father to choose this path and this gate told him one clear message. This, too, was part of his training.

While still a great distance from their house, Judah halted on the path and faced him. "Listen to me, my son. My work is not about how much money I can earn or what I can get from the people we served today. It's about how much I can give."

Eleazar shook his head, bewildered. "I don't understand, Father. When do you get paid for your services?"

"Hear me and listen well," the old man went on, his voice breaking with emotion. "If you have compassion for the sick, you will give whatever will ease their pain. Your skill. Words of comfort. Even your silver, if necessary. This day, you were not only learning from me. I was learning from you. I watched your face. I heard your sighs. From what I learned from you today, I will know what to teach you tomorrow."

Eleazar shrugged and lowered his gaze. He stared at his sandals, now soiled by the filthy roads he'd traveled.

"You can't pretend those people don't exist," Judah continued. "As a physician, your calling will be to heal the sick. The *sick*, Eleazar." The tone in his voice caused Eleazar to raise his head. He looked into his father's eyes, now hardened by a rise of anger. "It doesn't matter where they live or how much wealth they have. You must do your work faithfully and never prefer one person over another."

Eleazar swallowed but said nothing. What could he say? The argument in his head could never touch his father's heart.

"Tomorrow, we'll go to the Upper City," Judah said.

Fresh life surged through Eleazar, and he gave his father his full attention.

"That's right," the old man said, a hint of a smile on his lips. "You must have known, the rich also summon me." He gave a little laugh. "How else would I be able to support our family? Their gifts make up for what I gave away today and add a small fortune beyond. So, you see, my son? The Almighty honors a man's faithfulness with a promise of tenfold. Test Him and He will open the windows of blessing."

"We're going to the Upper City?" Eleazar said, having little thought of anything else his father had said.

Judah nodded. "Our first stop will be at the home of Ariel, the merchant. He's been a friend to me since I was your age. He's a man of great wealth, Eleazar, but he also has a meek and humble spirit. When we arrive, be sure to offer him a greeting. He's been suffering with a boil. I'll show you how to—"

Judah's voice trailed off. Eleazar had no interest in greetings or boils or even how much wealth they would carry away from the visit. Ariel had seven daughters, and they were all beauties. But, the loveliest was the youngest—a spirited, doe-eyed girl named Ruth. Eleazar's heartbeat quickened with every step he took toward home.

CHAPTER FIVE

*T*he next morning, Eleazar rose from his bed before the rooster crowed. Aside from his father's heavy breathing beyond the veil, the house was quiet. Unable to still his racing heart, he tossed off his blanket and hurried out to the courtyard. Shivering in the morning chill, he broke the ice in the laver, splashed cold water on his face and on his upper body and quickly dried himself.

Then he ran back inside, sprinkled a generous portion of his mother's scented oil on his neck and slipped into a clean tunic. He dipped his fingers in the aromatic oil and spread it through the mass of curls on his head. He felt his chin and frowned. No sign of stubble yet.

Eager for the promised visit to the Upper City and especially the house of Ariel, Eleazar paced the courtyard, a wave of unrest flooding through him. He pulled a few weeds from his mother's garden, glanced repeatedly at the open door of the house, then he passed through the gate and peered out at the horizon. A ribbon of gold lay beneath a string of clouds. A perfect day for the planned visit.

He was deciding whether to wake his father when Judah stumbled out of the house with a towel in his hand, and headed for the laver. Eleazar watched his father bathe with impatience, then he was momentarily distracted by the aroma of fig cakes warming on the hearth. He went inside and found his mother stirring a pot of lentils, the hefty steam coloring her cheeks a deep red.

Upon noticing him, Mara raised two of the fig cakes and offered them to him along with an understanding smile. There was no secret where he and Judah were going that day.

Judah returned to the house and settled on a cushion with a bowl of the lentils. Eleazar devoured the fig cakes, eager to get moving. But old Judah took his time, savored every steamy spoonful, and followed with a hardy swallow of goat's milk.

Finally, the old man left the kitchen and mounted the outer stair to the apothecary. He returned with a bulging leather scrip. Eleazar planted a kiss on his mother's cheek. Their eyes met in wordless encouragement, and Eleazar joined his father in the street. They headed up the hill toward the spread of rich mansions in the Upper City. The cobbled path in front of their own house slowly gave way to broad, polished limestone. Ivy-covered walls rose up on both sides of the road. Walled courtyards enfolded massive structures. Floral scents drifted into the street. As the road snaked farther upward, the whitewashed houses grew larger and more magnificent.

Ariel had great wealth. Eleazar was painfully aware of the difference between Ariel's standing and Judah's and their families' disparate social positions. He'd caught sight of Ruth and her sisters leaving the marketplace, their baskets laden with fresh fruits and vegetables, fish from the Great Sea, and bottles of olive oil and wine. Their clothing proclaimed their father's prosperity—long, flowing robes in a multitude of colors, shear veils draped loosely over their braided hair, bracelets of gold and silver on their arms, and jeweled sandals on their feet.

Whenever he walked to the temple for his lessons with the rabbi, he had passed by Ariel's home and had peered through the iron gate in hopes of catching sight of the beautiful young girl who lived there.

Today, he wouldn't merely walk past the dwelling. He'd step

inside that courtyard. He'd spend time with Ruth's father, perhaps impress the man as he assisted his father in caring for him. All the while he would keep a watchful eye out for Ruth.

When they reached Ariel's house, a lump came to Eleazar's throat, and his momentary confidence waned. He paused at the gate and caught his breath. Unlike the stone littered courtyard at his own home, a pavement of brown-and-purple marble stretched from one end to the other. Stone benches stood at intervals along the border. Several fountains carved from ivory spewed fresh water into large basins. Flowering vines encased two huge pillars at the entrance to the house, and a broad vegetable garden stretched to the far end, its flourishing crops quickly putting Mara's sickly herb garden to shame.

He swallowed and squeezed his eyes shut. Why had he thought he could impress a girl like Ruth? They came from two different worlds.

"Let's go in," Judah said, drawing Eleazar's attention back to the overwhelming spread of wealth.

He stepped ahead with less assurance. A huge curved doorway opened to the private living quarters. Mosaic tiles in many colors adorned the walls. There were more vines, more flowers in large urns, patches of green, yellow and gold adornments. Eleazar shook his head in awe. Not even his friend Achim's home could equal this magnificent dwelling. Like Ariel, Achim's father also traveled to foreign lands and brought back wares to sell in the marketplace, but his business fell short of Ariel's. Ruth's father dealt in costly products well-received by the elite of the city, while Achim's father sold lesser goods to the common people.

With his free hand Judah prodded Eleazar through the doorway and into the inner court. It was as if he had stepped foot inside Herod's palace. Huge walls, built of large, rose-colored stones towered on all sides. Elegantly carved birds, flowers, and butterflies adorned six pillars leading to doorways, each one opening to unseen quarters for servants, storage rooms, kitchens, and other areas known only to the very wealthy.

Eleazar lowered his eyes and examined his clothing. He was wearing his best linen tunic, the one he reserved for Sabbath services. It failed to compare with the magnificent attire Ariel wore to the Temple. And his sandals? The dirt from yesterday's journey into the Lower City still clung to the bottoms. Though he'd scrubbed them with all his might, he hadn't been able to wipe them clean.

Discouraged, Eleazar eyed his father with bitterness. The man stepped across the rich tiles with the same indifference he'd displayed at the homes of Shaul and Miriam and every one of the other miserable dogs they'd visited. It seemed no amount of wealth or poverty affected that man.

Two servant boys emerged at the far end of the inner court and directed them to a stone bench. They sat, side-by-side, and slipped out of their sandals. One of the boys knelt before Eleazar and bathed his feet in a basin of water with rose petals floating on top. Then, he wiped them dry with a towel, softer than anything he'd ever felt before. The other servant did the same for Judah.

With a wave of his hand, one of them beckoned them to follow, barefoot, up a long curved stairway to an upper room on the roof. Again, Eleazar was humbled by the spread of tiles that covered the expanse. To his left, a waist-high wall separated the women's bathing pool from the rest of the upper portion. To his right, a shelter created from palm branches and lattice boards stretched overhead. Beneath it was a magnificent chamber, fit for a king. Inside were three walls of purple curtains and in the middle of the room stood a raised bed built of polished ebony and elaborately carved with pomegranates and vines then overlaid with gold. Piled high on top was an assortment of blankets and pillows in bright reds and blues. Along the opposite wall stood two wooden seats, also of polished ebony, and spaced evenly around the chamber were eight oil lamps resting on tall pedestals. The glow from their flames bathed the entire room in a golden aura.

Eleazar took in his surroundings, and an overwhelming defeat settled on his heart. Then a groan drew his attention to the pile of pillows and blankets on the bed. The covers shifted and fell away and a large bulk of a man lifted his head. Eleazar recognized him immediately. Ariel's countenance, usually darkened from his many travels in bright sunlight, now had a pale, sickly appearance. Lines of anguish gathered on his forehead, and he moaned like a bull being led to the slaughtering altar.

"Judah, oh, Judah," the man wailed, his eyes on the old man. "At last, you've come. Tell me, why did you delay? I called for you three days ago. The pain has gotten worse. It's more than I can bear. It lingers through the day and holds my eyelids open all night long." With his voice high-pitched with anguish he continued his lamentation. "Please, my dear friend, work your magic. Heal this monstrous wound before I lose what remains of my strength and die before my time."

Judah stepped toward Ariel and snorted. "You should be a player on a Greek stage instead of a merchant, you poor man. I'm certain you would draw a large crowd with your excessive crying and wailing."

Ariel grunted. The anxious lines on his face eased a little, and he looked sheepishly at Judah.

"Only one week ago I visited you." Judah rebuked him, as if he were speaking to a child. "You complain for no reason. The boil on your shoulder must have begun to heal by now. Let me take a look."

Ariel breathed a long sigh. While Judah removed the bandages, the big man turned his eyes on Eleazar. He smiled with recognition.

"Come close, son," Ariel said, and he beckoned him with his free hand. Then he turned to Judah. "Is this Eleazar?"

Judah nodded and kept peeling away the bandages. "He's learning my trade."

"Wonderful. Why not let him practice on *me*?" He winced as Judah pulled the last bandage away. "I trust he might give far more sympathy than I get from his father."

Giving a shrug, Judah turned toward Eleazar and held out his scrip. "Take it," he said, his voice firm. "And listen to my instructions."

Eleazar hesitated for only a moment. This could be an opportunity to win Ariel's approval. He stepped forward and took the scrip, amazed that his hand didn't tremble as he might have expected it would.

He turned to one of the servant boys and did as he'd seen his father do many times during their visits in the Lower City. "Bring a pan of rose water, and some clean towels," he said to the boy.

The lad responded quickly, giving Eleazar an additional burst of confidence. He had taken charge now. No longer was he watching from a distance. He was performing the role of a physician, and he liked the feeling.

Then under his father's guidance, he cleansed Ariel's wound and applied a fresh poultice of figs soaked in olive oil. When he finished, Ariel sat up against the pile of pillows and smiled.

"I believe a fine, new physician is about to take over this city," the big man said. Eleazar beamed under the man's approving gaze. "Beware, you other doctors!" Ariel said with a chuckle. "This one will surpass all of you." He let out a sigh and looked at Judah. "You're a fortunate man to be blessed with a son who can follow in your footsteps. A son, Judah, while I have been cursed with a houseful of daughters. Seven, in all, but no son to inherit my trade. No male heir, save the husbands I choose for my daughters."

Husbands? Eleazar had been so intent on caring for Ariel's wound, he'd almost forgotten that somewhere beyond those massive walls was a young girl he'd admired from afar. Now he wondered, where was she?

As if reading the boy's mind, Ariel laughed. "Tell me, Judah, have you established a union for your son?"

His father shook his head. "No, I have not."

Ariel frowned. "According to our traditions, you should have taken care of that shortly after his birth, or at least by the time he weaned from his mother." He nodded toward Eleazar. "Perhaps you'll consider pledging him to one of my daughters."

Eleazar could hardly believe his ears. This man of great wealth had actually considered him. Discarded dreams renewed within his heart.

Ariel went on, unaware of Eleazar's pounding heart. "My eldest has already been married off, and three more have received contracts for betrothal," Ariel went on. "Make a choice, Judah, and I will honor it."

Eleazar stared at his father and silently willed him to speak on his behalf. But Judah said nothing and began to gather his belongings. He paused and gave Ariel a questioning look. "How can you tell me I've waited too long to pledge my son? Didn't you just offer me a choice of your daughters? Shouldn't they all have contracts by now?"

Ariel shook his head. "My three youngest have had many requests. I'm undecided. But, there is still time for an offer if you choose to make one."

But Judah merely laughed. "There's plenty of time, Ariel. I, too, could have answered several calls for a match. But I need to watch my son grow into the man he should become. Never mind tradition. Eleazar has a rebellious spirit. I will address the issue when he has matured to my liking and only after he has learned my trade and is ready to make a life for himself."

Judah's firm tone stirred defeat in Eleazar. Ariel was watching him. Had the man seen the disappointment in his eyes.

Ariel shrugged. "In that case, learn well, my boy. How fortunate you are to have this man as your father *and* as your teacher. Judah doesn't simply give a dose of medicine and go on his way, as some physicians do. He gives of himself. He sacrifices his time, his desires, even his money." He flashed a quick eye at Judah. "That's right, my friend, I've heard stories about your acts of kindness in the Lower City. Such deeds will not go unrewarded."

The big man turned again to Eleazar. "I've known your father since childhood. He's one of the most unselfish people I've ever met. Learn well from him. Follow his teaching as a physician, but, more than that follow his example as a man of integrity."

Eleazar stood in awe that a person of such great stature should speak so highly of his father. He looked at Judah, a bedraggled old man with shabby clothing and unkempt hair, and, once again, he saw a stranger. In this big house, in the presence of one of the richest men in Judea, Judah had risen to a place of high regard. It had been easier to think of the old man as a stubborn failure.

"You talk too much for someone who's supposed to be sick," Judah cut in.

He lifted his scrip to his shoulder, a sign they would be leaving. Anxiety coursed through Eleazar. He wasn't ready to leave. The opportunity to win Ariel had come and gone too quickly. If he could say a few words on his own behalf. But what? How could he convince Ariel to consider a match if Judah had already shut the door to such an opportunity? He could not go against his father.

"Talk too much?" Ariel said. "If I had been blessed with a gift of speaking, I would have convinced you months ago to accept the Council's invitation. Every man in the Sanhedrin agreed. They could have offered the seat to one of their own relatives, yet, they chose *you*."

The Sanhedrin? Eleazar stood in shock. Judah had been invited to join the Great Council, and he'd refused? Those men held great power. They made decisions that affected every citizen in Judea. And they had chosen Judah. But what had his father done? He'd rejected their call.

Eleazar stared in amazement at the old man, unable to speak.

"Give no mind to it," Judah said with a wave of his hand. "You need to rest, Ariel. I'll leave a potion, something to ease the pain and help you sleep. Perhaps when you awaken, your good senses will have returned."

Ariel reached for a leather pouch lying on a little table next to the bed. He withdrew five gold coins and handed them to

Judah. Then he beckoned Eleazar to come close. He pulled out another gold coin and pressed it in the boy's palm.

"Come back and see me," Ariel said, with a wink.

Eleazar mumbled a thank you and took a step back. He felt like he couldn't breathe. The visit had been far too short. And his father had taken away his one hope.

"Get some sleep, Ariel." Judah said, his voice gruff. "You'll soon be well and traveling again. Then, you can go to the coast, make yourself rich, and come home with another wound for me to heal."

Ariel was still laughing when Eleazar descended the stair to the lower court. His father was several steps ahead of him, but he took his time and savored the smoothness of the gold coin in his hand—his first wage as a physician's helper. Suddenly his thoughts were interrupted by a girl's melodic singing. He stopped on the bottom step and searched the inner court.

He found her sitting on a bench beside a potted plant, humming a fascinating tune. She was swathed in light blue veils from head to toe. Long lashes framed dark eyes that peered at him over the fold of cloth. A band of gold kept her veil in place, and a single curl, black as a raven's wing, had escaped near her left cheek.

A surge of heat swept over Eleazar. He couldn't take his eyes off of her. She stared back at him with startling boldness. Then she unhooked her veil and let it drop, releasing an ebony mane that fell past her shoulders in long waves. A dagger of sunlight pierced the branches of a palm tree and touched Ruth's face. Her cheeks glowed like polished bronze. The corners of her mouth turned upward, and a dimple appeared in her left cheek. Unexpectedly shaken, Eleazar turned away, scooped up his sandals, and, his heart pounding, he plunged into the street after his father.

CHAPTER SIX

*T*he road toward home took Eleazar farther away from Ariel's house and the beautiful Ruth. Somehow, he had not regained control of his pounding heart, but he couldn't shake the memory of the vision in Ariel's courtyard. He should have spoken to her, should have appeared strong and confident. Instead, he'd crumbled under the girl's steady gaze. Her mocking eyes had nearly destroyed him.

There was nothing more to do but continue down the hill, back in the direction from which they had come. Surely, they hadn't finished with the people in the Upper City. Surely, Judah had other patients to see.

Eleazar's concerns were dispelled moments later when Judah turned into a another courtyard a great distance down the hillside. Eleazar knew the dwelling well, for he had spent many hours in that house visiting Achim. He breathed easier now, knowing he was about to see his best friend. Achim's natural wit and happy spirit would certainly lift him up.

Judah paused at the door and turned toward Eleazar. "Zilpah has been complaining about her stomach again," he explained with a sad shake of his head. "I have a vial of her preferred medicine. Perhaps it will quiet her for a time, and Achim and his father will get some relief."

Eleazar had lost count of the number of times he'd delivered the dark brown liquid that seemed to dull Zilpah's pain. Though Judah had offered her newer medicines, the stubborn woman would accept nothing else.

Judah let out a chuckle, which surprised Eleazar. "I wonder if she truly suffers or if she just wants an escape." The old man shrugged. "No worry. It keeps her in a state of contentment, and that's what her husband wants."

Judah rapped on the doorpost. Seconds later, the door swung in, and Achim's round face appeared in the opening. His lips broke into a wide grin that tugged his freckles over flushed cheeks. His sparkling eyes reflected the azure sky above. Those clear blue eyes and flock of red hair had little in common with either of his parents, and Eleazar often wondered if the boy had come from a different heritage. Perhaps the rumors about Achim's ancestry bore some truth. The family had moved to Jerusalem from another place across the sea where his father still conducted business. Achim had no siblings, no other clues to his heritage. He could be a Gentile. He hadn't taken his temple training seriously. He'd learned a few verses of scripture and had dropped away, saying he had other plans for his future. He spent most of his time traveling with his father and learning the trade of a merchant. None of that mattered. He was the best friend Eleazar ever had.

Achim let out a sigh that sounded much like relief. "My mother's been awaiting your arrival," he said, eagerly beckoning them inside.

Zilpah lay on a couch by the window. She appeared to be sleeping, but at the sound of their footsteps she opened one eye.

Judah drew closer to her. "I've brought your medicine." He pulled the vial out of his bag and held it out to her.

Zilpah struggled to sit upright. Once stable, she grabbed the vial from Judah's outstretched hand and yanked the top off. Without a word of thanks or a promise of payment, she drank heartily of the foul-smelling liquid. Then smiling, she released a contented sigh and replaced the seal.

"My purse." She looked at Achim. He ran to his mother's personal closet and returned with a small leather pouch. She fumbled with the flap, withdrew several coins, and dropped them, one-by-one—*clink-clink-clink*—in Judah's open hand. He sorted out a fair price and returned the rest to Zilpah's purse.

"You're a descent man, Judah."

Strangely, Zilpah had the same tone of admiration Miriam had expressed only a few days ago. Eleazar frowned in puzzlement. What was this spell his father cast over everyone? Everyone, that is, except his own wife and children. It was as if he were two different people. One, a domineering rule-maker in the home, the other a true servant of the people, meek and mild and serving them from the heart.

Judah continued to speak with Zilpah. "I would not dream of cheating a friend. You know that, don't you?"

Zilpah was nodding and smiling.

So that was it. Judah wouldn't cheat a friend, but he'd deny his family riches and comfort. In that way, wasn't he cheating his own wife and children? None of this made any sense to Eleazar. He watched with interest as Zilpah succumbed to the power of the medicine.

Her eyes began to close. They flew open for only a moment, and she tried to speak, but she merely mumbled something incoherent. Then she swayed slightly, rolled her eyes, and fell back against her pillow.

Judah turned toward the door. It was time to leave. The visit was too short. Eleazar would have liked to linger there with his friend. Reluctantly, he bid Achim farewell and followed his father to the door.

"Our work is not yet finished," Judah explained, as though reading his son's mind. They continued down the hill and stopped at several other dwellings of little significance to Eleazar. People he didn't know had called for Judah's help. To Eleazar, the two most important visits were long past.

It amazed him that Judah came away from every home smiling

and quickening his step, as though his own good health grew stronger from helping strangers.

Shortly before sunset, they started toward home. Eleazar fell into despair as they left the glorious courtyards in the Upper City and journeyed farther down the hillside toward their own miserable dwelling. He couldn't help but compare his humble lot with the fortune of those he had visited that day. What's more, he found little satisfaction in the bulge of coins inside Judah's scrip. As he'd promised, Judah was providing what they needed. At least Mara would have nothing to complain about.

As they walked on in silence, Eleazar's mind drifted back to Ariel's courtyard and the lovely Ruth sitting there as though she'd been waiting for him. He smiled at the memory.

Suddenly, as they came around a bend in the road, a noisy shouting broke into Eleazar's thoughts. Three boys were standing in a half-circle in front of a wall. Though they had their backs to him he recognized one as Levi, his adversary from early childhood. He would not soon forget the day Levi taunted him in the Temple when he was reciting a passage from the Scriptures, and his voice unexpectedly squeaked. Levi got the other boys to make pig sounds, and they all laughed at him. Even Rabbi Heth appeared to stifle a smile as he reprimanded the boys.

Eleazar's face burned with anger as he remembered the humiliation. He stopped walking but kept his distance. Levi was tall for his age, a full head above the other two. As always, he appeared to be the leader. The three were cursing and waving their arms in the air. Eleazar looked at his father. The old man stood very still and narrowed his eyes, his attention on the three youth.

Levi picked up a stone and hurled it toward the wall. The others did the same. A squeal rose from the ground. Levi shouted another curse. The others did too.

There was a yelp, and the three burst out laughing. "Hit her again," one of them shouted.

"Adulteress!" Levi called out, and he flung another stone. "She is worthy of death."

Eleazar froze, but his father set down his scrip and moved closer to the boys. As Levi raised his arm to throw another stone, Judah grabbed his wrist and spun him around. In his hand was a rock as large as a man's fist. Startled, Levi spread his fingers and let it fall to the ground.

"What are you doing?" Judah held fast to Levi's arm.

The boy scowled at him. He tried to pull his arm away, but Judah had a firm grip. The other boys dropped their stones and stepped away from the wall. Eleazar looked past them. A tiny dog, it's shaggy, brown hair coated with blood, lay trembling on the pavement.

Judah's face had turned red. "Why are you attacking that helpless animal?"

Levi jerked his arm away and took a step back. He rubbed his wrist. "You hurt me." His black eyes flashed with anger. "Leave us alone, old man."

Judah's eyebrows came together, and he clenched his teeth. With a snap of his hand he waved the boys away from the wall. "Get out of here! Go. And don't do this evil again."

Two of the boys backed away from him. But Levi remained steadfast. He spat on the ground in front of Judah and sneered at him. "My father will hear about this. He's a member of the Council. He can bring judgment on you." He turned mocking eyes on Eleazar. "And on your miserable son."

Judah took a step toward Levi. "Go. Go home, before I throw a stone at *you!*" He bent over as though to pick up a stone.

The two boys scattered toward the Upper City. Levi made a nasty face, then he ran after the others.

Eleazar stared at his father. A smile crossed his lips. Once again, the old man had surprised him. Judah, the strong, angry ruler of their home, had rescued a little dog, and at the same time he had dealt with Eleazar's longtime enemy. A surge of admiration swept into Eleazar's heart, but only for a moment.

As the boys disappeared over the hill, Judah went to the little dog and lifted it in his arms. He pulled the animal to his chest and drew his cloak over its shivering form.

He cast a glance at Eleazar. "Get my scrip. Let's hurry home and see if we can keep this little dog alive."

Eleazar's long-held opinion of his father had begun to crumble over the last few days. He'd witnessed numerous acts of kindness and sacrifice. The moment they'd stepped foot out of their home, Eleazar had begun an awakening to a newfound truth. Judah had displayed a mix of strength and compassion unlike anything he'd ever seen before. His domineering father had become a little boy under the gaze of an old woman. The mighty physician had humbled himself in the homes of the needy. The pauper had stood tall in the homes of the rich, unmoved by powerful men like Ariel. And now, Eleazar had watched in awe as Judah flared in anger at a bunch of unruly boys and the next minute had gently cuddled an injured animal in his arms.

As Eleazar hurried along the road beside his father, he began to wonder about this man who had turned down the call of the Sanhedrin but cared about the welfare of a helpless animal. Fascinated, he determined to keep his eyes on Judah. Though he had no desire to stray from the plan he and his mother had devised for his future, perhaps he should consider what Ariel had said and learn what he could from the man he'd been living with for thirteen years but had never really known.

When they arrived home, Judah placed the dog's limp form in the center of the main room. He knelt beside the animal and examined it with a gentleness that belied the size of his big, clumsy hands. The rest of the family circled around them, all eyes on the little dog. At Judah's command, Mara brought a pile of rags and a basin of water. Eleazar set his father's scrip on the floor and lay it open. Young Simon reached out and patted the dog's head. Except for a subtle rise and fall of her abdomen, the animal lay deathly still.

Mara handed the pan of water to Judah. "What happened?"

Eleazar spoke up. "It was that brute Levi and his evil friends. They were yelling at this little dog, calling her an adulteress, and throwing stones at her. Look here." He pointed at an ugly gash above the dog's eye. "They could have blinded her."

Judah dabbed at the bloody wound and wrapped a strip of cloth around the dog's head. Then, one by one, he cleansed the other wounds.

Simon knelt nearby, his eyes filling with tears. "Will she live, Father?"

The old man nodded, but his face was lined with concern. "I pray she will. Those boys did a lot of damage, and—"

At that moment, the dog trembled and let out a piercing cry. An issue of blood poured from inside her. Judah reached into the bloody flow and lifted out two limp forms, so small he was able to hold both of them in one hand.

Eleazar caught his breath. Simon jumped back. "What is *that?*"

Judah shook his head. "The little dog was with child." He wrapped the dead babies in a napkin, then turned to his wife. "Mara, bring a cruse of wine. And hurry." He looked at Eleazar. "Reach into my scrip for the pouch of myrrh. We must ease her pain." Quickly, he faced Simon. "Gather these dirty rags, take them outside, and throw them in the burn pile. Then wash your hands at the laver."

As the family sprang into action, Judah continued to cleanse the wounds of the injured dog. Eleazar handed him the pouch of myrrh. Judah blended it with a splash of the wine from Mara, then he dripped the mixture in the little dog's mouth.

"This will help for a time." He gently stroked the dog's head. "Mara, get more towels. Make a bed for the dog." He gestured toward the boys' sleeping quarters. "Place it over there."

Simon had come back inside the house, and, hearing what his father had said, he let out a delighted shriek. "I'll do it. I'll make a place for her." He grabbed a handful of clean rags and started for his sleeping area.

Mara grabbed Simon's arm. "We can't keep this dirty animal in our home. Dogs have little use except to watch over flocks or to protect the courtyards of the rich." She glared at Judah.

"We don't have enough food for ourselves. And with the baby coming—" She placed a hand on her abdomen and pressed her lips firmly together.

"Please, Mother, let her stay." Simon tugged at her robe and turned hopeful eyes to her face.

Eleazar stood to his feet. "Father has done what he could. Let's put the dog out in the courtyard. If she survives the cold of night, she'll go away when she can."

Simon stamped his foot. "No!" He stepped between Eleazar and the dog. "I won't let you."

Judah wrapped the animal in a towel. He rose with the dog in his arms and faced Eleazar with determination in his eyes. "We will care for this animal until she's well." He turned his steel gray eyes at Mara. "I will decide if she stays or goes. But first, we must make certain that she lives."

Mumbling under her breath, Mara stepped aside. Simon hurried to his corner and fixed a tiny bed out of some straw and his handful of rags. Judah settled the little dog on the bedding, then backed away, a contented smile on his lips.

"Ishshah," he said with a nod. "*Woman*. Ishshah will be her name. For she has suffered the pain of childbirth."

"Ishshah!" Simon danced around the room, flapping his arms and shouting. "We have a dog, and her name is Ishshah. Our dog. *My* dog. Ishshah!"

"Be quiet!" Mara's harsh tone stopped the boy's dancing.

Simon's smile vanished. He tiptoed to his corner, knelt beside the sleeping dog, and stroked her head. "Ishshah," he whispered.

With the setting of the sun, darkness crept into the house. Judah took some lye and cleansed the floor where the dog had been lying. Then, he started for the courtyard to bathe himself.

"Mara!" he shouted from the courtyard. "Bring me a clean tunic and robe. Eleazar! take my scrip to the roof and place the medicines on the shelf. And hurry. The sun is about to set."

The meek and mild physician had vanished, and the ruler of the house had returned. Mara quickly responded with his clean clothing. Eleazar hurried up to the roof to dispose of the medicines. When he returned, Judah was there, refreshed and wearing a clean linen robe.

Mara removed a piece of flint from the shelf by the hearth and hurried about the room lighting the oil lamps. Their instant flame sent a glow against all four walls. She set out the plates and food for the evening meal, poured the wine, and set a loaf of bread in the center.

At that moment, a blast sounded from the temple. Judah strode to the east window, straightened his robe, and peered into the darkening sky.

"It is the Sabbath," he said.

CHAPTER SEVEN

The next morning, the house had settled into a damp chill. The lamps had burned out. Though it had been Mara's practice to trim the lamps several times during the night, she had let the nightly duty pass, unattended.

Judah and the boys rose from their beds, shivering. They bathed quickly and dressed in their temple attire. Eleazar stood very still and glanced about the room. Something was wrong. Mother was always the first one out the door for Sabbath services, but on this morning she had remained behind the curtain in her sleeping quarters.

Judah had emerged alone. "Your mother ails," he said. His customary gruff tone bore a hint of concern. "We will go to the temple without her."

Before leaving the dwelling, Simon paused for a last, lingering check on Ishshah.

Eleazar eyed his brother with impatience. "Come on. Father's already in the courtyard."

Simon bent over and gave the little dog a pat. His brow furrowed with concern. Then he turned away from his little dog and hurried outside.

The streets in the Upper City appeared to be more crowded than usual. King Herod had hired more than a thousand artisans to complete the work on the temple. The outer walls were nearly finished. Rabbi Heth had talked at length about Herod's temple. He told his gathering of youth that it already had surpassed the one Solomon built and the restoration completed by Zerubbabel. All Eleazar knew—and could see with his own eyes—was a magnificent complex. Instead of one building, there were several, including a huge, ornate palace where Herod stayed whenever he visited the city.

As they drew nearer to the massive stonework, Eleazar and his father and brother merged with a great river of people flowing up the broad stairs and into the main courtyard. The crowd grew thick with Jews who had come from other locations in Israel.

"It's because of the census," Judah snarled. "The Romans have levied yet another tax. Caesar Augustus has commanded that every citizen must go to his place of ancestry to register and pay a tax. Where will all that money go? Not to feed the poor, I am certain. It will go into Caesar's pocket."

Eleazar shouted above the noise of the crowd. "When will you register, Father?"

Judah shrugged. "If not for the law, I would avoid it. But, as the prophet wrote many years ago, we must obey the authority the Almighty has placed over us. Tomorrow I will go to the census taker and register. I will place the required tax on his table, and then I'll trust the Almighty to restore the money tenfold to us."

Once inside the temple court, Eleazar separated from his father and brother. He scanned the throng for Achim, shaded his eyes and searched from one end of the court to the other, uncertain if he would find his friend among so many worshipers.

Then he felt a hand on his shoulder and spun around. Achim stood before him, a wide grin brightening his freckled face, his blue eyes capturing the cloudless sky above.

Eleazar looked him over and smiled. "Look at you. Look at your robe." He spread his hands. "It could easily compete with Joseph's coat of many colors."

Achim twirled in a circle. His robe, a blend of twilled red

and gold threads billowed. The fringed hem fluttered and then went still.

Achim grinned with pride. "My father brought this from Egypt. It was sewn by the hands of slaves, Eleazar. Child slaves. Can you imagine? The gold threads were so sharp, they cut the little fingers as they sewed."

Eleazar eyed him with disgust. "There will be drops of blood in the weave."

Achim cocked his head. "The blood has been washed away."

Eleazar blinked back the brief hint of concern and looked away. "We have a new family member." He shot a sideways glance at Achim, then he picked up his pace and headed for the men's court.

Achim's eyes widened. "Has your mother given birth? Isn't it too soon?"

Eleazar shook his head and laughed aloud. "No, Achim. No baby yet. And you're right, it is too soon. This is a different kind of family member—a little dog my father and I found in the street after leaving your house yesterday."

Achim stopped walking and moved in front of Eleazar, their faces inches apart. The boy frowned in puzzlement. "What? You picked up a dirty little dog on the street? Dogs are everywhere, Eleazar. Why take one home?"

"Wait till you hear." He stared into Achim's eyes, intent on keeping his friend's attention. Then he lowered his voice as if about to tell a secret. He told him about the encounter with Levi and his friends.

Achim smiled mischievously. "I detest that Levi. He's no better than that wicked father of his. That whole family is pure evil."

Eleazar smiled. "My father was amazing. He chased those boys off. They ran like scared rabbits. Then he gently lifted the little dog from the street and carried her home." Then he gave Achim a sly look. "There's something else. Something I wanted to tell you when we came to your house, but there was no opportunity."

"You have a secret?" Achim's eyes sparkled with interest.

Eleazar nodded. "I saw Ruth yesterday. At the house of Ariel."
"Did you speak to her?"

A flush rose to Eleazar's cheeks. "There was no time." How could he tell his friend he'd lost his courage? "My father went there to treat Ariel's painful sore. I passed Ruth in the courtyard on our way out."

Achim gave him a knowing smile. "One day, you are going to speak to that girl. You merely need to—"

A blast from the pinnacle drowned out his next words. A multitude of people spread in all directions. The women and young children scurried toward their section behind the broad lattice wall. The men hurried up the long curve of stairs into the men's court where they vied for positions before the sacrificial altar. Eleazar had no idea what had become of his father and brother. He and Achim slipped through the throng of heavy cloaks and tasseled shawls and moved to the front of the crowd where they knelt on the pavement.

A slapping of bare feet drew his eyes upward. An attending priest mounted the stairs and strode toward the brass incense stand. The priest lit the incense in the bowl and sent a pungent flurry of smoke into the air. The ascending vapor spread through the main court and tickled Eleazar's nose. He blinked back a sting of tears, knowing the caustic irritation would stay with him for the rest of the morning.

He shifted his gaze to the laver and the sacrificial table. More priests entered. Men surged through the throng with their offerings of lambs and bulls. Eleazar's heart pounded with anticipation. Though he'd seen the bloody ritual time and time again, it still fascinated him. Sacrifice after sacrifice stained the sides of the sacrificial table. His eyes strayed past the priest and his bloody sword. He looked beyond the laver to the curtained wall that separated the Holy Place and the Holy of Holies. Yahweh's dwelling place on earth.

As he gazed at the curtain a wave of conviction surfaced over his rejection of the poor and the hopeless. He fought it with all the strength inside him. He had his own goals and they didn't include the kind of ministry his father had. With a surge of resolve, he set his focus on the future his mother had planned for him. If he remained strong, nothing would be able to deter him from his chosen path. Not Judah. Not the cries of the needy. Not even the all-seeing power behind the veil.

Two days later, Judah announced they would return to the home of Miriam.

Eleazar drew back. "Why, Father? We saw her only last week."

"I need to make sure the neighbor has fulfilled her promises." Judah stood firm. "And, I have more medicine to deliver, a new mixture of herbs I concocted only this morning."

As they left the house, Eleazar glanced back at the curtain dividing his parents' sleeping quarters from the rest of the house. His mother had been ailing through the night. He'd heard her moan, had listened as she moved about the kitchen, dragging her feet, a kettle simmering on the hearth, her unsteady breathing as she sipped the brew she had made.

Troubled, he plodded along the dusty road beside his father, his mind still on his mother's distress. "Should we have stayed at home today?" he said, and he eyed Judah with concern.

The old man shook his head. "She'll be fine. I left a mix of herbs on the hearth."

"But she—"

"Simon is there. She will be fine."

Judah's harsh tone silenced him. He continued walking but held his tongue, frustrated that the old man refused to hear him.

They arrived at Miriam's tiny hovel as the sun rose above the city wall. The roof of the house had been repaired, just as the neighbor had promised. Upon entering the house, a mixture of lemon and lye rose from the tiny household. The floor had been cleared of debris. Miriam's meager furnishings also had been repaired and cleaned. The old woman was wearing a pale linen smock and was sitting up in bed, a smile blossoming on her face at the sight of Judah.

"It seems the neighbor woman has followed my orders." Judah dropped to one knee beside Miriam's bed.

The old woman nodded. "Yes, my son. I've lacked nothing since your last visit. She brings water and bathes me daily. She provides clean clothing, and she brings a generous portion of their daily meal." Miriam chuckled. "Whatever did you say to her, Judah?"

"A few harsh words." Then, chuckling, he added, "and some coins."

Eleazar released a sigh, drawing Miriam's attention to him. Her eyes were gentle; her smile sweet. A spark of sympathy entered his heart. Seeing her again in such good spirits had a gentling affect on him. She was no longer a helpless old woman, but a friend of his father's. Within her deep blue eyes lay a wisdom beyond what he expected.

She held his gaze for only a moment. Then, as though understanding his discomfort, she looked at Judah and reached for his hand. "You've been so faithful, Judah. Why do you care for me as you do?" Miriam was shaking her head. Silver white curls fell against her cheeks. "My life is nearly over, Judah. It has little value now. You should not waste your time coming here when so many others need you."

"Your life has as much value as any other." Judah's voice was firm but tender. "Maybe even more."

Reaching into his scrip, the old man pulled out a vial of amber colored liquid. He placed it on a ledge carved into the stone wall beside Miriam's bed. Next to it, he set a large pouch.

"Medicine for your ailment. And—" He shoved his hand deeper into his scrip. "A good supply of bread, cheese, and roasted vegetables. And a horn of goat's milk."

Miriam began to sob. "Thank you," she mumbled into a handkerchief.

"Miriam, dear Miriam—" Judah rose to his feet and stroked her back.

Eleazar had rarely seen his father behave in such a manner. The tough old man had given in to his heart, but only on rare occasions. There was the day Simon was born. Judah had leaned over the baby's cradle while tears ran down his face.

Now he was bowing before this woman, and she'd called him "son." The relationship troubled Eleazar. He had questions. Lots of them. But would Judah ever tell him the whole story?

When they left Miriam's home, Judah paused again at the neighbor's door. They exchanged a few words, and there was again a tinkling of coins being dropped into the woman's open hand. More questions circled inside Eleazar's head. How could anyone demand payment for helping a neighbor? Even he, an admittedly headstrong youth, knew there was something wrong with such selfishness.

With some resolve, Eleazar expected they would head farther into the filthy darkness of the Lower City. Instead, when they left Miriam's street, his father turned upward, toward home.

"Why are you helping that old woman, Father? And why did she refer to you as her son?"

Judah gazed at him and breathed a long sigh. "My concern for Miriam goes beyond what usually happens between a physician and a sick old woman," he said, his voice soft. "After your grandmother died, it was Miriam who looked after our family. Your uncle Hiram and I were children, about the same ages as you and your brother, Simon. Miriam came daily to our home. She cooked our meals. She cleaned our house. She drew our water. On special occasions, she brought berries and fruit from the bushes and trees that grew on the hills outside the city. She went beyond the usual duties of a servant girl."

"She was your *servant*?" The reality hit Eleazar like a bolt of lightning.

"Yes, but more than that, she was my friend. After she finished her work, Miriam stayed into the night, playing games with us boys and telling us stories. We fell asleep to the music of her voice. Miriam treated us like her own children. She soothed our aches and pains, wiped our runny noses, and comforted our hearts. A servant? No. Not Miriam. She was a member of our family. A mother, a sister, even a grandmother. So, my son, you should be able to see why I care for her as I do. I can never fully repay her many kindnesses."

"Wouldn't it be easier to bring her into our home?" The thought struck Eleazar from out of nowhere, surprising even him.

"I considered having her live with us." Judah nodded pensively. "I wanted to care for her as she cared for us when we were young. But your mother created such a stir over having another mouth to feed, I had to close that door. I entrusted Miriam to her own children to care for her." He let out another sigh and frowned. "She never sees them. They've made a life for themselves in another place. They have forgotten about their mother, and they've neglected the laws that require them to look after her. So, whenever I work in the Lower City, I take care of Miriam, whatever she needs, as though caring for my own."

Eleazar thoughtfully considered his father's words. He understood now. Miriam had been a friend to his father, a servant in Judah's household, perhaps a grandmother to himself, if possible. She was no longer a stranger, a patient on his father's list. She was a human being.

"Is Miriam going to die?"

Judah nodded. "Soon," he said, his voice breaking. "I am trying to make her last days comfortable." He stopped walking and looked at Eleazar. "Can I trust you to help me do that?"

Eleazar nodded slowly.

He was still thinking about what his father had told him when they approached their own street. A crowd had gathered near their house. They wove past the neighbors and entered the courtyard. Simon came running from the house, his face streaked with tears, a wail erupting from his throat.

Judah dropped to his knees before his young son. "Simon, what's wrong?"

Sobbing and choking, Simon pointed toward the house. "Mama," was all he said.

Judah leapt to his feet and charged through the door. Eleazar followed close at his father's heels.

Inside, they found the neighborhood midwife in the center of the room, her face creased in anguish, the front of her apron stained with blood. Eleazar peered past her. The veil to his parents' quarters had been thrown open. His mother lay motionless on her bed, her hair a tangle of wet curls, the bedding beneath her a bright red. Her ashen face appeared like wax, her eyes were fixed on the ceiling. And on her abdomen lay a frail, lifeless baby girl.

Eleazar's head spun. Tears welled up in his eyes. Through the buzz in his ears he heard his father's anguished, "Mara. My Mara."

The old man fell upon the bed, sobbing. His body shook with intense agony. He continued to wail. "I should have remained at home. I should have been with you. Mara, my dear Mara."

Eleazar stared in disbelief. His mother was gone. And her infant child, born too soon, was dead.

Overwhelmed with grief, Eleazar fled from the house, past the crowd of busybodies, out into the street, and to a deserted hillside, where he collapsed in hopeless despair.

The rest of the day held more weeping, pacing, rending of cloaks, the irritating scratch of sackcloth, and the harsh scent of ashes mingled with tears. Neighbors rushed in and out of the house all day, their incessant wailing and whining lingered long after the mourners left.

That night, as Eleazar lay on his mat, he gazed out the window at a starless sky. His mother's words of guidance came flooding back to him. He pictured her face, the pride in her eyes, the smile as she helped him plan his future. Though she was gone, her words lived on in his heart.

In accordance with the law, the burial took place the next morning after Mara's death. The bodies of mother and baby were bathed, anointed with oil, sprinkled with aromatic herbs, and wrapped in linen cloths. Judah and his two sons led a procession of paid mourners and neighbors. They traveled along a dusty path to the family tomb outside the city. A harsh outpouring of lyres and tambourines filled the air. Judah's anguished cry rose above the noisy dirge. Eleazar wrapped an arm around his brother's shoulder, but the gesture only caused the little boy's heartrending sobs to grow louder. Eleazar's eyes gushed with tears as he looked with trepidation at the open tomb.

Four men bore the pallet that contained the bodies of Mara and her child. They settled the bodies inside the open grave and, with their heads bowed in reverence, they backed out of the opening and joined the crowd. The mourners' voices grew louder, their instruments grew noisier. Simon continued to weep, his little body trembling with uncontrolled grief. The men rolled a heavy stone across the grave's opening, and Eleazar breathed a final farewell to his mother and sister.

As the mourners continued to weep and wail in front of Mara's tomb, down the hillside in the town of Bethlehem a celebration was taking place. Instead of weeping and wailing, the people were rejoicing. A newborn babe had uttered his first cry. Shepherds had gathered there and were spreading the word. They claimed the Messiah had arrived. Villagers flocked to the site to see the miracle for themselves. The King, the Deliverer, the One called Emanuel had come at last.

CHAPTER EIGHT

As was customary, the family mourned openly for seven days. Neighbors heard the incessant wailing and sometimes joined in. Because he had come in contact with the dead, Judah also went through a full-body purification ritual. Then followed a period of private mourning, its length decided by the grieving family. For Judah's household, it went on for several days. Young Simon spent long hours curled up on his mat, with one arm draped over his little dog. Occasionally the boy emerged, ate a scrap of food or drank a little water, then he returned to his mat and the tiny dog that brought him only a little comfort.

Eleazar sat by the hearth and mourned quietly alone. He'd lost the one person who understood him, his only ally in his lifelong battle with his father. He stared into the fire and tried to block out the incessant scraping sounds of the old man's sandals pacing back and forth on the roof. Turning his attention to the pile of his mother's belongings, he pulled her chest from the heap and opened the lid. Inside lay the clothes she'd left behind, now to be given out to neighbors. He withdrew her combs, turned them over in his hands and removed a lone gray hair from the teeth of one.

He set the combs inside her pottery box. Then he lifted her favorite Sabbath dress, a blue linen robe with embroidered flowers around the hem. He pressed it to his cheek, savored the softness of the fine linen, and breathed deeply of his mother's lingering perfume. He returned the dress to the pile of clothing and reached for her jar of scented oil. At that moment, he thought he heard her voice calling his name from the courtyard. He looked through the open door at his mother's herb harden, now empty. Mara's plants had already begun to die. Tears came, and he fell back into mourning.

The house went momentarily silent. His father had stopped pacing. Then the sound of footsteps resonated on the outer stair. Quickly Eleazar slid the perfume and the pottery box behind him on the hearth. He shut the lid on his mother's chest and returned it to the pile. Grasping his two treasures, he hurried to his corner of the room, stepped over Simon who was now deep in sleep, and stuffed the items in a private nook behind his mat.

Several days passed before Judah was ready to return to his work. Eleazar spent time setting order to the medicines in his father's apothecary. When relatives of the sick came to the house, he handed them the needed powders and oils. At other times he settled in his corner by the hearth and read through his father's medical scrolls, torn bits of parchment with basic treatments for everything from a headache to a broken leg. Eleazar was certain the doctors beyond the Great Sea were practicing far better methods of healing. He'd heard about the Greeks and their wisdom in all fields of endeavor, particularly medicine.

While Eleazar renewed his dream to study abroad, his brother Simon had fallen into deep depression. The boy wept in his sleep, refused to eat a substantial meal, and avoided his friends who came to the door. Judah tried in vain to draw him out of his grief. He encouraged him to start lessons at the temple under Rabbi Heth. The boy wouldn't talk to his father, but turned away scowling. In desperation, the old man decided to send his youngest son to live with Uncle Hiram in Bethany. The man and his wife had no children of their own, so they willingly agreed to take young Simon into their home. Eleazar hated to see Simon leave, but his little brother was slowly dying, and he had to admit that such a change might save the boy's life.

On the day of Simon's departure, Eleazar went outside while his brother finished packing his belongings. Gray clouds had gathered overhead and cast a depressing pall over the courtyard. His mother's garden had fallen to ruin. Once filled with red and green flowering herbs, the patch of garden had turned to rubble. The vegetable plants had withered and there was no longer any fruit on the trees. It was as if all of nature had joined the family in mourning.

Uncle Hiram approached the gate with his donkey. Simon emerged from the house with Ishshah cradled in one arm and his other hand dragging a sack that held everything he owned. He handed the bundle to Uncle Hiram, then turned for a final farewell.

Judah reached out to give his son a hug. Simon stiffened and backed away. Instead Judah received a piercing glare from the boy's eyes.

Simon turned away from his father and drew close to Eleazar for a lingering embrace.

Eleazar clung to his brother. "Be safe, Simon. If you ever need anything, please come to me. I won't forget you. I won't turn you away."

Eleazar closed his eyes and tried to squeeze back a flow of tears. His brother slipped from his arms. Eleazar stepped back and watched helplessly as Simon joined their uncle at the gate. Nothing more was said. Judah's shoulders heaved with his silent sobbing. Hiram gave a quick wave, and they started off down the hill.

In Mara's absence, Judah hired a woman to come every day to cook and clean. Like a shadow, Endira slipped into the house at daybreak and escaped at dusk, leaving behind a swept and tidy home, clean clothes for the family, an assortment of dried fruits and meats, and a stack of fresh-baked breads on the hearth.

Judah dove into his work. With renewed enthusiasm Eleazar accompanied his father to the Upper City. And, with some reluctance, he also went along on Judah's occasional visits to the Lower City. In time, Eleazar began to relax in Miriam's presence and even enjoyed her humorous stories about his father and Uncle Hiram. On one occasion, he brought her the set of his mother's combs and even tucked them in her hair for her. She smiled up at him, the way she had smiled at his father, with unspoken love and appreciation.

He came away from each visit with words of wisdom rolling around in his head.

"Worries go down far better with hot soup," she'd said between sips of the broth Judah had brought.

At other times, she drew upon memories from her younger days and finished each tale with a proverb. "A half truth is a whole lie." And, "Youth is a crown of roses; old age a crown of willows."

Then there was Eleazar's favorite: "A cheerful heart is good medicine, but a crushed spirit dries up the bones."

Unexpectedly, he had grown to love the old woman, had begun to think of her as the grandmother he'd never known, and he looked forward to seeing her each week. Her stories about his father and Uncle Hiram made him laugh aloud. Others—sadder tales— nearly brought him to tears. Like the time young Judah fell from a tree and thought he'd never walk again. At last, Eleazar understood the nature of his father's increasing limp as they traveled up and down the hills of the city.

Through Miriam, Eleazar was gradually getting to know his father. No longer did he see him as a domineering tyrant.

Eleazar even began to anticipate Judah's visits with the lepers outside the city. He learned to look for the signs. Days before, Judah collected bundles of clothes from the relatives of dead people.

Once, he even filled a sack with Mara's clothing. Eleazar tried not to think about old Hilda wearing his mother's blue Sabbath dress. The moment the image came to his mind, he wiped it away.

Then there were the usual two packs of food and medicines. And when the time came for Judah to depart, he avoided Eleazar's gaze, spoke little, and busied himself with gathering the supplies together. It was then that Eleazar retreated to the upper room. He waited there until his father departed, confident that Judah would never again ask him to go along.

It was at just such a time when Judah paused before leaving and instructed Eleazar to straighten the apothecary. "Pay heed to what we need, and we'll go to the market tomorrow," he said. Then with a nod of his head, he left their home and headed for the city gate.

Eleazar finished his chore quickly. His father would be away for several more hours. Time for a visit with Achim. It had been a while since the two had gotten together. He hurried to his friend's house.

Achim greeted him at the door with a broad smile and open arms. His eyes sparkled like the blue of the sky, and he beckoned Eleazar inside with wave of his hand.

"I have something for you," Achim said, and it was obvious by the strain in his voice that he could hardly contain his excitement. "Something my father brought from across the sea."

Eleazar pressed his friend. "What is it? Tell me."

"You'll see. It's a surprise."

Achim led him into the main house. Eleazar kicked off his sandals and glided over the marble tiles. Several new furnishings had been added since his last visit. A waist-high wooden table on four legs, a huge closet with hinged doors, three bronze stands bearing oil lamps that cast an orange glow against the far wall.

They passed several open doorways. A visitor's area furnished with cushioned seats and a table for food and drink.

Eleazar craned his neck toward the kitchen. "Where's your mother?"

"She went to the marketplace with my father, to search for some meaningless treasure or to share the latest gossip with the other women."

Eleazar chuckled to himself. Achim's mother was known for her overzealous tongue.

The two mounted an inside stairway that led to Achim's private quarters on the roof. Unlike Eleazar's tiny corner that he once shared with Simon, Achim, an only child, had a broad rooftop retreat completely to himself. A large open porch spanned the outer court, and beyond a veil was Achim's covered sleeping area. As many times as Eleazar had entered that room, he was always struck with awe. It was no different now as he stepped through the curtain and swept his eyes over the raised bed, the hand-carved ebony table, floors overlaid with the cedars of Lebanon, and a tall cupboard with gold accents. A minty aroma permeated everything and had his head spinning as much from the overwhelming wealth as the intoxicating smell. At times like this he wondered how he and Achim had become such good friends.

Achim went to the cupboard and pulled the gold latch to open the door, exposing several shelves, most of them filled with colorful tunics, folded neatly and stacked in a row. There was Achim's coat of many colors, along with several others in rich blues and greens. Achim slipped his hand between the garments and withdrew several scrolls that seemed to be hidden there. He tossed them on the bed, and, with a wave of his hand, he invited Eleazar to join him there.

Eleazar stared in disbelief at the pile of parchments.

"What's the matter, Eleazar?" Achim laughed, and his face lit up like the sun. "Have you never seen scrolls before?"

"Of course I have, but these don't look at all like those we studied at the temple." He ran his hand over the long tubes. "This papyrus is smooth, not coarse. And strong. There are no ragged edges."

Still grinning, Achim unfurled one of the scrolls. Eleazar

leaned close. He recognized the square letters characteristic of Aramaic script. After spending hours over Hebrew letters, he welcomed the opportunity to read something in the common language of the day.

Tracing the letters with his finger, he read the page the traditional way, from the bottom right corner to the upper left. Then, he raised his head, his eyes wide. "These writings speak of illnesses and of possible cures."

Achim nodded. "Yes, my friend. They've been translated from the Greek."

Eleazar leaped onto the bed beside his friend. He lifted another scroll and quickly scanned the text. Then he tossed it aside and plucked another from the pile.

He could hardly contain his excitement. "These are treasures!" Grabbing another scroll, he read a few words aloud, looked up at Achim and smiled. His friend had given him the writings of the doctors of Alexandria. In his hands were the words of Hippocrates and other knowledgeable scholars, all translated into Aramaic.

"Do you know what this means, Achim?" Without waiting for his friend to respond, he answered the question himself. "This is what I've been needing. My father's scrolls contain simple instructions. These writings go beyond the common practices of Judea."

Achim laughed heartily. "Look." He pointed. "Here's one that describes broken bones and other injuries. And this one speaks of medicines unknown in this part of the world."

For the rest of the afternoon, with Achim looking over his shoulder, Eleazar poured over the parchments. Finally, he gave his friend a grateful hug.

"How can I ever repay you?"

"You can bring more of your father's medicine for my mother." Achim shrugged. "She complains day and night about her stomach pains. At other times, she chatters endlessly about the neighbors' business. Your father's mixture of herbs puts my mother to sleep, and it gives my father and me a few hours of peace."

"I'll bring some tomorrow," Eleazar promised. Then, gathering the scrolls in his arms, he headed for home. Along the way, he considered how his father might respond to his good fortune. Judah had little use for the medical practices outside of his own city. But it didn't really matter if Judah approved or disapproved. Achim had given Eleazar the tools he needed to pursue his dream. He'd taken the first step toward his promised future, and he wasn't about to turn back.

He entered the house to the aroma of lamb, coated with olive oil and garlic, and roasting by the fire. Endira had already set out a platter of raisin bread and a bowl of fresh-picked berries. The plump woman turned from the hearth, acknowledged his presence with a nod, and went back to her work. Few words ever passed between them, but Eleazar didn't care. She cooked his meals, washed his clothes, and swept the house clean, and that was sufficient.

Judah was nowhere to be seen, so Eleazar retreated to his corner and sorted through his scrolls. He settled on one and sat back against his pillow. The writing described a method of cutting open a woman's belly to withdraw a baby. He wondered if such a procedure might have saved his mother's life and the baby's too. He bit his lip. His father had no knowledge of such a possibility. If he'd known, perhaps he could have saved them. But no. The old man remained locked inside the medicines of the past.

Shaking his head, Eleazar continued reading. He looked up once to find Endira had left without saying a word. Then he heard the scraping of his father's feet in the courtyard.

His heart pounding, Eleazar rose from his mat and lifted the scrolls. His father entered the house, freshly washed and ready for supper. They settled on cushions in front of the spread of food left by Endira. Eleazar set the scrolls on the floor between them. Judah murmured a benediction, then dove into the lamb as though he hadn't eaten for days.

Even as he ate, the old man glanced at the scrolls, wrinkled his brow, then went back to his platter of food. He kept eating and said nothing. Eleazar grew more and more restless. He picked at his food and kept glancing from his father to the scrolls. Then, as Judah scraped up the last crumbs of bread, the old man narrowed his eyes and gestured toward the parchments.

Eleazar caught his father's silent question and responded. "A gift from Achim. They're scrolls. From Alexandria."

Judah pulled one from the pile, unrolled it and examined its contents. He stroked his beard pensively. Then he raised his head and gazed into Eleazar's eyes.

"So. You are moving ahead in your studies without my help."

"We can *both* study these," Eleazar offered. "The procedures go far beyond what the physicians in Judea practice. We can surpass them all." He looked hopefully into his father's face. "Together."

Judah's eyebrows rose. "Is that what you want? Do you seek to be the best physician in all Judea, to be honored for your wisdom and abilities? It seems you would prefer to serve man while ignoring the call of the Almighty—the call handed down by my father and his father before him."

His father's harsh words struck Eleazar's heart. Now he feared Judah might burn the scrolls.

"I don't want to be better than *everybody else*, Father. I only want to be better than *myself*. You've set me on the right path. I can learn more, not only from you but from these writings."

With a snap of his wrist, Judah dropped the scroll back onto the pile. Then, heaving a sigh, he rested a hand on Eleazar's shoulder. "All right, my son. You can have your scrolls, but only as long as they don't distract you from the lessons *I* will be teaching you. I don't want these writings to make you too proud to listen to my instruction. What I teach goes far beyond the schools and the scholars of Alexandria. They will teach you practices. I will teach you compassion. They will teach you to rely on instruments of their trade. I will teach you to rely on your heart."

Signaling an end to the conversation, Judah lifted his cup and sipped heartily of his goat's milk.

Eleazar scraped up the last of his meal. With his mother gone and Endira already out of the house, the cleanup would fall on him.

Eleazar turned his attention back to the pile of scrolls and smiled to himself. They promised an escape from his father's heavy hand, a path away from the miserable souls Judah served. He stood and began to gather the remnants of their meal, when someone rapped on the doorpost.

Who would come for healing at such an hour? He didn't move. Judah shuffled to the door. There stood a shabbily dressed, hunchbacked man with a somber look on his face. He drew close to Judah and whispered in his ear.

Eleazar continued to gather the scraps from the evening meal. He kept glancing at the man in the doorway. *Perhaps father will take care of his needs quickly, and he will go away.*

Their muffled voices ceased. The man left without so much as a vial of medicine. Judah stood very still just staring out at the departing figure. Eleazar caught his breath, aware that a terrible shadow had settled on their house.

"Father, what is it? What's happened? Is it Simon?"

Judah shook his head. "No, nothing has happened to your brother. It's bad news from the Lower City. That was Miriam's neighbor. He came here to tell me she has died." The old man bent low under an invisible weight. "His wife discovered her at midday. There was no time to summon us, no opportunity to heal her." Judah began to sob. "They prepared her body and buried her in a pauper's grave. A pauper's grave, Eleazar." The old man's eyes flooded over with tears. "She died alone." He shook his head. "Alone, Eleazar. No one should die alone. Least of all, Miriam."

A deep groan rose from Judah's throat. Startled, Eleazar dropped the platter he was holding. It clattered to the floor at his feet. He watched helplessly as with trembling hands his father tore his robe and released the tattered cloth at his sides.

The old man lifted his face toward heaven and filled the room with a pitiful wail. Then he fell to his knees and, rocking back and forth, wept as though his heart had been rent in two along with his robe. Judah's voice rose and fell in an unquenchable display of grief.

Except for the day his mother died, Eleazar had never seen his father in such a miserable state. He stood frozen, unsure of how to comfort the old man. Miriam meant more to his father than another sick person. She was a friend, a second mother, a wonderful old sage.

Holding his breath, he slipped past his father and quietly left the house. Outside, the cold darkness engulfed him. His father's wailing pierced the still air. Eleazar pressed his hands over his ears. Miriam had died. She was old. And sick. Wasn't she better off now, to be free, at last, from her sickbed and a life that had no purpose?

He looked around the courtyard, unsure of where to go or what to do. Tears came. They ran down his face. A terrible grief encompassed him. He cursed himself. Why did he care about that old woman? She was his father's friend, not his. He didn't know why, but somehow her death had pierced his heart. If this was the compassion his father had been trying to teach him, then he wanted none of it.

Stifling a sob, he ran from the courtyard and into the dark street. The bitter air struck his face like pellets of ice. He stumbled over the pavement, kept on going until he reached a secluded bend in the road. There, on a mound of dirt, he fell to the ground, buried his head in his hands, and let the tears flow without restraint.

CHAPTER NINE

To Eleazar's disappointment, his father continued the weekly journeys into the Lower City. Even though Miriam was gone and Shaul's broken leg had healed long ago, Judah continued to make himself available to the poor. There were many to be seen. As usual, they came home with little to show for their day's labor.

Judah's limping became worse over time. Some days, he remained at home, and those who were well enough to travel came to his door at all hours of the day and night. Some came on behalf of a sick relative. Others dragged themselves out of their sickbeds and arrived at the house, almost too sick to stand. Judah took care of all of them. No matter what the hour, he never sent anyone away without first trying to help. Eleazar had the task of mounting the outer stair to the upper room to fetch ointments, herbs, vials of oil, and various balms requested by his father. In payment, Judah graciously received whatever the visitor could afford.

A few times each month they packed a small bag of medicines and went to the Upper City where they answered calls from lawyers, tax collectors, merchants, and other men of high esteem. Eleazar accompanied his father with eagerness. This was the type of medicine he longed to practice. These people had bathed.

They paid well. Their maladies required simple cures, not like the filthy common people on the brink of death.

Nevertheless, wherever they went, whether to the homes of the elite or to the dregs of the earth, Eleazar heard the same accolades over and over again. They all loved "Judah ben Serach, the finest physician in all Judea."

He also put up with his father's long-winded descriptions of medical care, far removed from Achim's scrolls and the writings of more proficient doctors.

"We cleanse cuts with rose water, and we stitch the torn skin with horsehair," Judah said as they walked together. But Eleazar had learned the names of more potent medicines than rose water, and he'd read about coating the rough horsehair with candle wax to make it pass through the skin easier.

"Broken limbs must be bound. Do you remember Shaul?" Eleazar gave a sideways glance at his father. Of course, he remembered Shaul. They had spent many an afternoon at the man's house, long after his leg was healed.

"He was able to return to work within a few weeks," Judah said with an air of pride. Then he shook his head and the lines gathered on his forehead. "But not all broken legs mend as well. You have to watch for the signs, Eleazar. If someone's toes have turned black, they must be cut off. Then we need to bind the foot in order to save the rest of the leg."

All of Judah's instructions fell on deaf ears, for Eleazar already had learned better alternatives. Achim's scrolls had become his teacher, and he had little time for his father's babbling.

The men who wrote those words spoke of steel blades for slitting open the skin, sharp hooks that could be used for removing infected pieces of flesh, drills for relieving pressure in the skull, and special saws for severing a limb so perfectly that healing would follow. Such were the writings that stirred Eleazar's heart.

Still, he nodded his acceptance, temporarily appeasing his father and avoiding unnecessary arguments with the old man. Judah would never acknowledge the wisdom of doctors in a distant country. Eleazar knew that. For now, all he could do was pretend to agree with the old man while secretly hanging onto the scrolls Achim had given him.

They spoke of stronger medicines than anything they had in Judea, and a draining of the blood and other methods his father had not learned. His one dream now was to go to Alexandria where he could study under doctors who taught such procedures.

On one of their walks, Judah revived a painful memory for Eleazar. For some reason the old man found it necessary to talk about the problems associated with leprosy. Eleazar had avoided such a discussion from the day he'd encountered those hopeless souls. Now he could not escape Judah's sudden desire to talk about them.

"When a plague hits a dwelling, it's a terrible thing," Judah said, his tone grave. "The entire area must be cut off from visitors until the afflicted one heals. And, of course, if the priest declares the person unclean, you know what must be done."

Eleazar nodded but kept his eyes on the road ahead. "They must leave the city."

Judah grunted and then went on. "The separation might last for only seven days, as the law requires. But, at the end of that time if the spot has not healed, the priest will declare the person a leper and ban him—or her," he said with a twist of his head—"forever."

Eleazar didn't respond. Not a word of acknowledgement, not even a nod of his head. He stiffened his back and picked up his step. The old man seemed to understand his resistance.

"I tell you this for one reason, my son."

Eleazar kept walking.

"There's one more tool you need to have in your medical kit, and it's the most important one of all."

His interest slightly revived, he turned to look at his father.

Judah stopped walking and gazed into Eleazar's eyes. "It's compassion."

The word struck him like an overused proverb. How many

times was his father going to pound this same lesson into his head? He restrained a smirk but felt his patience continue to wane.

"Without compassion, you will merely be performing a simple physical healing," Judah went on, oblivious to Eleazar's sudden disinterest. "People need sympathy, encouragement, a gentle word, before they can get fully well. They need to know you care, Eleazar, that you understand their suffering." The old man grunted. "I'm afraid I haven't seen any such emotion displayed by you. I've watched you closely. You have skilled hands and a ready knowledge of medicines and diseases. But you do the work without offering one word of encouragement. Your fingers move, but your heart has frozen."

He stared back at his father and hardened his own gaze. Two pairs of steel gray eyes locked in a stubborn clash of wills.

"Don't you understand, Eleazar? This is why I've been taking you to visit the poorest of the poor. I wanted you to develop a heart for people who desperately need your care. I wanted you to know that our work is not dependent on how much money we earn or how famous we might become. It has to do with compassion for the hurting, no matter what their position in life."

Eleazar didn't blink. He stood straight and tall, his body rigid, his resistance evident. His father's persistence left him wanting Alexandria all the more. Compassion? He had no desire to be bound to the people of the Lower City. His mother's dream for him had been rekindled by the scrolls, and nothing would be able to turn him back from that dream.

He set his heart on going to Alexandria to study under the greatest physicians in the world. He wanted to visit the magnificent library and to fill his mind with lessons taught by great scholars. He knew what he had to do. He would continue to turn a deaf ear to his father's nonsense, all the while memorizing the writings in the scrolls and dreaming about the day when he could break free of Judah's control.

Then he awoke one morning to an entirely new problem.

Their female servant had not come to the house as was her usual custom.

"Endira is sick," Judah told him. "Her son came to tell us she would not be here today. You will have to fetch the water this morning."

Eleazar stared in disbelief. "Father, that is woman's work."

The old man turned his back to him. He bent near the hearth and turned a loaf of unleavened bread.

"Yes, it is woman's work, but only when there's a woman around to do it." Judah's tone was firm. "We need water, Eleazar. The jar is empty."

To be seen in public carrying a jar of water would bring the worst humiliation on him. "Please, Father, don't ask me to go. Can't we hire someone? I'll search the neighborhood for one of the young girls to come and help. Until Endira is well, we certainly can afford to pay someone a few coins."

Judah turned to face him. "It's mid-morning. The women already will have filled their water pots early today. If you go now, no one will see you. None of your friends will know you did woman's work."

Eleazar stiffened and clenched his teeth. Judah's brows went up. Then, the lines on the old man's face relaxed and he softened his tone.

"My son, you must learn to put away your pride. You have duties. Yesterday, your duty was to help the sick. Today, your duty is to fetch the water. It is no less honorable. Our life changed when your mother died. Since Simon left, it's only the two of us. We must help each other. Now, if you don't go for the water, we will have none for the remainder of the day, perhaps for several days."

Reluctantly, Eleazar lifted the empty jug to his shoulder and started for the door.

"Go to the Pool of Bethesda," his father called after him. "The water is fresher there, not stagnant like the filth in the nearby cistern. Until it rains again, you will have to go to the pool."

Eleazar released a sigh and started on the road to Siloam. On the way, he passed a party of young girls with water jars balanced on top of their heads. He cringed under their amused stares. Flushed with shame, he bit his lip and hurried off.

Upon reaching the pool, he moved toward the rock wall where the sparkling liquid gushed from between the stones, clean and fresh. Holding his jar beneath the flow, he scanned the area, comforted that he appeared to be alone. When the water reached the rim, he lifted the jar back onto his shoulder and turned to leave. But before he could take one step away from the pool, a girl's laughter startled him.

It was a familiar laugh. The lilting voice took him back to the home of Ariel. He slowly turned, scanned the area, and found Ruth sitting on a ledge a short distance from the pool. He hadn't noticed her when he'd arrived. He'd set his eyes on the pool and his mind on getting in and out of there quickly.

He stared into her glistening dark eyes. A smile crossed her lips. She looked even more beautiful than the day he'd seen her in Ariel's courtyard. She wore a bright purple dress, a noteworthy contrast against her creamy complexion and stark black hair. Her cheeks were flushed a deep pink. Her jeweled hands were folded on her lap, and her feet, adorned with toe rings and an ankle bracelet, dangled a few inches above the ground. She swung them back and forth, drawing his attention to the gems on her toes. Eleazar thought his heart was about to come out of his chest.

Swallowing hard, he shifted the jar to his other shoulder. "I— um—our servant girl didn't come today." He was stumbling over his words, but he rushed ahead anyway. "My mother is gone. I have no sister to do the chores." He shook his head. "This is not my regular duty. I'm a physician." He raised his chin, a surge of pride coming with the word *physician*.

She laughed again, and it sounded almost musical, like water bubbling from the rocks. She leaped off the ledge and took a step toward him. He backed away, spilling a little water from the jar.

"I already know you're a physician, Eleazar. Don't you remember? You came to my house and healed my father."

She took another step closer. He caught his breath.

Trembling, he lowered his jug to the ground and faced her. He swallowed and searched for something to say. "Your father is well?"

"Yes, he's gone off to another land—Alexandria—buying, selling, searching for something special for his daughters."

"Alexandria?" Eleazar forgot about the water jar.

"Oh, yes." Her smile broadened. "You know my father is a merchant. He often travels to Joppa, Caesarea, and other ports along the Great Sea. And when he crosses over, he goes to Alexandria."

She had captured Eleazar's full attention now. He looked past her sparkling black eyes, her flowing hair, her flushed face. The mere mention of Alexandria had his imagination spinning.

"I plan to go to Alexandria one day," he told her with confidence. "I want to study medicine there."

She nodded with understanding. "Many teachers go there from all over the world. Doctors too."

He plunged ahead with boldness. "I have a set of scrolls from Alexandria. My friend Achim gave them to me. I've read them over and over and have committed many of the teachings to memory."

Ruth smiled sweetly. "I've been to Alexandria." She spoke softly, pensively, as if she might be remembering. "My father sometimes takes me with him to visit my sister who lives there. It's an exciting place, Eleazar." She waved her hand and set off a tinkle of gold bracelets.

"Tell me more." He went to the ledge and sat, his eyes never leaving Ruth's face. "What are the smells, the sights, the sounds?"

She joined him there and sprang onto the rock beside him, but she kept a suitable distance away from him. Then she stared off beyond the water fountain.

He waited, his heart pounding with anticipation.

She moistened her lips and began to speak, her voice soft

and meditative. "A breeze drifts off the water and brings with it the smell of salted fish. If you get away from the shore, a new aroma arises from the flower gardens and the shops selling fresh-baked bread, and lamb roasting over a pit. People walk by and you catch the scents of various perfumes."

"The city," Eleazar prompted her. "What does the city look like?"

She lifted a shoulder. "Broad streets, rows of shops with all sorts of things for sale. Inns where people can buy a meal or spend the night. In the hills are many houses, including the one where my sister lives with her heathen husband." She let out a little giggle. "My sister chose the unbound lifestyle of the Greeks. Here, we are caught within so many laws and traditions. But there—in Alexandria—it doesn't matter if you are Jewish or Greek or Roman or from any other nation. Everyone blends together in one great crowd of cultures. Except for the stricter Jews who build their homes in a separate quarter, most of the people mingle in the streets and shops unconcerned about where they all came from.

Eleazar tried to imagine the city coming alive with all of Ruth's descriptions. In a brief time she had transported him across the sea to a place that until now had been only a dream.

"Go on," he said. "I want to know about the library and the school of medicine."

He was thrilled that they were at last talking, and it wasn't simply idle talk, but she had taken him on a journey to Alexandria.

"The library?" she said with a smile. "It's very large, with several rooms, a central garden, and schools, not only for medicine, but for astronomy and philosophy and law. Thousands of scrolls are housed there from many parts of the world." She frowned. "Years ago a great fire destroyed half of the city and a good part of the library. They were able to rescue many of the parchments, though they lost some to the flames. Then people added more to the collection as the years went by. It took a long time to restore the building."

Eleazar opened his heart to her. "I would like to study there one day. What is the school of medicine like?"

She answered with a little shrug. "The last time my father took me to Alexandria was about a year ago. The restoration was still going on. The work should be almost finished by now." Her eyes glistened with delight, and she gave him a half-smile. "That's your secret. Do you want to know *my* secret?"

He nodded.

"The university is open to people of any culture and of any status in life—including women. If I can convince my father, I would like to study literature. I love to read, and I want to be able to argue my position regarding the works of Plato and Aristotle."

Eleazar chuckled as he tried to imagine Ruth with a scroll in her hand and arguing with the most prominent scholars of the day. He admired her spirit. But once she returned to Judea, such schooling would fall away. Her lot in life was set. She would bear a houseful of children. Her interests would be in the home. But if she remained in Alexandria—

"I suppose you could stay with your sister," Eleazar offered. "Then, you could who go to the university. And you could argue with the scholars."

He released a laugh, then saw the hurt in her eyes. "I didn't mean—"

"Don't worry," she said, shaking her head with sadness. "My father would never allow me to stay with Abigail." She lowered her eyes.

His heart broke for her. He knew how much it hurts when someone shatters a dream.

"You mentioned Abigail's husband," he said in an effort to ease her pain. "It sounds like your father has accepted your sister's chosen life. Perhaps he'll be less strict with you as well."

Ruth raised her head. "She married the Greek against my father's wishes. At first he treated them as outcasts. But, in time, my father restored his relationship with Abigail. Now her husband assists him by seeking out bargains that come into the city. Ziba makes the purchases at the shore, and he ships the goods to Joppa, completing the entire labor in one day. With

Ziba's help, my father has been able to stay well ahead of the other merchants in Jerusalem. His business thrives because of my sister's choice of a husband. Nevertheless, I have no doubt, he would want to shelter me from their influence. And so, aside from a few controlled visits, my dream to live there cannot be fulfilled." Her dark eyes brightened. "But yours can."

A silence settled between them. Eleazar thought about his own father, likely watching the door for his return with the water. He leaped from the ledge. Tensing his arms, he lifted the water jug to his shoulder.

"I need to get this home. My father asked me to come for the water. This jar is far too heavy for any of the neighborhood girls to carry. It holds enough water for at least three days."

"Oh? Too heavy for a girl?" Ruth giggled loudly. She gestured toward a cluster of bushes.

There in the shadows Eleazar made out the outline of a shrouded figure. Ruth's handmaid. He'd seen her before. She was a cow of a girl, her large bones hidden behind layers of veils and her broad face partially wrapped in a shroud.

"Anna," Ruth commanded. "The water."

Ruth's handmaid emerged from the shadows. Resting on her shoulder was a jar nearly twice the size of his. He swallowed with embarrassment.

"Anna has served me since my tenth birthday," Ruth announced. "She lives with her parents in Bethany and comes daily to help me with anything I need her to do. In the morning she helps me bathe and dress, and she brings my meals. But, forgive me. Anna is more than a servant. She's my friend. My secret keeper. My companion. Do you see all the veils she wears? She comes from a modest family. I doubt her husband will see her face until their wedding night." Ruth giggled again, like she had revealed a secret.

Eleazar couldn't help but compare the two. The large servant was the exact opposite of Ruth, a fragile, delicate girl who needed protection. One looked like a work horse, the other, like a princess.

With that image in his mind, he turned to leave.

"When will I see you again?" Ruth boldly asked.

He smiled, for her boldness was the very quality that set her apart from the dull females in his neighborhood. He paused and considered a meeting.

"On the Sabbath, after the morning service." He lifted his chin. "Do you know the garden? Gethsemane?"

She nodded.

"There's an old olive tree, the oldest one in the garden. We can meet there, and you can tell me more about Alexandria." He raised his eyebrows.

She smiled and gave him a little wave, once again setting off a tinkle of bracelets.

As he departed, his head swam with joy. Silently, he thanked Endira for staying away that morning. If not for her absence, he would not have had this time with Ruth.

With the jug balanced on his shoulder, he hurried toward home. His heart pounded with the rhythm of his feet. Ruth could have summoned any young man in the city, but she'd paid attention to him. Hadn't her eyes flashed with passion when she talked about Alexandria? And hadn't she asked for another meeting with him?

He was remembering the things she'd said about Alexandria, when his thoughts were interrupted by two tall, slim figures coming down the street toward him. Their feet struck the pavement at a fast clip, the hems of their black robes slapped at the air. He recognized them immediately. Levi and his father! Quickly, he searched for a place where he might escape. They drew nearer. He considered turning around, but it was too late. They'd already caught sight of him. Levi's lips parted in an ugly sneer. Eleazar clenched his teeth and waited for the insult that was sure to come.

But just as Levi opened his mouth to speak, another figure sailed between them, blocking their path. An array of colors flashed before Eleazar's eyes as Achim shielded him from Levi and his father.

"I went to your house, this morning," Achim said, gasping for breath. "Your father told me how you offered to help with the water today." He spoke loud enough for Levi to hear. "What a nice thing to do, Eleazar. Only a secure young man would agree to such a chore." He shot a satisfied glance at Levi who passed by them just then. Achim raised his chin and patted Eleazar on his back. "Come on. I'll walk home with you."

Achim stepped in stride with Eleazar and hurried him away from the Pharisee and his son. Still, Eleazar caught part of Levi's last words— "woman's work, that's what he's doing." He decided to ignore the insult and moved on, grateful to have his best friend by his side.

Despite the weight of the jar, Eleazar picked up his pace. Achim huffed along beside him, his face flushed and moist with sweat.

Eleazar let out a laugh. "I'm the one carrying this jar, and *you* look as though you're about to fall over."

"I'm twice your size, Eleazar. I'm not accustomed to walking so fast, especially in the heat of the day." Achim struggled to catch his breath. "When I saw Levi and his father approaching you, I ran as fast as I could. I doubt you would have been able to avoid those two."

Eleazar managed a smile. "Thanks for interrupting what could have been a moment of shame."

"It's my duty as a true friend."

"Why did you go to my house?"

"I needed to buy some of that medicine my mother likes. Your father told me where I'd find you."

Eleazar's smile caught Achim's interest. The boy's eyebrows shot up. "What's happened?"

Eleazar's smile widened. "I saw Ruth today."

"What? Where?"

"I'll tell you everything when we get to my house. My father will be angry if I don't hurry."

After reaching home, Eleazar lowered the jar in its corner by the hearth. There was no sign of his father, so he and Achim retreated to Eleazar's private corner.

They settled on his mat, and Eleazar told his friend about his meeting with Ruth. "She wants to see me after services on the Sabbath." Eleazar could hardly contain his joy. "Do you believe the girl of my dreams wants to see me again?"

Achim laughed and patted his shoulder. "You fool. Don't you know nearly every girl in Jerusalem has her eye on you? You're tall and muscular. And you have that wonderful thick head of hair. It's no wonder Levi is jealous. He has a long, pointy nose and he's as skinny as a rod."

"Perhaps, but I don't have his money or his father's position. Aren't *those* the things girls look for when they're ready for a husband?"

"It's true, you don't have wealth and position right now, but as a physician you will be able to acquire both."

Eleazar shrugged. "I can only hope."

Suddenly Achim slapped his forehead. "I'm such a fool. I almost forgot why I came here. Will you sell me some of your father's dark-colored liquid, the one my mother uses to numb her pain? I've been away from home far too long."

The two hurried up the outer stair to the apothecary, Eleazar found a vial of Zilpah's medicine and handed it to his friend. Achim offered him a coin. Eleazar hesitated for a moment, then he reached out and accepted it.

As he descended the stairs, Achim called over his shoulder, "Let me know what happens on the Sabbath." He had a sly smile on his lips and a twinkle in his eyes.

Eleazar nodded, but he was far too elated to speak.

CHAPTER TEN

Clothed in his Sabbath best, his hair oiled and groomed, his body anointed with his mother's perfume, Eleazar went to the temple with his father. The old man kept glancing at him, a perplexed frown on his face. He never asked about the extra grooming, never questioned the aromatic scents wafting from his body.

Eleazar was ready with an answer. "I'm growing up, Father," was what he had rehearsed over and over again. He had no intention of telling the old man about his planned meeting with Ruth.

During the ceremonies, he was able to slip away into the crowd. His father would likely assume he had gone off with Achim.

When the service ended, he went from the temple to Gethsemane, his feet gliding over the cobbled roads like wings on fire. As he ascended the rise of the hill that led to the garden, his legs turned into flimsy reeds. An uncontrollable quiver surged through his body. He was going to see Ruth, and she was going to fill his heart with more stories about Alexandria.

The instant he passed through the gate, his cheeks grew hot, and his hands began to tremble. He cleared his throat and tried to dislodge the lump that had settled there.

Then he caught sight of Ruth standing by the old olive tree as she had promised. He stopped moving, stood very still, and admired the slim form in the pale yellow dress and the sheer green mantle. A thin band of gold crossed her forehead, and a single toe ring graced her right foot. Shiny black tresses framed her face, and she bore the same confident smile he'd seen before.

Taking a deep breath, he started toward her, his senses instantly sharpened by the scent of sweet calamus. He searched the clearing and breathed a sigh of relief. Ruth's handmaid hadn't come. They would be alone, a practice that was frowned upon by the adults in their city, but becoming more and more acceptable among the young people.

She held a small package. "I brought lunch," she said, giggling.

He nodded. "Let's walk a little." He gestured toward the path that wove among the trees in the garden.

Ruth nodded and stepped beside him, keeping a reasonable distance away from him. Eleazar struggled to find his voice. He felt her eyes on him, as though she were waiting for him to begin their talk. He straightened his back and struggled to find the right words.

"Tell me more about Alexandria," he said at last.

Ruth's face brightened. Her eyes sparkled, and she smiled, setting off the dimple in her left cheek.

"As I already told you, Eleazar, it's a wonderful place." Once again, she gazed off in the distance, as if she could see all the way to Alexandria. And she began to describe from memory the place that had captured her heart.

"There's a small island named Pharos and a lighthouse, the first thing you will see as you approach the coast." Already he was imagining a visit there, his ship drawing closer to shore. "It's a powerful structure," Ruth went on. "Tall and magnificent, with white marble sides that glisten in the sunlight. At night, its light sweeps across the sea and shines on the rocks close to shore, warning the approaching ships."

Settling on a ledge at the far end of the garden, Ruth patted the rock and signaled for him to join her. He sat beside her, grew quiet, and waited for her to continue her stories.

She opened her package and handed him a wedge of goat's cheese. As they dined on raisins and unleavened bread she brought Alexandria to the garden. He'd already envisioned the lighthouse, the waves crashing against the rocky shore, the shoreline, and the approaching ships. He could almost smell the salty air and feel the rocks beneath his feet.

"When you stand on the platform beneath the lighthouse, you will feel small and unimportant." Ruth went on. "Massive stone stairs ascend upward. There's only one door." She smiled sheepishly. "I've often dreamed of going through it." She tossed her head and shrugged. "No one can enter, of course, except the keeper of the lighthouse, so its interior remains a mystery to me, one that keeps drawing me back, if only in my mind. I like to imagine what amazing acts may have taken place inside that lighthouse over the years. Perhaps seamen were dragged inside after washing ashore from a shipwreck. Maybe robbers stowed their spoils there, or—even more exciting to me—perhaps two lovers met there in secret."

She paused then, and her face flushed a deep red. She avoided his gaze, adjusted her mantle, then, breathing a sigh, she continued.

"On the top of the lighthouse is a huge statue. Some say it was built in tribute to the Greek god Poseidon. I don't know for certain, but I like to imagine *someone* of great power is looking down on the sailors as they head out to sea." She faced Eleazar, her eyes dark and serious. "I *do* want them to be safe."

Eleazar was speechless. This girl was a mix of strength and weakness, alternately brazen and shy. In one moment, he wanted to run from her. The next, he wanted to protect her. At their first meeting she revealed a rebellious spirit that he was certain matched his own. But now he was getting to know the person inside. No longer was he drawn merely to her striking beauty. He was beginning to like the sensitive part of her that had emerged unexpectedly.

With her next words she took him beyond the lighthouse

to a narrow canal and a landing place where the passengers disembarked to shore and the sailors unloaded their wares.

"All day long, seamen toss bags and bundles onto the docks. Sometimes one of them tosses a bag a little too hard. There's the sound of breaking glass, and everyone stops working." She smiled and shook her head. "Then, someone makes a joke, they all laugh, and the careless tossing continues."

Eleazar shut his eyes and envisioned the shirtless seamen laboring on the docks. He could almost hear the cursing and the laughing and the songs in strange languages. Could almost smell the perspiration pouring off their backs.

Ruth paused and breathed a sigh. "For me, the best part of the day happens when the merchants arrive at the docks and the trading begins. They exchange gold and silver coins for fine silks, precious gems, pieces of furniture, sacks of grain, fine pottery, and bundles of ivory. Then they hurry off to their stalls to increase their profits. They return the next morning and load the ships with fresh supplies to take to other far-away places."

Eleazar thought about the goods that came from across the sea, items he'd seen on display in Jerusalem's marketplace. Within the Great Court of Gentiles with its spread of tables and booths, local merchants offered a variety of wares, some the traditional goods Eleazar had seen before, others unfamiliar items far superior to what the local artisans created. And there were medicines and foreign herbs and powders to make new mixtures, perhaps more potent than what was used before. Though his father chose not to sample those strange powders that came from across the sea, Eleazar would have liked to try them on the people they served. But for now, he would have to wait until the day he could take charge of his own work.

He looked at Ruth. She was unaware how much her talk encouraged him. Without knowing it she had given him something to hang onto. She flashed him a smile.

"Don't stop," Eleazar said. "I want to hear more."

She nodded and settled back against the moss-covered rock wall.

"At night, the dock falls curiously silent." Ruth's voice had softened to almost a whisper. "The only sounds are the scraping of the wooden ships against each other and the splash of the water kissing the shore. Our quarters are not far from the docks. I lie on my bed by an open window, and I breathe deeply of the salty air. Off in the distance, music pours from the inns and taverns, and drunken sailors sing and laugh. I fall asleep to the drone of their voices and the faint echoes of tambourines and lyres."

The images of the lighthouse and the ships instantly faded beneath a vision of Ruth lying on her bed. The image set Eleazar's heart to pounding again. His feelings for Ruth had gone far beyond a mere friendship. No longer could he still the stirrings that were taking place within him. Boldly, he reached for her hand. She didn't resist. A slight smile tugged at the corner of her mouth. There again was the dimple in her left cheek.

She was gazing at him, her eyes darkening. Then she slipped her hand from his, and her cheeks flushed. She bowed her head. He held his breath.

"Have I offended you?" he said.

She shook her head. Then she raised her face even with his and smiled. "You could never offend me, Eleazar."

They sat in silence and gazed into each other's eyes, an unspoken message traveling between them. Then, a shyness came over Ruth, and she looked away. Drawing a deep breath, she spoke further about the times she spent in Alexandria.

"During the day, my father takes me to the marketplace," she said, her voice lilting. "Two main roads are lined with all kinds of shops, and many smaller streets cross over and lead to the homes of the people who live there. I love to walk in and out of the shops, just to look at all the jewels and silks and fine pottery. My sister once spent all the money she had with her for a set of red Phoenician goblets. They sit on display in her kitchen." She laughed. "I have never seen anyone actually drink from one of them."

"You said many people live there. Are they mostly Greeks? People from other lands? Are there many Jews?"

She nodded. "Yes, many different cultures have settled there, including Jews who follow the strict letter of the law. They live in their own quarter, apart from the busy part of town. They avoid people of other cultures."

"Your sister married a Greek," he reminded her.

"True. Like Abigail, those women who are less strict in their faith have adopted many of the Greek ways. They wear head ornaments, necklaces, and gold bracelets that run all the way up their arms. They've pierced their nostrils, ears, and lips with expensive gem stones They blacken their eyelids, paint their lips and cheeks with red dye, and twist their hair into braids and pile them on their heads."

Ruth startled him then by leaping from the ledge. Like a butterfly freed from its cocoon, she twirled and danced, and sent her veil flapping in the breeze. Her ebony hair fluttered behind her like a ripple of black waves on a sea of glass.

Eleazar laughed with delight. "You are a rebellious girl, Ruth. If only your father could see you now."

She stopped dancing and drew close to him. Her eyes flashed with passion.

"We're the same, Eleazar ben Judah, you and I," she whispered. "I knew we were a match the first time we met." She pressed a finger to his lips to silence him. "Don't deny it. You're just as rebellious as I am, perhaps even more."

He drew back and looked away, aware of the flush that had risen to his face. Though he also had been aware of their bond, he had to admit the truth.

"I'm afraid we're *not* a good match, Ruth."

A dark pain clouded her eyes. "What do you mean?"

He shrugged and then responded with a frown. "There are differences. You live in a mansion in the Upper City. I live in a simple dwelling on a road to nowhere. Your father is a rich merchant. He travels to distant lands. He buys whatever he wants. My father is a hopeless minister to the poor, a man who gives to the needy while his own family lives in near poverty."

She shook her head as though to dismiss his words. "Eleazar, I'm not impressed by material wealth—or the lack of it. Your father may have chosen his destiny, but he has not set *yours*. We share the same spirit. In here." She pointed first to her heart and then to his. "What matters most is how we feel on the inside."

Eleazar gazed into her eyes. Within their depths, he found determination, and passion, and a fighting spirit, and he had to agree. They *were* alike in every way. They were a perfect match. *One day, Ruth, we will marry.*

"Let's make a promise," he said, and he reached for her hand.

She didn't resist but wrapped her fingers around his.

"When we're old enough, we'll marry, and we'll move to Alexandria."

She nodded, and her face lit up with a big smile.

He came away from their visit that day, determined to hold onto that promise. And he hoped she would, too.

And so, Eleazar continued meeting with Ruth, most of the time at Gethsemane, or sometimes they strolled openly through the marketplace with Ruth's handmaid trailing behind. They pretended to be a married couple shopping for grains and beans for their evening meal, and they stopped at Achim's father's stall and sorted through his spread of jewels and his collection of herbs and powders. On one such day, Eleazar pulled out the gold coin Ruth's father had given him, and he purchased a jeweled bracelet for her. Ruth's face flushed with surprise as she slid the bracelet on her arm and admired its sparkle under the glare of the midday sun.

Apart from such moments of joy, Eleazar's time at home fell into a dull routine. Endira took care of the household, and Eleazar accompanied his father in the streets or handed out medicines to people who came to their door.

Now and then, Uncle Hiram sent a messenger with a report about Eleazar's younger brother. Simon was learning his uncle's trade of basket weaving, content with the artistry and having no desire to follow his father into medicine. Eleazar wondered if he would recognize the boy now. They both had grown older and had set out on different paths in life.

Meanwhile, Eleazar and Ruth repeated their vow to marry one day. Unsure of what kind of reaction they might get from their parents, they continued to meet secretly. With much difficulty Eleazar maintained a proper distance. He rarely touched her, except to guide her over an uneven stretch of road, up a hill, or around a puddle in their path. He dreamed of gathering her in his arms and telling her how much he loved her, assured by the adoration in her eyes that she felt the same way about him.

Days passed. Weeks became months. Eleazar turned 18, then 19, then 20. What had begun as a sweet friendship had blossomed into a firm commitment. They began to make plans for their future, where they would live—in the Upper City—or perhaps in Alexandria.

With all his heart he wanted to claim Ruth as his bride. The day came when he could wait no longer. It was time to talk to his father.

CHAPTER ELEVEN

Word came from the village of Bethany. Eleazar's younger brother had arranged his own betrothal to a village girl, and he'd done so without consulting his father as his guardian Uncle Hiram had approved the union.

Eleazar was stunned. Simon was only 17. As the eldest, Eleazar should marry first. As far as he knew he had not been promised to anyone. Most families made such choices while their children were very young, sometimes immediately after birth. But for some reason, Judah had waited. Three years ago, Ariel had suggested a match. Judah had let the opportunity pass. Prompted by his brother's announcement, Eleazar decided to approach his father.

"Will you go to Ariel? He's your friend. He respects you. I doubt he will refuse our proposal."

"So." Judah eyed him with furrowed brow. "You have set your eyes on Ruth."

"Not only my eyes, Father, but my heart as well. You must agree it will be a good match—the son of a physician and the daughter of a wealthy merchant."

Judah hesitated. Eleazar held his breath. He stared at the old man, silently urging him to respond. His father turned away and walked over to the open window, simply stood there and looked out. Eleazar waited, his heart pounding, moisture gathering on his forehead. Judah turned around and faced him with sadness in his eyes.

Eleazar started toward his father and then stopped, overcome by a sense of loss.

"Yes, my son." Judah said at last, the lines on his forehead gathering. "Ruth is a fine young woman. I believe she will make an excellent match—for someone else."

Eleazar shook his head. "Not for someone else, Father. For *me*. Ruth has already agreed. We've been friends for several years. We've talked about a life together, where we want to live, how many children we'll have. We've made plans. We share the same hopes, the same dreams."

Judah's face had turned hard, like stone. When he spoke again, his voice sounded firm but gentle, the same mix of feelings the old man displayed when speaking to the poor and the needy.

"My son, I've known for some time about your secret meetings. Did you think no one would report to me?" He folded his arms across his chest. "You pursued that woman, sometimes without a guardian, and always without my approval. I should have spoken about the offense long ago."

A bitterness rose up inside Eleazar. He clenched his fists. "I don't understand, Father. Don't you want me to be happy?"

"Happy? I have nothing but your happiness in mind." Judah took a couple more steps and closed the gap between them. "You and Ruth are from two different worlds. Ariel and his family live in a magnificent home in the Upper City. Look around you, Eleazar. We have a humble existence."

Eleazar shook his head. "It doesn't matter. I doubt Ariel will object. Have you forgotten the day he offered one of his daughters? He would approve such a match."

"He was being a friend, nothing more," Judah growled.

"No. I don't believe that." Eleazar also raised his voice. "Ariel would never deny Ruth's happiness. When he learns we have promised ourselves to each other, he'll give us his blessing. I'm certain of it."

Eleazar hurried to his private corner and drew a pouch from under his mat. "Look, Father." He opened the pouch. " I've saved enough silver for a suitable bride price."

Judah set his jaw and stood firm. Eleazar's stomach tightened. How could his father refuse? A marriage contract with a family like Ariel's should have pleased the old man.

When Judah spoke again, his voice was flat and unyielding.

"My son, you are about to enter one of the three great events in a man's life—to be born, to die—and in the midst—to wed."

Eleazar stared at his father in disbelief. More meaningless talk.

Judah went on, unaware of Eleazar's mounting anger. "You have to be sensible, my son. It's important to marry someone who can bring the right balance to the union. Someone who fulfills what the other person lacks." The old man shook his head. "I'm sorry, Eleazar, but Ruth is not a good fit for you. Perhaps it's because you are too much alike."

Eleazar backed away and searched his father's face. A wall had gone up between them.

"I have followed you faithfully all these years." Eleazar counted off his acts of obedience on his fingers. "Week after week, I accompanied you into the Lower City. I kept my mouth shut when those helpless beggars paid you with scraps from their kitchens. I endured insults from other young men who fared far better in their professions. I listened to your every instruction, and I restrained my desire to go to school in Alexandria. Haven't I done everything you wanted?" Before Judah could answer, Eleazar closed in on him. "Why is it that now, at the most important time of my life, I cannot win your approval? Will you and I ever agree on anything?"

Eleazar was shouting now. He was fighting for the woman he loved. He couldn't give up. Not now. Not when his very future depended on one good word from his father.

Judah drew close and placed a hand on his son's shoulder. Eleazar backed out of his grasp. Though a cool breeze wafted through the open window, he couldn't breathe.

For a moment, he thought he saw tears forming in his father's eyes. With increased boldness he repeated his request.

"I'm asking you to approach Ariel, Father. I have never asked for anything before. I've been your obedient son. Now I beg you, please, don't deny me this one hope."

The old man shook his head despondently. "I'm sorry, my son. Your request comes too late."

"What do you mean?"

Judah breathed a heavy sigh. "I've already selected another, a more fitting bride for you, someone who will bring a balance to your rebellious spirit."

Eleazar took a step back. "Rebellious?"

"Yes, my son, you are rebellious. From the beginning, you have stood against me—both you and your mother. Did you think I didn't notice when the two of you went off by yourselves? I wanted you to follow the ways of my father and his father before him, but your mother had her own plans for your life. Instead of supporting me, she encouraged your rebellion."

"I worked by your side all these years, Father. Haven't I proved myself?"

"Not entirely. Your displeasure was evident. You openly despised Miriam and the other poor people in the Lower City. You hated the lepers on the hill. Somehow, I had to curb your rebellious spirit. So when it came time to choose a wife for you, I knew it should be someone whose nature is completely opposed to yours, someone with a meek and quiet spirit. Your choice—Ruth—would only join your rebellion."

Eleazar backed away. His next question momentarily caught in his throat.

"So you chose someone else? Without my knowledge?" He shook his head in confusion. "Who could possibly be better for me than Ruth?"

"Ruth!" Judah repeated the name with hostility in his voice. "The girl is trouble, Eleazar. Her own father confessed to me the difficulty he's had trying to raise her. She is far too headstrong.

I'm telling you, Ruth will bring nothing but trouble to our home." He kept shaking his head, and he stared at Eleazar with fire in his eyes. "No, my son. The one I have chosen is calm, sensible, yielding, a true example of the virtuous woman described in the proverbs."

Eleazar's head was swimming with names and faces. None of the women in the city appealed to him. Eleazar's hands were shaking. He was close to tears. "If not Ruth, then who, Father?"

Judah turned away and began to pace again. "I spent a great deal of time considering this decision, always keeping in mind what might be best for you. I thought of your work as a physician, your life in the city, and, most of all, your strong will. In the end, I chose someone who can restore an atmosphere of peace and tranquility to our home."

It didn't matter which young woman his father had chosen. Eleazar would refuse the match. He waited for the name, unprepared for what his father said next.

"I chose Anna, my son. You may know her. She serves in Ariel's household."

"Anna?!" Eleazar's mind raced back several years to the Pool of Siloam and his first encounter with Ruth and her handmaid. The miserable servant girl had emerged from the shadows, swathed in layers of cloth, an ox of a girl who paled next to Ruth's striking beauty. Anna. Their *guardian* who had trailed behind them during some of their walks. The lifeless, voiceless shadow that never left them at peace. He'd resented her from the start. She was always there, watching them. Now, his father wanted him to *marry* her?

"Are you aware, Father, that girl is big and homely, a mere slave who follows her mistress around like a helpless dog. Anna could never add a drop of peace and tranquility to this house." He folded his arms across his chest and took a firm stance. "I'll refuse." Again Eleazar raised his voice. "I won't marry anyone except Ruth. Anna can never—"

"You will marry the one I have chosen."

"No!"

Judah stopped pacing and stood face-to-face with him. He appeared to be controlling his anger, though it seethed in the depths of his eyes. "Anna is a wholesome, robust girl who will bear many children."

Eleazar shook his head vehemently. "Let her bear them for someone else."

"My son, my son. I have already visited Anna's family in Bethany. They have a well-kept home, full of love. Anna is trained in all the necessary household duties. She cooks. She sews. She tends to her chores in complete silence, never uttering a single complaint. As the proverb reminds us, *Who can find a virtuous woman? For her price is far above rubies.* Such is the person named Anna."

"I don't care. She is a stranger to me, a nobody with no future and no hope. Ruth and I share the same dreams."

"What *dreams?* Travels to some distant land?"

Eleazar stared back at him, astounded.

"Yes, my son, Ariel told me about your absurd plan to run off to Alexandria. He agreed with me. It's childish nonsense, nothing more."

"I *choose* the childish nonsense. I *choose* the dreams. I *choose* Ruth, and I reject Anna."

"Your protest comes too late. Anna's father has already agreed to the bride price, and we have only to sign the contract."

"The man is a potter, father. He has clay on his hands, not gold. He labors in the sun digging mud and soil from the ground. Then he spends long hours hunched over a wheel. This is not a suitable match. It's an insult."

"Nevertheless, the agreement has been made."

Eleazar felt a surge of heat. "I'll refuse. I'll do as Simon did and marry the woman of my choice *without* your consent. Ruth and I will marry, and you can do nothing to stop it."

He turned his back on his father and stomped across the room. He stopped at the open window, raised his eyes toward the heavens, and sent up a silent plea to the unseen power that resided there. Then, he turned around and faced the old man, his eyes aflame, his fists clenched.

"Believe what I say, Father. I will fight you on this. If you don't consider my wishes, I'll speak to the rabbi. I'll go before the Council if necessary. I'll find a way to overrule your decision, and I'll marry the woman I want."

Judah stood firm. "And you'll be labeled a rebellious son. The Council will laugh in your face. They might order a stoning. Do you want that?"

Eleazar ran a hand through his hair, now moist with sweat.

Still unmoved, Judah released a long sigh. "It's no use, Eleazar." He shook his head, and sadness returned to his eyes. "Oh, my son, my son," he said with a tenderness he rarely displayed.

Eleazar's heart leaped. He choked out his next words. "What do you mean, it's no use?"

"Haven't you heard?" Judah said with obvious compassion. "Ruth has been promised to another. To Levi bar Uzza. Their contract was sealed last week."

For the last time, they met in a sheltered alcove on the rocky slope of Gethsemane. A blast of cold air swept across the hillside. The olive trees languished in a frozen sleep, their branches heavy with frost.

Eleazar looked into Ruth's eyes. Rivers of tears spilled out and ran down her face. He brushed them away. More tears flowed. His own eyes blurred with moisture.

Ruth sobbed. "My heart is breaking. How could our parents deny us this one request?"

Eleazar stroked the side of her face. She placed her hand over his. Her fingers were icy cold.

He shook his head. Tears ran down his cheek and froze immediately. "You can't marry Levi. That man is a self-serving liar. He cheats his business partners and defrauds helpless widows in the midst of their grief. He follows in his father's evil footsteps. They deceive buyers by adding weight to the basket and double their income with every sale. They take money from the poor, and they steal from their friends." He kissed her fingertips. "You can't marry him, Ruth. That heartless man will be cruel to you."

She bowed her head and pressed her forehead against his chest. "It's hopeless, Eleazar," she said, her voice muffled by the fold of his robe. "My father has succumbed to Levi's deceit. That evil man convinced him the union would be good for business and profitable for both of them, with little regard for me."

"That's foolish. Your father doesn't do business the way Levi does. Ariel is an honest man."

"Levi is eager for the match. He visits our home daily, bringing gifts. While he's there, I vanish to other parts of the house, as far away as I can get from the empty chatter that passes between them." She raised her head and gazed into his eyes. "When my father looks at Levi, he sees a man of power and stature. I see an arrogant worm." She blinked back more tears. "There's so little time, Eleazar. Our wedding day has been set. When winter is over and the blossoms open on the trees, I will be Levi's wife."

Eleazar's throat tightened. He felt helpless. "Are you aware of the decision my father made?"

She nodded. "Anna is a fine girl. She served me well for many years. She will do the same for you, Eleazar."

"My father believes she'll quench my *rebellious spirit*." He spit out the last two words. "This decision has merely added fuel to it."

Ruth released a scornful laugh. "The Greeks speak of something they call *irony,* a twisting of truths so that what is expected is overcome by surprise. My father, the very man who showed me the world and encouraged my free spirit, the one who tempted me with visions of a life beyond Jerusalem, is the very one who now takes it all away."

Eleazar wrapped his arm around her trembling shoulders. She snuggled closer. Two women passed by them and clucked their tongues. Eleazar glared at them and held her fast.

"As long as we're free, I will not give up, Ruth." He leaned back and faced her with fresh resolve. "I have a plan. We can run away before our weddings take place. We can go to Alexandria and make our home there. As my wife, you'll be able to pursue the education you always wanted."

Ruth tilted her face and smiled at him. "I've dreamed of a life with you, Eleazar. For years I have thought of nothing else. But in pursuing our own happiness, we would hurt others. My mother would go to her deathbed. My father would disown me. I love him so much, I wouldn't survive his rejection. Except for my sister in Alexandria, I'd never see my family again."

"Yes, your sister. Didn't she already defy your father by marrying a Greek? And didn't he make peace with them?"

"Yes, but it was beneficial for my father. Now he has a business ally in Alexandria. Ziba readily supplies my father with items for the market. For that reason, and only that reason, my father accepted their marriage. But Abigail will never be able to come back to Jerusalem. If my sisters and I want to see her, we must go there."

"So your father tolerates your sister's choice of a husband, but he would turn his back on me, a Jew and a physician. And so he also would turn his back on you, his youngest daughter."

"*Your* father would turn his back on *you*, too, Eleazar."

He pulled away from her and shrugged. "He's rejected me through my entire life. Why should that change now?"

Ruth nodded pensively. "But there are others. What about Anna? My dear, sweet friend. She's so happy. She asked me to help her make a proper wedding dress. She's taken a job cooking for a family in Bethany, saving her own money, so she'll have a suitable dowry. Anna's passion has actually altered her appearance. She grows more lovely every day. If we deny her this joy, my heart would break along with hers."

"But I don't love Anna!" Eleazar backed away and threw up his hands. "How can I make her my wife when it will be *you* I'll be longing for, day and night, for the rest of my life? Is that fair to Anna?"

Ruth's resignation frightened him. Where was the fire? Where was that rebellious spirit his father had spoken about?

"It's hopeless, Eleazar." A frightening resolve had entered her voice. "I'm bound to another and so are you."

Eleazar ran his hand through his hair. He suddenly felt alone in their fight to be together. "I can't give you up, Ruth, especially not to *Levi*. As for Anna, I could never feel about her the way I feel about you. If we end this now, she would be free to marry someone else, someone who will love her as she deserves."

Ruth seemed pensive for a moment. A hint of hope entered Eleazar's heart. She quickly quelled it.

"You will suffer another loss, Eleazar, one that has great value for you. You would lose a place of honor in this city." More tears spilled from her eyes. "You would be denied the Council seat you have desired all your life."

Ruth's words struck Eleazar's heart. He hadn't forgotten about the Council seat. He'd merely set aside that dream while in the midst of this battle. But the promise had remained with him, hidden for the moment in the back of his mind.

While he longed to make Ruth his wife, he wasn't certain he could give up the dream his mother had set before him. He glanced about the garden. No one else was near. Still, he lowered his voice to a whisper. "I love you, Ruth, but to lose a seat with the Counsil? I don't know. Why can't I have you and that too?" He shook his head. "To qualify, I must be married, but only with the consent of my father. I must prove myself worthy of my profession. I must establish myself as someone with integrity and honor." His plan to run away began to fade. "What can I do, Ruth? Either way I lose something. It seems our fathers have won."

She looked away. He reached for her hand, but she pulled it free. She took a step back. The lines on her face instantly changed from longing to pained submission.

"How handsome you are, my beloved, And so pleasant!" Choking out the words, she quoted Solomon's bride. "By night on my bed I sought the one I love; I sought him, but I did not find him."

Then she slipped away from him and turned to leave. Eleazar watched her depart, helpless to make her stay. She hurried away, her robe billowing behind her, her footsteps quickening as she reached the bend in the path. A cry for her to stay lodged in his throat. The Council seat hovered like a ghost, and he gave in to the dream.

He blinked back another flow of tears, watched through blurred vision as she neared the edge of the garden. Then she was gone. All that remained were her tiny footprints on the frosty path and the lingering scent of calamus caught by the icy wind.

PART TWO
Eleazar, the Man

"Therefore shall a man leave his father and his mother, and shall cleave unto his wife: and they shall be one flesh."

Genesis 2:24

CHAPTER TWELVE
Jerusalem, A.D. 8

The days passed far too quickly for Eleazar. Winter's icy fingers destroyed his dream of a life with his beloved. The old man ignored his pleas and refused to approach Ariel with a contract. The day of Ruth's betrothal drew near, and he had no way of stopping it.

Then Spring came with its expected array of floral abundance. Red, yellow, and blue wildflowers dotted the landscape outside the city. Blossoming vines trailed over every courtyard in the Upper City. Their fragrance sailed down the hill to Eleazar's humble dwelling, nearly making him drunk with their scent. Among them, the warm, woody aroma of calamus remained as a subtle reminder of the love he would never possess.

Ruth and Levi married on a warm spring morning. Though Eleazar didn't attend the ceremony, visions of their union sent a dagger into his heart. Through his friends, he learned the couple had made their home in the Upper City, not far from Ariel's mansion.

Meanwhile, Eleazar's pending marriage to Anna was drawing near. With Ruth married he no longer pressed his father, for there was no one else he might consider. He turned his mind more intently on his work and his plans for the future. He determined to capture the attention of the Council. Everything he did, every word he spoke, every action, every success, even every failure, no matter how large or small, could bring his dream closer to fulfillment or tear it away. Once he had a wife and children, he would fit the requirements of such a calling.

The betrothal ritual at Anna's house plunged Eleazar into sudden despair. Reluctantly he went with Judah to Bethany to her parents' home, a humble dwelling inside a circle of similar homes, all of them simply built of clay and limestone with palm fronds scattered about the roofs.

Outside the entrance, under the shelter of a booth that was constructed of palm fronds and myrtle branches, stood a potter's wheel, braced by a huge stone inside a pit. All around the ground were the man's creations—bowls, pitchers, jars, pots and goblets, and a pile of tools—a paddle, several scrapers, and a knife made of flint. Off to one side, a mud-brick furnace oozed the remnants of that morning's fire.

Inside the house were three rooms—a kitchen and sitting area, and two curtained sections for sleeping. The girl remained behind her veil during Eleazar's entire visit. Whenever he looked her way, she lowered her eyes and furrowed her brow. Unlike Ruth, who shamelessly had exposed her beautiful face to him, Anna had never revealed her features, and she very likely wouldn't do so until their wedding day. From the little he saw, she could be as ugly as a dog. Though multiple veils had masked her face, they had not hidden her size. *Strong,* his father had said, and, while the old man envisioned a diligent housekeeper who would give him a multitude of grandchildren, Eleazar only saw a millstone around his neck, someone who might receive an occasional nod of gratitude from him and little more.

Eleazar barely discerned her footsteps, she tread so softly about the room. Without speaking a word, she prepared a platter of food under her mother's watchful eye. Then, she approached Eleazar, bent close to him and held out a serving of dried fruit and raisin bread. A hint of frankincense rose from beneath her veil. Eleazar winced at the pungent odor. It was reminiscent of the sacrificial offerings in the Temple. The acrid smell only served to increase his distaste for the girl.

He longed for the soothing fragrance of sweet calamus and the woman who wore its perfume. Her memory vanished then, and he was staring at the platter of food. Anna waited as he made his selections. He gathered the raisin bread and a few figs, then without a word he waved Anna off. She bowed and backed away in a submissive manner. Ruth would never have humbled herself in such a way. Offer a tray of food? Perhaps. But would she wait for him to make a selection? Probably not. If he didn't act quickly enough, he'd have to do without.

He took a bite of the pastry, and his eyes grew wide. The cake nearly melted in his mouth. The raisins were plump and sweet. The figs had a coating of honey and left a pleasant taste on his tongue.

At least the girl can cook, he thought.

A discussion between the two fathers had already begun. Anna retreated to a corner of the room and shrank within her mother's shadow. Though the two men had made the pact months ago, this meeting would seal the union. Eleazar felt a pounding in his chest. He reached up with one hand to still it. He considered leaping to his feet and calling a halt to the ritual. He could flee back to Jerusalem and plunge into his work, never to marry. But if he rejected the union now, it would bring disgrace on Anna and her family. His father would be furious with him, and the Council would have good reason to pass him by.

Judah pulled a pouch from his robe and offered the traditional bride price, 50 shekels of silver. At the same time, Anna's father brought forth a dowry on behalf of his daughter—two decorative urns and three vessels for cooking. Eleazar scowled at the meager exchange. A fleeting memory of the gold coin Ruth's father had pressed into his palm told him the gifts Ariel gave to Levi surpassed Anna's paltry dowry hundreds of times over.

He looked at his father. The old man was nodding his approval.

Then Judah reached for a stylus and signed the parchment.

His heart breaking, Eleazar needed a distraction. Once again he shifted his thoughts to the future. He could make the best of this marriage. He could move into a lavish home in the Upper City. He could purchase furnishings from across the sea and bestow fine clothing and jewels on his wife. The elders who gathered at the city gate would notice him. The Council members also would be watching. And one day, he would be able to walk into that secret room at the far end of the temple and assume his own seat of honor.

Eleazar pressed his lips together and watched in silence as the two fathers completed the contract. Then they stood, kissed each other on both cheeks, and turned their smiling faces toward Eleazar. Awkwardly, he rose and received their embrace. Anna's mother, a round-faced woman, rushed toward him and planted wet kisses on both of his cheeks.

"I am your mother now," she said and eyed him with pleasure.

Eleazar swallowed against the tightening of his throat. His mother was in the grave. There would be no regular visits with this one no matter what the law demanded. No further visits to this home until their wedding day. No more gifts, no questions, no promises.

He forced a smile, but, deep inside, he felt a growing emptiness. As he gazed across the room at his future bride, her eyes fastened to the floor, Ruth's face came before him once more, and inside he continued to weep for his lost love.

On the morning of Eleazar's wedding, the house of Judah ben Serach came alive with preparations. Hired servants scrubbed the pavement with lye, then scattered flower petals about the courtyard to overtake the acrid smell. Within minutes the aroma of myrrh, wild roses, and lilies permeated the air. Moments later serving tables and cushions encircled the perimeter. Endira and her helpers set out platters bearing mounds of figs, grapes, pomegranates, and apples. They scurried about, their arms laden with baskets of almonds and pistachios, pots of steaming lentils and barley, and platters stacked high with goat cheese. Endira's husband tended to the water pot that was filled with wine. And a lamb roasted over coals in the corner of the courtyard, it's pungent aroma floating across the courtyard and stirring Eleazar's appetite.

For the first time in Eleazar's life, Judah had used his money for one purpose other than to lavish it on the poor. A wedding feast for an unwilling groom had motivated the old man to empty his money jar with no regret.

Eleazar paused before the window and stared out over the courtyard. A cloudless sky announced a perfect day ahead. Everything was set for his wedding. A tear surfaced. He blinked it away. Heaving a sigh, he turned from the window and dipped his fingers in a jar of scented oils. He anointed his neck and chest, then slipped a pale blue tunic over his muscular frame, relishing its feathery feel as the sleeves slid over his arms. He tightened the hemp rope around his waist, then donned a new pair of sandals. Once again touching the scented oil, he ran his fingers through his hair and pulled several locks forward over his brow. Dressed in his finest robe, he stood before his mother's tall brass mirror and admired his reflection. He stared into his steel gray eyes and thick, curly hair and allowed himself a few moments of prideful musing.

Only recently had he become aware of his own good looks. The girls in the city stared at him from beneath their veils, often erupting in giggles and dropping their eyes whenever he glanced their way. Other young men taunted him about his muscles, their envy obvious.

"Eleazar!" The cry rose from the courtyard. Outside stood his best friend, Achim, along with Enos and Thomas. They wore colorful robes, woven headbands, and black-and-white striped tallits on their shoulders. Like Eleazar, they had groomed their beards and oiled their hair.

"The groom!" Enos announced, his thin face creased with wrinkles, his bony hands applauding.

Eleazar turned from the window and left the house. He entered the courtyard and stood before his three friends, his hands on his hips, his feet planted. He eyed them with an air of appraisal.

Breaking from the other two, Achim burst toward him, laughing. He arranged a garland of flowers on Eleazar's head. Thomas marched around him and looked him over closely. Though a head shorter than Eleazar and much stockier, Thomas moved with incredible agility. He stopped marching and broke into a wide grin.

"You look—" Thomas drew thoughtful fingers to his mouth. "Magnificent!"

Enos also stepped closer to Eleazar and peered into his face. "You're wrong, Thomas. This is not the face of a happy man." His angular brows slanted in feigned concern. "A groom should have a merry countenance. This one appears to be going to a funeral instead of a wedding."

Eleazar's three friends laughed together. He smiled and gave each of them a gentle punch in the arm.

Thomas frowned. "What is there to fear, my friend? Your father? An unruly crowd? The *bride?*"

"I fear nothing," Eleazar replied, straightening. "I'm getting married today. The ceremony will involve a ritual, nothing more. It brings no meaningful change to my life."

Enos raised one eyebrow and produced a half-smile.

"My friend, you will experience at least *one* major change. *Tonight.*" He gave a sly laugh. Achim joined in and poked Eleazar in the arm.

In contrast, Thomas became serious, even pensive. "Marriage can be a wonderful thing." He stepped in front of the other two. "Think about it, Eleazar. You'll be master of your own house. You'll have a wife who serves and obeys you. A quiver full of children to bring you joy."

"That coming from a man who has a gorgeous wife and four children!" Achim said.

Eleazar eyed Thomas with a touch of sadness. The man's obsession with the woman he married seemed shameful at times. He appeared weak, hardly the type of man the Council members would consider.

"And what about the single life?" Achim said, twirling. "A single man can travel the world and sample the women of other lands." He danced around the other three, waving his hands and shouting. "A single man is free from the watchful eye of a nagging wife, free from too many little ones pulling at his cloak and begging for sweets or coins. He can spend his money as he chooses. He can go where he wants, whenever he wants. He can roam the streets all night long, till sunup, without criticism. Yes, the single life can be quite enjoyable." He came to a stop in front of Eleazar.

The two stared at each other. One, happy to remain single, the other, secretly wishing he could.

He looked into Achim's sky-blue eyes and a flicker of understanding passed between them. Without hesitating, Achim grabbed Eleazar's arm and led him through the gate and along the path that would take them out of the city, over the Mount of Olives and down the ridge to the village of Bethany.

Enos and Thomas followed close behind. Back in the courtyard, the servants continued to rush about making preparations for the wedding feast. Endira's voice carried over the wall as she bellowed commands at her handmaids. There followed the clamor of dishes, the rhythmic slapping of bare feet, and the delighted squeals of youngsters running about the courtyard in expectation of a party.

CHAPTER THIRTEEN

Eleazar and Achim linked arms and continued down the road to Bethany. Thomas and Enos charged ahead of them and led the way with a merry dance. Eleazar caught Achim staring at him, a hint of concern in the young man's eyes.

"Be happy, Eleazar," Achim said, keeping his voice low. "This is your day. Forget what lies behind you and reach for the prize."

"The prize?"

"You've never kept your dream a secret, Eleazar, not from me. You've always had your eye on the Sanhedrin. Now is your chance to pursue it. You merely have to let go of the past and plunge ahead."

Eleazar stopped walking and looked into his friend's face. "The prize. The prize." He sighed. "Yes, Achim, but consider what I have sacrificed to get it." He shrugged and started walking again. "But, you couldn't possibly understand a broken heart."

Achim nearly stumbled on the path. He let out an annoyed grunt. "So you think I've never been in love? That I've never known heartbreak? That I have no feelings? If that's what you think, Eleazar, you're wrong."

He gave Achim a sideways glance and kept walking. "What are you saying?"

"I never told you about the girl I met in Joppa, two years ago."

"No, you didn't."

Achim stared off in the distance. "Her name was Hadassah." He smiled at the memory. "She had sun-streaked hair that hung to her waist, and her eyes captured the color of the sky. She was beautiful, too beautiful for me. I knew that. But for some strange reason, she liked me, Eleazar. She said I made her laugh."

It struck Eleazar that he'd been so consumed with his own loss he hadn't considered Achim might also have suffered a broken heart.

"I'm sorry, Achim. I never knew. What happened to her?"

"Our relationship was doomed to fail." Achim shook his head. "She was a Samaritan. Her family had moved to the coast so her father could work there as a shipbuilder. I met her while I was there picking up supplies for my father. Sadly, the man sheltered his daughter, did everything he could to keep us apart." Achim gave a little shrug. "There were religious differences, of course. He said my Jewish family would never accept his daughter, and he could never accept a Jew. I told him I'd consider transferring my allegiance to their faith. It made no difference. He married her off to the son of a silversmith, a man of great wealth and, most importantly, also a Samaritan. So you see, Eleazar, you're not alone in your grief. I, too, have nursed a broken heart."

Eleazar touched his friend's shoulder. "Why did you never tell me?"

"Ha! How could I? You were so starry-eyed over Ruth, I doubted you would *hear* me."

Eleazar slowed his pace. His friend had unwittingly told him something about himself he had never realized before. In the midst of his personal pursuits he had forgotten that others, including his best friend, also dreamed dreams and suffered painful losses.

"I'm sorry," was all he could say.

Achim tossed his head like he was tossing off an insult. "Let's not talk about that now. Today is *your* day. This isn't a time to weep over lost loves and mistakes of the past. There will be plenty of opportunities for us to talk about those things. And, we will, my friend. I promise. No more secrets."

As they neared Bethany, hot droplets formed on Eleazar's brow. His legs felt like pillars of clay. He stumbled and began to drag his feet. Achim pulled him along.

They reached the city gate. Thomas and Enos stepped aside and let Eleazar pass through first. Then the four of them entered the town's central court, festively decorated for the planned ritual. The moment Eleazar arrived, a crowd swarmed around him. Friends and strangers patted his back and shouted heartfelt blessings.

Then the guests parted, opening a path to the center of the courtyard. Eleazar's head spun. The sun beat down on him. He blinked his eyes and tried to focus. There were familiar faces. His father, standing close to Anna's parents. They smiled and swayed to the swelling music of flutes and lyres. His brother Simon stood nearby with his young wife. There was Uncle Hiram, and a group of ornately-clad young girls he guessed were Anna's friends.

At the far end, Anna sat like a statue, perched on a raised seat. As expected, she remained hidden beneath layers of veils. Even her eyes were concealed behind a sheer veil. She wore a pure white dress of fine linen, with a hint of blue around the hem. Her veil draped from her head down to her toes. She had a silver chain around her neck and no other jewelry. On her head rested a floral garland, similar to the one on Eleazar's brow.

He stopped walking, unable to take another step. He held his breath, considered turning around and running away. The music stopped. No one spoke.

Then Simon burst out of the crowd and stood in front of him. Eleazar stared back at his younger brother. For a moment, he saw his father in Simon's full face, his square jaw, and bushy eyebrows. Simon had grown into a man, a complete duplicate of their father.

Simon's lips curled into a friendly grin. "Your day has arrived, Eleazar. May blessings be upon you."

Eleazar thought it odd for Simon to be blessing *him* instead of the other way around. After all, *he* was the eldest. But with his younger brother having married months before, his actions would have been acceptable to this crowd.

Prompted by the stirrings of his heart, Eleazar wrapped his arms around his brother. He hadn't seen him in such a long time. Gone was the little boy whose mat had rested beside his at night. The little boy who hung on Eleazar's stories, spoken under the light of a full moon, had become a grown man, married and perhaps expecting children of his own.

Other men came forward and interrupted their reunion. They showered him with wishes of good fortune. A large hand gripped Eleazar's shoulder, and he turned to look into his father's steel gray eyes. Smiling with pride, the old man took Eleazar's arm and guided him toward his bride.

The crowd formed two long lines on either side of the path that led to Anna. The musicians resumed playing, their flutes and lyres filling the air with a melodic cadence. Children began to clap and cheer. Overcome with weakness, Eleazar forced himself to step ahead, slowly.

Suddenly, a familiar scent caught his attention. Was it sweet calamus? Swallowing hard, he turned slowly to his right and found himself face-to-face with Ruth.

Dark eyes, moist with fresh tears, stared back at him. Ruth's lips parted in a wistful smile, and she lowered her gaze. A hush settled over the gathering. Even the musicians halted their playing again.

A long arm, draped in dark purple, encircled Ruth's shoulder as Levi pulled his wife close to him. Eleazar tore his gaze away, and looked at his own bride, waiting at the end of the course. Anna rose from her seat, her dress spilled like a waterfall to the pavement around her. She took a couple steps toward him and paused.

Judah was breathing down Eleazar's neck. Turning toward the musicians, the old man clapped his hands twice. The music resumed. The festivities continued, and Judah guided Eleazar forward.

His own step rigid, Eleazar drew in front of his bride. He reached out, took her hand, and, as required, he uttered the proper words: "You are hereby consecrated to me." Then he paraded Anna inside the circle of wedding guests, nodding his head in salutation, as he had seen Thomas do at his wedding. The difference was, his friend had done so with noticeable joy, while Eleazar was feigning happiness. The guests fell in line and joined the procession. The music played, the tempo quickened, and the air filled with festivity.

Stepping ahead of their guests, Eleazar and Anna moved away from the courtyard and started toward Jerusalem, to the house of Judah where the ceremony would be completed. Without uttering a word to his bride, he guided her along the path, upward, into the city. They passed through the gate and continued up the hill toward Judah's house. The rituals would continue for three days, and then Eleazar would take over as head of the household. His body trembled as his dream of a happy marriage continued to crumble. In his heart, he had planned all those things with Ruth. Swallowing the lump in his throat, he pushed ahead, forced himself to move closer and closer to his destiny.

After everyone had gathered in Judah's courtyard, Anna's father spoke the seven traditional blessings over her. Then, as expected of him, Eleazar presented his bride with a gold ring and recited the words, "Behold, you are made holy for me according to the religion of Moses and of Israel." Another blessing was said over a cup of wine, which they shared, and then came the banquet. As tradition dictated, the next several days would be filled with feasting, drinking, and dancing, with guests leaving and returning several times to celebrate the union.

Eleazar pulled away from the crowd and reclined at a banquet table where he and Anna dined on strips of roast lamb, honeyed fig cakes, breads and fruit, and wine—lots of wine. Still masked,

Anna lifted her veil slightly to partake of the meal. The music continued to play, louder and with more fervor.

"Eleazar! Come!" Achim leaped toward Eleazar and pulled him to his feet. He dragged him to the middle of the courtyard and thrust him in the midst of several young men who were dancing. Sweat poured down their faces, but they continued moving, their exultant shouts ringing through the air. Now filled with wine, Eleazar moved freely among them, his feet tripping across the pavement. Someone shook a tambourine. The music grew louder, more intense. He reeled past his bride, his garland cocked to one side. Tears spilled from his eyes and blended with the perspiration running down his face. He didn't care. He kept spinning and dancing and kicking up his heels. Then, exhausted, he crumbled in a heap at Achim's feet, sobbing. Enos and Achim helped him up and dragged him back to his place beside Anna. The crowd of guests swam before his eyes. They continued talking and drinking and eating and dancing and smiling and laughing, all in a whirling blur. He scanned the crowd, hoping to see Ruth again. She wasn't there. Anna tugged at his robe. He turned to face her. This close, through her veil, he could see compassion in her eyes.

He swayed a bit, then looked down at his hands and examined his long, smooth fingers and his nails, clean and trimmed. *The hands of a physician,* he mused. He considered the promise of his new future, and he began to weep.

The revelry continued throughout the day. Eleazar's head throbbed with the music, the wine, and the knowledge that he was now a married man. By morning, his manhood would be complete.

With the setting of the sun, a bitter chill fell on the courtyard. Signaling an end to the festivities, Eleazar bid his guests farewell. Judah left to spend the night at his brother Hiram's house so that Eleazar and his bride could be alone.

Under Endira's direction, the servants cleaned the courtyard for the next day's celebration. In the morning, the guests would trickle in, eager for a look at the red-stained bed sheet hanging from Eleazar's window. A shout would go up, and the feasting and the drinking and the dancing would resume.

Alone in their bed chamber, Eleazar and Anna stood facing each other. Regretfully, he could summon no loving words to comfort her. With Ruth, he could speak freely. But not with this one. A mere ritual bound him to Anna. Nothing more.

She attempted to speak, her voice soft and trembling. "I will serve you well, Eleazar. I'll be a loyal wife. Your home will be run according to your wishes. Simply express your desires to me, and they will be done. I am your servant."

Eleazar could feel only pity for this woman. He sighed. "I have no doubt you will run our home well," he said with no emotion. "But, do not consider yourself a servant, Anna. This is not your parents' home. This is not Ariel's home where you worked as a servant girl. This is *your* home. *You* are the woman of *this* house. *You* will have servants to do your bidding."

She nodded and dropped her eyes. Her humble manner repulsed him. Where was the fire? Where was the fight? Yet he had no doubt that life would be easy with Anna as his wife. He stepped toward her, removed her veil and let it flutter to the floor. A solitary oil lamp cast a subtle glow on her face. She appeared flushed, even radiant. Her broad jaw took on a child-like softness. Her brown hair fell in ripples past her shoulders. Though she was tall and large-boned, the linen dress clung to her in long, delicate folds.

Neither of them spoke. Taking her outstretched hand, he gently led her to their bed.

CHAPTER FOURTEEN

$\mathcal{T}$aking charge of the home came easy to Eleazar. No longer would he be subject to his father's rule. Now he could make decisions for himself and for his wife. Judah would accept a lesser, advisory position in the home. Eleazar smiled. At last he had achieved his rightful place.

Though he still fell short of other physicians who had already established their work in the city, Eleazar was eager to apply what he had learned, not only from his father, but by diligently reading the scrolls Achim had given him. No longer would he serve the people of the Lower City. He turned his full attention to the Upper City, where residents would pay well for his services. If Judah wanted to continue caring for the poor, so be it. Eleazar would make his own way.

He had to build a different reputation for himself. If he wanted to increase his financial resources, he needed to start immediately. With the help of the Alexandrian scrolls and some mixtures of his own making, Eleazar progressed far beyond his father's limited methods. Months passed. He never lost sight of his dream to one day study in Alexandria. The day came when, having exhausted all resources available in Jerusalem, he decided to speak of his plan at the evening meal.

The sun had already set when Eleazar sat across from Judah at the four-legged table he had purchased along with four chairs from across the sea. Their home had gone through several changes with every new and unusual piece of furniture Eleazar could acquire. He leaned back, satisfied that he'd been able to transform their home into a palace of sorts.

The old man's stubborn lines had given way to the wrinkles of time. His stern lips, once pressed firmly together, seemed impotent now. Eleazar doubted his father would be able to argue with him at this stage of his life.

Anna brought two platters of food to the table and quietly settled on the seat beside her husband. After the usual blessing, Eleazar waited for his father to begin eating. Then he tore off a piece of bread, dipped it in the sauce, and savored the pungent taste of herbs and spices. Anna had proved herself a capable cook. He slid a piece of meat in his mouth, savored its salty flavor, then, with confidence, he plunged ahead with his plan.

"I want to go to Alexandria." Eleazar's eyes darted from his father to Anna.

Judah held a sliver of lamb in front of his mouth. Instead of taking a bite, he lowered it to the platter. Anna stared at Eleazar but showed no emotion.

"I can go for three months." Again Eleazar looked from his father to his wife. "It's a great opportunity. I'll be able to study under the greatest physicians in the world. I can learn to treat difficult illnesses using tools and medicines we've never had in Jerusalem. Such methods will bring me great success. I'll be able to cure more diseases, perhaps save more lives than ever before."

Judah's dull eyes came to life as a fire built within them. "You have no—"

Eleazar raised a hand and interrupted his father. "The sons of the Herodian kings have always run off to Rome to increase their education. Why can't we Jews do the same?" He took a breath, then leaned toward Judah. "I've already made my decision, Father. I'm merely asking for your blessing."

Judah took a long breath and responded with surprising calm.

"My son, have you considered where such a journey will end? You'll be living among strange cultures. As a physician, you'll be expected to treat Greeks and Romans and people from other nations. The Hellenists might entice you to go against your heritage. I doubt you are strong enough in your faith to withstand such influences."

Eleazar shook his head and chuckled at Judah's innocence. "Father, the world is changing all around us. Unlike you, I have no problem learning from Gentiles. Nor do I intend to restrict my services only to the Jews. If a person is ill, I won't stop to ask about his heritage before I try to cure him." He looked with sympathy at the old man. "Look around you, Father. Jerusalem already has opened its gates to other cultures. They trade with us in the marketplace. Many Jews have learned their language and their customs, which, I have to admit, are far superior to ours."

Judah's brow creased with concern, and he raised his hands, palms up. "There will come a day when the Hebrews and the Hellenists will clash, my son. What will you do then? Which side will you choose?"

"None, Father. I will serve them equally, but as a physician, nothing more."

"Eleazar, your practice already flourishes here in Jerusalem. The last census showed 25,000 people living in this city, enough for all the physicians and plenty for you. Why do you want to go away? What more can you learn in Alexandria that you haven't learned right here—from *me*?"

An uncomfortable silence settled over the table. Anna slid a platter of honey-soaked dates between them. Judah reached out and took one. Eleazar shoved the platter aside and leaned across the table toward his father.

"The physicians of Alexandria have advanced far beyond anything I've learned in this city. They've gone well past your instruction, Father. The Greek medicines surpass all that we have in our apothecary. The scrolls Achim gave me years ago merely served to whet my interest. Now, I hunger for more."

"My son, I've looked at those writings. Some of the treatments go against our religious traditions and may even involve witchcraft. I've waited patiently, hoping this foolish dream of yours would die. Now I see that it hasn't. You must heed my warning, Eleazar. Be content with what you have."

Eleazar shook his head, a fire building within him. "You're wrong, Father. What you see as witchcraft are merely cures that could mean the difference between life and death. Strange diseases, once thought incurable, now have names and choices for healing. I want to learn about them, Father, and yes, I want to test them on the people I serve. And I hope to develop my own medicines based on what I learn. To do that, I need to go to Alexandria. It's the center of study for many different fields—medicine, but also art and literature, philosophy and astronomy. I can expand my mind, learn things I never would in Jerusalem." He stood to his feet. "I'm going, Father. With or without your consent."

"But you want my blessing." Judah tilted his head, his eyes narrowing to mere slits.

"Yes, I want your blessing. It would comfort me to know you'll take care of Anna in my absence, and that, together, the two of you will provide medicines to the sick who come to our door. I need to know that you'll welcome me home in three months and that you'll take an interest in what I've learned."

Judah's brows came together at the center of his forehead.

"I'm leaving in two days." Eleazar's voice was firm.

"I say, *No!*" Judah's fist came down hard on the table. Eleazar started, but he didn't back down. He had reignited a flame within the old man, but an even greater one blazed inside himself.

Judah stood to his feet. "You will remain in this city and tend to the practice I established. *This* is where you need to be. *This* is where you will advance in your work, not in an unfamiliar land with heathens teaching you ungodly practices."

A surge of heat rushed to Eleazar's face. He was about to speak when Anna placed her hand on his arm. Calmly, she turned to face the old man.

"Eleazar must go to Alexandria, Father Judah." Her voice was sweet and respectful but surprisingly controlled. "As my husband said, I can help you with the medicines. I've assisted Eleazar many times with the blending of herbs and powders. I know how to make a poultice, and I've practiced the skills of a midwife. I have stood by and watched my husband deal with disappointment after disappointment. I'm sorry, Father Judah. You've taught him as much as you can, but he can learn far more in Alexandria."

She withdrew her hand from Eleazar's arm, and, with her eyes fastened on her husband, she spoke with a firmness that amazed him. He stood in awe, seeing a side of his wife that he had never noticed before.

"Eleazar, you will go to Alexandria." She smiled her approval. "Whether or not Father Judah gives his blessing, you have *my* blessing."

Judah stared at Anna and raised his eyebrows in surprise. Eleazar broke into a grin. Silently, he dared the old man to go against both of them.

Judah let out a sigh and nodded his assent. The old man lowered himself to his chair and bowed his head. Encouraged, Eleazar leaned toward his wife and planted a kiss on her forehead. Then he hurried out the door, eager to make preparations for his trip.

Anna watched her husband leave, confident that he would return a happy man, grateful to be able to fulfill his dream. Perhaps through this shared purpose she would win his favor after all.

She looked at Judah and smiled. The old man raised his head and stared back at her, an awareness flooding into his eyes.

"You've not told him?" Judah said, his voice tender.

She shook her head and rested her hand on her abdomen. "He said he would go for only three months. I'm confident he will come home in time for his first child to be born."

The next morning Eleazar went to the marketplace to tell his best friend he would be leaving for Alexandria. When he arrived, he saw Ruth standing by Achim's stall, looking through his display of jewelry. Her deep purple veils set off her black hair and her creamy skin. Eleazar looked around. There was no sign of Levi.

Weaving his way through the crowded plaza, he drew close to Ruth's side. The scent of calamus took him back several years to the garden of Gethsemane. His heart surged with remembered love.

"There's a pretty one." He pointed past Ruth's arm at a gold bracelet with ornate markings on it.

Ruth turned toward him. Her eyes lit up in surprise, and her quick smile sent his heart reeling.

"Eleazar," she breathed. "How are you?"

"I'm well—but lonely."

A hint of color rushed to Ruth's cheeks. She lowered her eyes and turned away from him. Though shocked by her sudden shyness, Eleazar reached for the gold bracelet and slipped it on her arm. She turned to face him, then, smiling, she held her arm up and wiggled her wrist. Sunlight bounced off the circle of gold. Her dark eyes flashed with appreciation.

"Achim!" Eleazar signaled his friend. "How much for the gold bracelet?"

Achim glanced up from his table of wares. "For you, Eleazar, ten denarii."

Ruth removed the bracelet and returned it to the table. "No, I can't—"

"Take five." Eleazar picked up the bracelet and slipped it back on Ruth's wrist, ignoring her protest.

"Seven and not a mite less." Achim stood firm though his lips had curled at the corners in a mocking grin.

"It's robbery." Eleazar laughed aloud and slammed the coins on the table. Achim nodded and picked up the pieces of silver, counting them one by one. His eyes darted back and forth between Eleazar and Ruth. Frowning he shook his head at Eleazar.

Ruth stared at the bracelet on her arm. She kept avoiding Eleazar's gaze. On an impulse, he pulled her to one side, away from the crowd.

"I have news." He could no longer contain his excitement. "I'm going to Alexandria, Ruth. At last, I'll be able to study under the greatest physicians in the world."

"That's wonderful, Eleazar." She spoke softly and kept her eyes on the bracelet.

He frowned. "Why don't you look at me?" He grabbed her shoulders. "What's the matter with you, Ruth? What's become of the girl who told me all those exciting stories about Alexandria? Where has she gone?"

An old woman brushed close to them. Her clucking tongue caused him to release his grip on Ruth.

Raising her eyes, Ruth smiled weakly. "When will you go?" Her voice was void of emotion.

"Tomorrow." He stared at her, confused by her lack of interest. "My friend Thomas has arranged a place for me to stay with his brother who lives there. I'll study the scrolls in the great library, and I'll learn under a physician his brother knows. This is my one chance, Ruth."

"Perhaps a few weeks in Alexandria will give you what you've always wanted." It was like she had accused him of some great sin.

He brushed off the slight and went on with his story. "My father and I argued about it at first. He finally conceded, but only after Anna intervened. You should have seen her, Ruth. She amazed both of us when she defended me."

"Anna." Ruth's voice became wistful. "How is my dear friend?"

"She's made a decent home for us, and she's learned enough about my work to be able to assist Judah while I'm gone." He nodded. "She's been a good wife."

"Of course, I never doubted that she would." Ruth fidgeted

with the bracelet, still avoiding his gaze. "Has she given you any children?"

Her question surprised him. Children? Such a thing hadn't been on his mind. "No children," he said. "So it seems the timing for this journey is good. I must go there now, before Anna conceives and such an opportunity is lost."

He paused and stared at her beautiful face. He'd forgotten how lovely she was. And now, having her so close, he spoke boldly. "Come with me, Ruth. Come to Alexandria. I've never forgotten our pledge. I loved you then, and I still love you."

Ruth backed away from him. "You mustn't speak this way, Eleazar. I'm married now. I have position among the women of the city. I have loyal friends, a houseful of servants, everything the wife of a successful merchant could want."

"And love? Do you have love, Ruth?"

She turned her new bracelet over and over on her wrist. "My husband doesn't show love the way you do. Levi is extremely jealous. When other men notice me, he stomps about in a rage. He must know my heart never belonged to him."

Her eyes met his and her former passion returned with a fire, then quickly vanished. Undaunted, Eleazar pressed on.

"Come to Alexandria. You said you have a sister who lives there. Make some excuse to Levi. Tell him you miss your sister. Come to Alexandria and be with me. Give me these few months, my dear one. Please come."

Ruth turned her face away. Eleazar looked around the marketplace. People milled about, involved in the business of buying and selling. They had no interest in this young couple in deep conversation.

"This could be our last chance for happiness." She turned toward him and shook her head, but he continued to plead with her. "We both live with someone we don't love. I was your husband long before you married Levi. And Anna? She is my housekeeper, nothing more. We made a pact, you and I. Have you forgotten?"

A large group of chattering women spilled toward Achim's stall, their shrill voices drowning out Eleazar's plea.

"Oh, Eleazar. What a pair of foolish children we were back then." She laughed, but pain flooded into her eyes. "We had our dream. Now we live in the real world. What you are asking is foolish, maybe even dangerous. If Levi should find out—"

"He won't. We'll be safe there, far across the sea."

She shook her head, then backed away. He reached for her but she quickly slipped into the crowd.

He tried to follow her, but the throng blocked his path. He caught one last glimpse of her, then her purple veils disappeared from view. Silently he cursed the man who had crushed her spirit.

𝓔leazar's voyage across the Great Sea brought an amazing sense of freedom. A renewed passion stirred within him, and he could hardly contain his joy. Several of the seamen on board the ship confirmed what Ruth had told him about the strange and wonderful land. They spoke of the mix of cultures, the bartering on the docks and in a massive marketplace, and best of all, they talked about the great library and its large store of scrolls and abounding opportunities for learning.

In some of their journeys, they had brought many scholars from other lands, as well as eager young men like Eleazar who wanted to study law, medicine, astronomy, and philosophy. Thrilled by their report, Eleazar set his gaze across the sea and watched for any sign of land.

An elderly man joined him at the rail. His balding head still had a few tufts of hair, and his weathered face spoke of many travels on the sea. He said his name was Solitus, and he was returning to his home in Alexandria. Solitus spoke Aramaic as fluently as his own native tongue. They shifted back and forth between the two languages, with Eleazar failing to grasp much of the Greek. At last, Solitus conceded to using Eleazar's more familiar language.

His heart aflame, Eleazar wanted to know more about the

city, this time from a man who lived there. They sought out a quiet place in the prow of the ship and settled on the floor with cups of steaming tea and some wafers the ship's cook provided. Eleazar gave the man his full attention. Solitus smiled and willingly spoke about his homeland.

"The city was named for Alexander the Great." The older man raised his chin with an air of pride. "Its magnificent design was the work of a Greek architect named Dinocrates. Though the city has, in recent years, become part of the Roman empire, the Hellenistic influences have remained."

He took a sip of the herbal drink. Eleazar did the same.

Then, giving Eleazar a wink, Solitus went on. "Unlike most cities, Alexandria contains a well-organized pattern of streets and cross streets which make it easy to navigate. Dinocrates' plans called for a broad central street in the midst of a very large agora. Shops line either side. People swarm there looking for bargains and unusual products from distant lands."

A thought struck Eleazar. "Will I have any trouble communicating with people from so many different cultures? After all, I am a Jew, and I was raised in the traditions of my faith. As you know, I speak a little Greek, having learned a few phrases in the marketplace back home. But how will I blend in with such a diverse crowd?"

Solitus shook his head and smiled. "You will not be alone. There's a large Jewish population, many of them descendants of those who came there during the Great Diaspora. Since that time, others have moved to Alexandria, eager to benefit from the trading that goes on there. Everyone adjusts well, and you will too."

Eleazar downed the last of his drink. "I must admit, I have always marveled over the ways of people of other cultures and other faiths. Despite the strict rules in Jerusalem, many of us younger Jews have strayed from the stricter laws of our forefathers. While we display a surface obedience to please our elders, our hearts have yearned for something less restraining."

Solitus laughed and patted him on the shoulder. "I expect you'll do quite well in Alexandria."

A shout came from the helm. "Land!"

Eleazar leaped to his feet and rushed to the rail. He looked out over the sea's blue-green expanse. Far ahead he caught sight of the lighthouse perched like a watch tower on the isle of Pharos, just as Ruth had described it. The structure's pure white sides reflected the sun's rays forcing him to shade his eyes against the glare.

The boat slowed and drifted past the island. All around, multiple sailing vessels loomed, their towering masts nearly disappearing into the clouds. The water rippled and splashed around the sides of the boat, and they slowly approached the shore. The serenity of the sea gave way to a furor of activity. Shirtless workmen tossed sacks of grain on the dock, the bundles landing with loud thumps. Their muscles rippled with every thrust, their backs glistened with sweat. Their damp brows were bound with strips of stained cloths.

Eleazar left the ship with Solitus' final words still in his head. *"You'll do quite well in Alexandria."*

He walked along the rocky shoreline and breathed in the sea air, a refreshing change from Judea's arid surroundings. There were no clouds of dust here, no sweltering heat, merely a mild breeze, like gentle fingers running through his hair.

His first order of business was to seek out Thomas' older brother, Minoa, and his wife, Pasha, a childless couple who lived in the Jewish quarter and had agreed to receive him into their home. They immediately asked about Minoa's younger brother, Thomas. Eleazar assured them that he and his family were doing well.

They showed Eleazar to a small room, sparsely furnished with a bed, a chair, a table for studying, and a solitary oil lamp.

"What more do I need?" he said, nodding with approval. "I'll spend most of my time at the library."

As he had expected, Minoa and Pasha adhered to the strict teachings of the Jewish law. While staying in their home he would have to do the same. But when he stepped out their door and walked the streets of Alexandria, he would become a student of Greek culture. Of this much he was certain. Minoa didn't own him, had merely provided a place for him to stay.

On his first night there, he ventured into a lively inn and connected with a group of young Jewish men who'd already immersed themselves in this strange culture. They lived in the Greek section, traded in the Greek shops, and spoke the Greek language. They even dressed like the Greeks with swaths of cloth draped over their left shoulders, their hair cropped into tight curls, and their chins shaved clean. Eleazar eyed them with awe. As long as he remained in Minoa's home, he would not have such liberty. For now, he set his heart on finding the right teacher.

Minoa arranged for him to meet an aging physician named Nikolaus. On his second day there, he rose early, and, without taking the time to eat anything, he hurried into the street and went directly to the library, eager to begin his studies.

He caught sight of the library almost immediately. Its great roof towered over the other structures in the city. It was the most impressive structure he had ever seen. A row of thick pillars bordered a broad stairway that led to two huge doors. Eleazar charged up the steps, two at a time. He passed through the massive doorway and went from the noise of the street outside to instant calm. People glided silently from one place to another, their whispered communications blending with the hushed scraping of their sandaled feet.

The main entry led to hallways and rows of classrooms, and beyond was a central, open-air garden, where students sat on marble benches, reading and speaking to each other in muted tones. Eleazar toured the grounds with fascination. Occasionally, a dignified older man passed through the area. Sometimes one stopped to say a few words to one of the students. The large expanse was filled with greenery and flowering shrubs. More doorways led to more classrooms, meeting halls, and laboratories. Above each door was a sign indicating what lay beyond. Eleazar eventually came to the one marked *Library*. He walked inside and came face-to-face with an inscription, *The place of the cure of the soul*. He smiled, for he had come there not only to learn more about his chosen occupation, but to clear his mind and his soul of all the doubts of his past.

This was a new beginning for Eleazar. With fresh eyes he took in the large room. All around were floor-to-ceiling shelves bearing hundreds of scrolls—maybe thousands. Would he ever be able to sort through them all? Surely, there must be some order to this vast collection.

He turned his attention away from the abundance of parchments and searched the area for signs of Nikolaus. Minoa had described him as "an older, balding man of slim stature, slightly bent, and having a purple blemish on the right side of his face." Eleazar didn't see anyone who fit the description, so he approached a young student who was seated on the floor against a far wall, his face buried in a scroll.

"Do you know where I might find the physician, Nikolaus?" Eleazar asked in stumbling Greek.

The student glanced up with annoyance and pointed to one of the side rooms. "Medicine." Then he went back to his study.

Eleazar entered the room marked *Medicine* and paused as he was struck with another overwhelming amount of scrolls on the shelves and piled in all four corners of the room. A gasp rose from his throat, and he shook his head in wonder. He suddenly felt very small and helpless.

Then he saw him, a man who fit Minoa's description, standing in the center of the room with his hands folded as though waiting for someone.

"Nikolaus?" Eleazar approached the tiny man, who greeted him with a smile.

"I am Nikolaus."

"I'm Eleazar ben Judah. Minoa sent me."

Nikolaus nodded, and his smile broadened, pulling the purple blemish to his hairline.

Eleazar accepted the man's kisses on both his cheeks. Then the older man gestured toward the wall of parchments. "If you want to understand the information in these scrolls, it will be to your advantage to perfect your knowledge of the Greek language," he said in perfect Aramaic.

Eleazar nodded, eager to begin his studies.

"Walk with me." Nikolaus led him around the room and pointed at one wall and then another. "This library was at one time even more magnificent than what you see today. There was a terrible fire in Julius Caesar's time. The library held an even greater collection of writings, more than 900,000 parchments, many of them brought here by the Ptolemies from conquests all over the world. The great fire destroyed many of those scrolls. Some of the young scholars rushed in and risked their lives to save as many as they could. Since then, others have worked diligently to rebuild the collection. As you can see, they've been quite successful."

Then, the little man paused, seemingly deep in thought. He pointed at the blemish on his face. "My reward for rescuing a mere handful of scrolls." Then a sadness filled his eyes. "I lost my best friend in that fire, and nearly lost my own life, as well. More than 40,000 scrolls burned that day. They covered many subjects, including medicine. Like you, I came here eager to find a cure for every known disease. I believed the scrolls held secrets to healing. Though many of the writings have been replaced, my lifelong friend was gone."

Eleazar felt instant compassion for this old man. He immediately thought of his own best friend, Achim. To lose a friend in such a tragic way would be unbearable.

Nikolaus then pointed at a pile of scrolls against the far wall. "After the fire, people from other lands began sending manuscripts to help rebuild the library. Philosophers, physicians, and scientists came from all over the world, eager to write what they had committed to memory. Over the years, they restored documents that were partially burned. And they added new lessons."

Nikolaus pulled a scroll from a nearby shelf. He spread open a detailed drawing of a human being—the muscles, the veins, the sinews, every layer of human flesh all the way down to the skeleton.

At that moment a blaze kindled inside Eleazar. He studied the page, drank in the details, and tried to commit them to memory.

"When can we begin my studies?"

The old man smiled. "Soon," he said, and rolled up the scroll.

"Nikolaus, I've waited my whole life for this opportunity. My father kept me trapped in Jerusalem where I learned only the basics of medicine. I don't want to waste one minute of my time while I'm here. Believe me when I say, I'm a willing pupil, perhaps the most eager student you'll ever have."

Nikolaus stared at him as though weighing his loyalty. Then he nodded. "I will give you a parchment that contains a simple study of Greek words for diseases and cures. Memorize them. Go to the marketplace. Test your knowledge of the Greek language on the merchants and the people who shop there. Join in the conversations as best you can. Soon, most likely within a few days, we'll begin to examine the writings of Hippocrates and other great men of medicine. Unless you conquer their language first, their descriptions will be meaningless to you."

"Yes, yes." Eleazar's heart was pounding. "Give me the scroll. I won't disappoint you, Nikolaus."

CHAPTER SIXTEEN

$\mathcal{D}$ays flew by faster than Eleazar would have liked. He did as Nikolaus had instructed—studied the Greek words, wrote them on parchment, committed them to memory while pacing in his room, recited them softly while walking on the city streets. He learned them well. He also spent time in the marketplace, and though he stumbled over the language and even brought a confused smile to the faces of some of the merchants, they helped him pronounce the words properly. His knowledge of the Greek language grew. When he returned to the library the following week, he submitted to a test with his teacher's approval. Nikolaus raised his eyebrows in amazement.

"You are making great strides, Eleazar. You've perfected your use of the Greek language, and you possess a rare ability to memorize these difficult diseases, far better than most of the students I've worked with.

Eleazar shrugged and flushed a little, but he couldn't deny the sense of pride that rippled through him. "I came here with one purpose—to study with you." He paused, then smiled with confidence. "I won't let you down, Nikolaus."

The little man returned his smile, then he pulled a scroll from a nearby shelf and exchanged it for the one in Eleazar's hand.

"Now you can move beyond your language study. This scroll

not only contains medical knowledge, but also drawings that will help you envision the names of body parts and what can happen to them. You'll need to master the various diseases and their cures, and many tools you've most likely never seen before. In a few days, you will accompany me into the city where you can observe my work."

Passion building inside him, Eleazar accepted the scroll from Nikolaus' hand and hurried into the garden to begin his study. He sat on a bench beneath a flowering vine, breathed deeply of the sweet aroma, and set his mind on the scroll. Hours passed. He took the scroll home and went directly to his room. Seeing his dedication, Minoa and Pasha did not disturb him but slipped into his room with a hot meal and left quietly.

After two days, he felt as though he had committed the words to memory. He went back to the library and searched for Nikolaus.

The old man greeted him with a satisfied nod. "Tomorrow, you will go with me into the city. I must perform a cutting."

A cutting? Eleazar had seen drawings, but now he would be able to observe a true man of medicine at work. He wondered that this little man, bent at the shoulders and with hands that trembled, could cut anybody without doing more damage to the wound. The thought was still on Eleazar's mind the next morning as they walked to the home of a common laborer who had injured his foot while unloading one of the ships. Nikolaus described the man's injury before they arrived at the house.

"I've labored hard to heal him," Nikolaus said, shaking his head, "But to no avail. All five of the man's toes were smashed and the edge of the wooden box tore open his ankle. His entire foot has turned purple. Now it seems the poison has begun to travel up his leg and is threatening his very life. I'm afraid we're going to have to remove most of his leg."

Even before the woman of the house opened the door to them, the man's agonized screams poured from the back room and sailed to their ears. His wife led them to the bed chamber where they found the poor soul writhing on a bed of soiled blankets. Nikolaus tried to explain that he was unable to heal the wound and that he would have to cut away the damaged portion.

The man flailed about on his bed, tossing his head from one side to the other and crying aloud. "No! Not my leg. How will I work? What is to become of my family?"

Eleazar was reminded of his father's care of Shaul the shepherd. The poor man had broken his leg after falling from his roof. Judah had healed the wound using crude methods. But this wasn't Shaul. And this wasn't Judah. It was a far worse injury, and the man's physician was Nikolaus. Would his father have been able to make such a decision?

Nikolaus instructed the man's wife to bring clean linen cloths, which he placed in Eleazar's hands. Then he approached the bed and removed a pouch from his bag. He blended a little powder with water from the man's bedside table. He got him to drink the potion. In a short time, the man fell into a noisy sleep. Then, beckoning Eleazar closer, the old physician cleansed the man's leg using a substance that stung Eleazar's eyes.

Nikolaus reached inside his bag and withdrew a carpenter's saw. Eleazar's eyes widened. He swallowed hard against the rise of bile from his stomach. He noticed the old physician's hands had stopped shaking. With nimble fingers, Nikolaus began to cut into the decayed limb. Blood oozed from the wound. Nikolaus signaled Eleazar to stem the flow. There was an unsettling scraping of blade against bone, then the limb dropped off. Without hesitation, the physician stitched up the dangling tissue with strands of horsehair. Then he drew the layers of skin over the man's knee and sewed them with a neat crossing of stitches. The man's face seemed so pale Eleazar thought he actually *had* died, but when he glanced at Nikolaus, the physician showed no sign of concern.

Afterward, Eleazar felt drained. Sweat poured from his brow, and, though the pounding in his chest had subsided, an uncontrollable weakness attacked his arms and legs. Meanwhile, the little physician hadn't oozed one bead of sweat. Working swiftly, he cleaned up the area and wrapped the severed limb inside the bloody cloths. He then summoned the man's wife, and gave instructions for her husband's care. Their talk swirled inside Eleazar's head and vanished. He doubted he would remember any of those instructions.

Nikolaus received a meager payment, a reminder of Judah's service to the poor people in the Lower City. Was this the way of all physicians, or only men like his father and Nikolaus?

The two of them bid farewell to the weeping woman, the severed limb tucked neatly under Nikolaus' arm. When they reached the street, Nikolaus leaned toward Eleazar.

"We'll dispose of this in the refuse area of the city." Then he strode on as though he'd just come from watching the games at an open-air theater.

Meanwhile, Eleazar had not been prepared for what he had just seen. The sanitation methods of the Greeks differed from those of his own people. He wondered about the spray of blood. The teachers of the law would have required him to wash himself and follow a cleansing ritual, perhaps offer a sacrifice. Nikolaus had not mentioned any of those rules. Unsure of how he was supposed to deal with such issues, Eleazar began to understand that while living in Alexandria his life was going to be different.

Even so, his father's words came back with full force. *My son, have you considered where such a journey will end? You'll be living among strange cultures. As a physician, you'll be expected to treat Greeks and Romans and people from other nations. The Hellenists might entice you to go against your heritage. I doubt you are strong enough in your faith to withstand such influences.*

His father's warnings troubled him. If he wanted to keep on with his studies he was going to have to choose. The methods of the Jews or the methods of the Greeks? The law or free will? The life he once knew or the one he now embraced? His father as his teacher? Or Nikolaus?

He glanced at the old man walking beside him. The trembling

had returned to Nikolaus' hands. He continued to speak about the medical procedure Eleazar had just witnessed. Nikolaus' voice had a slight tremor. Yet he kept talking as though the instruction meant more to him than the emotion that had come over him. The man was very old, probably close to 90. Could it be that he did not see Eleazar as merely a student who would learn from him and then go home? The truth hit Eleazar like a bolt of lightning. The old man was preparing him to take his place.

With each trip into the city, Eleazar became more confident in his own abilities. Nikolaus handed him more and more duties, until he was able to take over the treatments in many cases. His one desire was to be able to match and possibly even exceed the older physician's skills. Many times he came up with the right cure before Nikolaus had an opportunity to instruct him. He performed simple procedures under the old man's direction, and he looked forward to the day when Nikolaus would send him out alone.

His teacher occasionally began his instructions with these words. "Hear me now." And Eleazar knew he was about to get a word of advice apart from his medical schooling.

"Here me now," the old man said as they walked. "Be confident, but never trust only in yourself, for that is the moment when most men fail. Those you serve depend on your ability to approach them with humility and purpose."

Nevertheless, Eleazar's self-confidence soared. Not one of his patients had died following his treatment. Those he healed expressed their highest regard for him and dropped a great many coins in his hand. His initial fears melted away. On an impulse, while in the marketplace one afternoon, Eleazar purchased a wooden box with a handle for carrying. It was large enough to hold the tools he would need for his trips into the city. He filled it with knives, scissors, a drill, syringes, clamps, and an assortment of ointments and powders. He eyed his collection with satisfaction for they exceeded the meager contents in his father's apothecary. In a little more than a month, Eleazar was certain he had surpassed Judah's ability to cure the sick.

Then, unexpectedly, he heard his father's voice recite a proverb: *"Pride goes before destruction and a haughty spirit before the fall."*

He quickly shrugged it off, unable—or unwilling—to let it dampen his spirits.

If he wasn't on the streets with Nikolaus he was in the library deep into the books. Sometimes he went to a private reading area or to the central garden where he'd settle on a bench and unfurl a scroll. With the words filling his head, he let the rest of the world simply drift away.

He had settled in such a place one morning when a small voice interrupted his studies. Startled, he looked up and squinted at the shadow blocking the sunlight.

"What is it?" Eleazar didn't hide his annoyance.

"Are–are you Eleazar ben Judah?" the meek voice asked.

"Yes, I am. And who are you?"

"M–My name is Amed. I am a servant in the home of Ziba."

Eleazar lowered the scroll and straightened his back.

"My mistress, Abigail, requests your presence. A visitor has come from Jerusa—"

Eleazar tossed the manuscript to the floor and sprang to his feet. His heart pounding, he stepped toward the boy.

"Show me the way."

CHAPTER SEVENTEEN

*W*hen Eleazar reached Ziba's house, he rushed past the boy, burst through the door and came to a stop in front of Abigail holding a platter of fresh fruit in her hands. Startled, she nearly dropped the platter. She frowned at him then pointed toward an open door to the garden.

A vision of loveliness appeared in the doorway. "Ruth," he said, his throat tight with joy.

He slipped past Abigail and drew close to his beloved. Without a word she turned and led him into the garden. There, beneath a shelter of palm trees with flowering shrubs growing all around, he gazed at Ruth, hardly able to believe she was really there. A sheer green veil graced her hair, and her dress was of shimmering green and gold layers of silk. Her alabaster cheeks flushed a deep pink, and her dark eyes glistened with a rise of tears. Eleazar felt as though his heart had doubled in size.

A soft breeze swept off the sea and caught the scent of calamus. Her veil fluttered and fell away, leaving her hair to fall in long, dark waves to her shoulders. Eleazar reached out and swept a stray lock from her cheek, then he brushed her lips with his fingertips. She smiled. Gently he grabbed her arms and pulled her close. She surrendered to his embrace.

"I thought I'd never see you again," she whispered.

"Ruth. My dear Ruth. I can't believe you came. How is it you were able to arrange a visit?"

She backed away, took his hand, and led him to a marble bench within a bower of flowering plants. He glanced toward the house. Abigail was standing in the doorway, a troubled wrinkle on her brow.

"It was a sudden decision," Ruth explained, drawing his attention back to her. "Levi's business has taken him away from home for a while. Before he left, I begged him to let me visit my sister. It was a long time since I saw her last, and I missed her terribly. At last, he got tired of my pleading and sent me away."

"Does he know I'm here?"

"Possibly. Although he hasn't mentioned your name since your wedding, Levi keeps aware of everything that happens in Jerusalem. He knows everyone's business, and he knows how to use the information to his advantage."

Eleazar eyed her with concern. "I want to be with you, Ruth, but we must be careful. I don't want to bring Levi's judgment upon you."

She laughed, and the sound was like a stirring of little bells. Then she shook her head. "Eleazar, in this place we'll have a freedom that is unknown in Jerusalem. The Greek men have their wives and their mistresses."

He winced at the mention of mistresses. He didn't want to think of dear Ruth in such a low estate.

She tossed her head. "Women walk about with much liberty. They read. They get involved in political affairs. Here, we can choose. We can live within our Jewish laws, or we can accept the way of the Greeks."

He grinned. "Then I choose the way of the Greeks." Rising, he grabbed her hands and pulled her from the bench. Then he placed his hands on her waist, lifted her from the ground and twirled her about. Her girlish giggles thrilled him. For the moment he was back on Gethsemane again, playing with his love, with no concern for parents or rules or the sideways glances of strangers. They were in the privacy of a garden in a far-off land, and no one could steal his joy.

Squealing, Ruth wrapped her arms around his neck and clung to him. Then he set her down before him, kissed her forehead and both of her cheeks. And, for the first time in years, he dared to kiss her lips.

She blushed and backed away. "I'm so happy to be here," she breathed. "If only for a short time."

He frowned at her. "A short time? How short?"

She raised a shoulder. "I don't know. I'll stay as long as I can. For now, let's enjoy every minute we have."

"I agree," he said. "I don't want to think about you returning to Levi or to that miserable life you had in Jerusalem."

Her smile faded. "You can't know how difficult it's been. Once our contract was finalized and we said our vows, Levi put me on a shelf with all of his other possessions, only to be brought out when needed. His business dealings come first. Then he uses me for his own physical pleasure." She grunted with disgust. "Our intimacy is hardly intimate at all. And if a business deal doesn't go as he had hoped, I come away from our bed bruised and weary."

Eleazar clenched his fists, but held his anger as she went on.

"Not long ago, Levi was in a battle with other merchants over a widow's property. Her husband died, leaving her a large estate, and she had no family to rescue her. My husband bargains hard with such people. It pains me to stand by and watch him destroy a poor widow while she is yet in mourning. But that's what he does, and if he loses to another merchant, I pay a terrible price. He can't contain his anger."

Scowling, Eleazar let his anger fly. "If I learn of such things when I return, you can be sure I will go after Levi myself."

"You can't, Eleazar, or he will know the truth about us." Ruth stroked his arm, calming him. "Listen to me," she said. "Levi's greed will destroy him. The Council will hear about the way he treats the poor. Let *them* deal with him."

Eleazar felt a struggle going on inside him. He had no right to confront Levi, not while he was standing there with the man's wife, knowing he was falling into grievous sin.

Ruth reached up and stroked his cheek, and his guilt quickly melted away.

"You've grown thin." She searched his face. "Don't you eat? You care for others. Have you not been taking care of yourself?"

"I consume the manuscripts," he said with a shrug. "They provide sustenance enough for me. In the morning, I'm on the streets with my teacher, Nikolaus. I grab a bite between calls to the sick. Afterward, I rush to the library and study. In the evening, Minoa's wife brings me a little supper, and I plan my next day. That's my life." He paused. His eyes misted over, and she became a blur. "Until now," he added.

"And what will happen now that I'm here?" Ruth's eyes locked with his. "Will I interfere with this life you have established so well?"

He shook his head and wrapped his arms around her. "No, my love. I'll simply make a few changes. I'll be on the streets in the morning and at the library in the afternoon. But, my nights, dear Ruth, belong to you."

They went back to the bench and sat together. She had the smallest hint of a smile. He wished he could read her thoughts. She surprised him when she dared to lean her cheek against his arm. He held his breath, didn't move, didn't want to disrupt the sense of overwhelming comfort that came with her closeness. They sat for a long time, unmoving, in silence, their hands touching. He breathed in her perfume.

Then she raised her head. "I'll agree to your daily plan on one condition." He raised an eyebrow. "I insist you eat with us at my sister's house in the evenings. You won't be any use to anyone if you don't eat. Not to your mentor. Not to the sick people of Alexandria. And not to me. If you don't do this, you might be in need of a physician *yourself*."

"Eat with your sister? Did you see the way she looked at me when I came through her door? Daggers flew from her eyes."

"Don't worry, Eleazar. Abigail knows of our attachment, that we've loved each other since our youth. In fact, she resented my father for pledging me to Levi. I never kept my feelings a secret. Not from my sister. But you have to understand, she is concerned for my safety. In time, she will accept you. I'm certain of it."

She leaped from the bench and spun in a circle, her veils swirling about her in a blend of greens and golds. For the moment she looked like the young girl he first fell in love with in Gethsemane.

"Let's take a walk, Eleazar," she said, twirling this way and that way. "Let's go to the docks and watch the ships come in. Let's catch a ride on a sailboat to Pharos. Let's try to get inside the lighthouse." She stopped dancing and stood in front of him, her face aglow. "Let's do whatever we want and not think about Jerusalem or anything else."

Ruth was back. Not the meek and frightened woman he last saw in the Jerusalem marketplace, but the one he remembered from their youth. The free-spirited girl who dreamed the same dreams he dreamed.

"I'll come for you tonight," he said, grasping her arms. "We'll get away from your sister's watchful eye. We'll go for a walk and we'll talk."

Ruth nodded. "Tonight," she murmured. Then she walked him to the front gate and waved farewell.

The promise brought to his mind their first meeting at the well and their plan to meet again at Gethsemane. *"After the Sabbath service,"* she had said those many years ago. It was as if all that time apart had not happened at all. Now it was simply the word, "Tonight." A simple word but one he could hang onto for the rest of the day.

Reluctantly, he returned to the library and picked up the scroll he had left on the floor. He tried to resume reading where he'd left off, but his mind kept drifting back to Abigail's home and to Ruth.

He was still struggling with the text when Nikolaus appeared and summoned him for a visit in the city. Once more, Eleazar had to set his mind on the work before him. Ruth took her place in the back of his mind, always present but merely a faint promise for the moment.

This time, Nikolaus stood back while Eleazar tended to a man's stomach ailment. He blended herbs and honey into a mixture Nikolaus had taught him during his first week there. The man took a hardy drink, and within a short time he burst into tears, relieved that the pain had eased. Nikolaus nodded his approval.

They spent the rest of the afternoon in the city healing a variety of injuries and illnesses. By evening, Eleazar's feet were sore and his head was spinning with the names of unfamiliar herbs and spices.

He quickly bathed, donned a new shirt, and ran ointment through his hair. He gave his regrets to Pasha, saying he had been invited to the home of a friend. Then he hurried to Abigail's house. He found Ruth and Abigail in the kitchen making bread and arranging fruit on a platter. Avoiding Abigail's suspicious glare, he sped Ruth away from the house and into the street, then he took her hand and guided her to the middle of town.

They strolled along the broad central street of Alexandria. Shops with open doorways bordered each side, neatly spaced, distinctly unlike Jerusalem's disorderly arrangement of tables and stalls. Though Alexandria was crowded with people of many different cultures and dress, everyone walked by without jostling or bumping anyone else, giving only a passing nod or a smile. It was a pleasant change from the suffocating, elbow bumping throng so common in Jerusalem's marketplace.

Eleazar talked about his work, the new treatments he had learned, his growing attachment to Nikolaus. Ruth seemed to hang on every word.

"He treats me more like a son than a student," he said, slipping her hand in the crook of his arm. "Having no wife or children of his own, he is passing all of his knowledge onto me. He seems to gain pleasure from our time together. Because of Nikolaus, I will surpass every physician in Judea when I return."

Ruth's face brightened, and she laughed aloud. "Eleazar, you already *are* the best physician in Judea. People in the Upper City speak your name with high regard. How much better do you want to be?"

He smiled down at her. "My dear love, a good workman must *never* stop improving his trade, no matter how skilled he is."

"Eleazar." She spoke softly now, almost shyly. "I know you far better than anyone does. Once you've set your heart on a goal, you pursue it with such a passion nothing will stand in your way. When you want something, no one can stop you. I saw it in you, years ago. It's still there."

He understood with sadness. She was talking about the day he allowed her to walk away from him in Gethsemane. He'd made a choice, and she had accepted it.

He stopped walking and stepped in front of her. Tears flooded into her eyes. "Why didn't you come after me? Why didn't you stop my marriage to Levi?"

He shook his head. "I wanted to follow you, Ruth. At the time it seemed hopeless." He cupped her face in his hands. "I'll never again allow anything to come between us. You have my promise."

Ruth released a shaky breath. "And I had to let you pursue your dream. As long as I persisted, you would have had no future in Jerusalem. So, you see, my love, I had to walk away from you."

Moved by her confession, Eleazar wrapped his arms around her and pulled her close. "Do you forgive me then?"

She nodded. "Am I not here? Did I not risk everything to come to you?"

They held each other for a few moments, as people walked by, unaffected by their sudden show of affection. And Eleazar understood that behaviors that were unacceptable in his homeland were no cause for alarm in this place.

Taking Ruth by the hand, he guided her down the street, a satisfied smile on his face. The setting sun cast a glow on the open market, adding to the glimmers of light from tall lamps positioned along the sides of the street. He and Ruth merged with the flow of walkers.

He had passed these shops many times before, but they had never drawn him inside before. Colorful dresses and robes hung like curtains on bars in front of the stalls. Outdoor tables were laden with household idols, jewelry, woven baskets, and serving platters. Inside the shops more tables bore a variety of wares, many items unheard of in Jerusalem.

Cobblestone byways branched off from the main street and ran up hills lined with the homes of the residents. Roadside inns emitted aromas of blackened fish, roasted vegetables, and baked goods. Eleazar began to think about the meal that awaited them at the home of Ziba. Hopefully, when they returned he would receive a friendlier greeting than the one he got from Abigail earlier in the day.

As they walked arm-in-arm, he marveled that no one looked at them. Nearly every man had a woman on his arm, and nearly every woman danced along the street. A group of young adults, laughing and singing, passed by them, their arms linked.

Eleazar caught sight of a little shop with a beaded curtain across the doorway. He guided Ruth inside where they found two long tables, piled with colorful fabrics. Ruth strolled beside one of the tables and ran her fingers over the silken layers of cloth. She paused, and her hand came to rest on a sheer veil in many shades of blue. Eleazar lifted it from the table. He draped it over her hair and let the folds fall to her shoulders.

"It's beautiful," he said. "*You're* beautiful."

She blushed a deep pink. Wasting no time, he handed the shopkeeper a handful of coins. He didn't take time to barter, didn't stop when he heard the shopkeeper's confused, "Too much." He simply swept Ruth out to the street where he could admire her new veil in the light of the setting sun.

He tucked her hand in the crook of his arm. "It feels so good to be able to walk openly with you." He said, chuckling. "Parental contracts have no bearing over us here. For the moment, you belong to me."

Ruth stopped and turned to face him, her dark lashes fluttering beneath the glow of a street lamp. "Eleazar, don't you know? I've *always* belonged to you. That's never changed, and it never will. No matter where I go, or where I live—no matter how far away your work takes you—we belong to each other."

His heart surged with joy. On an impulse, he lifted her fingers to his lips and held them there.

"Look!" he called out to a passing couple. "Look at my love! Isn't she beautiful?"

They sang out their approval and moved on. Ruth blushed for the second time. Smiling and shaking her head, she took his hand and led him along the street toward the Delta area and the Via Canopica, the street where her sister lived.

"Abigail will have prepared a meal for us. And Ziba will be licking his lips. Let's not keep them waiting."

CHAPTER EIGHTEEN

At the home of Ziba, Eleazar dined on seared fish fresh from the sea, dried fruit and nuts, and a huge pile of grapes. Abigail's honeyed wheat cakes were a pleasant change from the unleavened bread he'd become accustomed to. He followed every bite of food with a long sip of red wine. For the first time in weeks he filled his stomach.

Ziba beamed as he watched his young guest grab a piece of bread and mop up a helping of stewed lentils. Abigail smiled, but she continued to keep a watchful eye on Eleazar and Ruth.

Though several years older than Ruth, Abigail possessed that same exotic beauty—dark eyes that flashed with an inner spirit, pouty kissable lips, and a full mane of ebony hair, though she had bound hers in a mass of curls in the manner of the Greeks. Her clothing too reflected the culture of the land. Layers of pink gauze hung from her shoulders, exposing bare arms adorned with gold and silver bracelets. Unlike Ruth, Abigail had stained her lips and cheeks with a bright red dye and she had marked her eyelids with a dark stain, a practice frowned upon by the Jews but readily accepted in this part of the world. Abigail had easily taken on the ways of her husband's culture.

Eleazar turned his eyes on Ruth and smiled at her natural beauty. He preferred her fresh, unpainted look, and he hoped she wouldn't change it as her sister had done. Though she'd been one of the more spirited girls in Jerusalem, she hadn't yet given in to the bold influences of cultures across the sea. Hopefully, she would keep the unspoiled yet vibrant disposition he had grown to love.

"Eleazar has been neglecting his stomach in favor of his studies." Ruth said. She slid another bowl in front of him. "He rarely takes time to eat a full meal. But that changes now. We will fatten him up. Don't you agree, Abigail? After all, we can't have Jerusalem's most sought-after physician needing a doctor, can we?"

Ziba let out a laugh and refilled Eleazar's cup. Then in a boisterous voice, he shouted, "You will eat nightly with us, my friend. Take care of your studies by day if you must. But, in the evenings you will dine here—at the house of Ziba."

Eleazar stared in wonder at his host. He hadn't expected to receive such a favorable welcome in this home. But, this big, hairy man had put him at ease from the moment he met him. The worried lines on Abigail's face also had begun to relax, and he hoped he was beginning to earn her acceptance as well.

To his left, Ruth offered him another piece of fish, a wedge of fruited bread, a handful of grapes. She spent more time taking care of him than feeding herself.

Ziba went on shoving food in his own mouth, his breath heavy with garlic and onions, his beard dripping with the dregs of wine. He talked about his work, the abundance of goods he had acquired for Abigail's father, and he laughed about the warring merchants, the drunken sailors, and the loose women who lingered at the inns. Eleazar laughed with him. Ruth and Abigail shared a look and shook their heads with disdain.

When dinner ended Eleazar leaned toward Ziba. "Thank you for your kindness." Then he looked at Abigail. "You prepared a wonderful meal." He waited for a response from her, but none came.

Abigail rose from the table and returned with a platter of sugared dates. She offered them first to her husband, then to

Eleazar. As he reached out and lifted a piece from the tray, he looked into her face.

"I need your approval," he mumbled.

Abigail hesitated. She lowered the platter to the table, then quietly returned to her seat. A troubled frown had creased her brow.

She released a sigh. "I don't disapprove of *you*, Eleazar. I'm concerned for my sister."

"Ruth is safe with me."

"It's not *you* I'm worried about. She has a husband, a brute of a man who wouldn't hesitate to bring shame upon her. Or worse. Levi could have her stoned for this transgression. One more thing. You have to remember, Eleazar, Ruth's visit here will be brief. One day she'll have to return to Jerusalem. Then what will happen? This visit will leave her wanting more, and her joy will turn to heartache."

Before he could respond, Ruth rose to her feet. "Abigail, I'm not a child. We haven't done anything wrong. We walk. We talk. That's all. My dear sister, I need to be with this man, if only for a short time. You once made a choice too, for Ziba. You must understand how I feel."

The stern lines on Abigail's face began to ease. She let out a long sigh and shook her head. "Please, Ruth. Eleazar. Be discreet. The city swarms with visitors. Word could get back to Levi—and to your wife, Eleazar."

Ziba gulped his wine and tore a piece of flesh from the fish on his plate. "Your secret is safe with us. Aphrodite will watch over you."

Eleazar stared at Ziba with interest. "Aphrodite?"

"The goddess of love." Ziba's eyes sparkled with mirth.

Eleazar shook his head. "I have but one God, my friend."

Ziba shrugged. "In any case, be cautious. Levi may have friends here. Stay clear of the Jewish quarter. Those people remain true to their traditions. They wouldn't delay to give a report." He chuckled, stuffed the fish in his mouth and licked his fingers.

He swallowed and locked eyes with Eleazar. "Keep to the main streets. Blend in with the crowd. Enjoy your time together. When Ruth returns to her life in Jerusalem, you, my friend, will go back to your studies." Ziba shrugged and dug into the rest of his food.

Eleazar reached for a handful of grapes and popped them, one at a time, into his mouth. He frowned as he pondered the idea of Ruth leaving. He hadn't considered that one day their time together would come to an end.

Abigail broke into his thoughts with a warning of her own. "Be alert to any sign of tension in the city. There have been seditious outbreaks. You don't want to be caught in the middle of one."

Eleazar nodded. "I witnessed a brawl outside the library one morning. A Greek and a Roman were arguing over a point of law. Their angry words soon turned into a terrible fight. They punched and kicked each other and tumbled into the street. Several young men moved in to stop them, but I stayed clear."

Ziba shook his head. "Too many opposing cultures in one place. Why can't they simply accept each other's differences and enjoy life—like I do?" He reached for a fig cake, crammed it into his mouth, and licked up the honey dripping from his fingers. A broad smile tugged at his lips, now coated with crumbs.

Eleazar glanced at Abigail. What he witnessed amazed him. She was staring at her husband with adoration in her eyes. She rose from her seat and approached Ziba, leaned close to him, and planted a kiss on his forehead. Ziba's eyes shone as he gazed into his wife's smiling face. He wrapped one arm around her waist and grinned.

Eleazar turned to Ruth. "Let's go into the garden."

Except for their walks in the city, Eleazar and Ruth met at the home of Ziba, always under Abigail's watchful eye. One night they went into the garden, and as they walked together under the glow of the torches, Eleazar drew closer to Ruth and breathed deeply of her calamus perfume. The warm and woodsy scent took him back to their meetings at Gethsemane.

Tonight she wore a soft, blue dress and the sheer, blue veil he had bought for her in the marketplace. A spark of light drew his eyes to a gold bracelet on her wrist. He recognized it as the one he'd bought at Achim's stall. He smiled, and his heart burst with love for her.

Sitting beside her on the marble seat, Eleazar tried to speak about his day's special moments, but his mind kept drifting to the nearness of her body and the soft feel of her hand in his. As they talked, she sometimes laughed and tossed her head. The brush of her hair against his neck sent a shiver down his arms. No longer was he content with their sitting and walking and talking. He wanted more.

"Nikolaus has taught me so much, my head is about to burst." He tried in vain to keep his thoughts on his work. "He won't allow any mistakes, which is a good thing. Meanwhile, I've made little progress in the pile of scrolls he assigned to me. No sooner do I finish studying one, and Nikolaus hands me five more. I doubt I'll be able to get through all of them before I return to Judea."

She tilted her head and grinned. "When you do return, Eleazar, you'll be one of the most capable physicians in the city. You traveled far from home to a place that offers everything you needed. Few men can claim such an accomplishment. Most of the physicians never left Judea. But you followed your dream."

Eleazar gave a modest shrug. "My dream means nothing unless you're in it, dear one. I've been busy here, it's true, but I've also been lonely, especially at night." He turned his upper body toward her. "As I lie on my bed, something is missing. Some*one* is missing."

Ruth dropped her gaze. She appeared to be struggling with the right words.

"Only you can fill the void in my life," he pressed.

She raised her face and stared into his eyes. "I don't remember you ever being so alive, Eleazar." Her voice was shaking as if she might be getting ready to tell him some bad news. "When we were children meeting on the hill outside the city, I saw your struggle. You wanted to fly, but your father restrained you. The man who sits beside me now is a happy, contented man, one who has accomplished everything he set out to do."

"Happy? Contented?" He grunted. "I suppose I am. For the first time in my life I'm not under my father's heavy hand." He grew quiet as he remembered how everything changed when his mother died. "My mother understood me best," he said, softly. "She knew what really mattered in my life. It was my mother who planted desires in my heart and encouraged me to pursue them. Now I'm following her plan. I'm living in Alexandria, and I'm learning my trade from a man who has become more of a father to me than Judah ever was."

Gently Eleazar slipped an arm around Ruth's shoulder. "I feel complete now, with you at my side.

She buried her head against his chest and began to sob. "The truth is, I wish I could stay here always, Eleazar. Jerusalem offers no place of honor for a woman who yearns for more. Here, women can own property. Back home, they *are* property. Here, women can be involved in politics. They can discuss issues on an equal level with men, they can study science, philosophy, and the arts. In Jerusalem, I'm reduced to one of my husband's possessions and nothing more. He rules me as heartlessly as he does the servants in our home. And no other man in the city—not even my father—would deny him that right."

"Then stay here, Ruth. Live with your sister. Don't go back."

He was surprised when he felt her hand wrap around his. For the first time since his arrival they had remained in the garden until Ziba's house went dark. There was no sign of Abigail. Ruth rose from the bench and led him toward her chamber. Eleazar's heart began to pound. Inside the dimly lit room, they stood inches apart. She stared up at his face, her dark eyes inviting him closer. Smiling sweetly she let her veil fall to the floor, and she melted into his arms.

CHAPTER NINETEEN

*T*he next morning, Eleazar moved his belongings from the home of Thomas' brother to Ziba's house. Minoa did not let him go without an explanation. He questioned Eleazar, his eyes narrowing in suspicion.

"You choose to abide in the home of a Greek while I have offered you free quarters?" His brow knitted together with deep lines. "What can you hope to learn in that house of sin? How can you keep the law while living with a heathen?"

Eleazar stood firm. "I thank you for your hospitality. But it's time I moved. Ziba's home is closer to the library. It will be far easier for me to continue my studies." He rested a hand on Minoa's shoulder. "Don't worry, my friend. I am strong in my faith. I'll be careful to adhere to the law."

Minoa slipped out of his grip and glared at him. "Could it be you have other reasons for such a decision? Take a warning, Eleazar. Your bad choices will come back to haunt you."

He nodded in acceptance of Minoa's warning. Then without looking back, he gathered up his belongings and left the house, a sliver of unease sinking into his heart.

For the next few weeks, Eleazar dove into his studies by day, and in the evenings he shed his physician's robe and became a visitor in the city with his love walking openly beside him. They visited the hippodrome, the theaters, and the gymnasium, where half-naked men competed for a prize. Afterward, in the dark of night, with Abigail turning her back on them, they clung together with only the moon and the stars to light their bed.

A fresh flame had burst within Eleazar, and he plunged into his work with a passion he hadn't known before. The writings of Hippocrates and other men of medicine came alive. He recorded medical notes on strips of parchment, memorized blends of herbs that could heal various illnesses, considered diseases that had previously been unknown to him, and through trial after trial he developed his own cures that worked on the individuals he cared for.

What he first had seen as an endless pile of scrolls had dwindled to only a few, and he acknowledged with sadness that he was nearing the end of his studies. Very soon he would have to return to Jerusalem. He would have to say good-bye to Nikolaus, whom he had grown to respect as a father, and to Abby and Ziba, his generous hosts. And most of all, to Ruth. The thought of losing her again sent daggers into his heart.

The moments he spent with his dearly beloved meant everything to him. *Ruth belongs to me*, he kept telling himself. *She never really belonged to Levi. Their marriage was unlawful, as was the one my father made with Anna's parents. Surely a person's heart bears more authority over a union than a piece of parchment and a ritual.*

He left their bed one morning before the sun had risen. Wearing only a loin cloth, he walked into the garden. His bare chest glistened with the early mist. His hair hung in damp curls to his shoulders. Off in the distance red streaks trailed across the horizon. Shadows of palm trees stood like sentries beyond the garden. His gaze moved past them, and he dreamed of a different future for him and Ruth, a future right here in Alexandria.

If they chose to remain, Ruth would never have to return to that monster, Levi. She would be safe here. As for Eleazar, he felt no desire to ever see Anna again, or his father. He and Ruth could purchase a house of their own. They could live as a married couple, raise their children, grow old together. He could work for Nikolaus. The man would welcome him. Already he had earned more money in these few months than he had gathered in an entire year working with his father in Jerusalem.

He would forget about the Council. He'd chosen that body of arrogance over Ruth once before. He would not make that mistake again.

With renewed confidence, Eleazar returned to Ruth's chamber, dressed in his clothes for work, and departed without waking her. He would tell her his plan that very night.

That evening, Eleazar hurried home, his heart aflame with his plan. He entered the house and found Abigail preparing the evening meal alone. A strange stillness had settled over the house. He set questioning eyes on Abigail. She turned her face away. He looked for Ruth. She wasn't in her chamber.

He found her in the garden. A storm was building on the horizon. Dark clouds swept overhead. A flash lit up the sky, then the world went black again. Eleazar sensed a harsh stirring in the air, and his heart told him it did not come from the coming storm. *It was right there in the garden.*

Ruth stood with her back to him. She raised one hand toward heaven as though in prayer. Her behavior perplexed him. He stood watching her and dared not to breathe. He started to walk toward her. At the scraping of his footstep against the tiles, she turned around and faced him.

A flash of lightning lit up the troubled lines on her face. Tears wet her cheeks. In her hand was a pure white flower she had pulled from a vine on the wall. She fingered the delicate petals, bruising them with her touch.

Eleazar's heart was pounding. "What has happened?"

She looked down at the flower in her hand, tore a petal loose and let it drop to the pavement. Eleazar's throat tightened. Beads of sweat formed on his brow.

"What is it, Ruth?" His own voice was trembling.

She gazed at him with the hollow eyes of a dead person. They were drained of the flame he had worked so hard to restore. Lines of red circled the rims of her eyes.

"It's time for me to go back to Jerusalem." She said, softly.

It felt like a two-edged sword had pierced his heart. "No, Ruth. You don't have to leave. Not now. Not ever. I've been thinking. We can stay here—in Alexandria. We can start a new life. You need never again return to that place or to that horrible man."

She smiled meekly and shook her head. "Oh, Eleazar. You're still holding onto a dream. You and I both knew our time together would be brief. I've been away far too long. Levi grows impatient. He sent word through a merchant friend that he wants me to return to Judea—immediately."

"But, I'm not ready to leave yet, Ruth. My studies—"

"Yes, your studies. You must set your mind on your studies. Forget about me, Eleazar. I have to go. I've already made my travel arrangements." Her eyes searched his face. "I'm leaving in the morning," she said, driving the sword deeper into his heart.

Eleazar stepped toward her. "I won't let you go. I've thought about this all day. I will fight for you, Ruth. I'll fight to keep you here."

"Oh, Eleazar," she said with a meek smile. "Our dream is merely that. A dream. It does not agree with what is true. I can't stay. I must leave right away."

Her fingers tugged at the flower in her hand. Its purity faded, and the petals dropped, one by one, to the pavement at her feet. Ruth's lashes were wet with tears, her cheeks were flushed. She released a long, shaky sigh.

"Eleazar, it seems—I need to tell you—I am with child."

He stepped back, his pulse racing. "Are you certain?"

She nodded and turned her face away. He reached out and pulled her close.

"All the more reason for you to stay." His heart was pounding almost out of his chest. "We can remain here as man and wife.

Our child will grow up in this city. We can forget about our life in Jerusalem and have more children. We can—"

"Eleazar, stop!" She pushed away from him. She released what was left of the bruised flower. It fell to the pavement between them. She kept shaking her head. More tears flooded from her eyes.

"Oh my love, my dear love," she said. "I have counted the weeks. The child isn't yours. It's Levi's."

CHAPTER TWENTY

Though he received many invitations to return to the home of Ziba, Eleazar did not go back after Ruth left. To go there now, without his love beside him, would be torture.

For the last few weeks of his stay in Alexandria, Nikolaus provided a room for him at his tiny quarters. As Ruth had encouraged him to do, he set his mind on his studies. It was the only way he could keep his mind clear.

Nikolaus watched Eleazar with concern in his eyes. "You read far into the night, and you rarely take a meal," he said, his voice harsh. "You must eat. You need nourishment to think clearly. And rest. You need lots of rest, my son. Hear me now. While you save others, your own body will surely fail if you don't take better care of it."

Eleazar heard Nikolaus' words and then discarded them. His goal now was to acquire as much medical knowledge as possible, and then he would return to Jerusalem and resume the life he had begun.

Another month passed. One evening as Eleazar was returning home from a sick call, a large figure leaped from the shadows. Great arms engulfed him, nearly crushing him. He let out a gasp and squirmed to free himself. He shifted his body to one side and prepared to beat off his assailant, when, under the glow of a street lamp, he looked straight into the man's face.

"Achim! You scoundrel. I was about to reach inside my scrip and pull out a blade."

Achim roared with laughter. Tears ran down his cheeks. "A blade? You considered using a blade on me?"

Eleazar breathed a sigh. "I didn't know it was you, my friend."

"I met with Nikolaus," Achim said. "He told me you would be coming home this way. I couldn't help myself, Eleazar. I had to surprise you."

Eleazar smiled for the first time in weeks. He set down his wooden scrip and wrapped his arms around his friend's large body.

"You've grown since I last saw you."

Again, they broke into loud laughter. Eleazar quickly forgot about his plan to rush home to do more reading. His best friend had come to Alexandria!

Achim placed a giant paw on Eleazar's shoulder. "We have much to talk about. I have news from home. But first, I'm starved. Let's fill our stomachs while we talk."

"There's a small inn by the harbor. Their cook sears the fish to perfection. They serve it with fresh leaks, lentils, and herbed bread. And they have the best wine in the city. You can lodge there for the night, if needed. But, I must warn you, the owner doesn't follow our dietary laws."

Achim shrugged. "I released myself from them long ago. How else could I carry on my business in foreign lands? A man has to eat."

They hurried, arm-in-arm, to the harbor. The inn swarmed with fishermen who reeked of their latest catch. They were tipping cups of wine, sloshing the liquid over the sides. Several broke into song and drew howls of laughter from others standing nearby.

Eleazar guided Achim to a quiet corner in the back. He beckoned to the innkeeper and requested a platter of food and two cruses of wine. Soon, the innkeeper returned with a stack of crusty fish, a bowl of lentil mash, herbed bread, and the wine.

They pounced on the meal like two starving dogs. Eleazar

lifted a piece of the bread and inhaled its aroma, then he bit into the fish, crusted with a blend of fresh garlic and bitter herbs. Achim stuffed his mouth with the lentil mash. The juices ran out the corners of his lips and into his beard. They ate in silence for several minutes, simply enjoying the meal. Then they tipped the wine to their lips and smiled with satisfaction.

Eleazar couldn't believe his best friend was sitting across the table from him. "What brings you to Alexandria?"

"Business, of course." Achim shrugged. "Most of the time I need only to go as far as Joppa. But now I'm seeking some rare spices that are available only in this city." He paused to consume another sliver of fish. "And," he added with a twinkle in his eye. "I needed an excuse to come and visit my friend."

Eleazar smiled. "Your visit should prove profitable. With my own eyes I've seen the merchandise coming off the ships. Huge sacks of grain, boxes filled with pottery, Phoenician glassware, and the precious oils and herbs you are seeking. If you keep watch at the shore you'll have your choice." He dipped a piece of bread in the lentil mash. "I've witnessed amazing sites at the shore. Only yesterday, a merchant stood on the rocks with a device that measures distances at sea. The sailors gathered around him like chicks surrounding a mother hen."

Achim laughed at the image. "Where can I find such a device?"

Eleazar took a bite of the bread. "The man had only one to sell. I'm telling you, Achim, you will have plenty of other unusual items to take back and sell in the Jerusalem marketplace."

Achim nodded. Then he sipped his wine in long gulps. "Mmmmm. There's a sweetness to this blend. Savor it, Eleazar. Drink. Eat. You look as though you've starved yourself nearly to death."

"Don't worry about me. I eat. But not with as much zeal as *you* do!"

They laughed together and drank together. Then, breathing a sigh, Eleazar allowed his grin to fade. He set down his cup and looked Achim in the eye.

"Nikolaus has offered me a position. He wants me to stay in Alexandria."

Achim sat back, alarm written on his face. Eleazar raised one hand to calm his friend.

"Don't worry. I have not yet accepted his offer, though it is tempting. I have work here—good work—and it pays well."

Ignoring Achim's knowing gaze, Eleazar reached for a piece of fish. He bit into its salty crispness, all the while feeling Achim's eyes on him. He needed to direct their conversation elsewhere.

"What of our friends, Enos and Thomas?"

"Ah, Enos," Achim wiped his mouth with the back of his hand. "His father urged the Council to accept him. He passed their examination, but, since he's only newly married, he was given one of the lesser, non-voting seats."

"And Thomas?"

"Thomas has a fertile wife." Achim chuckled. "She delivered another child last month. With the two oldest and their set of twins, that makes five."

Eleazar grimaced and shook his head in disbelief. "It surprised all of us when he married that woman. She came from a shameful part of the city. Her reputation was well-known, Achim. Yet, he wanted no other."

His friend shrugged. "Yes, but you know Thomas. He's not a good-looking fellow. He thought himself fortunate to have captured such a beauty. Even though she's borne him many children, he worries she might run off and resume her former life. I think he protects his claim on her by keeping her pregnant." He laughed, shook his head, and tore off a piece of bread.

Eleazar snickered. He made short work of the fish in his hand and washed it down with a long swallow of wine. Then he grew serious. Thomas was one of the few men who could wrest the Council seat away from him.

"Does he prosper in business?" he needed to know.

Achim nodded. "He does well as a silversmith. When Thomas forges a vessel, he doesn't merely fire it and set it aside to cool.

He finishes each piece with a special design of its own. And, he scratches his name on the base. His work is in high demand among the rich. His business thrives."

Eleazar tried to swallow his envy. "And what about the Council? Thomas is married. He has a good business. Has he been considered?" He eyed Achim over the rim of his cup.

Achim looked back at him, frowning. "His name came up several times. But his wife's past life could hinder a call. I suppose as long as he keeps her under control he has a chance. By the way, your name has been considered too, Eleazar. You seem to be a favorite among the members, all the more reason for you to return to Jerusalem as soon as possible."

My name? Who submitted my name?"

"You know him well. Ariel, Ruth's father."

Eleazar's eyebrows went up. "What? That man passed over me and chose Levi for his daughter's husband. Why in the name of heaven did he name *me?*"

"I can't answer that. I only know that for someone to receive a call from Ariel is a great honor. His opinion is well-respected. It would do you well to return to Jerusalem and let your presence be known."

"But I have more to learn, more to do *here*. I'm not ready to leave."

Achim tore a small loaf apart and offered half to Eleazar.

"You've had enough training to last a lifetime, my friend. Come back with me. I leave in two days. That should give you enough time to get your things together and settle your account with Nikolaus. Right now, the high priest and the Seventy are well, but if they lose a member they will fill the seat quickly. If you stay away too long, your spot could go to Thomas. Or someone else. Levi, perhaps."

"Levi? That scoundrel. Surely the members know of his ruthless business dealings. He takes advantage of poor widows, and he's known to ask more for his merchandise than others in his trade."

Eleazar grew quiet, his mind still on Ariel. The man had thought enough of him to bring up his name, but he didn't think him worthy enough to marry his daughter.

"And Ruth," he ventured to ask. "How is she?"

"She remains at home."

Achim lifted a piece of the bread to his mouth and devoured it. Then he pulled the flesh off another fish. After he stripped it clean, he lowered the skeleton to the plate. Eleazar watched him closely. The sparkle had left his friend's eyes.

"There's something else. What is it, Achim? Tell me."

Achim seemed to be stalling as he tore off another piece of bread and dipped it in the mash. He raised the sop to his mouth, licked his lips, and swallowed. When he spoke, it was with deep sorrow.

"I told you I have news from Jerusalem. Your father ails. Anna cares for him as best she can. She's proved herself to be wise in the use of the medicines. She serves people who come to the door for help, and she keeps Judah comfortable and well-fed. Nevertheless, poor Judah grows increasingly weaker with each passing day."

Eleazar shrugged. "I taught Anna well. She's merely following my instructions. As for my father, I'm content to leave him in her care. I was finished with him long ago."

"Anna's a fine woman," Achim said, his eyes fixed on him. "I don't think you ever appreciated what a treasure you have in her."

Eleazar shook his head and frowned. "There is another, Achim. You know that. No one will ever take Ruth's place in my heart."

"Yes, and it's a devotion that can only lead to your fall."

"I need to tell you, Ruth was here—for nearly a month."

Achim was about to shove another piece of fish in his mouth. He dropped it to the platter.

"Are you insane?!" Achim's outburst startled a group of fishermen sitting nearby. They grew suddenly quiet. Turning, he glared at them and forced them back to their own business.

Eleazar leaned toward his friend and lowered his voice.

"We spent a lot of time together. We walked. We talked. We shared the same bed." He ignored the stunned expression on Achim's face. "That's right, my friend. I love her. I want her to be my wife. Don't the scriptures say a man should enjoy life with the woman he loves? Ruth is the one I love."

"Eleazar, Ruth is married to Levi, and she's going to deliver his child. You must stop this insanity. What you feel for Ruth is left over from your childhood. You're not young people anymore. You are both married. To someone else." He leaned toward him and placed a hand on Eleazar's arm. "Listen to me. The best of your life is waiting for you at home. You have a wonderful wife."

"I can't help it, Achim. On my return to Jerusalem, I'm going to see what can be done. There are laws, legal ways to annul a marriage. Or in this case, two marriages."

"Don't be a fool, Eleazar. You have no complaint against Anna. And, the laws that apply to a man divorcing his wife do not apply to a woman. In the end, Ruth will lose. It could mean her very life."

"Achim, Achim, Achim." He kept shaking his head as he dragged out the words. "Please, just be my friend."

Their eyes met in a silent battle of wills. Then Achim let out a sigh. His blue eyes clouded over, and he uttered his next words with deep sadness in his voice.

"My friend, you've been away for so long and so busy with your studies, you couldn't have known." Achim shook his head. "And then this affair with Ruth? Eleazar, things have changed in your home, as well. Anna is getting ready to deliver your own child in three months." He chuckled and shook Eleazar's arm as if trying to awaken him from sleep. "You're going to be a *father*, my friend. A *father*."

Eleazar leaned back against the wall. His head felt light, and the room began to turn in many directions.

After a long silence, he found the words. "Anna? With child?" Overcome, he lowered his head to the table. "Then, my fate is sealed. I have no other choice but to return to Judea with you."

CHAPTER TWENTY-ONE

*E*leazar paced in his courtyard. Heavy aromas rose from the garden Anna had planted. The thick scent turned his stomach. His entire body tensed with each outburst from inside the house. All day long Anna's anguish had continued, and it seemed like it would never end. During her first pangs of childbirth, Eleazar had remained close by his wife's side. Hoping to ease her pain, he had given her a cup of water to which he'd added a little opium, a drug he had brought back from Alexandria. Then he had slipped out of the house and had left his wife and child in the care of the midwife.

With the onset of night, a sliver of moon ascended and cast a shimmering beam against the garden wall. A web of shadows stretched across the pavement. Eleazar stepped over them, on them, around them, his footsteps quickening with each scream from the open window.

He laughed at himself. He had dealt with numerous childbirths in Alexandria, without the slightest trembling of hands. Nikolaus had taught him how to cut a baby free from the womb, a method used by the Romans since the time of Julius Caesar. Most of the time, the newborns entered the world through a natural process. But at such moments, when the child struggled for release, Eleazar had freed the child and had preserved the mother's health as well.

But here, in his own house, with his wife screaming in his face, he'd felt like a helpless child. And so he had retreated to the courtyard.

He'd found Judah there, seated on the pavement against a wall. The old man followed Eleazar's pacing with a smile on his lips.

"It's the way of the woman and the way of the child," Judah told him. "And, it's the way the Almighty ordained it."

At that moment, Anna let out an ear-piercing scream.

"Praise be to Yahweh for not making me a woman," Judah said, his gravely voice even more grating in recent years. Then he eyed Eleazar with mirth in his eyes. "Why do you fret so, Eleazar? Anna's not like your mother." He snorted. "Anna is strong. Your mother was frail and unsuitable for childbearing. She lost two in the early months, and, after birthing you and your brother, she suffered badly when your sister was born far too early. But, rest your mind, my son. Anna will be fine. Your child has gone its full course. And Anna has proved herself strong. You'll see. She will live to give you many more children."

Eleazar nodded. "Do you think it will be a boy, Father? I want a son, a firstborn male to follow in our path."

Judah shrugged. "The midwife believes it is a boy. She looked for the signs, the rounded shape of Anna's belly, the sickness during her first few months. Only the Almighty knows for sure."

Eleazar turned away and leaned against the doorpost. He kept one ear turned toward the open window.

The night crept on. At the first hint of daylight, he heard a cry unlike the shrieks that had poured from his wife's mouth during the night. This wail rose from Anna's throat like the cry of a wounded animal. Immediately, there followed another cry, softer and weaker than the first. Eleazar froze and kept his eyes on the open door. Moments later, the midwife appeared, her hair hanging in wet ringlets, her apron stained with blood. She shook the towel in her hand, then tossed it aside and smiled.

"It's a girl," she announced. "A beautiful, perfect baby girl."

The midwife disappeared into the house, leaving Eleazar

speechless. He had prayed for a son. He tore at his robe, raised his chin toward the heavens, and sent up a cry of his own.

Judah struggled to his feet and approached him.

"It is not a shame to give birth to a daughter," the old man said. "Think of Ariel. The poor man has seven daughters and no sons. But you'll have more children, Eleazar. Perhaps your *next* child will be a boy."

He kept shaking his head, unable to grasp such a promise.

"Go to Anna," Judah said, his voice soft. " Go inside and greet your little girl. Comfort your wife. Behave as the husband and father the Almighty created you to be."

Forcing himself to accept his loss, Eleazar stepped inside the house and walked into the quarters he shared with his wife. The birthing stool had been kicked aside, and Anna now lay on their bed with one arm holding their child. A pink face peeked out above the swaddling. Eleazar gazed at mother and child. A part of him was in awe that he had produced this tiny babe. Another part of him despised the girl. Anna's eyes glistened with happy tears. She beckoned him closer.

"She's thin, like you, Eleazar. She has long arms and legs. And, she has your silver gray eyes and your full head of curls."

Eleazar knelt beside the bed, his eyes on the little one. His heart softened slightly as he leaned closer to his newborn babe. With two fingers he stroked the child's brow and caressed her cheek. "She appears to be healthy."

Anna nodded. "Yes, the midwife took great care applying the oil on her little arms and legs. And she swaddled her gently but snug enough to keep out the cold."

Anna turned sad eyes on him. "I'm sorry I didn't give you a son, Eleazar. Perhaps next time?" She smiled sweetly.

Next time? With Anna? "Yes," he agreed. "Perhaps next time."

Anna shifted a little to get more comfortable. Then she drew the baby closer to her chest. "I'd like to name her Mara, after your mother." She raised hopeful eyebrows. "If that is your wish."

Eleazar nodded. "Yes, Mara is a fitting name."

He rose to his feet, and walked out of the house.

His mind drifted to the Upper City to the home of Levi bar Uzza, where Ruth had concealed her own disfigurement. Soon she also would travail in agony. A child would come forth, and Ruth would present Levi with *his* firstborn. Eleazar shuddered at the thought.

Word spread throughout Judea. One of the Seventy had died, and the Council members were about to fill the empty seat. Three names had come before them: Eleazar, Thomas, and Levi. Eleazar heard the news along with everyone else.

He couldn't simply sit back and let his future fall in the hands of old men. He began to conceive a plan.

It was a crisp fall day when he approached the gate in front of Thomas' house. He hesitated outside the door, almost turned and left. Then, setting his jaw, he tapped the wooden post, signaling his arrival.

He needed to know if Thomas wanted the position as desperately as *he* did. What could Council membership mean to this humble silversmith? Though Thomas' work prospered, he possessed no decision-making ability. He was a man who worked with his hands, not his mind. Eleazar, on the other hand, used his mind daily in his work. He had to determine the source of a person's illness, had to choose the right medicine, had to return to the home many times after to make sure the cure had done its job.

Eleazar's time spent in Alexandria had set him apart from the other young men in the city. Thomas was a weak-willed husband who submitted to his wife's demands. She spent his money in the marketplace satisfying her own desires, while Thomas followed her there like a cow being pulled by the ring in his nose.

Meanwhile, Eleazar kept Anna at home, in the kitchen, tending to meals and caring for their baby. Now that he'd returned from Alexandria, he kept control of the moneybag. Even

Judah had lost his authority and had settled into the life of a doting grandfather.

Now Eleazar had taken control of yet another yearning in his life, his desire for a seat in the Great Council.

He tapped again on the doorpost. A lovely face appeared in the opening. Deborah, Thomas' wife. Though she had birthed five children, she appeared young and radiant. Her honey-colored tresses were drawn into a knot at the back of her head, though a few curls trailed freely at the sides of her face. Though she wore a loose-fitting smock, there was no doubt that a full-breasted woman was hidden beneath the fabric.

He smiled. She blushed and lowered her eyes. Then she stepped away from the door and allowed Eleazar to pass through.

He found Thomas sitting cross-legged at the hearth. A fire blazed, filling the room with warmth. Scattered on the floor around Thomas were several pieces of crafted silver, works of art fashioned by his own hands. Eleazar surveyed the array of decorative bowls, cups, and urns. Such craftsmanship would bring a fine price in the Upper City.

Thomas acknowledged Eleazar's presence with a nod but continued pouring molten silver into a clay mold. With able hands, he drizzled the gleaming liquid around the inner edge, spreading it thin and adorning it with a row of beading around the lip. His face was flushed from the heat of the fire, but his hands remained steady, and his eyes were fixed on the work in his hands. Drops of sweat had formed on his brow and the back of his neck had turned red. He turned his face toward Eleazar, and with a quick wave of his hand, beckoned him to sit.

"I'll be finished in a moment." Thomas returned his attention to the mold. "This one is for a special customer—for Enos' father."

Eleazar settled on a cushion a safe distance from the fire.

Without stopping his work, Thomas called out to his wife. "Deborah! A cool drink for my friend."

Like a gentle breeze, Thomas' wife slipped into the room, dipped a cup in a stone water pot in the corner and offered the cup to Eleazar. As he received it, her fingers brushed the side of his hand, then she quickly turned away. He fought the impulse to watch her depart, but kept his eyes on Thomas.

So the silversmith was creating a gift for Enos' father, the man who had recommended him to the Council. Surely, the gesture would guarantee him at least one vote.

Wiping the residue from the bottom of the mold, Thomas struggled to his feet, walked toward the window, and set his creation on the ledge to cool.

He turned to Eleazar. "Let's go outside where the air is fresh."

Thomas had grown thicker around the middle since Eleazar had last seen him. He'd always been heavy, but now his stomach was so big he looked like he was about to give birth. His breath came in labored puffs, and his feet scraped against the pavement as if he had trouble walking even a short distance.

Eleazar followed his friend outside and sat beside him on a stone bench. He sipped his water but kept his eyes on Thomas. A child's squeal drew his attention to the other end of the courtyard. Thomas' children were chasing each other in happy circles.

Deborah came through the doorway carrying a silver tray with two silver cups of wine and a mound of purple grapes. She had let her hair down. It fell in long waves past her shoulders. Eleazar reached for a cup on the tray, then stared into her deep blue eyes. She returned his gaze. No wonder Thomas was jealous. This woman was like the one in Proverbs, *a honeycomb with a mouth smoother than oil*. She could invite a man closer simply with a wink of her eye.

Eleazar knew better than to follow after such a woman. There was only one for him. But Deborah could be the one flaw in Thomas' life that would deny her husband the Council seat.

With swaying hips, Deborah went back into the house. Thomas watched after her until she was out of sight. Eleazar pitied the poor man. To be bound to a woman in such a way would only lead to his destruction.

"My wife holds my future in her hands," Thomas admitted,

as though he'd read Eleazar's mind. "The men of the Sanhedrin select members who are strong leaders in their homes. If Deborah ever strayed, if she gave them any reason to doubt her faithfulness to our marriage, I would never be able to please those men."

Eleazar nodded. "That's true, Thomas, but you don't have to worry. Do you?"

"No. No. To my knowledge, Deborah has always been faithful. But I see the way men look at her, and it troubles me. Look at me, Eleazar. I'm not handsome like you. I don't have Enos' wisdom. Or Achim's wonderful way with people. I'm a simple silversmith with a wife who looks like an angel."

"Yes, but consider your accomplishments, Thomas. You create magnificent works of art. You are a success in the city, a man who has earned the respect of the Council, simply through his own success."

Thomas nodded, but a sadness had settled in his eyes.

Not to be dissuaded from his plan, Eleazar pressed on. "Look at your beautiful family. Aren't they proof enough of Deborah's loyalty?" He gestured toward the children and noticed with interest that not one of them bore any resemblance to their father. Nor did they resemble each other.

"You've done well, Thomas."

Thomas sipped his wine, then coddled the cup in his hands. "So what brings you to my humble home?"

Eleazar ate a few grapes. "I'd like to purchase one of your silver platters for my wife. Your work is finer than anything I have ever seen, not even during my stay in Alexandria. Your craftsmanship far exceeds the work of all other artisans in Jerusalem and beyond."

Thomas bowed his head in humility. "You're too kind, my friend." He took another sip of wine. "And how is Anna? And your little baby?"

"They are well."

"And your work? I've heard about your success."

Thomas' kind words troubled him. As much as he coveted that Council seat, he began to change his mind. He had come there to find out what kind of marriage this man and his wife had. There was no doubt, the woman had a wandering eye, and Thomas was aflame with jealousy. But what kind of pain did Eleazar want to inflict to assure his own success? He struggled with the thought for only a moment.

"Tell me, was your time at the home of my brother gracious?" Thomas asked.

"Yes, Minoa and his wife provided fine lodging. They also arranged a mentor for me, a knowledgeable Greek physician named Nikolaus."

Thomas smiled with admiration. "You did well, Eleazar. Your knowledge of medicine is badly needed here in Judea. I doubt any other physician can match your abilities now that you've studied with the finest." Thomas looked him in the eye. "Eleazar, you and I have one thing in common."

"And what is that, my friend?"

"You know very well what I'm talking about. We both desire a seat in the Sanhedrin. It seems we have become rivals." Thomas frowned. Already a wedge had come between them.

"Yes, such a problem does put a wall between friends, doesn't it?"

"While I don't want to defeat *you*, Eleazar, I *do* want the position. The truth is, I *need* it, if only to show my wife I have some value, that she did right to marry me."

"You must know we will never be true adversaries." Even as Eleazar said the words, a sword pierced his heart. He couldn't deny the truth. Not only were they adversaries, but he would do whatever he could to win. Deborah had unknowingly provided him with the best weapon of all. Now he only needed to approach the one person who could help him carry out his plan.

"Well, my friend, show me a selection of platters, so I can buy one for my wife." Eleazar set aside his cup and rose from the bench.

Thomas led the way into the house, and Eleazar looked over

a collection of silver pieces. He chose a large platter with scroll-work circling the outer edge.

"Anna will love this."

He paid Thomas his asking price, with no bartering, and was about to leave when his friend stopped him.

"Wait, Eleazar." Thomas went over to the hearth and lifted a silver cup from the pile. "I made this especially for you." The flame on the hearth flashed against the side of the cup in Thomas' hand.

Eleazar received the cup and eyed it closely. It was magnificent. He turned it over in his hand and a lump came to his throat. Inscribed on the base was Thomas' name and the words, *"For Eleazar, Friends Forever."*

CHAPTER TWENTY-TWO

*E*leazar wasted no time. The Council met daily in the Chamber of Hewn Stones inside the Temple complex. They could announce an opening at any moment.

With great haste he searched through the shelves of his apothecary, shoved aside the sacks of powder, the vials of oil, and the pouches of herbs he'd brought from Alexandria. At the back of the shelf rested an unopened bottle of the medicine Achim's mother favored. Tucking it inside the fold of his robe, he slipped out of the house and hurried along the path to Zilpah's house. His heartbeat throbbed in time with his pounding footsteps. A spark of guilt nagged at the back of his mind. He quickly dismissed it. He reached her door, stopped to catch his breath, and rapped on the post.

There was the shuffle of feet. Then the door cracked open, and a pair of eyes like ripe olives stared out at him.

"Who's there?" Zilpah must have been home alone.

The woman was widowed two years before when Achim's father fell from his horse and smashed his skull on a rock. Now she depended solely on her son to provide for her. As he did often, Achim had gone away, traveling as a merchant and enjoying his single life. Zilpah rarely opened the door when she was alone. But when she saw the vial in Eleazar's hand, she broke into a grin.

"For your stomach ailment." Eleazar held the vial out to her.

She grabbed the bottle and backed away from the door. Her tangled hair and puffy eyes were a sure sign she'd been sleeping. She wore a loose-fitting garment that bulged in places where she had grown fat. Scurrying across the room, she withdrew several coins from a jar on a shelf in the corner.

Eleazar waved away her payment. "It's a gift, an extra bottle from my apothecary. Consider it a reward for a service Achim did for me long ago."

Zilpah pressed the vial to her breast. "This is life to me." Tears rushed to her eyes. "With Achim gone and his father long dead, I have no one to prepare my herbal drinks. Many nights I lay writhing on my bed. This will help me sleep, Eleazar. Thank you."

Holding up one hand in an attempt to delay her from drinking, Eleazar smiled with feigned kindness. "I heard Achim went to the coast. Would you like a little company?"

The old woman's grin widened. Company?! Why *wouldn't* she want company? Zilpah was known throughout the city as someone who enjoyed talking about her neighbors, and Eleazar had provided a willing ear. With a sweep of her hand she invited him to sit on her couch beside her.

"A cup of water?" She rushed off and dipped a silver cup into the pot by the hearth. Her hand shook as she released the cup into his hand spilling some of the liquid on his robe.

Except for a narrow stream of light pouring through the window, the room lay in shadows. Zilpah tossed aside her rumpled blankets and sat beside him.

"It's good to see you, Eleazar." She gripped the little bottle tightly, as if she feared he might take it away. "Tell me, what is happening in the city?"

This woman hungered for two things, his father's herbs to dull her senses and a tasty rumor to awaken them. He silently vowed to give her both.

Zilpah opened the vial. He hoped she wouldn't drink until he had accomplished what he'd come to do.

"Your wife is well?"

"Yes, we have a daughter, but I guess Achim must have told you that."

Zilpah nodded and stared off at nothing in particular, still gripping the bottle of medicine.

"How I wish my Achim had married like you and Thomas did. I want grandchildren. Achim is my only child, the only one who can provide me with little ones to hold on my knee. But—" She sighed. "It seems he's chosen a life of simple pleasures, with no wife and no children to restrain him."

A tear spilled down her cheek. Eleazar bit his lower lip. Perhaps he should leave.

Zilpah sniffed the opening of the bottle, but still she didn't drink. "Achim is a man of the world," she said with a touch of resentment. "He stays home for only one day, and he's gone for several. He wanders off to lands unknown to me, like his father and his father before him. And what of me? I remain here, alone, with no husband to keep me warm, no grandchildren to play at my feet, no life as other women know it."

"You have friends," Eleazar offered.

"Yes." She pursed her lips with annoyance. "Neighborhood busybodies, always waiting for the next morsel of news I can give them."

Rising, she continued to clutch the vial but went to the hearth and returned with a silver plate and slices of raisin bread.

"Eat." She thrust the plate in front of him. "My raisin bread is the best in the city. My friend Rachel has tried to outdo me, but she fails every time." Zilpah laughed. "Rachel's raisins are bitter. Mine are delicately sweet." She winked at him, then she lowered her voice to a whisper and stared into his eyes. "I use a secret blend of herbs and oils."

Eleazar bit into a piece of Zilpah's prized bread and nodded his approval.

"Isn't Rachel married to Hoshea, the priest?" he said, feigning interest.

Zilpah brightened. "She is. But have you seen how she dress-es? Her clothing is far too ornate for her husband's position. A priest's wife must display modesty. Rachel flaunts her fine cloth-ing and jewels with little concern for Hoshea's image. What's more, she can't make a decent raisin bread." She took a sip from the vial.

Eleazar chuckled under his breath. The woman was perfect—a willing ear and a mouth to spread whatever she heard, possibly with a little more seasoning. He only needed to wait for the right opportunity.

Zilpah needed little provocation. She moved from one rumor to another, feeding him stories about people they both knew, as well as people known only to her. Neighbors, servants of neighbors, merchants, government officials, priests, "the cruel Romans, spineless Jews, wicked Samaritans, ignorant Gentiles, and heartless Pharisees." She had a label for each of them.

Eleazar drank a little wine. With each tale, he bobbed his head, urging her on. After a while, he reached for the last piece of raisin bread, then he stared at the silver plate.

"Isn't this one of Thomas' creations?"

"Oh yes. Isn't it beautiful? Achim purchased it for me a few months ago. Thomas' work has been in great demand throughout Judea. I'm fortunate to have one of his finer works of art."

Eleazar acknowledged with a nod. "I went to Thomas' house only yesterday to buy one of these for my wife. He truly is a busy man, hardly has time for his friends. Between selling his wares and keeping an eye on his wife—"

As he had hoped, the mention of Thomas' wife brought Zilpah upright. Her eyebrows flew up, and she grinned like she was about to reveal another secret.

"That woman flirts with every man she meets." It was as if her tongue had suddenly caught fire. "I've seen her myself, in the marketplace, behind porticos in the temple, even in the streets. The mother of five children and she struts about like a common whore. Everyone suspects, of course, but *I* have seen with my own eyes. I caught her with a local innkeeper one afternoon. The two of them disappeared inside the inn for far too long. And what about that young lawyer who helped Thomas with his financial affairs? Deborah was the one who hired him. He went to their home when Thomas was away selling his wares in the market-place. I suspect the man's visits went beyond money matters."

Eleazar allowed her to ramble on, her voice rising with every remembrance that spewed from her mouth. "I don't know how she gets away with her lewd behavior." Zilpah shook her head with disgust. "No one has brought her before the Council. How can they? She hides her mischief well. Besides, people love Thomas far too much to bring such a curse on his home. And the poor man ignores the truth."

She took a deep breath, long enough for Eleazar to feed the fire. "Word is that Thomas rescued Deborah from a disgraceful life. But how could he expect her to change? And to be honest, maybe she hasn't." He took a sip of wine and eyed Zilpah over the rim of his cup. "Have you seen their children?" He was almost whispering now. "Not one of them resembles Thomas."

"They're bastards, every one."

Eleazar nodded and finished his drink, then, content that he had planted enough seeds, he stood up, released the tray and cup into Zilpah's hands, and bid her goodbye. She sat open-mouthed on her couch, like she wasn't finished talking yet. Without anoth-er word, he slipped out the door, knowing she'd make fast work of the vial of medicine and be asleep in seconds.

Once outside, he picked up his stride and headed down the hill for home. But when he reached a bend in the road he stopped walking. A recitation from his youth had returned with amazing force, and the psalmist's warning struck his heart cold. *Lord, who may dwell in your sanctuary? Who may live on your holy hill? He whose walk is blameless, and who does what is righteous, who speaks the truth from his heart and has no slander on his tongue, who does his neighbor no harm and casts no slur on his fellow man.*

He had no idea why that passage of scripture had suddenly

come to mind. Now he wondered, what had he done? Thomas was one of his closest friends. They had known each other since their youth. They had studied together at the Temple. Had played in the hills as little boys. Had been present at each other's wedding. Did he really want the Council seat that much?

And what of Deborah? What if she'd done nothing wrong?

Then there were the children. Did they resemble Thomas or didn't they? Mathias had Thomas' wide, brown eyes. Amos was short and heavy, like his father. And what of little Katra? Her mop of unruly hair was much like her father's. So also with the twins. Had Eleazar merely seen what he wanted to see that afternoon? Had he purposely blocked out the truth?

Doubts battled within his heart. He considered going back to Zilpah's house and correcting the wrong he had done. But, it was too late. Zilpah would not listen to him now. She preferred dirt over soap. The merciless wheel had already begun to turn, and there was no way to stop it.

By the time the rumor reached Eleazar's ears, it had multiplied. Though unproven, the story held enough weight to keep the Council from considering Thomas. Now their decision had settled on either Eleazar or Levi. With his adversary's self-serving reputation well-known, Eleazar felt confident the treasured seat would soon be his.

CHAPTER TWENTY-THREE

*N*ews poured from the city gate. The wife of Levi had given him a son. Eleazar was on his way to the marketplace when he heard. Unable to contain his envy, he staggered past a table of wares and backed into a dark corner of the courtyard. The merchant there busied himself with his goods, but he kept a suspicious eye on Eleazar.

His face grew hot. He clenched his fists. Ruth had borne a son. *A son.* She should have been *his* wife. The boy should have been *his* son. Angry tears flooded into his eyes.

He burst out in the open, wove through the crowd, and made his way to Achim's stall. He drew close to his friend.

Achim looked back at him with sympathy in his eyes. "So you've heard."

"Levi is shouting the news from the rooftops." Eleazar tried to keep his voice low, but it was impossible to contain his rage. "The beautiful woman I love belongs to that brute of a man who, as we speak, is fighting against me for one of the highest honors in the city. Now they have a son, while I live with a homely housekeeper who gave me, what? A daughter!"

Achim placed a hand on Eleazar's shoulder. He shook his head. "My friend, you have much to be thankful for. Why don't you see your good fortune? In your mind Levi has everything you wanted. But that is not the truth. The people of Jerusalem have declared you one of the most skilled physicians in all Judea. Ruth is lovely, yes. But the woman you married has inner value. Anna is loyal. She causes you no trouble. She works hard to make a good home for you. Tell me, how many women would have sent their husbands to Alexandria for three months so he could fulfill his dream? You cry because she gave you a daughter instead of a son. Your little Mara is a lovely baby, certain to grow into a fine young woman. Eleazar, *you* are the one to be envied. Not Levi."

Achim's words of assurance hung in the air. Eleazar shook his head.

Achim stepped away from him and put his hands together, as though in prayer. He waved them up and down in front of Eleazar's face.

"Tell me, what can I do to help you, my friend? How can I make you see how fortunate you are? I have traveled for most of my life. I have no wife to comfort me, no children to bring me joy. And my mother is about to drive me crazy with her endless chatter. So what can I do to help you find happiness, and if not happiness, at least contentment?"

"You can arrange a meeting for me with Ruth." Eleazar spoke quickly, without thinking. He ignored the sneer on Achim's lips. "Wait until after she passes her purification period. According to the law, she must remain confined for a month following her son's circumcision. One day she'll come to the marketplace. She likes to shop at your stall. She'll come to purchase something, perhaps a piece of jewelry to brighten her day after being confined for so long. Talk to her. Tell her I want to see her."

Achim was shaking his head.

"Do this for me," Eleazar persisted. "And I will never ask you for anything again."

Achim blew out a labored breath. "My friend, do you know what you're asking? Step away from your heart for a moment and see the danger that awaits you. Listen to me. Don't attempt to relive what you had with Ruth in Alexandria. She belongs to another man. Honor their marriage, or you'll bring trouble on both of you."

"I can't help myself, Achim. Ruth has a hold on me, like a disease that has no cure. I only know I come to life when she's near me, and when she's away from me, a part of me dies."

Again Achim shook his head. "If you're discontented at home, I can arrange for an evening with one of the local harlots, someone who can help you forget Ruth and get on with your life. These women won't cleave to you. They cost little. And they are discreet."

Eleazar's eyes widened in unbelief. "Don't you understand? I am not looking for a woman of the streets. My feelings for Ruth go beyond physical pleasure. I *love* her, Achim. My heart belongs to her, as does my body, my mind, and my whole being."

He was certain he saw tears in Achim's eyes.

"Listen, Achim. When Ruth's month of purification is over, you'll be one of the first to see her. Ask her to meet with me. Arrange a time and a place. If you really *are* my friend, you will do this.

The lines on Achim's forehead gathered in a troubled web. He gazed back at Eleazar, and shook his head. "I want you to know, Eleazar, if I do this for you, it will be against my will." He released a long sigh. "May God forgive me."

He patted Achim's shoulder. "It will be all right, my friend. You'll see. It's a meeting, that's all. Mere words will pass between us. Nothing more."

A month passed. On most evenings, after his work was done, Eleazar paced the upper floor, his mind counting the days when Ruth would come out of her purification period. He held onto Achim's promise, confident his friend would not let him down.

It was during a busy morning, when several people had lined up at his door asking for medicines, that a young Hebrew came through the gate into the courtyard.

"Yes? What is it?" He didn't attempt to hide his displeasure. This poorly dressed boy had interrupted his work. But why? To beg free medicine for an ailing relative in the Lower City?

"Achim, the merchant, calls for you." The boy's voice was so low Eleazar strained to hear it.

"What did you say?"

The young Hebrew lowered his gaze. "Achim has called for you."

Eleazar set down the vial in his hand, nearly spilling its contents. He passed the line of people in the courtyard and approached the boy. "Achim called for me?" He needed to be certain. "Did he give a message?"

The boy nervously shook his head. "He—he said to come. That is all." He turned to leave.

Ignoring the crowd, Eleazar started for the gate.

Judah had been standing by the entrance. He took a step and blocked Eleazar's path. "You have sick calls," he said, his voice gruff.

Eleazar flew past his father. The old man's angry shout faded along with the confused murmurs rising from the people in the courtyard.

He ran up the hill toward the marketplace, wove through the throng, and hurried to Achim's stall.

Upon noticing him, Achim set aside the handful of gemstones and drew close to him. "Remember, I warned you."

"What do you mean? What has happened?"

Achim's breathing grew heavy. "Ruth came to the square this morning." Achim kept his voice low. His eyes darted nervously at his customers. "I caught sight of her, over there." He nodded toward a vegetable stand.

Eleazar could hardly contain himself. "Did you speak to her?"

"I did." Achim tightened his lips.

"What did she say? Did she ask about me? Did you mention my request?"

"Eleazar, calm yourself. She asked about you before I could even speak your name."

A surge of hope filled his heart. "Tell me what she said."

"She asked if you are well and if your work prospers. She also asked about your family, and she showed a sincere concern for Anna and your daughter."

"Of course. She always liked Anna. My wife served in her household for many years. But, what did she say about *me*?"

"Eleazar, you're behaving like a child." Achim breathed a sigh. "Look. I did what I promised. I called for you the moment she came to the marketplace. That should be enough."

"Stop it, Achim. I don't need you to judge me. Just tell me. Does she miss me as I miss her?"

He raised a shoulder. "I can't say for certain."

"What did she say about a meeting? Did you ask her?"

"I asked her." Achim looked away as though unable to deal with the helpless plea in Eleazar's eyes. Then he looked back and, his countenance softening with compassion, he shook his head. "She refused."

"She refused?! Why, Achim? Why did she refuse a simple meeting? Surely there would be no harm in that."

"She said she will not endanger your life. What's more, she's concerned for her child now. She doesn't want to risk losing him."

Eleazar felt the world drop from under his feet. He gripped the edge of Achim's stall. "You should have pleaded with her, Achim. You know what she means to me."

Achim kept shaking his head, his blue eyes swimming in sadness.

Biting his lip, Eleazar turned away and staggered into the crowd, but not before he heard Achim's anxious warning.

"Forget her, Eleazar. Get on with your life."

Forget Ruth? Impossible. Once again, he plunged into his work, though now and then he allowed a vision of her face to come before him. On nights when he yearned for Ruth to come to his bed, it was Anna he turned to.

In time, Anna was expecting another child. Eleazar prayed daily for a son. He wished he had a mix of herbs that might assure it, but there was nothing in his apothecary that could promise a male child.

Judah grew older and more feeble. His ability to stand for long periods lessened with each passing month. Eventually, the old man retreated to a stack of pillows by the hearth. To Eleazar's relief, his father no longer went to the Lower City, and his visits to the leper caves had ceased long ago.

One day, as dusk began to fall, Enos barged into Eleazar's home. His face was drawn. Dark circles framed his eyes. Tears spilled onto his beard.

The family was together in the main room of the house. Little Mara slept in her crib by the hearth.

"Eleazar!" Enos called out. "Eleazar!" Then he bent low and gasped for air.

Rushing to his side, Eleazar guided his friend to a pile of cushions and lowered him there.

"Enos, what is it? What's happened?"

Anna was seated at her loom, weaving a fresh cover for their bed. She stopped working and stared at Eleazar's friend, her face lined with concern. Judah sat upright on his cushions, his eyes fastened on their visitor.

Enos wiped the moisture from his cheeks. At last, he spoke. "It's Thomas," he sobbed. "Our good friend is dead, Eleazar. He took his own life, this very morning."

"Thomas? Why would he *do* such a thing?"

Enos pulled out a handkerchief, mopped his brow and blew his nose. "That poor man. A rumor had circulated throughout the city. Someone said his wife had been unfaithful. Not only once, but many times."

"What? That's absurd!" Eleazar's heartbeat quickened. He burned with guilt. He had not meant for Thomas to die—only to be rejected by the Council.

Enos wiped more tears from his face and then went on.

"Thomas believed the lie. He grieved for days, refused to let anyone into his home. Finally, in a fit of despair, he poured a cup of molten silver down his throat. Down his throat, Eleazar. It was a horrible way to die. He must have suffered terribly."

Eleazar stood to his feet. "Why wasn't I summoned? I'm a physician. I might have been able to help."

Enos shook his head. "There was nothing you could do. By the time Deborah found him, he was already dead."

Eleazar fell to his knees, his head spinning. He beat his chest. It was his fault. He had brought this horrible pain on his friend.

"Why would anyone spread such a vicious rumor?" Enos choked out his grief. "They said his wife had several lovers over the years, that none of the children were his. Deborah insisted there was no truth in it. After she found him, lying by the hearth, she went out of her mind, almost took her own life. If not for the children, she would have died with her husband." Enos gazed into Eleazar's eyes. "She really did love Thomas."

Overcome with guilt, Eleazar bent low and wrapped his arms around his knees, pulled them close to his chest, and he lowered his head to the floor. He didn't try to restrain his sobs. Enos stroked his back. They cried together, rocking back and forth, one in utter despair, the other suffering with remorse.

When their weeping subsided, Eleazar staggered to his feet and tore his outer robe in two pieces. His anguished cry filled the room. While he was grieving over the loss of a friend, even more than that he was regretting what he had done.

Anna was weeping softly at her loom. She raised her face. "I heard the rumor last week." Her voice broke. "I was in the marketplace when word came to me, but I dismissed it immediately. Deborah is a friend. She spoke often of her husband and praised him for changing her life."

Judah stumbled to Anna's side and placed a hand on her shoulder. Then the old man turned toward Eleazar, his steel gray eyes piercing into Eleazar's very soul. He shrank under his father's steady gaze. When Judah spoke, his voice was harsh.

"Cursed be the wagging tongue that destroyed that man and his family. And cursed be the fools who listened to such filth and then built upon it."

Enos choked his agreement. "The final blow came with the response of the Council. Though they considered the report to be mere gossip, it was enough to eliminate Thomas from their choices. In one day, Thomas lost everything. It's no wonder he ended his life."

Enos mopped his face again and faced Eleazar. "Now it's between you and Levi, my friend. My father told me the Council is considering you equally."

Judah straightened. "Has anyone traced the rumor to its source?"

Enos extended his arms, palms up. "No one knows for certain. One of the women blamed Achim's mother. We all know what a cruel tongue she has. Others are saying Zilpah merely passed on what she heard from someone else. In any case, she denied having any part in it. I, myself, tried to put Thomas at ease. But, as you know, he was always troubled about his wife, afraid she might go back to her old life. How can anyone reason with a man like that? The thought of her lying with someone else tormented him."

Judah pounded his fist in his other hand. "Idle talk destroys more than the person talked about. It also destroys the speaker and the listener, no matter if it be a woman—or a man." He shifted his gaze to Eleazar.

The room grew quiet. Eleazar tried to ignore his father's accusing stare.

He turned to Enos. "Please, tell Deborah, I want to help her family however I can. Let me know what I can do. Anything, Enos. Anything at all."

Enos nodded. "I'm going to Achim's house now. He is quite distraught over this news, especially since his mother was named."

The two men embraced and Enos disappeared into the night, leaving Eleazar to mop the sweat from his brow.

Judah approached him. He drew close enough to keep his words between the two of them. "My son, is there anything you need to tell me?"

Eleazar faced his father. Their eyes met in a stony gaze.

"Why do you ask?"

A vial of my special medicine disappeared from the shelf more than a week ago. I assumed you took it to Achim's mother. She's the only one who asks for it."

Eleazar shrugged. "It's possible. I–I don't recall."

"With Thomas' dying in this manner, the Council will not let this evil rest. If they question the old woman further, she will have to admit who passed the story to her. It would not look good for a man of stature to be accused of women's idle talk."

Eleazar let out a nervous laugh. "Why would you think it was a man?"

"I don't know, Eleazar. Is there something you need to tell me?"

His stomach tightening, Eleazar stepped around the old man and went to a table where there was a cruse of wine. He poured some of the red liquid into a silver goblet and gulped it down. He started to pour another when an engraving along the base caught his eye. It bore Thomas' signature and the words, *For Eleazar. Friends Forever.*

The cup slipped from Eleazar's hand and crashed to the floor. He turned and looked at his father. The old man was still watching him, his eyes narrowed, but he said nothing.

CHAPTER TWENTY-FOUR

A solemn funeral was held for Thomas. Afterward, Deborah and the children vanished from their neighborhood.

Achim's mother charged Eleazar for passing the gossip to her, but because of her reputation as a tale-bearer and Eleazar's standing as a valued physician, few people believed her. The accusation died along with several other ugly rumors that had poured from her lips. Still, the Council removed Eleazar's name from their choices and awarded the open seat to Levi bar Uzza.

Eleazar continued his work in the Upper City, gaining more praises for his knowledge of Greek medicines. He prospered in wealth and fame. The public praises helped to ease the guilt he had borne over Thomas' death. In the end, he reasoned with himself and concluded he hadn't forced the man to kill himself. It was Thomas' decision.

Soon, another baby's cry rose from Anna's bedroom window. To Eleazar's delight, his wife had delivered a boy.

"Son of My Right Hand," he shouted, and he began to plan the child's future.

On the day of the boy's circumcision, Eleazar stood proudly in the temple and presented his eight-day-old son to the priest. As required, he made an offering of five shekels. Anna stood nearby holding their daughter. Judah also had managed the long, difficult walk to the Temple. Now he drew close to the priest, his watery gray eyes on the baby. With trembling fingers, the old man reached out and pulled back a corner of the swaddling cloth. In a gravely voice that echoed off the temple walls, Judah proclaimed a blessing on his grandson.

"I prayed for this child, and the Almighty answered. He will be strong. Healthy. A physician of the highest sort, just as his father, his grandfather, and his ancestors before them."

Chanting a prayer, the temple priest stepped between them, a knife in one hand. The flame from a nearby oil lamp flashed off the blade. Eleazar lifted the boy and waited for the sweep of the priest's hand that would deliver his son into the covenant of Israel.

The priest cried out, "Lord, raise up this offspring in the sight of his father and mother. And may his name be called—" He glanced at Eleazar.

Then, as the priest brought down the blade, Eleazar shouted, "Benjamin! His name is Benjamin."

When Anna's purification had passed, she accompanied Eleazar to the temple once again. This time they brought with them the required sacrifice—a young, unblemished lamb, which Eleazar bore across his shoulders. Anna carried Benjamin and a cage containing a live pigeon. Three-year-old Mara followed with one hand clinging to her mother's robe. While Anna and the children watched from behind the lattice in the women's court, Eleazar joined the priest at the slaughtering table.

The priest uttered a prayer and, with one quick movement, he slashed the animal's throat. Blood spewed out. With great speed, the priest skinned the animal and severed its limbs. He saved a generous portion for the priesthood, then he placed the remaining meat in the fire, last of all tossing the lamb's head and entrails into the blaze. The aroma of seared meat filled the temple court.

With the sacrifice completed, Eleazar went to the women's court and took the cage from Anna. Removing the pigeon, he pressed its wings against its body so it wouldn't escape and took it to the priest. As he walked away from the women's court, he heard Mara ask, "Mother, why do the animals have to die?"

"It's for a sacrifice," Anna explained, her voice soft. "To purge your mother of impurities. You'll understand when you are older, my child. There has to be a blood sacrifice. There's no other way to appease our righteous God."

His daughter's question and Anna's answer stirred a growing doubt in Eleazar's heart. While in Alexandria he had strayed from the teachings of his ancestors. Since arriving back in Judea, he'd been trying to remember the commands he had learned as a youth, all the while fighting the urge to discard them completely. He was a physician. He was trained to save lives. To take part in the merciless killing of animals no longer made sense to him. What's more, the killings never fully satisfied the guilt that festered inside him.

He approached the priest and handed him the pigeon. The bird pulled one wing free of the priest's grip. It flapped in vain for its release, then let out a screech as the priest tucked the wing back inside his hand and tightened his hold. With trained fingers, he pinched off the pigeon's head, killing it instantly. With the bird's headless body lurching about and blood flying everywhere, the priest mounted the temple stairs and hurled the bloody flow at the four corners of the altar. Then, he dropped the pigeon into the fire, sending off a spray of sparks as the flames consumed it. The stench of smoldering feathers hit the air, followed by the more savory aroma of burnt flesh. Finally, the bones sizzled, cracked apart and scattered to the bottom of the bowl.

Uttering more ceremonial words, the priest bowed repeatedly. Afterward, he turned away from the altar and went to the women's court with Eleazar close behind.

"You have been cleansed," the priest announced to Anna. "You may go now and resume your duties as this man's wife."

They walked home in silence. Soft sobs rose from their confused little girl. Eleazar refused to still her questions. Nor did he look at his wife, not even once. Anna followed close behind him, her sandaled feet softly scraping the pavement. When they arrived in the courtyard, she reached out to touch his arm. He turned to look at her for the first time since leaving the temple.

"We can have more sons." She looked at him with hope in her eyes. "Once a woman has one son, she often produces another."

Pulling away, Eleazar turned from the open gate. "I'm going to the Upper City," he called over his shoulder. "It's time we moved to another house."

Achim had told Eleazar about a sprawling estate farther up the hill. The owner had abandoned it to move to a more prominent home near the Roman settlement. To Anna, the move would likely promise more children. But Eleazar saw it as a way to get closer to the rich people he served in the Upper City. Perhaps the Council might consider him once again. But there was another reason for the sudden pounding of his heart. The place he had in mind was two courtyards below the home of Levi.

The family of Eleazar ben Judah settled in a large stone mansion high on the hillside, a few streets away from the royal palace. The vast courtyard had separate housing for the servants he planned to hire, and a large storage room for tools and garden implements.

In the center was a large basin and fountain for bathing. The courtyard floor was paved with giant marble squares that had red and green veins running through them. Flowering vines trailed up thick stone walls around the inside, and a heavy iron gate sealed off the only entrance. There also was a large well for drawing water, several marble benches, and gardens bearing every kind of fruit and vegetable.

A separate grazing area and adjoining stable provided space for four horses, two donkeys, and three milking goats. Eleazar planned to acquire those animals, along with chickens and a rooster.

The main building had six halls leading to separate bedchambers. Each room had a latticed window that faced east in the direction of the temple. Judah's room was situated close to the kitchen. It had a wooden door, providing the old man a place where he could pray at his leisure.

With Achim's provisions from afar, Eleazar furnished his home with raised beds, tables, chairs, and other items new to Jerusalem. Except for her clothes and jewelry, Anna left behind everything she owned in the former house, as Eleazar had insisted, knowing the neighbors would make quick work of them. He replaced everything with new treasures from across the sea.

In addition to a large oven at the far end of the courtyard, Anna's inside cooking area contained a separate oven with a stone hearth for keeping foods warm. An assortment of pans and pottery filled an entire wall of shelves. In the corner stood two stone water pots, a wine vat, and several barrels for storing beans and flour. Eleazar surprised Anna by installing limestone commodes in all of the bedrooms, with the drainage flowing underground to the garden.

Though Anna had never complained about the meager furnishings in their former house, Eleazar felt a sense of pride in being able to provide her with such comforts. The former servant girl would now live like a queen. For a moment he remembered the promise he had made to his mother. Now he was fulfilling that promise to his wife.

Eleazar's private place was on the roof. An outer stair spiraled upward to a giant rooftop apothecary. There was a seating area where Eleazar could be alone to study or to pray. A separate wall partitioned off a group of guest quarters. And when Eleazar stood by the rail, he could look out over the city of Jerusalem and feel his success. He had realized his mother's dream. He had gained fame and fortune. He had surpassed the life his father had planned for him. If he continued along the same path, another Council seat would one day be within his grasp.

On her first day in her new home, Anna stood in the doorway and held her breath. Then, quietly entering, she cast her eyes from one side of the room to the other, carefully moving about, running her hands over the furnishings, the linen draperies, the ornate bowls and pans. Eleazar folded his arms and watched her, wishing he could have done the same for Ruth.

The children's handmaid followed Anna inside. Wide-eyed, the girl cuddled baby Benjamin to her breast. Little Mara darted about the room, sitting here, jumping there, then she disappeared into one of the bedrooms.

Eleazar hired five more servants to help with the cooking and the cleaning of the house and grounds. Then he went out and hired a young boy to run errands, feed the animals, and keep the stables clean.

"Do we really need all those servants?" Anna resisted, her eyes wide.

He nodded and gave her a stern warning.

"Enjoy your home, Anna," he said with little emotion. "The servants will do as you command. Just see to it that I'm not troubled with household problems. My work will keep me busy enough."

Anna nodded, but her troubled eyes wanted something more. Eleazar could guess what she lacked. Anna had come from a loving home—far different from the cold and sterile house where he had grown up. While her parents had openly showed their love for one another, Eleazar's mother had been like a dripping faucet complaining about her lot in life, and his father had repeatedly neglected his family's needs so he could serve the poor. No wonder Eleazar didn't know how to love his wife as he should.

Something else blocked the flow of his emotions. His love for Ruth held him captive. He was unable to break free, nor did he want to.

That evening, while his wife busied herself with the evening meal, Eleazar went up to his rooftop retreat and stared out over the other houses. He breathed deeply of the fresh mountain air. Amidst the clatter of pans and dishes below, he heard his wife humming. Then came her gentle commands to the servants, followed by Mara's squeals of delight. He sighed with satisfaction. At last, he had escaped from his childhood and that miserable excuse of a home. Never again would he have to walk amidst the filth in the Lower City.

But even as he pondered his success, even as he boasted inwardly over all that he had accomplished, he remembered the words of Nikolaus. *"Hear me now. Be confident, but never trust only in yourself, for that is the moment when most men fail."*

Eleazar bit his lower lip. How could he feel good about his success and still remain humble? When would he ever be able to claim to have it all? As he continued to ponder this, the scent of calamus drifted on a breeze from the house of Levi, only two doors up the hill. At that moment, nothing else mattered—not his wealth, not his position in the city, not even the rewards that lay within his reach. It all seemed worthless without the woman he could never have.

CHAPTER TWENTY-FIVE

Three years passed. Eleazar was on the roof sorting through his supply of medicines, when he heard a footstep in the lower court. He peered over the side. A boy of about 10 years of age stood looking up at him. He was dressed in a rich toga with gold threads woven around the hem. His hair was cropped close to his head, forming a crown of tight curls in the manner of the Greeks and the Romans. He wore leather sandals, and he bore the stature of one who served in a wealthy household.

In flawless Aramaic, the boy announced his mission. "Your services are needed at Antonia."

Eleazar eyed the boy with suspicion. Why would someone in the royal palace summon a Jewish physician? His reputation was widespread. Perhaps even the foreigners had heard of his ability to heal the sick. In any case, he could not refuse.

He tossed a few medicines into his scrip, flung the bag over his shoulder, and descended the stairs. Giving the boy a nod, he followed him out of the courtyard and along the road that led to Antonia in the northwest corner of the city.

Upon reaching the royal palace, Eleazar gazed in awe at the magnificent structure, nearly 7,000 cubits long and with three towering pillars that seemed to disappear into the clouds. He followed the boy through a giant archway and approached two separate groups of buildings. Those on one side were used only by King Herod and his followers, and those on the other side contained banquet halls, housing for Roman officials, guest quarters, and a huge barracks that could hold 600 Roman soldiers. Eleazar suddenly felt very small.

The boy led him through a large, flourishing garden where several bronze fountains spewed water on the flowers and plants, and an untold number of life-size marble statues bore the images of Roman heroes. His heartbeat throbbing in his ears, Eleazar wondered what authority had called him to this place.

The boy beckoned him from the top of a marble stairway. Eleazar mounted the smooth steps. Then they moved into a large hall, where mosaic artwork stretched from floor to ceiling on both sides. Images of birds, snakes, lions, and half-naked women surrounded him. In between the works of art were closed doors, trimmed in gold around the edges. As he walked past them, Eleazar turned his ear toward each room. From inside came whispered conversations, an occasional outburst of laughter, the strains of lyres and flutes, the clatter of dishes, giggles, and drunken babble.

They reached the end of the hall. Before them was a large red door. A Roman soldier stepped aside and allowed them to enter.

Not even the time he'd spent in Alexandria had prepared Eleazar for the display of wealth on the other side of that door. He stood very still and took in the entire chamber—thick curtains hung from the walls and a woven rug stretched from one end to the other. There were gold-plated chairs and multiple pillows in all shades of the rainbow scattered about the room. Carved ivory tables were laden with platters of grapes, figs, a roast pig, a mound of breads, and bottles of dark red wine. Seven torches stood about the room and set off a subtle glow.

Four male servants, all youngsters, were clad in short togas like the boy who had summoned him. They stood like sentries as though waiting for their next command. Their eyes were on a raised bed where a huge man, his skin as white as marble, reclined amidst a pile of blankets and pillows. Layers of flesh bulged from the openings in his toga. His arms and legs resembled raw bread dough, and his stomach rose and fell with each breath. His face was layered, with one layer forming his brow, the next the folds under his eyes, and the last his cheeks and chin. There seemed to be no neck.

The big man set his eyes on Eleazar and his fat lips spread in a smile. "Eleazar ben Judah, they say you are the best physician in all Judea. They also say you are not strict in your adherence to the oral laws of your people."

Eleazar raised his eyebrows. "They?"

"My guards. They spend much time in the marketplace. They listen closely to the talk and they report anything of interest to me. Sometimes, with great detail." He raised himself up on one elbow. "I know you studied in Alexandria with one of the most knowledgeable physicians in the world. I know you don't object to treating people of other cultures. And, most important of all, I'm told your ability to heal surpasses that of all the other physicians in Jerusalem."

Eleazar responded with caution. "If a person is ill I do my best to bring him to good health. It matters not to me if he is a Jew or a Greek—or a Roman." He said the last with a sting of bitterness. "As a physician I am called to offer healing of the body, no matter who it is."

The man grunted and beckoned one of his servants. He whispered something in his ear and waved him off.

Eleazar stared with disgust at the man. Strip away his power and all that remained was a lump of human flesh, with no purpose but to cater to Caesar. "I don't have much time," he said with impatience. "Tell me, what is your ailment?"

The Roman sat up straight and flung his flabby legs over the side of the bed. They dangled like two, dimpled lumps of clay.

"Ailment?" The Roman burst out laughing. "Is *that* what the boy told you?"

Eleazar remained steadfast. "He merely said someone needed my services. I assumed—"

"You assumed? Be careful not to assume anything in the presence of a Roman." The man's eyes glistened with mirth, and he laughed aloud. Then he lost his smile and stared at Eleazar, his eyes narrowing.

An uncomfortable silence settled between them. Eleazar straightened his back and locked eyes with the man. The air in the room became thick with discomfort. Eleazar held his gaze. Then the Roman shifted slightly and cocked his head, like someone does when they're about to surrender.

"I'm Marcus." The smile returned but it seemed forced. "For the next few months I will reside in your city under King Herod's rule, and I will oversee the tax collection and other duties that are unpopular with your people. Does that offend you?"

"I have no concern with your duties."

"Good." He continued to keep his eyes on Eleazar. "My personal physician has been called back to Rome, so I am seeking another, someone who will drop everything whenever I summon him."

Eleazar eyed him with suspicion. "So, you have no ailment, no immediate need for a physician, yet you feel justified in interrupting my work?"

He expected Marcus to flare up at him. But the man merely chuckled. "I'm as healthy as an ox."

"Then I must depart. My services are needed elsewhere by people who really *are* sick." Eleazar turned toward the door.

A guard blocked his path.

"Don't go!" Marcus' outburst sounded more like a plea than a command. "I *do* have need of your services. Please, stay."

The guard placed his hand on the hilt of his sword. Eleazar turned and faced Marcus. He opened his mouth to speak, but Marcus raised his hand and silenced him.

"Physician, please bear with me." The Roman's tone had turned shamefully meek. "Though I have no immediate sickness, I need your help. My responsibilities are great, but my needs are simple. And," he added with a fresh air of confidence, "you will be well-paid for your services."

Eleazar doubted he could be any use to this man.

"Perhaps my generosity will speak more loudly." Marcus opened a leather pouch and poured gold coins in his palm. Several slipped through his fingers and onto the floor. Eleazar recalled the one gold coin Ariel had dropped in his palm many years ago. His heartbeat quickened.

"I can pay well for your services, physician." Marcus heaved a long sigh. "I have exhausted my supply of medicines. I have a special need for the mash that is made from poppy seeds. When prepared properly, it dulls my senses and helps me deal with the duties I face each day. Are you familiar with this medicine?" He raised his eyebrows.

Eleazar nodded. "Yes, I am familiar. The Greeks call it opium."

"Of course, you are a physician who has been trained well in the art of his profession. I have no doubt you are eager to ease the pain of those who depend on you."

The man tilted his head like a woman might when pleading with her husband to buy a precious gem or a jar of her favorite perfume. Though disgusted by the image, he continued to listen, for the man had caught his attention with the gold coins.

"Perhaps you will consider providing *me* with a supply from your store?" Marcus dropped the coins back inside the pouch. "Surely you can get an abundance from your merchant friend. I believe his name is Achim?"

A darkness entered Eleazar's heart. This Roman knew far too much about his personal life.

He cleared his throat and straightened his shoulders. "I understand your need, Marcus. But you are Herod's servant. You carry out his wishes and, in the end, you persecute the Jews—*my* people. Why should I help *you*?"

Eleazar's remark brought a shocked silence to the room. Spurred by a sense of power, he continued his denunciation. "You're a pampered worm, Marcus. You get pleasure by controlling others." He glanced at the line of meek young men who stood nearby. He shook his head. "I'm afraid you have wasted your time, Roman. I need to leave."

Marcus nearly lurched off of his bed. "Do you know I have the power to have you imprisoned? Or worse?"

Eleazar stepped closer to the man's bed. He slowly shook his head. "I don't fear you, Marcus. You have no power over me, for I have friends in high places as well. Yes, you can try to destroy me. But I need only to put my cause before the Sanhedrin. Do you really want that kind of humiliation? How will such shame ensure your authority here?"

Again, he started to turn away, but Marcus grabbed his sleeve. "Perhaps what I have to say will change your mind."

Curious, he stopped and faced the man. "What do you mean?"

Marcus smiled and released Eleazar's sleeve. "I speak of a certain woman—the wife of another Jew—a person who holds much interest for you. I believe her name is Ruth."

The hairs on the back of Eleazar's neck stood on end. "What are you saying?"

Marcus drew his legs up on the bed and shifted back onto his pile of pillows, a satisfied smile on his face. "Perhaps, if given the opportunity, you would like to resume the secret meetings the two of you had in Alexandria."

Eleazar backed away, stunned.

Marcus' smile broadened. "You have nothing to fear from me, physician. Perhaps instead you will thank me. Besides as much gold as you can carry, I can provide a private room where you and your concubine can meet discreetly, away from the wagging tongues of your precious Jews."

The possibility of having Ruth back in his life brought Eleazar to a halt. To be able to hold her again, to kiss her and lie with her would bring him such happiness. He only had to provide this ox of a man with a supply of opium. A very simple request. He stood very still and considered the man's offer. As long as Marcus remained faithful to his promise and kept the meetings secret, there would be no threat. But if he ever crossed the man— He reached into his scrip, withdrew a small pouch, and offered it to the Roman.

Marcus' thick lips watered at the corners as he reached inside the pouch and pinched a portion of the white powder. He touched it to his tongue, his eyes on Eleazar. Then he nodded, gave Eleazar another smile, and held out the pouch of gold coins.

"The boy who summoned you will show you a private room. So long as you continue to fill my need, no one will bother you there."

Then Marcus turned over and put his back to Eleazar. Their meeting had ended.

Gripping the pouch of gold coins, Eleazar left the room, his head swimming with the possibilities. He had traded his honor as a physician for his personal needs. Once again, his passion for Ruth was pulling him away from what was right and honest and sensible.

Eleazar followed the servant down the hall. The boy opened a door. Eleazar's concerns vanished the moment he looked inside the bedchamber and beyond, a private garden. He paused in the doorway and tried to imagine Ruth standing there. His confidence renewed, he hurried from the palace. He soared down the outer stairs, past the guards, and into the street. As he followed the winding road back to his house, he became increasingly aware of the many courtyards he passed along the way. Within those walls, hundreds—perhaps thousands—of Jews depended on him for healing. The truth of what he had done drove a sharp sword into his heart. He'd made a pact with the devil himself, and he didn't know how to let it go, or if he wanted to.

CHAPTER TWENTY-SIX

everal days later, Eleazar was in the courtyard sampling the berries that grew on the shrubs in the far corner. He pursed his lips. The tiny pearls had a bitter-sweet taste.

"Wait another week to harvest them," he told his young servant. "They will sweeten by then. For now, gather some herbs and take them to Anna for drying."

The boy nodded and headed for the large patch of greenery where a variety of herbs grew. Anna had done a fine job planting her garden. Leeks and garlic, parsley and mint, plus every vegetable on the face of the earth and several trees that were already bearing fruit. Eleazar sighed with contentment. His lavish courtyard could rival any other in the Upper City. He thought about his mother's meager patch of herbs and wilted vegetables and wished she could have enjoyed the abundance he now saw before him.

He heard a footstep at the main building. Anna was standing in the doorway, her face aglow. "I have good news," she said. "Simon has summoned us for a visit."

"Simon?" He hadn't seen his brother in months. He looked past Anna and peered through the open doorway. Judah was inside reclining on a mound of pillows. He looked back at Anna. "Send word that we'll be there," he said, loud enough for his father to hear.

Judah stirred slightly. "You can go without me," he mumbled. "I will not step foot in your brother's house."

Eleazar shook his head in disgust. "Father, why do you insist on keeping this distance from your youngest son? Many years have passed since Simon left. It's obvious he wants to repair this chasm that exists between you."

Judah struggled to his feet.

"Your brother's summons means nothing to me," he growled. "Simon blamed me for your mother's death. Then he punished me by staying away."

"He was only a boy when he left, Father. He was grieving. We *all* were grieving. He's a grown man now. Come with us and listen to what he has to say."

"My answer is, *No!* When Simon left, he chose his uncle's occupation. He married the woman of his choice without seeking my approval. *I* didn't divide our family. *He* did. And have you forgotten how he behaved at your wedding? Your brother ignored me. He stepped across my path as I was about to offer you my blessing. Then *he* invoked the blessing in my place. It was the greatest insult a father could bear."

Eleazar released a long sigh. So, it had come to this. Now he was the parent, and his father was the stubborn child.

"Listen to me." He summoned as much control as he could. "Simon has taken a difficult step to restore our family. It must have taken a lot for him to humble himself in this way. Now it's up to you, Father. I beg you, stop this useless war with your youngest son."

Judah stood firm. "I will not step foot in his house. My complaint is not only with Simon. My own brother turned against me. Hiram kept silent all those years. He never informed me of Simon's plans, his work, his marriage. Hiram's death ended any hope for reconciliation."

Silent until now, Anna stepped between them. She gazed into Eleazar's face.

"It's not right to argue with your father." She lowered her

voice so Judah couldn't hear. "Give him time, my husband. As the day draws near for our visit, Judah may change his mind and go with us. Be patient. He's an old man, but he continues to think like someone half his age, clearly and with purpose. And, yes, like a stubborn child."

Eleazar turned sharply away from his wife. He had not asked her opinion. Anna's place was in the kitchen, or with the children, or in his bed if the need arose. He started up the stairs to his apothecary and left his wife and his father to their own thoughts, caring little what they might be.

The day came for Eleazar's journey to the home of his brother Simon in Bethany. Anna went along, riding on a donkey. Mara and Benjamin ran ahead of them, eager to find out if they had any cousins.

The visit began amidst tears and joyous laughter. Eleazar's children ran off with Simon's son and daughter in a flurry of shrieks and giggles. The two brothers embraced.

"It's been far too long," Eleazar said. He backed away to get a better look at Simon. The truth was, they looked nothing at all like brothers. While Eleazar was tall and slim, like their mother, Simon had inherited his father's short, stocky frame, his broad jaw, and his big hands.

Simon gazed past his brother toward the open road. Disappointment swept over his face.

"He refused to come, Simon. He's a stubborn man."

"He still thinks I blame him for our mother's death, doesn't he?"

Eleazar nodded. "What's worse, I believe he also blames himself. You're simply a reminder that he failed her."

"I behaved unfairly. But I did away with those feelings a long time ago." He shrugged. "I always knew in my heart that our father wouldn't purposely harm anyone, especially not our mother. If you recall, his obsession with the poor became a curse to our family. If he hadn't left her alone that day—"

Eleazar rested his hand on his brother's shoulder. "I'm afraid we'll never know why the old man behaves as he does. He seems to have no feelings beyond his care of the hopeless. Tell me, Simon, did our uncle ever talk about our father's strange ways? Did he tell you what the old man was like as a child?"

"No. Now that Uncle Hiram is gone, I'm afraid their history was buried with him. The truth can only come from our father, but don't expect it, Eleazar." He patted Eleazar on the shoulder and led him inside the house. They sat beside the hearth, where the fire dispelled the autumn chill. The scent of drying herbs filled the air. Simon's wife brought them a tray of cakes and a hot brew. Then she and Anna retreated to a side room, their female chatter muffled by a curtain pulled across the doorway. An occasional high-pitched giggle emanated from beyond the veil.

Eleazar weighed the problem and came up with a solution. "Perhaps it's time you came to Jerusalem. Confront our father. *Make* him listen to you."

Simon shook his head. "I doubt I'd be well-received. Did you see how Father avoided me at your wedding? I hadn't seen him since the day I left home. Even in the midst of your celebration he never spoke to me, never even acknowledged my presence."

"He believes you avoided *him*. In fact, he told me you stepped ahead of him to offer me a blessing."

"He waited too long!" Simon leaped to his feet, his face flushed red. "*Someone* had to do it."

"So this division between you continues. It seems you and the old man are both stubborn."

Eleazar breathed a heavy sigh. It was at that moment that he realized Simon not only looked like his father, he'd also inherited his nature. He decided to say nothing more about it.

Turning his attention to Simon's home, Eleazar marveled at all his brother had accomplished. "You've provided well for your wife and children. Fine furnishings. A well-stocked kitchen. You have everything you need."

Simon grinned. "Your words mean a lot to me, Eleazar. I'm

aware of your success as a physician. Someone like you—praising me—I am speechless."

"Show me your work," Eleazar said, rising from the hearth.

"I keep a ready supply over here, in the corner." Simon gestured toward a pile of baskets and bowls, woven from palm branches. "They sell almost as fast as I can make them."

He lifted one basket after another and held them up before Eleazar. He turned each one on its side, then tapped the bottom to demonstrate its strength. He grinned with pride.

"Be sure to let Anna choose one before you leave." He stared at Eleazar with admiration. "It seems we both have found success, my brother, you even more than anyone I know."

Eleazar brushed away his brother's praise with a wave of his hand. "If not for my time in Alexandria, I would be no better than any of the other physicians who strive for attention in Jerusalem. Not only did I learn more about medicine, but I was able to perfect my knowledge of the Greek language. I labored long hours over heavily written scrolls. I trudged many miles through a maze of streets to the homes of the sick. My mentor, Nikolaus, told me I had advanced faster than any of his other students. He even offered me a position, which, of course, I had to refuse."

"And your life in Jerusalem is good?"

"I moved my family to the Upper City." He watched his brother for a sign of envy. Simon merely smiled. He cast his eyes around the dwelling again, satisfied that his brother's home, compared to his own lavish estate, appeared quite humble.

Simon took Eleazar by the arm and led him out the door and through the courtyard. "Let me tell you about my most recent venture." Simon sounded like he was about to share a secret. "It could also be of profit to you, Eleazar."

Pulling their cloaks tighter against the chill, they strolled, side-by-side, along the rise of the hill. Though nearly barren at this time of year, in the spring Bethany's expanse would come alive with green grass and an array of white, yellow, and red flowers.

For now, the stony path crunched beneath their sandals as they walked farther from the house.

"A venture?" Eleazar's curiosity was aroused.

Simon grinned. "I've invested all of my savings, every single coin I owned, and the profits have already started coming in. I do nothing at all except wait."

Eleazar frowned. "What sort of business allows you to sit back and collect the rewards with no effort on your part?"

"I know, it sounds absurd, doesn't it?" Simon laughed aloud. "Nevertheless, several of my friends already have enjoyed huge profits. We simply provide the funds. Eventually, caravans bring merchandise from the coast. The local merchants take the items to the marketplace in Jerusalem. After the sale, we get our money back with interest."

Eleazar stopped walking. He gazed at his brother with concern. "I don't understand. Don't the merchants have enough money of their own to handle such dealings?"

Simon shrugged. The innocent smile on his brother's face disturbed Eleazar.

"Tell me, Simon. Who holds the purse strings? And who decides what everyone's share will be?"

"It's all planned in advance by a very prominent businessman in Jerusalem. He's a member of the Sanhedrin, so he must be an honest man. I believe you know him, Eleazar. His name is Levi bar Uzza."

"Levi?!" Eleazar choked out his rival's name. "How can you be so foolish, Simon? That man is a swindler. Have you forgotten what he did to your little dog, Ishshah?"

Simon eyes widened in disbelief. "Levi was a child back then. We all did stupid things when we were children. He's a grown man now. He's successful. I only know of his ability to earn money. Lots of it. He's one of the richest men in the city."

"Yes, at other people's loss. He takes advantage of widows soon after their husbands die. He oppresses orphans. And he has not proved himself worthy of his wife." The truth struck Eleazar like a huge rock falling on him from the highest mountain. He knew of many Pharisees and scribes who practiced business the same way, but only one of them pestered his conscience. Levi, the one who had stolen his love away.

"I haven't suffered any losses." Simon persisted, still smiling.

"Give him time, my brother. He sets a plan in place, wins your confidence, and like a cobra, he strikes without warning. Just when you begin to feel comfortable with your arrangement, Levi makes his move. He fattens his own money pouch and leaves the innocent wanting. You need to withdraw your funds *now*, before it's too late."

Simon smiled sweetly at him. "Eleazar, Eleazar. Don't fret so. My money is safe. Besides, it's already too late. As we speak, Levi is organizing another caravan from the coast. The documents are in order. I've signed over all my money. Be patient. You will see. In two months the profits will flow in, and I'll be a rich man."

Eleazar shook his head slowly. Sadness engulfed him. Like his brother said, it was too late. If his suspicions proved correct, he would deal with Levi himself, perhaps take the issue before the Sanhedrin. Somehow, he had to protect Simon's interests. Knowing the merciless way Levi conducted business, his brother could lose everything he owned.

CHAPTER TWENTY-SEVEN

Several days passed and Eleazar busied himself with calls from the sick while he continued to try to make sense of his visit with Marcus. He'd set aside one day every week to refresh the items in his apothecary. It was on such a day, late in the afternoon, as Eleazar was sorting through a shipment from the coast, when he caught sight of a little handmaid standing in the courtyard.

Eleazar descended the stairs from the upper room, a vial of liquid in his hand—medicine for his father. He stepped closer to the girl and towered over her. She shrank back and lowered her eyes.

He thought about the pile of medicines on the roof. "What do you want?" His voice sounded harsh, but he didn't care. He had no time for sick calls today.

"My mistress is requesting your services." Trembling, she gazed up at him with fear-filled eyes. "It's urgent, sir. Please, bring your medical scrip to the house of Levi."

The house of Levi? The girl had said her mistress had called for him. Eleazar rushed up the stairs, opened his scrip, and made a hasty check of the contents. The vial he'd been holding slipped from his hand and crashed to the floor. A dark green liquid spilled across the stone pavement. Ignoring it, Eleazar filled his bag with medicines. Then he stumbled down the stairs and lunged ahead of the girl. The house of Levi was only two doors away.

Seconds later, Eleazar arrived in Levi's courtyard. Several servants had gathered quietly by the entry, their faces white with concern. Eleazar felt their eyes following him as he passed by them to the main house.

The young girl ran ahead of him and led the way through the central quarters. A stab of envy entered his heart as he passed the lavish furnishings that far surpassed those in his own home. His time in Alexandria had made him aware of what the world outside of Judea offered. Yet, despite his efforts to supply his home with the best the merchants could provide, Levi had outdone him once again.

Eleazar followed the handmaid through a curtained doorway into a private chamber. He found Levi there, his long fingers gripping Ruth's shoulders as she knelt next to the bed with her head bowed. He looked past her at a boy of about six years of age. It was Malachi, the son born to Levi and Ruth. The son that should have been his.

At the sound of his footstep, Ruth lifted her head and turned to face him. Lines of worry creased her brow. Her dark eyes were rimmed with red. Tears ran down her cheeks.

He stepped closer to the bed and let his scrip slide to the floor. Malachi lay very still. The color had left the boy's face. His eyes were shut. For a moment, Eleazar thought the child had died. Then the tiny lips parted and released the hint of a breath.

Eleazar turned and looked into the face of his longtime adversary. Levi's stern demeanor had melted away. His dark eyes, usually filled with threats or accusations, were now swimming in tears. He looked every bit like a distressed father, wringing his hands, his shoulders stooped beneath an invisible weight.

"Eleazar. Please, help my son. My personal physician could do nothing. I sent him away. At the pleading of my wife I called for you. Since the time you studied in Alexandria your medical ability has lifted you above the others. I beg you, do whatever you can to help my boy."

Eleazar hesitated. Of all the people in Jerusalem, this was the one man he had no desire to help. Then he looked at Ruth, her sad eyes pleading with him to stay.

He sighed with resignation. "Tell me what happened."

Levi gestured toward the upper floor. "My foolish son was walking on the rooftop ledge, showing off in front of his friends. They urged him on from the courtyard below." He pointed at a spot in the courtyard. "Malachi lost his footing and tumbled over the side. The railing did not prevent his fall. Look." Levi's long fingers separated the boys hair and revealed a swelling behind his right ear. "Here is the mark where he struck the pavement."

Eleazar moved closer, took a long look at the injury, and then began to remove the child's clothing. He checked every part of the boy's limp body, searching for more injuries. Dark purple bruises covered his arms, his back, and his buttocks. His legs moved easily under Eleazar's gentle guidance.

"There don't appear to be any breaks," he said.

Ruth's sigh of relief touched his heart.

Leaning closer to the boy's face, he pulled back Malachi's eyelids, one at a time, and peered into those dark eyes. A glaze had clouded them, and his pupils had grown larger than what was acceptable.

"He's in a deep sleep," Eleazar said. "I doubt I can rouse him."

Ruth caught her breath and began to sob.

"Take care." Eleazar kept his voice soft. "I'll do everything in my power to revive your son." He looked at Levi, but he had directed his words to Ruth—to comfort her, to win her approval, to let her know he still cared.

Drawing on his training in Alexandria, Eleazar recalled another time when a young child had tumbled from the back of a running donkey. The lad had cracked his skull on a rock, leaving a knot as large as a pomegranate on the back of his head. Nikolaus had moved quickly. The aging physician drilled a hole in the location of the injury and immediately relieved the pressure. To Nikolaus, it was a common medical procedure. To Eleazar, it was a miracle. The boy recovered after a few days of bed rest and was out riding again, with his hair shaved off and his brow wrapped in a bandage.

Eleazar had never attempted such an operation. He stared at the boy, hesitant to even try. Then he looked at Ruth again and succumbed to the pain in her heart.

He opened his scrip and searched through the tools he had acquired over the years. What he needed lay on the bottom, unused until now and hidden beneath more necessary items. He withdrew the drill and tested it's workings.

Ruth let out a gasp. "No." She lay across her son, as though protecting him.

Eleazar turned to Levi. "Move a lamp closer to the bed, then get me some hemp ropes to bind your son so he won't move. Have the servants gather some clean, dry cloths and three pans of fresh water." A thrill went through him. For the first time in his life he was giving orders to Levi, and it felt good.

Levi hurried out of the bedchamber. When the room was set up as Eleazar had requested, he cleansed his hands with lye and water and applied a cleansing ointment to the drill. Carefully, he turned the boy on his side and shaved the hair from around the wound. Then he took one of the clean cloths and soaked it with sulphur. The sharp odor filled the room and brought fresh tears to Ruth's eyes.

He glanced at Levi. "Bind him. Then hold him still. Do not allow him to move."

Levi bound the boy's arms and legs with the hemp rope. Then he gripped his son's head and held it fast. Ruth leaned across the bed and fell across Malachi's stomach. Sobbing, she pressed her face against his side. Eleazar poured more of the purifying drops on the tip of the drill, the way Nikolaus had taught him. Then he positioned the end over the boy's wound and froze.

He held his breath. What if he failed? What if, instead of saving the boy's life, he ended it? He couldn't bear to hurt Ruth in such a horrifying way. Perhaps if they waited another day Malachi might revive on his own. His eyes moved from Malachi to

Ruth. She lifted her head and stared at him with trust swimming in her eyes. Turning his attention back to the boy, he took another breath. Then, steadying his hands, he began to turn the drill.

He turned the handle slowly at first, broke through the outer layer of bone with a loud crunch, then went deeper, and deeper, until a pale liquid oozed from the wound. Satisfied he'd relieved the pressure, he sewed up the opening and covered the boy's wound with more medicine and strips of clean cloth.

Then he stepped back and allowed Ruth and Levi to close in. "Now we wait," Eleazar said with an air of finality.

Levi bent close and shook his head. "He's still badly swollen." He straightened and turned to look at Eleazar. A scowl had returned to his face. He crossed his arms and glared in silent accusation.

"The swelling will go down in a few days," Eleazar assured him. "Keep watch through the night. Take four-hour vigils with the servants. Do not leave the boy unattended at any time. If you see any blood, call for me immediately.

Unable to stop sobbing, Ruth reached out and clasped the boy's hand. "It's my punishment."

Eleazar glanced at Levi. The man was eying his wife with disgust. "Punishment?" Levi snarled. "Stop behaving like a stupid woman. You didn't do anything to our son. He fell. It was an accident. Now control yourself, woman. We'll do as the physician has said. We'll watch Malachi through the night.

Eleazar cringed at Levi's harsh response to a woman who was caught in the throes of grief and concern. Ruth would get no sympathy in this house that night. Then he considered Levi, and the hairs on the back of his neck stood on end. The man's heart had returned to its cloak of ice.

Levi stared back at him and challenged him to leave. He pulled some coins from a leather pouch and tossed them on the bed. "For your services." Then he strode from the room.

From the main quarters came the rattle of bottles and wineskins. Then there was silence.

In the stillness of Malachi's bed chamber, Eleazar found himself alone with the boy and his mother. He held his breath and listened. Malachi's labored breathing blended with Ruth's faint humming of a familiar children's song. He touched her shoulder. She stopped humming and looked up at him. Even in her distressed state, with her nose red and her eyes nearly swollen shut, she looked beautiful to him.

She tilted her head and gazed into his eyes, her own eyes overflowing. "This is my rightful punishment," she said, her voice breaking.

"No. You're wrong, Ruth. The Almighty doesn't hurt people this way. He doesn't punish the children for their parents' sins. Your husband said it was an accident. It's not a curse. Not a judgment." He shook his head. "You have nothing to fear."

She turned away from him and ran her fingers over Malachi's arms and legs. She kissed his cheek, his brow, his lips, all the while whispering words of comfort to her sleeping son.

It was time for Eleazar to leave. If he delayed, Levi would grow suspicious.

He gazed at Ruth, and his heart ached for her. "I'll return tomorrow to check on your son." She didn't look up, didn't see him leave the house.

In the morning, before the sun burned the dew from the pavement, Eleazar returned to the house of Levi. The boy was still asleep, but his breathing came easier, and a rosy color had returned to his cheeks. Still, he needed constant watching.

Ruth had remained at her son's bedside. She looked as though she hadn't slept. Her dress was wrinkled. Her hair hung in matted spirals past her shoulders. Her skin had lost its radiance. Eleazar wanted to gather her in his arms and comfort her. She managed a slight smile and rose awkwardly to her feet.

She turned to a servant girl who stood in the shadows. "Bring some clean linen cloths and a pan of rose water."

After washing her face and hands, Ruth requested a pitcher of herb tea and two cups. The servant girl rushed out again and returned several minutes later with a tray.

Ruth handed one of the cups to Eleazar. "Thank you for coming to the aid of my son," she said with a touch of shyness. "Levi's personal physician tried one remedy after another, but Malachi grew worse as the hours passed. I begged my husband to send for you. I didn't care what Levi thought. I knew you could help."

Eleazar drank a little of the sweet liquid. "You did the right thing, Ruth. Nothing could have kept me away, not even Levi."

"Yes. But my husband has treated you harshly in the past. I wasn't certain you'd want to do anything for *him*."

Eleazar smiled. "No, not for him. But for you I would do anything. I would even subject myself to the man's insults, if necessary."

At that moment, Levi stepped into the room. "No insults will be coming your way today." His voice was calm, even friendly. He drew close to Malachi's bedside. "Has my son revived?" Gone was the troubled father. Levi appeared refreshed, like he'd slept well and now had resumed his business-like stature.

Eleazar clenched his jaw and restrained his ire. "Your son sleeps restfully."

Levi turned to Ruth. "I am needed in the city. Report to me any changes when I return." Then he shook his head. "Get some rest, woman. You look terrible."

Ruth bowed her head. Eleazar would have liked to grab the man's throat. Levi had crushed Ruth's spirit, and he could do nothing to restore it. Sighing, Eleazar returned the cup to the servant's tray. He shook his head and started for the door.

"Keep your health," he said to Ruth, pausing beside her. "Not only for your sake, but for your son's. He's going to need you while he recovers."

She gazed into his eyes, and for a moment her former spirit flashed to life, then it quickly disappeared. He thought about the Roman's offer, then forced the dream to the back of his mind. For now Ruth needed to keep her attention on her son. Eleazar could wait a few more days.

For the next week, Eleazar didn't handle any sick calls in the city, but merely cared for his visitors at home. He wanted to remain available in the event Ruth called for him. He made several visits to Levi's home, more often than he had done for anyone else who needed his services. Each time he saw Ruth, his love for her grew, until he could think of nothing else when he was away.

As he expected, Anna also visited Ruth's home. As Ruth's former handmaid and a longtime friend, it was natural for Anna to show concern. She brought fresh-baked breads and some vegetables from her garden. This pleased Eleazar, for Levi would also be appeased. He was a physician, but they also were neighbors, showing their concern and nothing more.

After the week had passed, word came at the break of dawn that Levi's son had awakened. Eleazar grabbed his scrip and hurried up the hill. He found Malachi sitting up in bed, sipping broth from a ceramic bowl. Ruth sat on the side of her son's bed, tipping the bowl to his lips. For the first time in days, she was smiling.

Eleazar moved closer and carefully pulled away the bandage on the back of the boy's head. The bruising had turned from dark blue to light purple. The swelling had subsided. He looked into the boy's eyes, his ears, his mouth, the inside of his throat. He stepped back and released a long sigh. Then he smiled and gave Ruth an approving nod.

"You've done well as your son's nurse," he said. Then he turned his attention to the boy. "So, Malachi." Eleazar tried to sound stern. "I hope you will stay away from the edge of the roof now."

Malachi nodded and grinned sheepishly.

"Do you know what I did to help you?" He looked into the boy's eyes. They were shining black, like his mother's.

"You put a hole in my head." Malachi laughed. "My mother told me."

"Yes, and do you know why I did that?"

Malachi blinked and shook his head slightly.

"I wanted to relieve the pressure from your injury."

"So, what am I? The boy with a hole in his head?" Malachi laughed again.

Ruth laughed with her son and gave him a little squeeze. Eleazar watched with pleasure, thrilled to see his beloved happy again, and pleased that he had been able to restore her joy.

He frowned at Malachi, but kept smiling. "For now, yes, you're the boy with a hole in his head. It goes with the foolishness that put you in this bed in the first place. Now rest. Perhaps tomorrow I will take away that horrible name. There will be no more boy with a hole in his head. Just Malachi."

He turned to Ruth. "Keep him in bed for a few more days." Then he dared to ask, "Is the boy's father at home?"

"No, he's been called to the city on business."

"Can we talk? In the courtyard?"

Ruth gave a last, lingering look at her son, then she followed him into the courtyard. Eleazar scanned the area. Confident they were alone, he drew close to her and spoke barely above a whisper.

"My dear one, seeing you again has rekindled the flame in my heart. Your face comes before me often during my day. I have missed you."

"Eleazar, I've missed you too," she breathed. Her admission got his heart beating faster. "Since I left Alexandria, I've struggled with my feelings for you. Levi's cruel behavior makes me want to run to the safety of your arms and never leave."

"Why do you stay with him? You could return to your father's house. If he's mean to you, the Sanhedrin needs to know about it."

She shook her head with sadness. "It's hopeless. My father would never bring Levi before the Sanhedrin. They are in business. Don't you see? I'm a prisoner in my own home. My only joy comes from Malachi."

He leaned closer. "Then meet with me, Ruth. Privately."

"That's not possible. What we had in Alexandria is in the past. We can't go back. I would lose my son. And you have much to lose too."

"You don't understand. We don't have to leave Jerusalem." He lowered his voice to a mere whisper. "I've found a place where we can meet discretely. It's a good distance away from anyone who knows us. It's in the Roman quarter. Grant me one meeting. Only one. Then decide." Even as he said it, he knew one meeting would never be enough for him.

"The Roman quarter?" She frowned, and her dark eyes filled with fear.

"Yes, but it's safe. And private."

She glanced toward the room where her boy lay resting. Eleazar grabbed her hand. "One time," he pleaded.

She let out a sigh. "I will meet with you once, but only so we can talk. On the evening of the first day of the week Levi always takes care of business in the city. He's gone for several hours. I can slip out of the house for a while. But I must be firm, Eleazar. It has to be this one time, and one time only. Now," she said, pulling her hand away. "Tell me where."

CHAPTER TWENTY-EIGHT

Eleazar felt as though the first day of the week would never come. At last, as the sun began to set, he left his house and hurried to Antonia, his heart pounding with the beat of his flying footsteps.

He instructed the outside guard to watch for Ruth and to direct her to his private chamber, then he tucked a few coins in the man's hand assuring his silence. In exchange for an additional pouch of opium, Marcus had arranged for a platter of dried fruit and a cruise of wine. Eleazar's attention moved past the table of provisions and to the far corner of the room where stood a bed covered with plush pillows and a sheepskin blanket.

An open door led to a garden, smaller than the one at Abigail's house, and more private. Towering walls and an assortment of trees and shrubs framed the area and kept out curious eyes. There was one bench with enough room for a man and his maiden to sit comfortably.

Though the evening brought a crisp chill, perspiration began to form on Eleazar's forehead and on the back of his neck. He mopped his brow, straightened his robe and tightened the cord at his waist. He paced, stopped to listen, and paced again, his ear ever turned toward the hall.

A footstep drew his attention to the door. It opened, and Ruth stood in the entrance, her slight form framed by the torches that glowed in the hall behind her. A sheer veil clung to her shapely body, enhanced by the effects of motherhood. She wore a second veil across her face with only her dark eyes exposed above the fold. Eleazar was grateful that she took care to hide her face so she wouldn't be recognized as she made her way to the palace.

He stepped toward her, reached for her hand, and drew her into the room. Before she could protest, he pulled the veil from her face and kissed her.

Ruth pushed him away. "You promised we would talk." Though her words were firm, her eyes beckoned him to kiss her again.

With his hands on both her arms, Eleazar pulled her close and held her to his chest. She didn't resist.

"I think you already knew I could never settle for mere words." He kissed her forehead.

She let out a trembling sigh. "Nor could I," she admitted. "My life has been loveless for so long, I had forgotten what the touch of a caring man felt like. My husband has no gentleness in him. He is greedy and demanding, the same way he deals with money and business. I mean nothing to him except to increase his stature in the city." She gazed into Eleazar's eyes. "It's been a lonely life, my love."

"You don't have to be lonely ever again, Ruth. Nor will I. Our time together will make up for our loveless marriages."

Eleazar took a step back and gazed into Ruth's beautiful face. She'd grown lovelier with each passing year. She was no longer a high-spirited young girl, but a graceful woman and the mother of a young son.

"I've arranged for us to meet twice a month in this place." He held up his hand. "Don't deny me this one joy, Ruth. And, don't deny yourself."

She smiled and melted into his arms. "I'll come here whenever you want me, Eleazar. Nothing can keep me away. Nothing."

Two weeks later, Anna crushed Eleazar's dream with four life-changing words.

"I am with child." Her face was beaming. His heart nearly stopped. He stepped back and could feel the blood draining from his face.

This would be their third child. Mara was now six, a few months older than Ruth's son, Malachi. And young Benjamin had turned three. Since having a son, Eleazar had been content with having only two children. He hadn't considered another. He rarely touched Anna anymore, and he grieved over the few evenings he'd spent in her bed. Now that he had Ruth in his life again, he saw no need to pursue affection at home.

Anna's announcement brought a knot to his stomach. *Another child?* He acknowledged her happy news with a nod, then he left her standing in the kitchen, troubled lines creasing her brow, and he retreated to the rooftop alone.

That evening, under Anna's direction, the servants prepared a large supper. Eleazar dined in silence, offering few praises for the rich foods his wife had selected. He ignored the puzzled look on his wife's face. His daughter, Mara, approached him with a plate of bread and cheese. She smiled shyly at him. It struck him that he hardly knew his daughter. He stared into her round eyes and lifted a piece of bread and a wedge of cheese from the plate, bringing a wide grin to her face.

She was a beautiful child, and except for the eyes, she looked more like him than like her mother. Brown curls cascaded down her back, and she had Eleazar's wiry frame. He had already considered a union for his firstborn child. Enos' son, Hareem, would make a good match. Hareem's grandfather held a top position in the Sanhedrin. Eleazar expected such a union would prompt the older man to name him for the next open seat.

Mara walked away, obviously satisfied with her father's brief attention. His eyes strayed to Benjamin, who was huddled close to his grandfather on a pile of pillows by the hearth. A plate of food rested on the youngster's lap. Benjamin picked through the slices of meat and offered them to the old man. Judah opened his mouth wide and accepted each morsel with a smile. He kept one arm around Benjamin's tiny shoulders, and with his other hand he gestured while speaking in soft tones only the boy could hear. Eleazar watched them with curiosity and wondered how he had missed the growth of their bond.

He felt a surge of envy. Without his knowledge the two had entered a world of their own, and he had easily been excluded.

With Anna pregnant again, his one relief was that she would not be available to him, at least for another year. He could now be faithful to the only one who held his heart. He and Ruth would meet as planned, and no one would be the wiser for it.

Months passed. By day, Eleazar performed his duties as a physician, sometimes receiving the sick at his house and at other times visiting them in their homes. Occasionally, he met with the prominent men at the city gate. It was important that he stay alert to what was happening in Jerusalem. The Romans had converged on Judea in full force. Soldiers were everywhere, enforcing the Roman laws and keeping peace between cultures. Caesar had taken control of all civic matters. A web of thick paved roads fanned out from Jerusalem in all directions. They were built to withstand the heavy carts and wagons bearing Roman soldiers and their loads of supplies.

Eleazar had little interest in the Romans, except for the one who had provided a private meeting place for him and Ruth. Twice a month, on the first day of the week, as planned, Eleazar met Ruth in their private chamber at the palace. On those nights, he left the house early, before Anna could ask him where he was going. Sometimes, he didn't even stay for supper.

Meanwhile, he kept Marcus content with a flow of the man's favorite drug.

Then one night, as Eleazar was returning home from the palace, he found the midwife at his door. The third child was not due for several weeks. Thoughts of his mother came flooding back. In a panic, he pushed past the old woman and entered the bedchamber where Anna lay writhing in a pool of blood.

He lunged toward his wife. "Anna, what's wrong? It's not your time."

She grimaced and reached for her husband's cloak. Catching one of the folds, she pulled him closer. Then she moaned and shut her eyes.

Eleazar knelt beside her bed. With knowing hands, he felt the contour of his wife's abdomen. The child had dropped into the pathway, but had stalled there, sideways. He continued to feel for movement.

He looked at the midwife. "The child lives," he said, a ray of hope surfacing.

The midwife stood helpless with a towel in her hand. Lines of concern crossed her face.

Perspiration formed on Eleazar's brow. He had observed this kind of distress before, in Alexandria. Nikolaus knew what to do. The old physician had cut the baby free. But this was not someone else's wife, not someone else's child. They were *his*.

Anna moaned again, and her eyes fluttered open. "Save our baby," she whispered. "Don't bother about me, Eleazar. Help our child."

He held his breath and searched his memory for what Nikolaus had done.

"I'll have to cut the baby free," he said.

The midwife let out a gasp. Anna writhed in agony. He couldn't waste another moment. Leaping to his feet, he commanded the midwife to heat a pot of water and to bring clean towels. She hurried off.

Eleazar raced to the upper room. He searched the shelves, knocked over bottles, shoved sacks of powder to the floor. Then, he found it, one small pouch of opium, the last of his supply. He hesitated. Achim's caravan wouldn't arrive for at least two more weeks. He'd been saving this for Marcus. A shriek rose from the room below. Clutching the pouch in one hand and his wooden medical kit in the other, Eleazar stumbled down the stairs to his wife.

At her bedside he blended some of the opium with water until it was completely dissolved. He held the bowl to Anna's lips, allowed her to sip it all, then he waited for her to drift off to sleep. Meanwhile, he set his tools in a row. First the horsehair and needle, then the sterile wrappings and other cloths to mop up the flow of blood. Then he unwrapped the blade from a clean towel, purified it with sulphur, and held it ready.

Minutes later, Anna was breathing the breath of sleep. Within minutes, he cut the child free. He placed his newborn daughter in the arms of the midwife and began to stitch Anna's wound. It ran the length of her abdomen and would leave an ugly scar. Carefully, he worked each stitch until each layer of flesh was well-sealed. Then he doused a strip of cloth with medicine and placed it over the scar. He lay several other cloths over his wife's abdomen and secured them there.

The midwife was still holding the child, a baby girl. He looked closely at the newborn and found her frail and ashen.

"Wrap her tightly in her swaddling cloth," he commanded.

The midwife turned aside to take care of the child. He called after her, "Keep her warm. This one came too early. She will need extra care, if she survives at all."

With Anna sound asleep, Eleazar went out into the courtyard and breathed deeply of the night air. He gazed into the heavens at the spread of stars, a welcome retreat from the ordeal inside the house. Again, he thought about his mother and how he and Judah had found her at home, travailing.

Perhaps I'm not very different from my father, after all, he thought to himself. *Where was he when my mother struggled in childbirth? He was with Miriam. And, where was I when my own wife needed me? I was with Ruth.*

Tormented by the reality, he ran his hand through his hair, walked to the edge of the courtyard and looked out at the deserted street. Suddenly, he felt the weight of his many mistakes. One day he was going to have to face them all. But how could he turn all the evil he had done into good? There seemed to be nowhere to hide from the judgment of an angry God.

Anna's body had been weakened by the cutting. She would never again be able to bear another child. Eleazar wondered how he might break the news. For her own good they would have to avoid the marriage bed. To her, it would be one more rejection from a husband she already knew had never loved her. But, for him, it promised the freedom to pursue such pleasures with Ruth. For now, he would do what he could to care for the stranger in his bed. He would help Anna to heal and in doing so perhaps ease his guilt a little.

Anna thrashed on her bed throughout the night. She burned with fever, wailed about the pain in her abdomen. Eleazar rationed out the remaining opium. He winced as he watched the last of it pass between his wife's lips. There would be none for Marcus for the next two weeks or longer.

The midwife came daily to attend to Anna's needs. Eleazar also hired a nurse to take care of the baby. Anna's scar had turned red. Infection had set in. From a bitter mold he prepared a medicine that was popular among the Egyptians. He spread it over her scar and covered the wound with clean linen, then he repeated the process several times a day. He didn't leave the house for fear she might die.

The midwife brought a bowl of broth she had made from onions and fresh greens. Eleazar held the bowl to his wife's lips. Anna drank a little. Then, lacking strength, she fell back against her pillow. Eleazar hovered like an eagle over its nest. He didn't want his wife to die. She had become a vital part of his life. What's more, the children needed her.

Every now and then, Mara and Benjamin peeked through the open door. When Eleazar looked up they fled like frightened birds. He realized with shame that they feared him more than they were worried about their mother's sickness.

On the sixth day, he entered the bedchamber to find Anna sitting up, her eyes clear, her hair washed and combed. The midwife stood nearby, her arms crossed in front of her, and a satisfied grin on her lips.

"My baby." Such were the first words out of Anna's mouth. She held out her empty hands. "I want to hold my baby."

Eleazar summoned the nurse.

After the newborn child had been placed in her arms, Anna smiled and looked at Eleazar, a mother's joy evident. "I'd like to name her Abi. It's a simple name. Only three letters. Tiny, like she is."

"Why not Abigail?" Eleazar brought up the popular name. He thought of Ruth's sister. The woman was strong, lively, a treasure. Perhaps the name would bestow such qualities on his own child.

"No, not Abigail," Anna insisted. "Simply Abi."

Eleazar nodded his agreement. He looked down at the frail infant's purple face and skinny arms and legs and doubted she would survive anyway.

He had only one word of advice for his wife. " Nurse her until she's satisfied and do it often."

From that moment on, Anna gave nearly all of her attention to the little one. She discharged the nurse and began to feed the baby her own milk. It was as if she'd made it her personal mission to save the child's life. Eleazar hoped the child might live, for Anna's sake.

When he told his wife she could never attempt to bear another child, she fell into a state of mourning. No longer did she look at him with shining hope in her eyes. There would be no more children. No more touching and no more sleeping in the same bed. She sat for hours, cuddling the newborn to her breast, humming softly, and leaving Mara in the care of their handmaid while Benjamin spent every waking hour with his grandfather. The color left Anna's cheeks, and the glow departed from her eyes. Gray strands began to appear throughout her hair. She looked older than her years, and more haggard. She seemed to be finding joy in only one person, her fragile little daughter, Abi.

Eleazar escaped the heavy cloud that hung over his home and returned to his work in the city. He also resumed his meetings with Ruth, though he hadn't kept his part of the agreement with Marcus. But he couldn't avoid the Roman forever. The day came when the Roman summoned him to his private chamber and demanded more opiates.

"I've waited three long weeks for my medicine," he growled. "Now you tell me it will be another week?"

"The caravan has been delayed." Eleazar stood firm, but he could feel his confidence slipping. Achim had not promised the shipment would arrive soon, nor was he certain he would be able to bring back any opium. "I can only try," Achim had said.

"What of the supply you already had?" the Roman pressed.

"My wife had a difficult childbirth. I had no choice but to use the remaining pouch to save her life."

The Roman snickered. "Your wife?! *Your wife?!* What is this sudden interest in a woman you've neglected in favor of your mistress? You would have been better off if she had died rather than waste my medicine on her."

Eleazar felt a surge of heat rise to his neck and face. He would have liked to beat that barbarian into a bloody mess. He held his temper, if only because he didn't want to lose his times with Ruth.

"We had an agreement." Marcus leaned toward him, an angry scowl on his face. "I've kept my part of our bargain."

Eleazar should never have trusted the Roman. Now the man owned him in a way that he couldn't escape. He glanced at the guard standing by the door, the sword halfway out of its sheath.

Eleazar considered his store of medicines. "Perhaps something else will do until the opium arrives."

Marcus shook his head. "They are less potent, meaningless medicines that merely mask the pain for a few minutes."

Eleazar nodded. "I'll do what I can."

"You have one day," Marcus said, a smirk on his lips. "Bring me my medicine, or our agreement will end, and you will face the wrath of an angry husband."

Then he lifted a silver cup to his lips and drank heartily. The purple liquid ran down his chin. He wiped it away with the back of his hand, then he gulped down the remaining drops. He lowered the cup and curled his lip into a sneer. But his smile quickly faded.

"Go now, Jew! And don't come back without my medicine."

With that, Marcus winked, chuckled, and leaned back against his pillow. Eleazar swallowed his anger and left the room with Marcus' boisterous laughter following him down the hall.

CHAPTER TWENTY-NINE

The next morning, Eleazar hurried to the marketplace. Perhaps Achim had returned from the coast with a fresh load of supplies, including the precious opium Marcus craved. But when he arrived, his friend's stall wasn't in its usual place. He searched the area and finally caught sight of Achim setting up his wares in a remote corner of the square, apart from the usual clamor.

Weaving through the crowd, Eleazar dodged the vendors who were calling out to him and kept his eyes on Achim. Why had his friend moved his wares away from the flow of shoppers? There was something distressingly different about Achim. His blue eyes had lost their sparkle. It was as if a cloud had passed over him. His face was ashen. No laughter poured from his lips. Nor did he speak with the people who approached his stall. No booming voice bartered for a higher price. He simply moved items around on his table as though in a trance, hardly looked at his buyers, merely put out his hand to accept whatever they wanted to pay.

Gone was the smiling merchant who used to dance about with bursts of energy, waving his arms and bobbing his head and laughing aloud. The Achim Eleazar knew had all but disappeared within the shadows.

As Eleazar walked closer to the stall, he noticed Achim's

hands were shaking. A woman offered him a few shekels for a jeweled necklace. Instead of pressing for more, as he normally would, he accepted the meager amount. Eleazar frowned with concern. In only three or four weeks, his friend's appearance had changed from a robust and vibrant seller of goods to a cowering beggar.

Achim looked up at Eleazar and offered a weak smile. "*Shalom*, my friend."

There was no boisterous welcome. No friendly waving of his arms. Even his clothing looked drab, not the usual colorful array so common with Achim, but more like unkempt bedclothes.

Eleazar stepped up to the stall. "Peace to you as well, Achim. I've been waiting for your return from the coast." He leaned across the table, closer to his friend. "But first, tell me what's wrong. You seem—different."

Achim turned his face away and busied himself with his wares, mindlessly moving items from one place to another, then moving them back again.

"Did you have a profitable journey?" Eleazar pressed.

"I did," Achim mumbled. "Come. Choose something nice for Anna." He waved his hand over an array of gemstones. "She will be giving birth soon, no?

"Our child came early, Achim. She's a frail little girl. I'm not certain she will survive. Her weight is far below what it should be." He shrugged. "Perhaps you have something we might feed her, some powder or oil to give her strength."

"Surely, her mother's milk is the best remedy," Achim said. "Wait a while longer and see how she does. I have nothing here to rival what comes from a woman's breast."

An old woman barged in front of Eleazar, selected a bracelet from Achim's table and offered him a price that was far too low for such a treasure. More people rushed up behind her. Word must have spread through the marketplace that one of the merchants was practically giving things away. Achim didn't argue with the woman but reached out and accepted her offer.

She slipped the bracelet on her arm and walked away, a satisfied grin on her face.

Eleazar spread his arms and rested his palms on each end of the table in an attempt to block any more people from taking advantage of his friend.

"I could use some powdered ivory," he said, loud enough for the people behind him to hear. "It's been useful in treating a variety of ailments—fever, snakebite, vomiting, headaches, and a wide assortment of—" He stopped talking. It appeared that Achim had not been listening to him at all.

Achim simply nodded and reached under the table. He brought up a sheepskin pouch in his left hand. "From India." He almost smiled. Then his left hand began to shake, and the pouch slipped to the ground. Eleazar bent to pick it up. As he rose, he came face-to-face with his friend. He drew in a sharp breath. Troubled lines on Achim's brow confirmed his fears. Achim was deathly sick.

More customers came up behind Eleazar and reached past him. They grabbed at jewels and small pieces of pottery, ornaments for their homes, layers of silk for their clothing. Aflame with anger, Eleazar spun around and threw his hands up.

"Leave! Get away from here. Can't you see this man is not well? I said, Leave!"

Stunned, they backed away and began to depart in different directions.

He turned his attention back to Achim, who had started putting his wares away in their sacks. Eleazar looked over what remained on the table and picked up a gold ring with a large emerald in the center.

Achim named a foolishly low price. Eleazar paid him three times the amount and added a handful of coins for the powdered ivory. Then he edged closer and lowered his voice.

"Did you bring any opium, Achim? I need a good supply of it."

Achim locked eyes with him. "It's for the Roman, isn't it?"

Eleazar nodded.

Achim shook his head with displeasure. He reached under the table and brought out another pouch. "This will lead to your end," he warned.

Eleazar checked the contents, nodded, and offered a suitable payment.

Achim slipped his hands behind his back. "For you, no cost."

Eleazar placed the money on the table. Then he stepped around to the other side and drew closer to his friend. Achim took a step back.

Eleazar moved closer, backing his friend against the wall. Achim looked down. Beads of perspiration oozed from beneath the turban onto his brow.

"Tell me the truth, Achim. What has happened to you?" Eleazar searched Achim's ashen face. "Are you ill?"

Achim looked him in the eye and let out a troubled sigh. His shoulders sagged, and tears spilled from his blue eyes.

"I suppose I should have called on you, Eleazar. I've developed a weakness in my left hand. You saw the pouch fall to the ground. I have no feeling in that hand, none at all."

"Is there anything else?"

With his right hand, Achim pulled down the collar of his cloak exposing a patch of rotted skin on one side of his neck.

"There are more," Achim said with sadness. "Too many to count and hidden beneath my cloak."

A cold chill surged through Eleazar. He recognized the signs. Numbness and unexplainable sores. He remembered the caves where his father took him so many years ago. Serus the priest had a lesion on his neck. The scrolls he'd studied in Alexandria touched briefly on the disease. Often, no visible sign appeared for weeks, or even months. But once it manifested itself it moved quickly. The disease ate away at the skin leaving behind ugly sores, like the one on Serus' neck and like this one on Achim's neck. The numbness also would spread in time. Injured fingers and toes would go unnoticed and eventually they would drop off.

His head spinning and his stomach churning, Eleazar recalled

Hilda, the old woman who'd soiled him with her vomit. His heart sank. Though he wanted to deny the truth, he had no doubt his friend had been struck with the dreaded disease.

Eleazar's mind rushed to his apothecary. "I have some medicines at home," he told Achim. "I'll run back and check my shelves." He held up the pouch of powdered ivory. "Perhaps this will help. I'll prepare a balm for you and return here as fast as my feet can carry me. Wait for me, my friend. Gather up your wares, but don't leave."

Achim shrugged. His lips moved but no words came out.

Blinking back anxious tears, Eleazar spun away and hurried toward home. Upon reaching his house, he charged through the open door, into the main room, and headed straight for Judah's chamber.

"Father! Father! I need your help."

Eleazar found the old man in a huddle with young Benjamin, a pile of pillows arranged comfortably around them. Benjamin stared at his father with a wrinkle of annoyance on his brow. Judah held a small knife in one hand. In his other hand he held a piece of wood that had begun to take on the appearance of a small horse.

"Benjamin, leave," Eleazar commanded. "I need to talk to your grandfather."

The boy turned anxious eyes on him. "F–father. P–P–Papa has almost f–finished c-carving my toy."

Eleazar cringed at the sound of his son's stammering. Only recently, Benjamin had developed the flaw. Not even he, a great physician, had succeeded in finding a cure.

"Go out!" he growled.

Benjamin scrambled to his feet and left the room, clutching a wooden horse that had no legs or tail.

In a panic, Eleazar turned to his father. "I need your help, Father. My friend, Achim, suffers with some type of infection.

It looks like what I saw years ago on the lepers outside the city. You spent much time with them, Father. Did you have any success with the medicines you prepared? Did you ever heal anyone or did you see some sign of improvement? Anything, Father. Please, help."

Judah set down the knife and ran his hand through his full crop of graying hair.

"Achim?"

Eleazar nodded.

The old man shook his head, a moist sadness filling his eyes. "You've seen the sores?"

"I have. And he has a strange numbness in his left hand. He can't hold onto anything."

Judah rose to his feet and stumbled across the room. "Let's go up to the apothecary," he said. "Perhaps, we'll find something there."

Pausing for a moment at the bottom of the steps, the old man gripped the rail and then started up with Eleazar close behind. The journey up the stairs was slow and tedious. Eleazar's heart was racing faster than the old man's footsteps.

In the upper room, Eleazar threw back the curtain, exposing several shelves littered with vials, pouches, bowls, mortars, pestles, and cruses of oil. Stepping back, he allowed Judah to search through the supply.

The old man's hands trembled. He spilled a vial of liquid. He dropped a pouch of herbs. He sniffed different bundles, pressed his finger to a powder and placed it on his tongue. Eleazar stepped from one foot to the other, anxious to return to the marketplace. Then, to his relief, the old man nodded his head and made a selection. His hands still shaking, Judah awkwardly mixed the herb with a splash of olive oil.

"Have Achim drink this. I can't promise a cure, my son, but it's all I can remember."

"I bought some powdered ivory, Father." Eleazar held up the pouch.

Judah nodded. "Make a poultice and apply it to his sores."

Eleazar worked quickly, mixing part of the ivory and some water into a thick paste. He held the mixture before his father. Again, Judah nodded his approval.

Eleazar shook his head in wonder. After all his years of training—the trip to Alexandria, the books, the scrolls, the note-taking, the memorizations, the long hours following Nikolaus around the city—when he needed a remedy to help his best friend, his one hope lay with the simple brain of an aging physician.

Judah's shuffling feet made the journey down the stairs even more distressing than the climb up. Eleazar backed down in front of the old man, balancing the medicines in one hand and bracing Judah's arm with the other, so the old man wouldn't fall. With each labored step, he held his breath, eager to be on his way. They finally reached the bottom. Eleazar helped his father get settled in his chamber. Then he ran into the street and raced back to the marketplace.

The entire square was buzzing with more activity than when Eleazar had left. A group of veiled women bearing baskets of produce blocked his path to the far end where he had last seen Achim's stall. He wove through the crowd, bumping people's arms, taking care not to drop the precious medicines. When, at last, he reached the secluded corner, he stood in shock. Achim's stall was gone. He looked around the square, thinking he'd chosen the wrong place. There was no sign of his friend.

One by one, he asked the merchants in nearby stalls if they had seen where Achim went. They knew nothing. He stood very still, just staring at the empty space. Other vendors had started closing in on the location with their overabundance of goods. Eleazar backed away.

Turning, he hurried in the direction of Achim's house. He took long strides along the winding street, stumbled over a break in the pavement, then, panting for breath, he reached the house.

He pounded on the door. There was only silence. He pounded again. Achim's mother opened the door a crack. Seeing Eleazar, she snorted and retreated inside without a word.

"Please, Zilpah. Is Achim at home? I need to see him."

The urgency in his voice drew her back to the door, and though she remained hidden, she answered him. "He's gone to see the priest. Now leave me alone."

"Mattathias," Eleazar murmured. Of course. Such examinations were given to the old priest. He envisioned Achim at the temple now, showing his blemish and speaking of the numbness in his left hand. He imagined him listening to Mattathias' judgment. He envisioned Achim accepting the seven-day quarantine. He needed to stop his friend before he disappeared from the city, needed to try his father's medicines on him.

Eleazar ran up the hill toward the temple. Though he was gasping for air, he lunged up the broad steps and ran to the men's court. When he arrived there, he found a young priest polishing the cedar railings.

"Where is the priest named Mattathias?"

Startled, the priest turned to look at him. He frowned with annoyance. "Mattathias is lighting the lamps near the women's court." Then he turned his back on Eleazar and went back to work.

Outside the women's court, Eleazar spotted the frail, old priest with his long, ropelike beard and familiar white band around his brow. His long garment was also white, and around his waist was a belt woven from strands of hemp. With a steady hand, the old priest lit the final saucer and sent a tongue of acrid smoke into the atmosphere.

Eleazar walked toward him. Mattathias recognized him immediately. "And, what can I do for you, physician?"

"I'm concerned for a friend. Achim, the merchant. Has he come to see you?"

"Achim." Mattathias nodded. "Yes. Yes. He came to the temple a short while ago. I examined him myself."

"I saw him earlier today in the marketplace." Eleazar strained to keep from bursting out in sobs. "He showed me his affliction. I hurried home to prepare a medicine for him." He held up the vial. "When I returned, Achim had vanished along with all of his wares."

A sadness filled the old priest's eyes. Reaching out with both hands, he gripped Eleazar's shoulders. "I'm afraid your friend's condition appears hopeless." Mattathias frowned. "For year's I've served as the examiner for such diseases. I've seen this infection before. I regret to tell you it looks to be a fast-moving leprosy. There are several signs. The numbness in Achim's fingers. And the sores on his neck. They are beginning to change color, as did several patches on his scalp beneath his turban. Achim has the most aggressive form of the disease. I fear not even you can save him."

Eleazar stepped back. "I can't accept this." He shook his head. "I *won't* accept it. I've seen a good many infections myself, Mattathias. Some have been simple wounds that went away with treatment. As a merchant Achim travels great distances. He could have been infected during one of his journeys. Such things often heal in time."

Eleazar squirmed under Mattathias' sympathetic gaze.

"I'm sorry, Eleazar. I hope Achim's time in quarantine will prove me wrong, that he will return healed and in good health, but all of the signs—"

"Where is he? I want to see him. Has he left the city?"

"No. He chose the quarantine room." Mattathias gestured with a wave of his hand. "There. The cubical in the far corner where he can receive meals from the priests. But, I must advise you, he can see no one. Not even you, Eleazar. In seven days, he'll come out and be reexamined in accordance with the law. Hopefully, as you suggest, the sores will have healed and the numbness will have subsided. If that happens, I can pronounce him clean, and your friend can perform the necessary cleansing rituals. But you must wait seven days. It's the law. Seven days, my friend."

Mattathias ended with an air of finality. But Eleazar did not want to give up on his friend.

"If I can't see him, please, Mattathias, would you pass these medicines through the opening where he receives his food?"

Mattathias stroked his beard.

"My father once ministered to the lepers on the hill," Eleazar pressed. "He helped me make these preparations. This one is for Achim to drink. This other one must be applied to his sores."

Releasing a sigh, Mattathias accepted the medicines, but he uttered one more word of counsel.

"Prepare yourself, my son. You can do nothing more except pray for Yahweh's help. Offer a sacrifice, and pray for a miracle. Without it, I see little hope. "Come back in a week."

Mattathias turned away and carried the medicines to the quarantine chamber.

Eleazar watched him depart. *Pray? Pray to someone I've never known? How can I expect Yahweh to hear my prayer, when I've ignored Him for most of my life? Must I repent of the sins I've committed and assume He's going to forgive me? How many more sacrifices will I have to make beyond what I've already offered?*

Feeling defeated, Eleazar walked out of the temple, his head down, his heart breaking. Achim may very well have leprosy. Then a spark of truth struck him, and he had to admit, he, too, had become a leper of sorts, if only on the inside. His heart was full of sores from a lifetime of wrong choices and sinful deeds. A leper? He was the worst of them.

A week later, Eleazar returned to the temple and again sought out Mattathias. He waited in the outer court until he heard the old man's labored step rising from a narrow hallway at the far end. He turned to see Mattathias approaching.

The priest's sad face sent a chill down Eleazar's spine.

"I'm sorry," Mattathias whispered.

"What about the medicines? Did Achim use them? Did he show any sign of improvement?"

His face grim, Mattathias appeared to struggle for an answer. When he spoke, his voice trembled. "My son, there has been no change. It appears Achim's condition has grown worse. I had no other choice but to send him away."

Eleazar let out a resounding, "No!" His agonized cry bounced off the temple walls and drew the attention of several priests who were on their knees cleansing the pavement. Tears surfaced, and Eleazar sobbed unashamedly. He covered his face with his hands, bowed from his waist and swayed back and forth, finally crumbling into a ball at the priest's feet.

Mattathias stroked his back and murmured words of comfort, but they did little to ease Eleazar's anguish. Rising, he tore his robe down the middle and continued to wail. "Achim. My friend."

The old priest wrapped an arm around Eleazar's shoulder. "Come. Come with me into the priest's chamber. You can find solace there. You can collect your thoughts and pray for peace."

Pray? There was that word again. A useless word to Eleazar. He had never benefited from prayer. Never found peace in all of the sacrifices and ordinances and laws of Moses. What good would prayer do his friend now?

He stumbled alongside Mattathias, blinded by his tears, the pavement tilting beneath his feet. He entered the tiny room and fell to the floor. He stayed there for a long time, wanting to pray, but words wouldn't come. When he emerged, the sun had arched high in the sky. It's merciless rays beat down on the open court.

Eleazar left the temple and went out of the city. He passed the elders at the gate without acknowledging their greetings. He descended into the Kidron Valley and proceeded up the hill to the Mount of Olives. Squinting against the sun, he looked toward the east. Far off in the distance, the mauve colored hills of Moab lay strung along the horizon. Closer to Jerusalem on the nearby ridge were the leper caves. They still existed, still welcomed the afflicted into their gaping holes.

He stood there for a long time just staring at those dark caves and remembering the shrouded figures that resided there. His heart ached. Perhaps Achim had made his way to the caves. Or he could be wandering around in the wilderness like so many of them did. He'd never be able to find him now.

CHAPTER THIRTY

Another Sabbath passed. Eleazar slipped out of the house with the pouch of opium in one hand and the ring he had purchased in the other. He went directly to the palace, boldly entered Marcus' chamber, and thrust the pouch into the Roman's hand.

Marcus checked the contents. Satisfied, he smiled with disdain and waved Eleazar away.

Eleazar was thankful for the brief visit. He'd come to see Ruth, not Marcus, and the only reason he entered the Roman's chamber was to hand over the pouch. He left in a hurry and went directly to the garden room and his love.

When Ruth arrived, Eleazar rushed toward her and kissed her forehead, her cheeks, her mouth. Then he took a step back and opened his hand. The dancing candlelight put sparks on the green stone. Ruth laughed with delight. Her adoring gaze set Eleazar's heart to pounding. He slipped the ring on her second finger, a perfect fit.

Ruth held her hand high and admired his gift. "I will treasure this more than all of your other presents. This will be my marriage ring." She lowered her hand and stared into his face. "We don't need a contract or parental approval, Eleazar. We only need each other."

Eleazar took her hand. "Sit with me." He led her through the open door to the garden. They walked together along the marble path and settled on a stone bench beneath a flowering almond tree, its pink blossoms dropping in a steady rainfall. Eleazar raised her hand to his lips and held it there.

He needed to tell her about Achim's disease, needed to share his pain with her. He sighed heavily, for no one understood his heart as Ruth did.

"My friend Achim is ill." He choked out the first words, then he took another breath. "He's left the city. The priest declared him a leper."

"A leper?" Ruth gasped. "I don't understand. When did this happen?"

Tears surfaced and stung his eyes. "I wanted to help, but I could do nothing to save him."

Eleazar did not restrain his own flow of tears. Ruth began to weep with him. They wrapped their arms around each other and cried without shame. Bending low, Eleazar rested his head on Ruth's lap and continued to sob out his pain. His entire body trembled with the release of his grief. His shoulders lurched with each burst of sorrow. Ruth stroked his back. She placed a cool hand on his forehead. She didn't speak a word, simply held him close. There would be no love-making tonight. Just two people clinging to each other, their broken hearts bound together in deep lamentation.

When it came time to leave, Ruth pressed her palm against his chest. "I have some news of my own." Her lashes were wet with tears. She had the slightest hint of a smile on her lips.

"News? What news?"

"After hearing your news about Achim I wasn't going to say anything tonight." She brightened slightly. "But I'm bursting with joy, Eleazar, and perhaps what I have to tell you will ease your pain."

"What is it, my love? Speak to me."

Ruth gazed into his eyes. Then she spoke the words that would alter their lives forever.

"It seems I am with child again."

He sought her face for more. "Is it—Levi's?"

Ruth shook her head and laughed, her eyes sparkling. "The child is yours, Eleazar."

"*My* child? You're certain? This child is *mine*?"

Ruth laughed again, and her whole face lit up.

Now, in the midst of intense grief, Eleazar's beloved had brought him unexpected joy. His heart pounding, he embraced her, gently, at first, then with unrestrained passion.

"Do you know what this means, Ruth? It means we're eternally bound together. We're going to be a family."

"Yes, I believe the same. No matter what happens, we will have something no one can ever take away from us. We will have a child of our own."

Eleazar then asked the question that was pressing on his mind. "And, what of Levi? Will he suspect infidelity?"

"I'm waiting for the right time. I want to make sure he will think the child is his."

Eleazar stepped back. His joy faded slightly. "How do you know for certain this child is mine?"

Ruth hadn't stopped smiling. She looked at him now as though talking to an innocent child. "Eleazar, you must understand. Though I've done so unwillingly, I have submitted to Levi according to his desire. I had no choice. But I've counted the days and the weeks. I'm certain this child is yours. When Levi does the numbering using the dates *I* will give him, he will be convinced the child is his." She reached for his hand. "But you and I will know the truth. It's *our* child, Eleazar. I have no doubt."

Eleazar's surge of jealousy diminished. Of course, Ruth had to fulfill her nightly duty to her husband. How could he expect otherwise? But now Ruth was going to bear *his* child, and nothing else mattered. A cunning smile crept across his lips. And Levi would never know.

"Now listen," Ruth went on. "I'm nearing the time when I must go hide myself. Once my condition is evident, I will have to remain at home."

"And afterward? When the child arrives will you return to me? Will you bring my son—or daughter—and allow me to embrace the proof of our love?"

"Of course, I will. Nothing will keep me from you."

While awaiting the birth of his child, Eleazar dove into his work. He visited the sick, increased the stock of medicines in his apothecary, and studied a new pile of medical scrolls by the light of a candle at night.

One afternoon as dusk was approaching, Eleazar finished calling on the sick and started for home. Suddenly a hand came out of the shadows and gripped his shoulder. He spun around to see a familiar face.

"Enos! You startled me." He laughed and patted his friend on the back.

Enos didn't laugh. Instead, his face was lined with concern.

"What have you done?" Enos' tone was sharp. "Don't you know you've come under the watchful eye of the Council?"

Eleazar frowned at him. "What are you talking about? I've been dealing with sick people all day." He lifted his medical box. "I'm on my way home." He gestured with his free arm. "Come on. Walk with me."

"There's talk you made a deal with Marcus. The Sanhedrin frowns on such behavior. Don't you know Jews must separate themselves from those barbarians? If you've entered the home of a Gentile, you must submit to a ceremonial cleansing."

"I don't follow those rules. I'm a physician. I am called to heal."

"My father asked me to find out what I can. He said you've been seen entering the palace regularly. He wants to know why. What kind of agreement do you have with that worthless Roman?"

"I provide medicines, that's all, the same way I do for everyone else. You know I have no issues with people of other cultures. Many Jews have accepted the Helenistic teachings. I am one of them."

"That kind of talk could end your chance for a Council seat."

"The 70 have to consider everything. I'm a prominent physician. I take care of my aging father. And I have a growing family. Those things should satisfy them.

"Marcus already has a personal physician. Why would he call on you?"

Eleazar shrugged. "He sent his physician away months ago. Be at ease, Enos. And tell your father he can be at ease too. There is no problem, no conspiracy. I'm simply doing my work as a physician, nothing more."

"Eleazar, the man isn't ill. He entertains worthless Romans who claim to be his friends. He's a fat glutton who oppresses the poor. He drains the population of their livelihood through taxes, and he spends the money on himself and his endless parties. What business do *you* have with him? Please, Eleazar, give me something I can tell my father. Help me put this rumor to rest."

"I told you, Enos, I give him medicine for simple ailments. And, he pays me well."

Enos shook his head. "How could you have gotten involved with him? You must know a conflict has arisen between the Romans and the Jews. Our people grow tired of those oppressors. Some are planning a rebellion. They call themselves Zealots. They want to take back our city and be rid of Rome forever."

"Enos, you know I have never been involved in political conflicts. I dislike the Roman rule as much as any other Jew. But I don't get mixed up in government affairs. Nor will I support the Zealots. I simply pay my taxes and live my life."

A flicker of doubt entered Eleazar's heart. He stopped walking and looked at his friend. "My association with Marcus should not affect the Council's decision."

Enos stared into his eyes. "I'm telling you, Eleazar, if you want to become a member of the Sanhedrin, you need to walk in the same manner as the other members."

Eleazar placed a comforting hand on Enos' shoulder.

"Then I will start to take more of an interest in the government," he said, smiling. "Even so, my main goal will continue to be to serve the sick. No matter *who* they are. Surely, they can't deny me the duty I have as a physician."

"Then, that will be my report to the Council. And you'd better pray they are contented with it."

Several months passed. Purim was upon them. A light snow had dusted the city streets. Eleazar loaded his wife and children on a cart, hitched it to their horse and led the animal down an icy path to the home of Simon in Bethany. It had been two years since he had last seen his brother. Now Simon had invited his family to celebrate the Purim meal and the traditional exchange of gifts. Eleazar had packed a solid gold urn stuffed full of candied dates, pomegranates, and a variety of nuts. Anna had made a fruit bread to share with the family.

When they arrived in Simon's courtyard, Eleazar's mood changed from joyous expectation to troubling concern. His brother greeted them outside the house, his face drawn, his shoulders hunched. His eyes were red and swollen as if he hadn't slept for days.

He peered over Eleazar's shoulder. "I had hoped Father would come."

Eleazar shook his head sadly. "I'm sorry. That stubborn man chose to remain at home by the window that faces the temple. There's something unholy about a man who prays day and night yet continues to reject his youngest son. Our father fed the poor and tended to lepers, but he won't throw a single crumb to the child of his loins."

Simon shrugged. Dismissing his pain with a wave of his hand, he linked his arm in Eleazar's and led him inside the house. Eleazar gave him the urn and Simon presented him with one of his large woven baskets filled with beans and lentils and yellow gourds from his garden.

Simon's wife, Marita, beckoned the family to sit at their table where she'd already laid out platters of breads and pastries, a pan bubbling over with lentil stew, and a generous pile of roasted leeks and potatoes. The aromas filled the room and drew Eleazar's eyes to the lavish spread.

The children flooded into the house, Eleazar's three and Simon's two. They dropped to the floor on one side of the low table, plumping their pillows, laughing and jostling against one another. The adults gathered around the other side, where they could visit apart from the children's play.

As they dined, Eleazar kept an eye on his son, Benjamin, who was sitting next to Simon's daughter, Rachel, still a child, but beginning to blossom. The young girl didn't seem to mind Benjamin's stammering. In fact, Rachel sat very still and waited patiently for the boy to complete every sentence. She giggled at times over something silly he said. But, she didn't make fun of him. Nor did she pressure him to hurry his speech.

Eleazar turned to Simon. "It's time we considered blending our families. I would like to propose a marriage contract between my Benjamin and your Rachel."

The two children stopped chattering and stared wide-eyed at Eleazar. The two mothers grinned and squeezed each other's hand. Simon was the only one not smiling.

"Do you realize what you're asking," Simon gestured toward the hearth where a pile of unfinished baskets lay, their crumbling sides evidence of Simon's lack of supplies.

"Look around you, Eleazar. Do you see how things are with us? We are poor. You are rich. This food came from our garden. You have enough money to buy whatever you want in the marketplace. I can't even buy enough straw to complete a single basket." He shook his head. "Benjamin should not wed below his stature."

Eleazar's frown deepened. "I don't understand, Simon. Two years ago, you had the promise of great wealth. Remember your deal with Levi? Did he not fulfill his part of the agreement?"

Simon reached for a piece of bread but didn't bite into it. He avoided Eleazar's gaze.

"I invested everything I had." Simon chewed on the bread and swallowed. "It's gone. All of it. Levi sent me a worthless excuse through one of his servants. The boy said his master's creditors had failed to provide, and so he had no choice but to spill his losses on the rest of us. I sought him out. I needed to know more. I went to his home in the city. He refused me entrance."

"Why didn't you come to me? I live only two doors away from that thief. You had to pass by my house to get to his. Why didn't you stop? I would have gone with you."

Simon tossed his head to one side. "I wanted to handle it myself, Eleazar. Besides, I didn't want Father to know."

"But the man stole from you."

"I have no proof. Levi's word means nothing. Nor does his name on a contract. He does whatever is best for him, and the rest of us suffer."

"You had a contract? Where is it? I want to see it."

Simon shrugged. "I signed a piece of parchment. It meant little to me. Remember, Eleazar, after our mother died, I left home at such a young age I had to let my studies go. Unlike you, I never learned to read well. Instead, I pursued our uncle's trade and did quite well at it. Perhaps, if I could have read the contract I would have used better judgment."

"It doesn't matter whether or not you can read. How could you have trusted Levi? Show me the parchment."

Simon shrank under Eleazar's angry stare. The women ate in silence. The children also stopped their play.

"It's too late." Simon choked out the words. He looked sheepishly at Eleazar. "Levi carried the contract away with him. I cannot pursue him in the courts. Even if I did, what good would it do? He always has the backing of the Council. You can be sure Levi has even deceived the Seventy and gotten away with it."

"And, what about the other men who took part in the deal? What has become of them?"

Simon let out a heavy sigh. "Fools, like me. They too lost everything. One of them was dragged off to prison for not paying his debts. Except for my baskets, I fear I would have joined him there."

Eleazar's heart began racing. He would love to bring Levi before the Council and expose his evil. A bad report about Levi could bring about his removal from membership.

He looked at Simon and a surge of pity flowed through him. For now he'd have to forget about Levi and simply do something to raise his brother from his losses.

"Let me help you, Simon. I'm your next of kin. Whatever I have also belongs to you. I'm rich. I have enough money for both of us. I can provide whatever you need, money for straw and whatever else you want, plus a suitable dowry for your daughter. Then Rachel can be bound to Benjamin."

Simon clenched his jaw. "Haven't you heard me, Eleazar? Rachel must remain without a promise until I can restore my funds. I won't have it any other way."

Ignoring his brother's refusal, Eleazar reached inside his robe and withdrew a leather pouch. Spreading it open, he dumped a pile of gold and silver coins on the table. The children screamed with delight.

"There will be more," Eleazar assured his brother.

Tears welled up in Simon's eyes. "I can't expect you to pay for my mistakes."

"Consider it a loan, an investment in your business, whatever you want to call it. You can get the materials you need to make more baskets. When you sell them, we *both* will profit. Forget about Levi. Put your mistake behind you and move ahead."

Openly humbled, Simon leaned toward his brother and embraced him.

Looking over Simon's shoulder, Eleazar caught a view of Benjamin and Rachel, their heads close together. Their intimacy sparked a memory of himself with a young, spirited girl in Gethsemane so many years ago. He pushed away from Simon and looked his brother in the eye.

"In a few years our children will be of age. By that time, your finances will be secure, and we can plan a wedding unlike any other."

Early the next morning, Eleazar returned to Simon's house carrying a large moneybag. This time, he came leading a donkey, and on its back sat Judah.

Eleazar helped his father slide off the animal. The old man's step faltered as he shuffled toward Simon's door. Simon emerged from the house, his mouth open in amazement. Squinting against the sunlight, Judah's youngest son took a step toward his father. He hesitated, then with three quick strides, he fell into Judah's open arms and wept without restraint.

"Abba." The word broke from Simon's throat.

The two held a long embrace. Eleazar looked on, his lips parted in a satisfied smile. With that one hug decades of hostility melted away, and father and son were restored

Stepping back, Judah faced his youngest. "Simon," he said, his voice hoarse. "I waited far too long to come to you. Can you forgive a bitter old man?"

Simon's countenance softened. Wrapping one arm around his father's shoulder, he led him toward the house. "Come, Father. I want you to meet my family."

Eleazar followed them. His eyes flooded with tears as Judah bent on one knee and embraced his grandchildren for the very first time.

CHAPTER THIRTY-ONE
A.D. 29

A steamy summer evening sent waves of heat rising from the cobbled path in the Upper City. Eleazar trudged toward home, his scrip of medicines dangling from one shoulder, his eyes burning, his entire body weary from far too many sick calls. He felt drained and was eager to recline at home on a mound of pillows. He thought of the supper Anna and her servants were preparing—roast lamb, vegetables steaming on the hearth, and Anna's famed raisin and nut bread.

He had almost reached his gate, when a young female darted from the side of the road and blocked his path. He recognized her at once. *Ruth's handmaid.* She was the same young servant who had summoned him to Malachi's bedside several years ago. His heartbeat quickened.

The girl lowered her chin shyly and peered at him with round, dark eyes. "My mistress—she sent me to tell you—I–I mean, she wanted you to know—"

"Speak up, girl. Tell me what?" The blood had rushed to Eleazar's head. Already worn from a heavy workload, his impatience began to boil.

"She–she has borne a daughter." She paused as the news sank in. "The child's name is Martha."

A daughter? Ruth had borne him a baby girl? Disappointment surged into his heart. She'd given Levi a son and had given him a daughter. Would he never surpass that man at anything?

Then he thought about his beloved Ruth, the love of his life. His disappointment immediately subsided and was supplanted by an overwhelming sense of joy. So Ruth had given him a daughter. He loved the babe already, for she was the offspring of their unbroken love.

He quickly came to his senses. "Is the mother well?"

"She is." The girl raised her head and smiled.

"And the child?"

"She also does well. Do you have a response for my mistress?"

"Tell her—" His lower lip quivered, and a lump formed in his throat. He fought against the sobbing that was sure to come. "Tell her, the news brings me great joy."

Eleazar quickly turned his back on the girl and entered his courtyard with tears streaming down his face.

Six months passed. It seemed like an eternity to Eleazar as he waited for more word from Ruth. Then, one morning, he spotted her in the marketplace, walking with her handmaid. Ruth had a linen-wrapped bundle strapped to her chest. Her handmaid bore a large basket laden with fresh vegetables. As he approached them, the handmaid separated from Ruth and busied herself at a nearby stall.

"Ruth," he whispered as he drew near.

She looked up at him, her eyes melting in instant adoration.

"Your child," she breathed, and she pulled back a corner of the linen, exposing an angelic pink face.

"Martha. My dearly beloved Martha," he murmured. "She's beautiful, Ruth. She's an exact image of her mother. Look. She already has your hair, black as a raven's, and your skin, like ivory, pure and unblemished."

"And your eyes," Ruth said. "They're silver gray, the one clue that she came from your loins."

He frowned with concern. "Your husband has no suspicions?"

"None expressed. I told him my grandfather had gray eyes. It hardly mattered to him. The man is so consumed with his business dealings, he rarely even notices *me* anymore. And poor Malachi. He yearns for a father's attention. I fear when he approaches manhood his only learning will have come from me and our male servants."

Ruth's concern for her son touched Eleazar's heart. At the same time, her complaint about Levi's lack of interest in the boy stirred his own feelings of guilt. Hadn't he done the same with Benjamin who now got all of his teaching from Judah?

"I regret I have not done much better with my own children," Eleazar admitted. "Mara has already grown into a young woman. Several of my friends have approached me and have suggested a match with their sons. I have yet to make a decision, but I am leaning toward Enos' son. Then there's my Benjamin. He has turned to his grandfather for guidance. The two have bonded to such a length it's impossible for me to get close to my son. It's my own fault. I let the moments slip away from me."

She placed a hand on his arm. "That's tragic, Eleazar. Sometimes we learn such things too late. Perhaps in future days you will be able to heal this division between you and the boy."

He smiled at her innocence. Heal this division? How? When an identical division had existed between himself and his own father for years.

"The greatest tragedy in my home is little Abi." He shook his head despondently. "She remains frail, almost sickly. I fear for her life. I've checked every medicine in my store, but I've found nothing to help her grow and thrive. If she survives to womanhood, what man will want her? I fear she's destined to be a childless spinster should she live that long."

"I'm very sorry," Ruth said with sincere sympathy.

He offered a grateful smile and shrugged. "Thankfully, Anna and Judah have been able to keep our home safe and flourishing. I have provided material wealth—everything they need—but I have denied them myself. Now a wall has gone up, and I don't know how to tear it down." He shook his head. "I neglected my family and plunged into my work, and now I'm reaping the punishment for my mistakes."

Ruth gave him a half-smile. "Mistakes? Was I one of your mistakes?"

"No Ruth, no. You were the one thing in my life that was *not* a mistake."

A sadness clouded her face. "I drew you away from your home. I am as much to blame as you are."

"Listen to me. You're not to blame. In the midst of all my wanderings, you have given me joy. And now we have a baby of our own. I won't make the same mistake with *this* child. Martha will know she is loved."

Smiling, Ruth removed the baby from her pack and placed her in Eleazar's arms. The almost weightless child encased in a light blanket softened his heart. He drew little Martha close to his chest and pressed his lips against her forehead. He breathed deeply of her scent. She stared back at him, and, like Ruth had said, her silver gray eyes mirrored his own. One small hand emerged from the wrappings. Martha's tiny fingers grasped his beard and tugged. Eleazar grinned, and his heart throbbed with tenderness.

He turned his attention to Ruth. "Bring her to me at the palace. Allow me to enjoy my daughter as often as possible."

Ruth nodded. "I will."

Eleazar relinquished the child into her mother's arms. "But come with caution," he warned. "Marcus grows weary. He asks for stronger medicines. Some are difficult to obtain. I long for the day when he and his followers return to Rome."

"When that happens, we'll find another place," Ruth offered.

Touching his fingertips to his mouth, he pressed them to the baby's forehead then to Ruth's lips. He mouthed the words, *I love you.* Then he tore himself away from the two most important people in his life.

A.D. 30

Ruth remained true to her promise. When she and Eleazar resumed their visits she also brought Martha along. Eleazar's heart surged with joy at the sight of them. On such evenings, he put aside his daily concerns and entered another world, one that he and Ruth had created for themselves, an escape from the lives that had been forced upon them against their wishes.

Months passed. The child grew. Eleazar watched her struggle to walk. He heard the first word out of her mouth. *Abba.* It thrilled him. From that first day in the marketplace, Eleazar determined he would bond with this child as he had not done with his other three. Martha's face had begun to take on more of her mother's features. Her shiny black curls and cream-colored skin reminded him of Ruth in her younger days. Then, there were those silver gray eyes, and, though Eleazar found pleasure in them, he feared Levi might look into them one day and see the truth.

At every visit Martha lunged into her father's arms, confident he'd catch her as she left the floor. Life couldn't get much better. Until, one night, Ruth came alone. A darkness had fallen over her usual joyous spirit.

Eleazar set aside the gift he had purchased for the child. "Where's Martha?" His eyes darted toward the open door.

Ruth raised a hand to calm him. "We must talk."

His heart pounding, he grabbed her shoulders. "Has something happened to Martha? Do you need my services? Where is she?"

Ruth slipped out of his grasp. "Martha is well, Eleazar. My handmaid is caring for her at home."

"Then why didn't you bring her? What's wrong?"

For years, he'd been able to read Ruth's thoughts. He knew when her husband had abused her. He knew when Levi was away. He even suspected when the man had drawn her into his bed. What's more, without her saying a word, he knew when she was happy, when she was sad, even when she was annoyed with him. No matter how hard she tried, Ruth had never been able to keep her feelings a secret from him. Now, for the first time, he couldn't read her mind.

"Something's wrong. Tell me, Ruth, before I burst."

"Eleazar—" Her eyes flooded with tears. He waited, his stomach tightening into a hard knot. She started to turn away, as if she found it unbearable to have him look at her.

Then she faced him and boldly said, "I can no longer meet with you."

"What?" He grabbed her arm. "Why, Ruth? What's happened? Has Levi found out about us?"

She shook her head and slipped out of his grasp. "Levi knows nothing. Please understand, Eleazar. It isn't about Levi. It isn't even about *you*. It's about me and remorse over our sin."

"Our sin? You never thought of our time together as sin. Why now?"

Eleazar could feel her pulling away from him. He reached for her hand. She drew it back. An invisible barrier had risen between them. Though he longed for an answer he wasn't prepared for the one she was about to give him.

"I had an encounter the other day—at the temple." Her voice softened with tenderness. "I don't understand it all," she went on. "But I do know my life has changed, Eleazar. I see things more clearly now. My sin rose up before me and condemned me. And, just as quickly, it was replaced by overwhelming peace."

Ruth smiled, but it wasn't the familiar adoring smile that delighted him. This smile was different. It was longsuffering, and the tone of her voice was distant, yet it bore a certain strength Ruth had never shown before.

"Eleazar, what we've been doing is wrong." She held up a hand to stop his protest. "We've always known the truth, but we've continued to ignore it. I can no longer be a part of such wrongdoing, nor can I encourage you in this sin."

"Please, Ruth, don't throw away what we have. I dealt with the guilt a long time ago. Through no fault of our own we were bound to the wrong people from the beginning. *We* didn't make the mistake. Our parents did. Now, I beg you, consider what we have had these few years. Consider Martha. Isn't she the offspring of a perfect love?"

Ruth shook her head. "Stop, Eleazar. We've been deceiving ourselves. We knew the law, and we disregarded it."

"The law? And, what has the law done for us except to make us feel guilty for pursuing happiness? We have made a place for ourselves that has been good and whole and right."

"But it's *not* right for me. Not anymore." Her sharp tone startled him. "The truth is—" She lowered her gaze as though unable to look him in the eye. "I've taken a good look at myself. Eleazar, I'm no better than a common harlot."

He burned with anger. "Don't reproach yourself this way! I've never thought of you as a harlot, nor will I stand here and allow you to claim such a vile condemnation."

Ruth backed away from him. Keeping her voice soft, she continued to speak.

"Eleazar, I have loved you with an everlasting love. She placed her hands over her heart. "In return, I've received a love I never dreamed possible. You're strong, yet gentle, and so calming when I need you to be. You have not failed me since our youth. I'll cherish our time together for the rest of my life. But these private meetings must stop. When I leave here tonight, it will be the last time you will see me. Or Martha."

Eleazar reached out to her. She evaded his grasp.

"I don't understand, Ruth. Why have you changed?"

She looked away from him, then, her eyes met his, and she spoke the words that would shatter his heart. "I went to the temple the other day and as I walked through Solomon's Porch, my eyes were drawn to the most extraordinary man."

A flood of heat rushed to Eleazar's face.

Ruth's eyes took on a distant look that confused him. "He

was an unusual man. People said he was a healer from Galilee, a miracle worker." She spoke almost in a whisper now.

Eleazar scowled. "Healer? Miracle worker? Did he study in Alexandria, as *I* did? Did he carry a scrip filled with the newest medicines and physician's tools? Take me to him, and I'll match wits with him."

Ruth laughed, and he bristled. "You shouldn't feel threatened, Eleazar," she said. "Others referred to him as Teacher, Master, and Rabbi. One man even used the word *Messiah.* Then one of his companions spoke his name—Jesus." She said it with such love in her voice Eleazar burned with envy.

"Jesus? That's an overused name in our country. If he's so special why does he have a common name? Tell me, did you speak to him? Did he approach you?"

"I didn't speak to him, Eleazar. I never met him."

"Then, how has he won your heart away from me?"

Her eyes aglow, Ruth shrugged off Eleazar's jealousy and continued to speak with tenderness about the man in the temple.

"He was just standing there in Solomon's Porch, speaking to a large crowd, including scribes and Pharisees who had gathered there. They were questioning him. Some of their voices sounded angry. But he remained calm and in control. I watched him from a distance. I stepped behind one of the pillars and hid in the shadows."

"Did he frighten you? Did you feel threatened?"

Ruth shook her head and smiled sweetly. "No, I wasn't frightened. Not by him. But a strange peace fell over the gathering, like the gentle calm that precedes a storm. At that moment, several men dragged a woman into the courtyard and forced her to the ground at Jesus' feet. Her dress was muddied and torn, and her face and hands were covered with dirt. I couldn't help but feel great pity for her. The men accused her of adultery and demanded that Jesus give his approval for a stoning. How strange that these men of renown in their costly robes, with phylacteries displayed on their arms, should commit the woman's judgment to this humble visitor who wore only a modest teacher's robe and a linen mantle on his head. Yet that is what they did. They challenged him to declare judgment on that poor woman."

Eleazar began to pace, looking up occasionally at Ruth as she continued to plague him with her story.

"I felt sorry for the woman. She was so broken. She didn't try to defend herself but submitted to the angry mob. Those men disgraced her before a great number of people."

Eleazar seethed with anger. "I don't understand what this has to do with us. So a group of prominent citizens demanded a word of judgment from this nobody from Galilee. Why should that matter to us? A woman was caught in the act of adultery. She was brought to judgment and deserved to be stoned. This happens all the time in Judea. Why do you care? Was she a friend? Was she an important woman in the city? What made this stoning different from all the others?"

Concern wrinkled Ruth's forehead. She sighed.

"No, Eleazar, I didn't know her. In fact I had never seen her before. But I felt drawn to her. Those men wanted her stoned for the sin of adultery, a sin I also have committed—with you. That could have been *me* being dragged there, to the center of Solomon's Porch, for everyone to see and for our years of sinfulness to be exposed."

Eleazar ran a hand through his hair. "You speak foolishness, Ruth. You're *not* that harlot. You haven't given yourself to lots of men. Only to one, and rightfully so. What we've had is special. How can you compare yourself with a simple whore?"

"I don't know if she had multiple lovers or only one. Admit it, Eleazar, her transgression is similar to ours. Perhaps her parents also kept her away from the one she loved. But take your mind off of her and look at what *we've* done. *We* fell into sin. *I* am an adulteress. I have defiled my marriage bed. I have betrayed my husband. I have robbed my friend Anna of the life she should have had with you. I have kept you from your children. If I'm not an adulteress, Eleazar, then who is?"

"I'm not going to listen to this." Eleazar spun away from her. He walked into the garden, his steps hard against the marble floor.

She followed him there. "Eleazar—" she pleaded.

He turned to face her. "Don't throw away what we have. Do you think I will let you go so easily? How can you expect me to never see you again, to never hold my little Martha again? Forget about the woman in the courtyard and look into my eyes. See the love that resides there. Hear the pleading of my voice."

She answered him calmly, her voice firm and in control.

"Eleazar, it's too late. I've already made up my mind, and I can't turn back. I watched that woman, broken and submitting to Jesus' judgment. Each of her accusers held a stone. They waited for one word of condemnation from him. Just one."

Ruth's eyes darkened. "I trembled there in the shadows. It was the middle of the day, stifling hot, yet I was shaking. I held my breath and waited for the stones to fly. In my heart I knew that whatever judgment this man passed on that woman he also was passing it on me."

"Did they stone her?" Eleazar asked, then held his breath.

"Jesus looked into the eyes of the woman's accusers. Those self-righteous men melted under his gaze. Then he did something really strange. He bent to the ground, and with his finger he wrote something in the dust. I was too far away to see what he had written, but those men could see it. He stood up and spoke to them with authority, saying that whoever had no sin should be the first to cast a stone. He stooped down again and wrote something else. Their response was amazing. One by one, they dropped their stones and left the courtyard, until the woman knelt alone before Jesus."

Eleazar pictured the scene. Angry men had been turned into cowering dogs. A woman who had sinned had been released from judgment. And what of the man who had commanded such power?

"What Jesus did next touched my heart," Ruth said. Tears filled her eyes and began to spill down her face. "He spoke so softly I had to strain to hear him. He asked the woman where her accusers were. She looked about. In a voice so weak I could barely discern it, she told him the men had left. Then, Jesus said—and I'll never forget his words—'Neither do I accuse you. Go and sin no more.'"

Ruth began to sob. "Go and sin no more, Eleazar. Go and sin no more. His words pierced my very soul. There I was, hidden from view, yet Jesus' words soared across the courtyard and reached me there behind the pillar. Don't you understand? The words he spoke to the adulteress he also spoke to *me*."

Eleazar shook his head. He couldn't breathe.

"He let the woman go?! He heard the evidence against her, and he still let her go? This goes against all that is righteous. Those men of the city had proof of that woman's sin. They didn't need his permission to stone her. They could have gone directly before the Council. Yet, they came to *him*? I'm afraid you've been deceived, my love. First of all, those men didn't follow the law as it was written. Then they allowed *this stranger* to make the judgment, when they themselves had all the power they needed."

"I know it sounds strange, Eleazar, but that's exactly what happened. In the end, Jesus freed me from something that has troubled my heart for years."

An icy fear struck Eleazar. All the other times, whenever something had interfered with their bond, he and Ruth always found a way to be together again. Now, it seemed, he could lose her again, and this time he sensed she wouldn't be back. In a panic he tried to think of a way to make her stay. Though she stood directly in front of him, he could feel her slipping farther and farther away.

"This man has bewitched you, Ruth." Eleazar was desperate. "He's a charlatan, a sorcerer! Please, come to your senses. Don't be deceived. He's not our judge. Don't allow him to tear you away from me."

Ruth reached up and stroked Eleazar's cheek. Her dark eyes melted with love for him.

"I'm going to leave now," she said. "I will always hold you in my heart, but I won't be back. Don't attempt to see me again. Or Martha. Get on with your life, Eleazar. Make Anna happy. Restore yourself to your family, before it's too late."

She backed away from him. He expected to see more tears in her eyes. Instead, they had a peaceful glow that perplexed him. He stepped toward her. She backed away and started for the door. On the surface he tried to be strong, but inside he was crumbling like a shattered piece of limestone.

"I'll always love you Eleazar. *Shalom*."

Helpless, he watched her depart.

CHAPTER THIRTY-TWO

Eleazar had no reason to return to the palace. But by staying away, he had cut off Marcus' supply of opiates. The Roman sent a messenger with a threat. *I'll make you suffer like you never thought possible.* What could the man do? Kill him? Death would be a welcome release now that he'd lost Ruth.

He turned his attention to his work, suffered through the complaints of the sick, sat for hours at the bedsides of the dying, and handed out medicines until his store was empty. Few things mattered anymore. His children didn't know him. Anna filled her days with the care of the baby. Even Judah had disappeared within his own little world, a world that only allowed Benjamin inside. But, most of all, Ruth was out of his reach.

He resented the man called Jesus. Though he had never seen him, Eleazar thought him nothing more than a magician. Other people shared his opinion. They said he did miracles by trickery. But there were those who insisted Jesus had not merely come from Galilee. He had come from heaven, they said. They told stories about his miraculous birth. They hurried to join the crowds whenever he came to Judea. They sat on a hillside and listened to him talk. Some had even witnessed healings and exorcisms.

"He's God in the flesh," one man said.

Eleazar sneered with contempt. They would never be able to convince him the man was anything more than a fraud.

When at home he spent hours at a table in his rooftop apothecary, reading newly acquired scrolls, experimenting with herbs and potions, and pining away over his lost love. During such a moment, when he was sitting under the canopy with his head buried in a scroll, he heard the slapping of Anna's bare feet on the stairs. He ignored her, hoping she'd go away. But she drew close to him and waited in silence.

At length he raised his head. "What is it?" He didn't try to hide his annoyance.

Anna folded her hands in front of her. "Enos' mother came to our home for a visit."

He stared back at her. In one hand he held a piece of parchment. In the other he gripped a stylus, a sign to his wife that he needed to get back to work.

"She has proposed a betrothal." Anna smiled expectantly.

Eleazar dropped the stylus and raised his eyebrows, but he said nothing.

"She offered a match between her son, Hareem, and our daughter, Mara."

Enos' son! He'd been waiting for this very moment. He turned his upper body toward his wife and gave her his full attention.

"Such a match would be favorable," she said. "Think about it, Eleazar. A marriage between the daughter of a successful physician and the grandson of an esteemed Council member."

His head swam with the possibility. The Sanhedrin would likely dismiss any suspicions they'd held against Eleazar. Surely, they could overlook his failures—the rumor that brought about Thomas' death, the visits to Marcus in the palace, and, going back even further, his rejection of his father's guidance in favor of schooling in Alexandria.

They would begin to look at his accomplishments, his dedication to serving the sick, and the sacrifices he'd made at the temple, often surpassing other men with his offerings of unblemished calves and sheep, not to mention the handfuls of coins he dropped in the offering box. With Enos' father speaking on his behalf, the members would be sure to consider him.

The proposal of marriage set ablaze a fresh spirit in Eleazar. He was about to give his blessing when Ruth's face came before him and brought to his mind the disagreement he'd had with his father, years ago. While he had chosen Ruth, Judah had selected another.

He stared into his wife's hopeful face. "Does she love him?"

Anna's brows went up. Her eyes twinkled with mirth.

"Love him? Why do you ask, Eleazar? Such decisions are made by the parents."

"Have you asked Mara if she loves Hareem?" he insisted.

"No, why would I do such a thing?"

Eleazar felt his neck grow hot.

"Does it seem unreasonable for me to ask if my daughter loves the young man?" His impatience mounted. "Forget tradition. Forget about what *you* want. The scriptures speak of many situations when men and women were joined in marriage because they chose their mate. Didn't Michal plead with her father to give her to David long before he became king? And what about Solomon? He chose numerous wives and concubines without seeking his parents' approval."

Anna stared at him in confusion.

He set his jaw, determined she would obey his only wish.

She chewed her bottom lip and wrung her hands. "Mara barely knows the boy." Her voice was weak. "I know a little about him. He's a fine young man who will provide well for her. Whether or not she loves him doesn't matter. She will *grow* to love him—in time."

He looked at his wife as if seeing her for the first time. He'd assumed she'd loved him from the beginning. After all, he was a strong, handsome physician with a promising future. He never imagined that this woman had *grown* to love him.

"Summon Mara!" he commanded. "I'll ask her myself."

Noticeably stunned, Anna scurried down the stairs. Minutes later, she returned with Mara close at her heels. The girl stood before her father, her hands clasped at her waist. Her gray eyes, like his own, clouded with uncertainty, a hint of fear within their depths. Could it be he had turned into such a threatening figure in his own house that his eldest daughter trembled at the sight of him? Why couldn't she wrap her arms around his neck as little Martha had? He let out a sigh and leaned toward her.

"Do you want to marry the son of Enos?" He spoke as gently as he could.

Mara shrugged. She smiled shyly.

"Do you *love* him?"

She giggled and looked at her mother.

A hot anger rose within him. He rose to his feet.

"Child! I'm handing this decision to *you*. What do *you* want to do?"

Her smile vanished. She stood, speechless, fear flooding into her eyes. Anna rushed to her daughter's side and wrapped an arm around her shoulder.

He brushed his hands together. "I am washing my hands of this. Mara must decide for herself what she wants." He turned away from them and went back to his scroll.

It came as great relief to Eleazar when the women from both families went ahead without his approval and began making preparations for Mara's wedding. There followed the customary visit by Enos and his wife who brought a generous bride price, while Eleazar presented a lavish dowry on behalf of his daughter. He willingly signed the marriage contract.

Eleazar's home buzzed with activity for weeks. The women's voices rose in a constant chatter as they discussed the bride's attire, the feast, the food, the musicians, and the guest list. Eventually, he could no longer endure all the noise. He left the house and took a walk outside the city, hoping for a few minutes of blessed quiet and fresh air.

He followed a path over the Mount of Olives and meandered downhill toward the town of Bethany. He considered visiting his brother Simon, then changed his mind and continued on. The path dropped in a sharp descent to the Jericho road. He stepped over the ruts, kicked aside a cluster of dusty stones, and continued along the paved highway, hardly aware of the people who passed him on their way to the Holy City. This was a well-traveled road, used more by the Romans than by the local population. Men in armor had flooded into the city, an obvious sign that Caesar's authority had increased in Judea. Not only had Marcus remained in the city, but more of his kind came in, flaunting their authority, persecuting the Jews with more laws. They increased taxes, and kept a wary eye on the Jewish citizens. If the day ever came when he filled a seat in the Sanhedrin, he would use his authority to put pressure on the Roman officials. He would convince them to be more sensitive to Jewish customs.

Once again Eleazar had begun to dream about the Council seat. In losing Ruth, the door to the Sanhedrin had reopened to him. It was more of a possibility now. He was pondering this when a shrouded figure appeared a great distance down the road. The shadowy form came toward him. Like many of the afflicted, he was hunched over and he walked with a painful limp. As he drew near, he moved off the path so Eleazar could pass him with plenty of room.

He stared at the man, unable to pull his eyes away. There was something familiar about the shape of his body and the patch of red hair at the rim of his veil. A name rose to Eleazar's throat and lodged there. Before he could speak it, the man drew his mantle tighter across his face and called out the familiar warning, "Unclean."

Eleazar stopped walking. He knew the voice. A chill traveled down his spine. Above the fold of cloth a pair of sky-blue eyes stared back at him. They flashed with recognition, then they clouded over, and the man walked on.

Stunned, Eleazar watched him go. Then the leper turned. Their eyes met again. Eleazar took a step in his direction. The stranger raised his left hand. Three fingers were missing. "Unclean," he repeated. Then he shuffled off.

Eleazar stood gazing after him. Unable to move, he kept watching as the shrouded figure headed for the leper caves on the hill. Hot tears rose to Eleazar's eyes. He blinked them back, but they returned like a flood and streamed down his face. He stared down at his elegant purple robe, trimmed in gold, with bright red fringe circling the hem. He shifted his gaze to the figure in the tattered cloak, a distant shadow now, stumbling up the hillside to those black openings on the ridge. With a heavy heart Eleazar turned away and started for home.

It was the first day of the Feast of Booths. Anna and the girls had gone to the market to purchase items for the weeklong observance. Eleazar passed through the house and found Benjamin sitting at Judah's feet, a stylus in the boy's hand, a scroll unraveled on his lap. At 17, the lad was continuing his training in the scriptures under the scribes at the temple. His apprenticeship as a physician was long overdue. Yet, instead of pursuing his father's work, he had chosen another path. He wanted to be a scribe, but not the kind who made judgments in the courts, merely someone who would copy the scriptures and the words of more skilled orators, never having to expose his stammering tongue. His grandfather had approved of the boy's decision. Now Judah had assumed the role of Benjamin's guide and was helping him through his temple studies. Though pricked to the heart, Eleazar didn't object.

Most days, after returning from sick calls, he retreated to the upper room and sorted through his medicines, mentally noting what he needed to replace. The smell of lye floated up from the courtyard. A lamb turned on a spit over an open fire. Servants hurried about, cleansing the house and arranging the table for Eleazar's family. A festive atmosphere prevailed.

Suddenly, a frantic voice rose from the bottom of the stairs. "Eleazar! Eleazar!"

He had a fleeting memory of Enos barging through the door of his house with news of Thomas' death. His friend's voice carried the same frantic sound. He leaned over the wall and caught sight of Enos mounting the outer stair, his bony chest heaving with every step.

"I came as quickly as I could." Enos stopped at the top and labored to catch his breath.

"What is it? What has happened?"

"Oh, Eleazar." Enos nearly fell into his arms. "My friend. My dear friend."

Eleazar eyed him with puzzlement. "Come. Sit here. Rest yourself." He guided Enos to a stone bench, then he settled beside him.

"Calm yourself, Enos. Speak to me."

Enos shook his head and opened his mouth to speak. But words didn't come.

Eleazar waited, his impatience mounting.

Enos pressed his knuckles to his eyes. "Oh, Eleazar, Eleazar. A terrible thing has happened."

A cold chill raced through him. "Tell me, Enos. What is it?"

Enos turned toward him, his face flushed. "It's Ruth."

"Ruth!?" A cold chill ran down Eleazar's spine.

"My friend, word came from the elders at the gate. Ruth has been accused of adultery." Enos shook his head with sadness. "The Roman, Marcus, has been spreading rumors that little Martha is not Levi's child but was conceived through an adulterous union. Levi confronted Ruth, and she didn't deny it."

Eleazar's eyes widened. In a panic, he sprang to his feet and started for the stairs.

"Where is she? I'll go to her. I'll tell them it's a lie."

Enos came up behind him. "No, Eleazar. Don't be foolish."

"I have to protect her. She's innocent, Enos." He turned and looked into his friend's face. "I'm to blame." The admission came easier than he would have expected.

Enos shook his head. "You shouldn't expose yourself, Eleazar. Marcus never mentioned your name."

The Roman's threat came rushing back to him. *I'll make you suffer like you never thought possible.* Of course. What could cause him greater pain than to stand by and watch his lovely Ruth pay for his sin?

"I'll declare my part in this. Perhaps, they'll let her go free if I tell them I forced her."

"It's too late, Eleazar. Levi has already brought his wife before the Council. He dragged her through the streets, and when they reached the temple, he called for my father and demanded the members pass judgment upon her without delay."

Eleazar pictured his beautiful Ruth, marred by the dirt of the road, humiliated, disgraced, because of him.

"The Council members challenged her. For her father's sake, they gave her an opportunity to deny any fault, to say she'd been forced against her will." Enos shook his head. "Though they pressed her to speak the man's name, she refused. In the end, they sentenced her to be stoned to death."

"No! Not Ruth." He grabbed Enos' arms. "Listen to me. *I* am at fault. I pushed and pleaded and pursued her until she gave in. The judgment should fall on *me*, not on Ruth."

"Eleazar, to her last breath she never once spoke your name. She wanted you to be free, to continue your work and your life in the city." He backed away. "You need to honor her decision. It would do no good to expose yourself now. As for me, your secret is safe."

Eleazar released his friend, dropped to his knees, and sobbed into his hands. Enos wrapped his arms around him.

"I always knew you loved her, Eleazar. Though I wasn't certain anything had happened between the two of you, I thought perhaps it had." He stroked his back. "You have to let her go."

Eleazar rocked back and forth, agony coursing through every part of his body. Tears flowed like a river and he wailed his grief over the rooftops.

Then he pushed away from Enos and rose to his feet, his anguish turning to bitter hatred.

"It's because of that prophet, the man called Jesus," he cried out. "He put foolish thoughts in Ruth's head. She told me she had seen him in the temple. She listened to his promises. He tore her away from me, Enos. He tore her away from me."

A thought struck Eleazar. "What about Ruth's father?" he said, disgust rising within him. "He's a member of the Sanhedrin. Couldn't he *do* something? Couldn't he save her?"

Enos shook his head. "Ariel could do nothing. Though he's one of the Seventy, they barred him outside the chamber until after the vote. He stood there in the center of the court, helpless, as several others carried out the stoning. A great many people gathered to watch the spectacle, but no one would go against the Council. No one could save her, not even her father."

Eleazar wept openly, more tears spilling from his eyes. He sent a grievous wail over the rooftops, with no concern if anyone heard him.

Then he turned back to Enos. "What has become of her? I must go and claim her body. I need to give her a proper burial."

Enos wiped tears from his own face. "No, Eleazar. It's too late. When it was over, she lay bleeding on the pavement. People spat on her as they walked by. Ariel rushed in and gathered his daughter in his arms. He was weeping and wailing like a little child. Then, he took her away for a private burial."

Eleazar bowed his head in despair. The thought of his beautiful Ruth bloodied and bruised, lying in the dirt of the road brought unspeakable grief to his heart.

"Ruth. Ruth. My dear Ruth," he sobbed. "May the Almighty bring judgment on me for causing this to happen to her."

Another thought struck him, and he grabbed Enos' arm. "What about the child? What's to become of Martha?"

"The child?" Enos clenched his teeth. "That monster Levi called her filthy names and tossed her into the street."

"She's only five!" Eleazar shouted. "The love of my life is dead, and my child suffers unbearable shame."

"Your child?" Enos choked out the words. "The child is yours? Oh, Eleazar, this is far worse than I thought."

"I have to do something. I have to go and find her."

Enos grabbed his arms and held him fast. "Enough, Eleazar. You cannot expose yourself in this manner. Think about your profession. Think about the Council. Think about your family. It would do no good to involve yourself now."

Eleazar pushed out of Enos' grasp. "My Ruth is dead, and our child is lost in the city. And I stand here, helpless to do anything about it."

A scraping of feet drew his attention to the bottom of the stairs. Anna was standing there, her eyes fixed on him. The pained look on her face told Eleazar she had heard everything. Before he could speak, she spun away and fled into the street.

The sun was beginning to set. The servants had laid out the evening meal. Still, Anna had not returned. Eleazar paced the floor, torn between declaring his fault before the Council or remaining silent, as Enos had advised. *"She wanted you to be free, to continue your work and your life in the city. You need to honor her decision."* With her dying breath, Ruth had protected him.

His thoughts turned to Anna. One more innocent person was suffering for his sins. He considered going out in the streets to look for her. By this time, she could have reported him to the Council. She had every right to accuse him.

As the sun began its final descent beyond the city wall, a trumpet blast sounded from the pinnacle of the temple. He walked into the courtyard and stopped short of the gate, his eyes widened at what he found there.

Anna came through the entry gripping the hand of a little five-year-old girl. Shiny black curls framed the child's angelic face. She stared at him with silver gray eyes, a mirror image of his own.

Anna took a step toward him. "I searched the neighborhood and found her in the care of Ruth's handmaid. That kind servant had slipped into the street mere seconds after Levi threw out the child. She was taking her to the home of a friend when I met them on the way."

Eleazar froze. He gazed through tear-filled eyes at his little daughter. Anna gave him a nod, and he stepped forward and fell on his knees before Martha. He smoothed the dirty wrinkles from her dress, brushed off the loose soil from her tear-stained cheeks. Shamelessly, he wrapped his arms around his little girl and yielded fresh tears. He didn't try to hide his pain. The damage had been done. Now all he could do was pour love on his child and protect her from anymore harm.

"Martha, my child, my beautiful little girl," he sobbed.

She slid her tiny arms around his neck, like she used to. His heart broke.

Anna's comforting voice penetrated his sobs. "There's no need to grieve any longer, Eleazar. You can rest in peace, my husband."

He looked into her face. Through a blur of tears he saw she was smiling down at him.

"The child will remain with us," she said. "No one needs to know your secret. I want to do this as a kindness to my friend, Ruth. Martha will be *our* child, now. Yours and mine."

CHAPTER THIRTY-THREE

*R*uth's family held a private funeral for her. Eleazar watched from the hill, his heart breaking with every step the mourners took toward the open tomb.

After losing Ruth, Eleazar's life would have seemed hopeless except for one thing. Little Martha. Her laughter echoed throughout the house, pulling him from his misery into a life he'd never experienced before. He had no time to grieve. Martha's happy innocence drew the family together in a way Eleazar could never have done. Even frail Abi came out of her shell and played handmaid to the newest member of the family. Benjamin also spent time squatting on the floor with Martha, sharing with her the little wooden animals his grandfather had carved for him. Anna honored her promise and treated the child as one of her own. And Eleazar? His behavior changed overnight. He hurried home from his work in the city every evening, eager to have his youngest leap into his arms and cry, "Abba!"

Winter came and went. Mara's wedding passed with little effort. Eleazar's eldest daughter and Enos' son settled in a home of their own, also in the Upper City. To Eleazar's dismay, Benjamin continued to cling to his grandfather. Because the boy's stammering did not subside, Eleazar agreed to allow him to continue his studies with the temple scribes. As a copier of the scriptures, he would not be forced to speak. In the evenings Eleazar found his son sitting by the hearth translating the holy texts into Aramaic, the more common language of the day. Sometimes he caught Judah peering over the boy's shoulder, the old man's face beaming with pride.

Eleazar eyed Benjamin's work with troubled interest. One afternoon he looked over the boy's shoulder at the parchment on his lap. He grabbed the stylus from Benjamin's hand and demanded his full attention.

"Why do you pursue such a profession? Don't you know you'll be keeping company with Pharisees? They will command more and more of you. As a physician you would be able to make your own way. But this kind of work will place you under the control of others."

Benjamin looked with innocence into Eleazar's stern face.

"Not all s-scribes do the w-will of the Pharisees, Father. I answer to the r-rabbi. I write the t-truth. The authorities accept my w-weakness in speech and leave me to the making of c-c-c-copies. That's all I w-want to do."

With a heavy heart, Eleazar returned the stylus to the boy's hand, gave him a pat on the head, and left him to his chosen profession.

So it was that Eleazar continued his own work with no son to carry on the family trade. He left the house alone every morning and returned at night, weary and wanting only a quick meal and a soft bed.

The months flew by. Martha turned six. Then seven. Benjamin sank into almost complete silence and spent long hours writing. Abi remained frail and awkward. Only little Martha brought life to their home, filling the quiet air with shrill laughter and happy chatter. An amazing joy followed her from one room to another. She rarely asked about her mother anymore, but whenever she did, both Eleazar and Anna spoke only high praises of the beautiful Ruth.

For reasons unknown to him, Eleazar had not yet been summoned to take a Council seat, although several seats had been

vacated and filled over the past few years. Then, one evening
during supper, a request by Anna sent him into a rage.

"We need to make a contract," she said. "Abi has been of age
for sometime."

"What is this madness?" Eleazar raised his voice, startling
everyone in the room.

To his surprise Anna persisted. "We need to consider her
future, Eleazar. We've waited far too long. I was beginning to
think all hope was gone, until today. Now it seems she's been
approached for betrothal."

Eleazar lifted a piece of bread. He held it in front of his mouth
but didn't take a bite. He burst out laughing. "Abi? Who would
consider this mouse of a girl?"

Abi sat very still, her eyes lowered, her face flushed a deep red.

"A messenger came to our home this afternoon," Anna went
on. "He was from the house of Levi."

The name brought Eleazar to his feet.

"Who from *that* house wants to marry our daughter? One of
Levi's servants? That smelly boy who looks after his animals?"

Eleazar turned away from the pain in Abi's eyes.

Anna stood and faced him, her eyes aflame. "Eleazar, please!
Our daughter is blossoming before your eyes. All you see is a
sickly little girl, but others see a beautiful young woman, ready
for marriage. While you look on her frailty, others see a tender
flower. Yes, she's quiet and painfully small. But she has a sweetness about her. Not every man wants a free-spirited woman."

Eleazar drew back. For the first time in their marriage, Anna
had hinted at his unfaithfulness with Ruth. He struggled for a
response. But before he could say anything, Anna spoke again,
a little sharper this time.

"You ask who in Levi's household wants to marry our daughter? It's not one of the servants, as you believe. It's none other
than the man's own son, Malachi, the boy you healed from a
head injury many years ago. He has grown, Eleazar, and he's set
his heart on our Abi."

Eleazar tensed. "I will not consent to such a match. How do you know the boy wasn't forever harmed by that injury? Perhaps Levi wants to be rid of him at our expense."

He looked at Abi. A tear crept out of the corner of her eye.

"You're wrong, Eleazar." Anna dared to challenge him. "Malachi no longer shows any sign of injury. You did well in your healing of him. I've spoken with Malachi. He's a smart boy who works under his father and has proved himself successful as a merchant."

Eleazar's mind raced over memories of Levi—as a boy, as a man, as the thief who nearly destroyed Simon, as Ruth's abusive husband. He wanted no part with that man.

"Send word in the morning. My answer is no." He stared at Anna's angry scowl, then turned his eyes on Abi, who had already begun to weep. "I said, no." He pounded the table. "No. No. *No!*"

Judah, who usually ate in silence, lifted his head. "The match is a favorable one, Eleazar."

He turned his wrath on his father. "Do you think I want to send my daughter to that household? Levi's the scoundrel who swindled Simon and so many others. Do you not remember how your youngest son struggled to restore his fortune? Malachi will be the image of his father—a deceiver of widows and orphans, with no remorse for those he hurts. I don't want our Abi to live in that household."

From out of nowhere, Abi's meek little voice broke through Eleazar's shouting. He turned toward her, his eyes wide. The poor child rarely spoke in his presence.

"Abba," she said, her eyes brimming with tears. "Please, hear me. Malachi isn't like his father. He's a wonderful person, honest and trustworthy—like his mother was."

Like his mother? Abi's words pierced his heart. Years ago, when he had rushed to Levi's house to heal the boy, he had gone there for Ruth, not for Levi—not even for Malachi, but for Ruth. It was Ruth's plea that had drawn him to the boy's bedside. It was for her sake he had dared to try such a risky method to release the pressure on the boy's brain. And now Malachi had grown up and he wanted to marry Abi.

"Father, I love him."

Love him? Eleazar's head throbbed with doubts. He could continue to deny the request, and Abi would likely go through life an unmarried woman, disgraced, childless, and alone. Or, he could welcome Ruth's son into the family, perhaps convince the boy to become a physician. But, such a request could only bring more wrath from Malachi's father.

The eyes of the family were on him as he struggled with a decision that could affect the rest of Abi's life. Levi's pointed nose and beady eyes rose up before him.

Eleazar turned toward Anna. "This time it will not happen as it did when you women made plans for Mara's wedding. This time I will not sign the contract, not with that man sitting across the table from me."

He stormed from the room. Over his shoulder he shouted his final decision. "This union will *not* take place. Send word at once."

Abi retreated to her quarters. Eleazar refused to change his mind. With little success, he covered his ears and tried to block out the endless wailing that poured from Abi's room. He suspected she might die of grief. When his daughter, at last, emerged, her eyes were red and swollen. She sat at the table and picked at her food. She grew more sickly as the days passed. She did her household chores as though in a trance, gliding from one part of the house to another, pausing now and then at her mother's side. Anna's eyes sent invisible daggers at him. Still, he would not give in.

Eleazar's troubles increased one morning while he was on the rooftop, selecting medicines to toss into his scrip and discarding those that had aged. It was then that he noticed a red mark on his left forearm. He frowned at it. Several possibilities went through his mind. Perhaps he had gotten too close to the fire pit the other day. Or had he spilled a harsh liquid on his arm? He couldn't recall.

He applied a paste of powdered ivory to the blemish, then he pulled his sleeve over it and went about his work, expecting to find the sore gone in a few days.

But a week later, the blemish had spread up his arm and had begun to resemble the one he had seen on Achim's neck. That night, he lay awake beside Anna, unable to sleep. He rolled from one side to the other.

She awakened. "Is everything all right."

"Yes, go back to sleep."

She rolled over and put her back to him.

There was no question what he had to do. In the morning he would go to the priest. He would show Mattathias the blemish and let him decide his fate.

PART THREE
Seven Days Of The Leper

"And if the priest see that, behold, the scab spreadeth in the skin, then the priest shall pronounce him unclean: it is a leprosy."

Leviticus 13:8

CHAPTER THIRTY-FOUR
The First Day
A.D. 30, The Tenth of Nisan

The law was clear. Eleazar had no choice but to obey it. After a sleepless night, he rose from his bed and, careful not to awaken his family, he quietly packed a bag with a change of clothing, a sheepskin of goat's milk, and enough food for seven days. He returned to his quarters and whispered to his wife, awakening her from a sound sleep. She stared wide-eyed as he told her about the blemish.

"Do not be concerned, Anna. I will follow the law and accept the prescribed separation. If I am healed, I will return in seven days."

"And if not?" She trembled like a frightened child.

"Be at peace. As a physician I see this blemish as nothing more than a mild infection. Nevertheless, cleanse yourself and discard our bedding. I must leave now."

Before she could respond, he turned his back to her and hurried to Martha's bedchamber. His daughter lay in a tight little ball with her knees tucked up to her chest. He pulled her blanket up to her shoulders and blew her a kiss. Tears came. He blinked them back and set his jaw.

Fearing he might awaken her with his weeping, he hurried

out of her room and went to Benjamin's corner by the hearth. He selected one of his son's scrolls, and without looking at the text, he tucked it under his arm. Then he grabbed the bag he had packed and took one last look around the dwelling. Anna was standing in the doorway of their bedchamber, her face wrought with despair, tears running down her cheeks. He turned his face away and went out the door. In the courtyard he was instantly struck by a blast of cool morning air.

Anna called after him, but he kept walking. She cried out again, fainter this time. He picked up his pace and hurried away from his home.

As he trudged upward along the cobbled path toward the temple, a sliver of sunlight carved into the black of night. The entire city lay sleeping. By the time he reached the temple complex, the sky had turned gray, then white, then a soft blue. Soon the shofar would sound from the pinnacle, and the streets would fill with merchants and beggars and people of all stations of life.

He reached the temple courtyard and found it nearly empty. A young priest was tending to the oil lamps. At the scrape of his sandal, the priest turned to look at him.

"May I be of service?"

Eleazar eyed the youth with interest. He appeared to be no older than Benjamin.

"I seek an audience with Mattathias."

A look of concern crossed the boy's forehead. And no wonder. Mattathias held the most undesirable of all the temple duties. For most of his older years he was the priest who examined strange blemishes. He'd made a judgment on Achim's wound. Now he would do the same for Eleazar.

The young priest swept his eyes over Eleazar's purple robe, the embroidered front, the fringed hem, and his thick leather sandals. Without a word, he turned away and, his bare feet slapping the pavement, disappeared among the porticos.

Eleazar began to pace. His labored breathing sent puffs of vapor into the chill morning air. The pungent odor of burnt carcasses rose from the altar beyond the separation gate—a reminder of the endless sacrifices that took place at the temple only last night. He grunted. What good would such offerings do him now?

The slow padding of bare feet drew his attention to the far end of the courtyard. Old Mattathias emerged from the shadows and hobbled toward him. His shoulders were bent beneath a tan robe that fell to his ankles. His long full beard stretched almost to the corded belt around his waist. Eleazar was overcome with a mix of pity and anxiety. The withered old man coming toward him could offer nothing more than an opinion, never a cure.

Mattathias beamed in recognition, but his welcoming smile quickly faded. "Physician, what brings you here? I know of no priest needing medical care. Tell me, who summoned you?"

"No one summoned me. I am here of my own choosing."

Mattathias' dark eyes narrowed with interest. "Perhaps, you have come to *seek* help, rather than to offer it." The wrinkles on his forehead deepened.

Three priests hurried past, their bare feet gliding noiselessly over the tiles.

Eleazar stepped closer to Mattathias and lowered his voice. "Can we talk? In private?"

The old priest gestured toward a far corner of the court. "Over there."

Together, they moved into the shadows. Eleazar lowered his belongings to the floor and faced the priest. He towered over the little man, yet, he felt small and helpless in his presence. His future depended on whatever judgment the priest pronounced on him.

Mattathias folded his hands and said nothing, but his eyes locked with Eleazar's, and he waited for him to speak.

Eleazar took a deep breath and released it with a shake of his head. "Mattathias, I've contracted an infection of some sort." He shrugged. "It's a small wound, but a stubborn one. Though I've tried every remedy in my store, I could not remove the blemish.

Now it has grown and even changed shape. And it's a different color, having gone from brown to purple to pink, and now to white. Even the hairs on my arm have turned lighter."

Mattathias stroked the corners of his mouth. "Where is this blemish? Must I examine you in private?"

"No. I need only to raise my sleeve." Eleazar drew back the dark purple cloth. The priest's grimace sent a chill into his heart.

"How long have you had this wound?"

"Several days," Eleazar admitted. "I would have come sooner, but I was certain I could cure it. I applied a salve, a simple paste I made from ivory. Then I tried a mixture of herbs from Alexandria. The spot spread until it was twice the size as at the start."

"Do you have any feeling?"

Eleazar shook his head.

The old priest frowned. "My son, are there any other signs of infection on your body?"

"No other. Only this stubborn mark."

"Tell me, do you know how you acquired this? Think about the sick people you care for. Have you been close to anyone who may have traveled a great distance? Perhaps someone who came from a foreign land and had a similar affliction."

He shook his head. "I can think of no one."

"Has anyone died in your care?"

"No. Everyone is doing well."

Mattathias drew closer and lowered his voice. "Have you had contact with a leper?"

Eleazar sighed with resignation. "None that I am aware of." Immediately, he was taken back more than thirty years to a ridge of caves outside Jerusalem.

"There was one time." He paused as he remembered the nightmare. "It was a long time ago."

Mattathias cocked his head and his face awakened with curiosity.

"I was thirteen years old," Eleazar told him. "My father was instructing me in the work of a physician. I did not believe he would begin my training in the worst possible place on earth. He took me to the leper caves on the hill."

Mattathias sucked in a breath of air. "My son, why did your father do such a thing?"

Eleazar raised a shoulder and sighed. "You know how Judah is. His service to the helpless has always come before anything else—even his own family." He spoke with such bitterness he feared Mattathias would take offense.

Instead, the old priest gave him a comforting nod. "Eleazar, you can do nothing about the past. I doubt this mark came from what happened to you long ago. You're a physician, the finest in all Judea. Consider the medicines you handle. Did you spill something on your arm?"

He shook his head slowly, thoughtfully. "None that I recall."

"And you say you tried several cures?"

He nodded.

Mattathias straightened. "Then we have no other choice but to follow the law. I am pronouncing a seven-day separation."

Though the priest's decision came as no surprise, Eleazar buried his face in his hands. For the first time since he discovered the spot, he released the anguish that he'd been holding inside. Every sob sent a shudder through his entire being. He wept bitterly and without shame.

"My–my family." Eleazar choked out his concern. "Will I ever see them again?"

Mattathias shrugged. "I pray that you will."

Eleazar let out a bitter laugh. "Only one week ago, the Sanhedrin sent a messenger to my home. They have a vacancy. I am one of their choices to fill it. Do you understand what that means, Mattathias? For most of my life I have dreamed of being counted among the Seventy. Now the seat is within my reach and I—"

"Eleazar, your healing will come easier if you find peace. Listen to me. During your week of quarantine, I want you to set your mind on good things. Think about returning home to your family.

The seat of honor will still be there in a week. It's important that you keep your thoughts hopeful."

He pointed at the scroll Eleazar had brought along. "What is this?"

"It belongs to my son, Benjamin." He lifted the rolled parchment. "It seems my son prefers the work of a scribe rather than to follow the profession of his father. This is merely a section of scripture he copied." He tilted his head. "It may help me to pass the time."

He unrolled the parchment and showed the script to the priest.

"Ah," Mattathias sighed. "This writing comes from the works of Isaiah. His words should bring you comfort." The old priest took a closer look. "This is fine work. You say your son, Benjamin, made this copy?"

Eleazar lowered his gaze. "I confess I've understood my son too late. I have not made it easy for him to pursue his own way."

"Perhaps you will have another opportunity."

"Perhaps." He rolled up the scroll.

Mattathias folded his hands. "Let this period of separation be a time for meditation. Let the words of the prophet help you draw near to Yahweh."

They stood facing each other. Mattathias pointed at a dark place beyond the women's court.

"I can offer you a place—a private room we use for this purpose. It's vacant now."

Eleazar knew about that miserable chamber where diseased people spent long and lonely days while they awaited their reexamination.

"My friend Achim spent seven days in that room, many years ago."

Mattathias' eyes brightened with the memory. "Yes, I remember him well. A man of rare spirit. He always made me laugh. It pained me to have to confine him."

"His end was not a pleasant one."

The light in the old priest's eyes dimmed. "No, it was not." Then he extended his hands. "Will you stay?"

Eleazar shook his head.

"The quarters are regularly cleansed," the priest urged.

"No."

"You are aware of the alternative."

He nodded. "The wilderness. At least I'll be able to take a breath of fresh air."

He was surprised to see tears running between the wrinkles on Mattathias' face. The old man cleared his throat. "It's your decision, Eleazar. But, if you're certain—"

Eleazar nodded.

"There's a cave on the Ophel Ridge. You must pass through the Dung Gate and follow the path over the Mount of Olives, then turn east toward the rising of the sun. You'll find the cave on an upper level, beyond a large cluster of hyssop. Others have spent their week of separation there. I expect it will be empty now. Most likely, you will be alone until your reexamination."

"Thank you, Mattathias."

"At the end of seven days, come back to see me. I will again look at the blemish." The priest smiled, but a sadness filled his eyes. "Remember, Yahweh does not forsake those who cry out to him in prayer, if they do so with a true heart."

Eleazar snorted. "A true heart? I don't know what that is anymore. I fear my own heart has been overcome with the very disease I dread. A different kind of leprosy has grown inside me, Mattathias, one that cannot be cured with salves and ointments. Now I have been cursed with an outward presence of the very disease that has grown inside me for years." He shook his head sadly. "I've been a leper all this time, and I never knew it."

Mattathias nodded with understanding. "It's like what the Psalmist wrote. *My life is spent with grief and my years with sighing. My strength fails me because of my iniquity, and my bones are consumed.*"

Eleazar stared into the man's watery eyes. He knew what he had to do. He pulled a veil from his pack, wrapped it around his forehead, drew the end across his lips, and tucked it inside the fold above his left ear. Mentally, he'd been rehearsing the word he was required to say to anyone he met on the path.

Unclean.

In the past, he'd heard it mouthed by lepers he'd come upon during his journeys outside the city. It was always the same. A cloaked figure would emerge in the distance, hunched and scraping the ground with his feet. The man would draw closer. Above the strip of cloth that covered his lips appeared red, tear-filled eyes. He would stumble off the path into the dirt and weeds in order to clear the way for the healthy.

Now Eleazar would be one of them, at least for a week, and perhaps longer.

With a sigh, he picked up his scrip and uttered a meek *"Shalom"* to Mattathias. Then he turned away.

"Go in peace," the priest called after him.

Eleazar approached the outer stairway, stopped walking, and looked back. Mattathias' sad eyes were still on him. The old priest raised a hand to wave, then he turned away and disappeared into the shadows.

CHAPTER THIRTY-FIVE

Eleazar began his journey into exile. He followed a narrow, winding path downward into the Lower City and wove between two endless rows of dirty hovels. Near the Dung Gate the odor of smoldering refuse unleashed boyhood memories of visits to this forsaken part of Jerusalem.

His father had dragged him down this very path. Hollow eyes had watched them from between tattered curtains. Filthy children had thundered into the streets begging for alms. Occasionally, to Eleazar's disgust, his father would lead him into one of those dark, foul-smelling homes and tend to some poor soul who had no ability to pay.

Judah's ministry to the poor had plagued Eleazar from the first day he entered his training until he was old enough to go off on his own. Then he visited homes only in the Upper City, where he could emerge clean and smelling like fresh mint, and with a handful of gold coins in his scrip.

He huffed out his shame. Somehow his life had changed, and now he was the forsaken one, and the people of the Lower City were the healthy. If any of those beggars should approach him now, he'd have to send them away with the warning, *"Unclean."*

Unclean, he mused. *Even those cursed beggars are better off than I am.*

People passed him and looked the other way. He moved on. It was as if the leper's curse had already ended his life, like he no longer existed.

As he reached the Dung Gate, the shofar blasted its morning call from the pinnacle of the temple. The gate swung in. He stepped out onto the hillside and inhaled deeply of the fresh mountain air. Squinting at the streak of sunlight in the distance, he continued along the stony trail between clumps of grass, still wet with dew. He rounded the side of the Mount of Olives. The haze lifted, and the sun painted daggers of light on the sandy floor of the desert. Bright red poppies awakened to the sunlight, and clusters of white and purple wildflowers tumbled among a scattering of rocks on the hillside.

The setting's peaceful aura momentarily soothed Eleazar's anxiety. He paused to watch the desert come to life. Then, from somewhere down below came the faint sound of tambourines and flutes mingled with spirited voices.

Eleazar scowled. *A party at this ungodly hour? A wedding perhaps?*

A clamor at the bottom of the hill drew his attention to a large group of people coming from the direction of Bethphage to the south of the Mount of Olives. Their instruments sent rhythmic tones into the air. Men, women, and children leaped about in a frenzy, waving palm branches and spreading their coats on the path in front of—what? A man riding a colt? The comical display had Eleazar chuckling for the first time in days.

Curious, he strained his ear and tried to make sense of the recurring refrain. "Hosanna; Blessed is the King of Israel that comes in the name of the Lord."

He shook his head. Such acclaim should be reserved for the Messiah. But, no Savior of the people would enter the city on a colt.

Perhaps they were mocking the Roman official who had recently settled in Judea. The procurator called Pilate could never win the hearts of the Jewish people. He might as well go back to Rome.

His interest pricked, Eleazar turned from the ridge and followed the crowd. The man on the colt paused on the crest of a hill and sat motionless, his eyes on Jerusalem. The chanting ceased. The air grew thick and quiet.

Eleazar flinched. The man was weeping. Then, he spoke and his voice sounded like a rush of water. "O, Jerusalem. If you, even you, had only known on this day what would bring you peace, but now it is hidden from your eyes."

"Who is he?" Eleazar said aloud to no one in particular.

"His name is Jesus." The response came from a man at the edge of the crowd. "He's the Prophet from Galilee. The Healer. The King of the Jews."

Eleazar glared at the man on the colt. He wore a teacher's clothing—a simple blue robe with a fringed border. He flaunted no jewels. No crown. *A prophet? This man could never be a prophet. Or a healer. And surely not a king.*

Jesus. The name stirred a bitter memory. So this was the man Ruth had seen in the temple court. If not for him, she would still be alive.

The man at the edge of the crowd came toward him. Eleazar raised his hand. "Unclean!" he called out for the first time. The man backed away and disappeared into the crowd.

Setting his jaw, Eleazar turned and resumed his journey to the Ophel Ridge. When he looked back, the man on the colt had disappeared over the rise and had moved closer to the city's East Gate. The crowd of fools had gone after him.

"The Healer," the man had said. Now Eleazar wondered, should he have followed the crowd? Should he have sought a miracle from this Jesus? *Perhaps*— he shook off the thought and continued walking in the opposite direction.

Eleazar stepped along the dip of land that led to the southern ridge. He mounted another rise, came upon the large cluster of hyssop, then he located the cave, a miserable hole in the side of the hill. He hesitated at the opening, struck by a long-discarded memory of the caves along the limestone ridge. It was there, as a youth, that he first met the forbidden ones who lingered at death's door.

Heaving a sigh, Eleazar set his belongings on the ground outside the cave. He stepped closer to the opening. A cold sweat overtook him. He touched the back of his neck. His hand came away moist. He wiped it clean on his robe. How sad that this swath of costly purple cloth should now serve as a towel.

He sighed with forced acceptance and stepped into the darkness. A fluttering came from somewhere overhead. Something flew past his head—a bat or a bird—and stirred his veil.

As his eyes became used to the darkness, he looked about him at the rock walls. There were no signs of life. Only a dusty floor, a pile of stones, and a branch of hyssop, remnants left behind by the cave's last inhabitant.

He grabbed the hyssop and swept the floor free of gravel and dust. He discarded the branch on the hillside and moved his meager belongings inside the cave. He gathered the rocks in a circle and piled some twigs in the center, then he pulled a flint and a cruse of oil from his scrip and soon had a small fire going. The flame lit up the inside of the cave, and he saw it was empty except for his own possessions.

Squatting before the fire, he removed a handful of raisins, a piece of unleavened bread, and a wedge of goat's cheese from his pack. His first bite carried him back to a corner of Gethsemane and the beautiful Ruth sharing her lunch with him. He remembered her sweet, young face, how she lit up when she talked about Alexandria, a tiny dimple appearing in her left cheek, and her lips parted in lively conversation.

Once on fire with the spirit of youth, here in the cave he had become a lonely old man, clinging hopelessly to the past. Ruth's image began to fade.

He finished the meal, folded his pack into a pillow and reclined on the floor of the cave. He prayed for merciful sleep.

He didn't bother to wipe away the tear that had oozed from the corner of his eye. It dried on his cheek.

At the home of Eleazar, Anna staggered out of the house, through the courtyard, and onto the cobbled street. There, in the dust of the road, she flung herself face down and scratched at the earth with her fingernails. She tossed dirt on her head and let out a tormented wail that drew neighbors from their homes. With parched lips she released a cry from the depths of her throat.

"My God, my God," she cried out. "Why has this horrible affliction come upon us? Is this a righteous judgment? Must our lives be destroyed? How can I continue without my husband? How can my children go on without their father? What will become of us? Have mercy, Dear Lord. Have mercy. Please, heal Eleazar. Cleanse him. Hear the plea of this poor woman, your humble servant."

Tears streamed down Anna's cheeks. She rose to her knees and rocked back and forth in pained lamentation. Behind her stood Benjamin, helpless to comfort her. More neighbors flooded into the street. A dozen pairs of eyes were on her. She ignored them and kept on wailing. But one pair of eyes caught her attention. Dark, threatening eyes. They belonged to a tall, slim man who had emerged from his home two doors up the hill.

Anna drew herself up and looked into the face of Levi bar Uzza. Unlike the kind faces on the rest of the crowd, Levi allowed a sneer to cross his lips. She stared back at him, pleading, but she received no pity from those piercing black eyes.

Eleazar spent the rest of the day gathering hyssop and palm branches to make a more comfortable bed for the night. He also searched the hillside for berries, and he filled an empty goat's horn with water from a nearby well. The heat of the day pressed upon him until he was forced to shed the outer cloak and the veil that separated the clean from the unclean.

Late in the day, he sat on the edge of the cliff and ate another meal. His thoughts strayed to his family, seated around the costly table he had purchased, eating roast lamb and an abundance of vegetables from Anna's garden. Judah would have taken Eleazar's place at the head of the table, and little Martha would be asking where Abba had gone.

He cried easily, something he'd rarely done before. A man with a hard heart had little need for tears. Now he was overflowing with them.

Prayers wouldn't come, though he'd committed to memory a great many of them. For unknown reasons he couldn't summon a single Psalm or petition, couldn't recall the promises of Isaiah or the lamentations of Jeremiah. The scriptures he'd recited as a youth had vanished amidst his medical studies, for he'd had no use for them—until now.

The setting of the sun changed Eleazar's world from searing heat to bitter cold. He slipped back into his cloak and used the veil for more warmth, covering himself with it as he lay on his bed of hyssop and palm branches. Through the long, freezing night, he remained by the fire, grateful for the warmth it provided. The quiet of the day quickly gave way to the sounds of night creatures. He fell asleep to the distant howl of jackals, the screech of a hawk, and the shrill singing of locusts.

Eleazar rose to the first rays of sunlight. He reached for his scrip and went outside the cave to the ridge. Pressing his hand against the small of his back, he lowered himself to the ground with a heavy sigh and dropped his feet over the side. He was facing east. An orange glow created a halo around the mountains of Moab. He took in the sight, amazed that he had never stopped to enjoy the glorious vision before.

He reached in his scrip and withdrew a wrapping of fig cakes and a horn of goat's milk. He consumed two of the cakes and wrapped the remaining four in the piece of linen. Brushing the crumbs from his beard, he uncapped the horn and poured the warm milk down his throat.

Feeling refreshed, he looked around him at the barren desert and the desolate hillside. Except for a few berry bushes and tufts of grass, the wilderness before him spoke of disease and death. Few creatures could survive out there during a drought. Only those tiny animals that could burrow into the soil had any hope of seeing another day.

Though his bones ached from a fitful night, he made it to his feet and went back inside the cave. He picked up Benjamin's roll

of parchment and carried it outside. Then he sat with his back
against the rock wall, beneath a ledge that would shelter him
from the glare of the rising sun, for it would soon be overhead.
He spread the scroll and began to read the words of the prophet
Isaiah as Benjamin had recorded them.

*Have you not known? Have you not heard, that the everlasting
God, the Lord, the Creator of the ends of the earth, faints not, neither
is weary? There is no searching of his understanding.*

Eleazar paused from his reading. With Isaiah's words swimming around in his head, he gazed out at the parched wilderness,
the mauve colored mountains in the distance, and the ribbon
of road that led to Jericho.

He shook his head. He might never understand the One who
spoke all of that into existence, the Creator who also held the
power to speak it all away. He wondered if Yahweh might also
speak away the blemish on his arm. If he could reach the ears of
an unseen God, would he obtain His mercy? Or was it too late?

Eleazar read on.

*He gives power to the faint; and to them that have no might he
increases strength.*

He looked toward the heavens and cried aloud, "Where is this
strength, O Lord? Where is this power that is able to restore me?
Tell me where? And why? That is my question now. Why has
this horrible affliction come upon me? Why have you brought
such bitter judgment into my life at such a time as this?"

The text blurred. He wiped away his tears then clenched his
fists and began to rock back and forth. An agonizing wail rose
from the pit of his stomach and filled his throat. His tormented
cry echoed off the rock wall. It sailed across the wasteland,
even reaching, it seemed, the distant hills of Moab. For the
first time in his life, Eleazar was helpless. In the past, he had
boldly ignored the commands of Moses. He had shunned his
father's authority. He had depended solely on his own strength
and had paid little heed to the advice of his elders. Not his
father or the rabbi, not even Nikolaus, or any other human

being had been able to guide him away from his life of sin. It was true what he'd said to Mattathias. The spot on his arm was merely an outward manifestation of what had been growing inside him for years. The truth was, he had always been a leper, if only in his heart.

Oh, to experience a miracle and the healing power of a merciful God. To have Yahweh's kindness pour down upon his wretched soul and rescue him from himself. He looked again at the scroll. The person who first penned those words was a man of God, far more righteous than he was. Now he was trying to make those ancient words his own in hopes he might awaken the Creator of heaven and earth to his need.

Eleazar stared out at the wilderness and waited, but no voice broke through the gathering clouds like it did for the prophets of old. No hand came down to touch his wound. No spirit of comfort embraced him. He'd never felt so alone.

The rising sun splashed color on Anna's garden inside the courtyard. The house was bathed in golden hues. Birds chirped their welcoming song, and the household of Eleazar ben Judah awoke to another day.

Anna knelt in the center of the floor with a large silk cloth spread before her. On top was a pile of her precious jewels. Martha squatted at Anna's side and plunged her fingers into the glittering array of gemstones and pearls. She lifted a couple bracelets and slipped them on her wrist. Benjamin sat quietly in the corner, a scroll spread open on his lap, a stylus in his hand.

Judah emerged from his quarters, his ailing feet bound with rags. Anna looked into his questioning eyes and went back to sorting through her treasures.

"What is this?" Judah gestured toward Anna's collection.

"I'm getting ready to make a sacrifice for my husband." She glanced at him, but continued to look through the pieces. "I must appease Yahweh with an offering, one that costs me dearly. I will entreat him to restore Eleazar to us. My jewelry and perhaps a lamb should get Yahweh's attention."

Judah drew closer.

A sob parted her lips. "From the time I worked as a servant girl, I have longed to own such adornments." One-by-one she held up the items. "This ring. This bracelet. These gold earrings. This collection of toe rings." She lay them back on the cloth and shook her head. "When I married Eleazar, my life changed. He was as giving as a husband could be. He provided everything our family needed and beyond."

"Everything but himself," Judah grunted.

Anna shook her head and glared at the old man. "My husband was generous and kind. Look at these treasures. Look at this beautiful house. Look at our children." She straightened. "Now it's *my* turn to give back to Eleazar. Perhaps Yahweh will turn a merciful ear to a woman who denies herself all this luxury." She waved her hand over the spread of jewels.

Judah shook his head. "Do you want money? Take the moneybag hidden behind the water jug. Take as much as you want and give it as an offering in the temple."

"Don't you understand?" Anna eyed him in disbelief. "It's not about money. A proper offering must come through sacrifice. There has to be a sense of loss. There must be pain. Otherwise it is meaningless."

"There m—may be another way, M—mother," Benjamin said from his corner. Setting aside his scroll, he rose to his feet. "The p—prophet Jesus is in the city. It's been said he heals the s—sick, the lame, the b—blind, even lepers. The sick p—person doesn't have to be in his p-presence. He can heal from afar. We should find him. W—we can ask him to heal F—father."

Anna scowled at her son. "Jesus? I've heard of that man. Don't be deceived, my son. They say he uses magic and only *pretends* to heal people. His companions follow him like little children. They support his claims. But, they're all liars."

"No, M—mother. I was there, y-yesterday, in the t—temple. He's a good man. He c—confronted the m—moneychangers. He t—tossed their t—tables to the ground and scattered their c—coins."

Anna leaned toward him, her cheeks flushed with rage. "All the more reason to doubt him. Where were the priests? Didn't they take him into account?"

"Th—they stood off at a d—distance, watching."

"If he has offended them, his life will be in danger," Anna raised her voice. "So will the lives of those who follow him. Heed my warning, Benjamin. Stay away from that man."

"But, M—mother—"

"I command you to keep your distance, Benjamin. With the Passover approaching, there's a mixed crowd in the city. Riots have already broken out. This Jesus seems to incite them all the more. Keep away from him, my son, and stay safe."

Anna stared into Benjamin's eyes and sent him a silent warning. But the boy turned away from her and looked to his grandfather.

Judah put a hand on his grandson's shoulder. "I would like to see this Jesus for myself," he said to Anna's amazement. "You will take me there tomorrow morning, Benjamin."

"Father Judah—" she began to protest.

The old man raised a hand and silenced her. "I will make a judgment. I will listen to this Jesus speak. When he's finished, if I have doubts, we will stay clear of him and his followers. But if I am content, we will approach him and ask him to restore Eleazar to good health."

Anna looked from Judah to her son and back to Judah. "How can you—"

"The boy will be safe with me," the old man assured her.

"W—will you join us M—mother?"

She let out a sigh and pressed her lips tightly together.

"Do what you must, and *I* will do what I must. I'm going to sell these precious jewels to Levi. I'll take the money to the temple in the morning. But I won't be going there to see your prophet, Benjamin."

Judah flew into a rage. "Sell to Levi? What are you thinking, woman? That man is a thief. He won't pay you what your jewels are worth. You can go into the city tomorrow and find another merchant who will treat you more fairly."

"Levi lives nearby. I can do this quickly tomorrow morning—"

She glanced up at him. "I'll place the money in the offering box, and I'll say a prayer to Yahweh. That will accomplish much more than your prophet can."

"Why wait until tomorrow, Anna? Why not play the fool today?"

"Levi isn't at home. I saw him leave by the upper road."

"He's evil."

"It doesn't matter. The sacrifice won't be Levi's. It will be *mine*."

Anna pulled the corners of the cloth over her jewelry and secured it with a knot.

"I'll sell *all* of them," she said with a firmness Judah wouldn't be able to oppose. "Early tomorrow morning, I'll go to the house of Levi, and I'll accept whatever price he offers. I've made up my mind, Father Judah. Don't try to stop me."

$\mathcal{I}$n the early morning hours, before the sun rose above the distant mountains, Eleazar descended the hill and looked for a place to bathe himself. He found a flow of water trickling from the cliff wall. He looked about. Assured that he was alone, he removed his outer garments and splashed the chilly water on his chest and face. To his dismay, the mark on his arm had remained.

Shivering, he slipped back into his cloak and started to return to the cave, but stopped short of it. Though it had provided suitable shelter, it had proved to be a lonely place. He'd spent the first day of his separation in utter loneliness, grieving over his past sins and regretting his self-serving ignorance of the needs of others. Should he survive this terrible illness, he vowed to spend more time with his children and to take better care of Anna and his father. He would work hard to provide for the family, and he would pursue friendships with people of prominence, especially those members of the Sanhedrin—people like Enos and Ariel and the men who sat at the city gate.

For now, he craved the company of other people. Like Job, he felt abandoned, emptied of everything he owned, alone and uncertain about his future.

He needed to talk to someone who might understand. Another leper, perhaps. Possibly Achim, if he could find him. The thought of seeing his old friend again sparked fresh life in Eleazar. He looked out at the landscape, the distant hills with their gaping leper caves, and, closer to the city, the road where he had encountered the shrouded figure who reminded him of his lost friend. The man had left the road and had disappeared into the hills. Eleazar looked in the direction where he had gone. If it really was Achim, he needed to find him.

With a new sense of purpose, he gathered his remaining food into his leather scrip, secured his other pack and the scroll in a corner of the cave, and draping his mantle around his shoulders, he walked toward the ridge and the leper caves where his father had taken him long ago.

Anna found Levi pacing in his courtyard, his robe fluttering with his heavy footsteps, as he went back and forth over the marble slabs. The frown on his forehead told her he was deep in thought. The phylactery on his arm stood open. In one hand he gripped a tiny strip of parchment. He held it high and glanced at it now and then. His voice rising and falling with a flood of passion, he spoke the words of scripture.

Take heed to yourselves, that your heart be not deceived, and you turn aside, and serve other gods, and worship them; And then the Lord's wrath be kindled against you.

Anna scowled at the man's false show of faith. A true man of God would have committed those verses to memory.

Hearing her footstep, the man turned and let his angry gaze fall on Anna.

"What do you want, woman?"

For a moment, Anna felt like the young servant girl she once was, shy and withdrawn. She reminded herself that as the wife of a prominent physician, she had acquired equal stature with the man in the fluttering robe.

She straightened her shoulders and returned his gaze. "Why are you troubled, Levi?" Her voice was firm as stone and steady.

Surprised by her boldness, Levi took a step back.

She held his gaze, all fear leaving her as she considered her purpose for coming there, to rescue her husband from a dreadful disease.

"T—troubled? I'm not troubled," he said, and his hand began to shake. "I'm simply dealing with an encounter I had at the temple yesterday."

"Tell me about it," she said sweetly. She shifted the bundle of jewels in her arms.

"There's a false prophet in our midst." Levi's voice had turned cold. "The man claims to be a healer. He leads the people away from our traditions. He promises a better life, a more perfect kingdom."

So Levi had met the man Benjamin had spoken about. Anna began to wonder what sort of person could throw Levi into such a fit. She raised her eyebrows.

"My son Benjamin told me about that man. He said he over-turned the tables of the money changers the other day." Anna laughed to herself. The entire city knew Levi owned one of those tables. He exchanged Hebrew shekels for Roman denarii, often walking away with the better deal.

"Yes, my table as well!" Levi confessed. "I had sorted all my money, the clean from the unclean, the Hebrew coins on one side of my table and the foreign coins on the other. That man accused us of taking unfair advantage of the people. He claimed the temple was his Father's house. His *father*?! Blasphemy!"

"Did you question him?" Anna knew Levi would not let such an opportunity pass him by.

"We surrounded the liar. We needed to expose him before his following grew. I posed several important questions myself." Levi stuck out his chest and raised his chin. "He questioned our interpretation of the law. He called us hypocrites. Hypocrites!? We have position in this city. We have importance. We have authority, while he is—" he paused and spun toward her. "He is *nobody!*"

Anna shuddered. Levi had the power to inflict unbelievable pain on his enemies. She felt a touch of pity for the stranger from Galilee. Perhaps he was innocent, a humble servant of the people, merely spreading good will.

"What will you do now?" She feared his answer.

Vengeance flamed in Levi's eyes. "I won't rest until that man is imprisoned and put to death. The Council will be meeting soon. I'll take this before them. The temple priests also will get involved. We'll put an end to that man's false teachings and we'll charge him with insurrection."

A chill ran through Anna. She'd heard enough. Drawing a deep breath, she lifted the bundle in her arms. "I've brought some jewels for your approval. Perhaps you will offer me a good price?"

Levi frowned. She untied the knot and opened the cloth. The lines on his face eased and he smiled. Raising his eyebrows, he tucked the tiny parchment inside the phylactery, and he beckoned Anna to follow him inside the house.

The sun continued its upward climb, beating the landscape with its harsh rays and stealing all of the air. Eleazar raised his hand to block the glare, tried to keep sight of the ridge. Wildflowers grew on either side of the road. A blanket of poppies, soft pink campions, and bright blue cornflowers would have a short life in this wasteland. Much like those wildflowers, Eleazar felt his own hopes withering.

A flock of swifts darted overhead, their high-pitched cries shattering the stillness. Lizards, startled by Eleazar's footstep, scattered into the brush. He soon came upon the stretch of road where he had seen the shrouded figure with the blue eyes. He left the path, followed the man's route, and mounted the cliff to the familiar row of caves.

He paused for a moment and stared at the bleak openings.

For a moment he was that thirteen-year-old boy again, facing a horrible encounter. A passage from the Psalms came floating back to his mind, long forgotten since his youth because it meant little to him then, but now the truth of it struck him hard.

I am counted with them that go down into the pit: I am as a man that has no strength. Free among the dead, like the slain that lie in the grave, whom you rememberest no more: and they are cut off from thy hand.

Swallowing, he drew near to the ledge and caught sight of the shadows of three men. Two of them sat leaning against the rock wall. The third, a tall, robust man, stood in front of them with his back to Eleazar. The two sat quietly, their attention on the tall one. None of the figures resembled Achim. A crunch of stones under Eleazar's feet caused the tall man to turn around. His clothing, though black like the others, appeared to be new. He'd bound a bright red band around his forehead, and over his shoulder hung an embroidered mantle with a scarlet fringe. His face was brown from the sun, not ashen like the others. His thick brows came to a point over a straight nose, and he had shaved his jaw clean.

"*Shalom.* Peace, my friend," he said, smiling.

Eleazar hesitated. "I am—unclean." The word stuck in his throat.

The man nodded. "Of course you are." His voice was pleasant, not threatening. "Why else would you come to this forsaken place?" He gestured toward the caves.

Despite Eleazar's warning, the man rushed toward him. "Join us. We were in the midst of an argument about tithing. Are you for it, or against it?"

Eleazar shook his head. "I have no opinion," he said.

"Come. Join us anyway," the tall man said, his voice friendly. He nodded toward the two men sitting against the wall. "This is Joachim ... and Bartilaus. And, my name is Reuben. I'm a physician from the valley near Jericho, a servant to these unfortunates."

Eleazar breathed a little easier. "My name is Eleazar ben Judah. I'm a citizen of Jerusalem, and I'm also a physician."

Reuben's eyes grew wide. "Aaah. Eleazar? Your reputation has preceded you. I am honored."

Eleazar had no knowledge that his reputation had gone beyond the city's gates. Little good such fame would do him now.

"It seems I am no longer the physician but the patient," he confessed.

A cloud of concern settled on Reuben's face. "You've been afflicted?"

"My arm has an infection, and I have begun the required seven-day separation."

Reuben drew closer. "Let me take a look."

Eleazar frowned. "I told you, I am unclean."

Could it be that this physician also suffered from the disease? Eleazar lowered his scrip to the ground and drew back his sleeve.

"I'm unclean," Eleazar repeated, thinking the man had not heard him.

"It's of no concern to me," was Reuben's surprising reply. "I have an opinion about the law of separation, that perhaps it prevents the healthy from helping the weak. I have lived with lepers, tended to their wounds, shared food with them. Yet I've never acquired the disease. Perhaps the Almighty has separated me for this work." He smiled and gripped Eleazar's arm. "Be at ease, my friend. There is no need for concern."

To Eleazar, this was a welcome relief. "I've always been the healer, never once the patient. I presumed the disease afflicted only the poor, the careless, or those who lived in squalor."

Reuben chuckled. "Leprosy does not choose its victims according to a man's position in life. Even people of high esteem have fallen under its curse. Do you recall the story about Yahweh cursing Miriam with leprosy for complaining against her brother Moses? And what about Naaman, a respected army captain? He was afflicted and then was healed by washing in the Jordan. Maybe *all* lepers should try that," he said, laughing. Then, he drew close to Eleazar. "I have seen with my own eyes the disease ravishing the rich and the poor alike. There is no respect of persons."

Reuben lowered Eleazar's sleeve and released his grip. Eleazar boiled with indignation. "You speak lightly of a life-threatening illness," he said through clenched teeth. "I may never see my family again."

"My friend, I spoke without thinking. In truth, there is nothing you can do except wait and pray. You may be one of the fortunate ones."

"You couldn't possibly understand a disease you've never had. You can't know what it's like to have the messenger of death hanging over your head."

"Eleazar, I've cared for these poor souls for seven years. Though not a sign of it has appeared on my body that doesn't mean I won't have it next week. Or tomorrow. Or this very day. When I return to the valley, I will go through the necessary purification rituals, and then I will go about my business of helping others. My life is no longer my own. A terrible event ended my dream, and so I've committed my life to this service."

"Service?" Eleazar was astonished. "You would risk your life for a mere service?" He shook his head. "My father pursued a similar path. He also referred to his visits to this place as a *service*. Though he never acquired the disease, my mother and my brother and I paid the price."

Eleazar's bitter words drew surprised stares from the two men by the wall. He drew closer to Reuben and lowered his voice. "I warn you, physician, you are endangering your life, and that of your family, if you have one. Why don't you go back to Jericho and forget about these poor souls?"

Reuben straightened, and the lines on his forehead deepened. "The disease is everywhere, Eleazar, even in Jericho. My service continues there." He stepped back and tilted his head. "And what about you, my friend? Aren't *you* endangering your life? Except for this minor irritation on your skin, you appear quite healthy. Why didn't you enter the temple chamber or go off by yourself during your seven days? Why come here?"

Eleazar shrugged. "I spent one night alone, in a cave on the

Ophel Ridge. It was a lonely, deserted place. I needed to talk to someone, anyone who might understand. So I left the cave and came here hoping to find an old friend, a leper by the name of Achim."

Reuben brightened. "Achim? The merchant? I know him well."

Eleazar's spirit came to life. "Achim was my best friend from our youth. He was declared a leper several years ago. He left Jerusalem without a word to me. Once I thought I passed him on the road leading to these caves. That's why I came here, Reuben, to find my friend."

The sparkle in Reuben's eyes faded. "Oh, Eleazar," he said, a sadness washing over his face. "I fear your friend has the worst type of the disease, the kind that moves quickly. The sores have consumed his entire body. Achim suffers terribly, and I'm afraid his time grows short."

Tears came easily to Eleazar. He didn't try to halt their flow but let them run down his cheeks and into his beard. A sob erupted from his throat. He staggered to the wall, reached out and planted his palm against the stony surface, tried to keep standing but slowly sank to his knees.

Reuben came up behind him and rested a hand on his shoulder. "Perhaps it will help you to see him again."

He nodded and sobbed out a plea. "Where is he?"

Reuben pointed toward Jericho. "There's a place on this side of the Jordan where a group of lepers have made their home. They raise their own crops—mostly wheat and barley and corn. They keep goats and sheep and fowl." He softened his voice. "Achim has been living among them."

Renewed passion surged through Eleazar. "Can you take me there? Today? Now?"

Reuben nodded. "It will be dark soon. Spend the night with us. I brought food from Jericho. You can refresh yourself and get a good night's sleep. If we leave early tomorrow morning we can reach the village by dusk, ahead of the Passover.

CHAPTER THIRTY-EIGHT

That afternoon, Anna made her way to the temple. In one hand, she clutched the meager payment Levi had given her for her precious jewels. She'd suffered a great loss, but it didn't matter. After all, wasn't that part of the sacrifice? Didn't she have to feel pain in order to approach Yahweh with a plea for his help?

She entered the outer court and found it packed with people. She weaved through the throng toward the offering box at the far end of Solomon's porch. Priests stood on either side of it, their eyes fastened to the opening. An old woman shuffled ahead of Anna and crept closer to the temple treasury. With painful effort the woman knelt before the box, dropped two coins in, and bowed her head to the pavement.

A blue-robed figured moved up beside her. "Do you see this poor widow?" he said, his voice tender yet filled with authority. "She has put in more than anyone else. All these people have given abundantly out of their wealth. But she, out of her poverty, has given everything she had."

Anna froze before the money box. Surely, her sacrifice would be meaningless now. She hadn't given everything she had, only a portion of it. She still owned a large house, a chest full of fine clothing, a well-stocked kitchen, and so much more.

She was still standing there, the handful of coins stuck to

her hand, when the man walked away and the crowd surged after him. They lunged past Anna, nearly causing her to fall. Dropping her donation into the box, she turned and followed after them.

"Who is he?" someone asked.

"They say he's a prophet," another voice answered.

"He's a simple carpenter," said another. "From Nazareth."

"No. He's a miracle worker."

More voices rose up.

"He's a healer."

"He cured my brother of a plague."

"They say he can raise the dead."

The praises kept coming. Anna's head began to spin.

"He's not merely a man. He's more than that."

"The Son of God!"

"The Messiah!"

Hearing that, she stepped away from the madness and stared after the crowd.

"They call him Jesus. *Savior*," a woman said with reverence.

A Pharisee strode by. Long tassels hung from the four corners of his mantle. A phylactery was fastened to his upper arm. "Blasphemer!" he shouted at the woman.

"Shhh! He's going to speak." A man pointed toward the porticos.

A hush settled over the crowd. Anna craned her neck. The man called Jesus stood on a rise of steps at the far end. She looked about the gathering, a curious mix of Jews and Gentiles. Positioned about the court were Roman soldiers easily recognized in their plumed helmets and leather tunics. Each had a short sword strapped to his waist, a javelin in one hand and a shield in the other. The sunlight glinted off the metal ornaments on their breastplates. They stood very still and watched the crowd, chins raised in prideful command.

Temple priests, Pharisees and scribes, many of them members of the Great Council, filed into the court. They joined together in a chain of self-importance on one side of the courtyard. Levi bar Uzza entered their midst, his lips pressed together, his black eyes narrowed at the speaker.

Also in the crowd were followers of Herod, Jews who had traded their loyalty for political favors. They were held in disdain by other Jews who had remained loyal to the traditions of their faith.

The temple scribes huddled together with the priests. Moments later, they sent their disciples to the front. They gathered around Jesus.

"Is it right to pay taxes to Caesar, or is it not?" one of them cried out.

Jesus asked him to show him a coin. The man did so. "Whose image and seal are inscribed here?" Jesus said, raising the coin so all could see it.

Anna smiled with amazement. Jesus had responded with a question of his own. *How clever.*

The profile of Tiberius Caesar, emperor of Rome, was clearly etched on the face of the coin. "Give to Caesar what rightfully belongs to him," Jesus said. "And give to God what is rightfully His."

Joyous shouts went up from a portion of the crowd. Anna, being taller than most women, drew herself up and peered over the veiled heads. A group of young men had gathered close to where Jesus stood. Anna flinched. Her own son, Benjamin, was among them. She looked for Judah and found him leaning against a far wall, his eyes on the speaker instead of on her son.

What kind of man was this who could draw Judah from his comfort at home to walk on tired feet to such a place? She looked at Jesus and wondered if this man could, indeed, restore Eleazar. And if so, what good were her sacrifices? Her coins? Her precious jewels? What of the perfect lamb that would face death on her behalf during the Passover sacrifices? Would any of those gifts capture Yahwah's attention?

Anna kept her eyes on Jesus. The Jewish leaders moved in and began to examine him. When he showed no fear, they became incensed against him.

Unmoved by their threats, Jesus turned away from them and spoke to the crowd.

"Watch out for the teachers of the law. They walk around in flowing robes and enjoy the attention that is bestowed upon them. They claim the most important seats at meetings and banquets. They put on a demonstration of righteousness, make lengthy prayers, and display their phylacteries for all to see. But they, themselves, break the very laws they teach. They are hypocrites, deceivers, blind guides."

The richly robed men spun away and left the temple, their robes fluttering and their shawls flying. Levi departed with them. The scribes and priests also left in the direction of Caiaphas' home.

So, Anna mused, *Now they will gather behind closed doors and decide among themselves what should be done with this stranger.*

A cold chill passed through her heart. Never before had she seen anyone stand up against the religious leaders. She looked again at Jesus. He was speaking softly to a group of young men. Greeks. She knew them by their short tunics, their shaved beards and their cropped hair. The cords of their sandals wound up their calves almost to their knees.

"The hour has come for the Son of Man to be glorified," Jesus told the crowd.

An joyous shout went up.

He spoke at length. No one tried to stop him. When he finished he declared, "Father, glorify your name!"

There was a stirring of wind among the pillars. Anna shuddered and drew her veil closer.

"Was that thunder?" a woman asked.

Anna looked toward the heavens.

"No. See?" A man pointed. "The sky is clear."

"I heard a voice," another woman whispered. "Like that of an angel."

"You dream, woman." The man's remark drew laughter from his companions.

"No," the woman insisted. "The voice clearly said, T*his is my beloved Son, in whom I am well pleased.*"

Anna trembled. Was that the truth? Or blasphemy?"

More conversation continued between Jesus and the people. When it ended, Jesus descended the steps and headed for the temple gate. Men and women thronged around him. Then the crowd began to disperse. Some followed after Jesus and his friends. Others stood in groups, talking among themselves, their arms waving, their voices strained. People were crying. And laughing. And shouting.

Anna recognized some of the men in one group. They belonged to the alliance known as the zealous ones. They approached the Herodian Jews and began to call out accusations at them. The Herodians struck back with angry words. Their arguments grew louder and more violent. Fists flew. Blades flashed in the sunlight. The sound of metal against metal rang out. From their watch by the gate, the Roman soldiers moved in, their swords drawn.

Anna searched the crowd. Judah remained by the wall, but where was Benjamin? Then she found him in the crowd that was following Jesus through the gate. Leaping forward, Anna tried to reach her son. She fought against the surge of bodies.

"Benjamin!" she cried out, her voice fading in the uproar. "Benjamin!"

She struggled against the people who were moving in all directions. She caught sight of Benjamin again and threw herself into the crowd. She drew closer to him. She pushed her way into the jostling throng and reached out. His cloak was inches from her fingers. Then someone blocked her path. She stumbled, then watched, helpless, as Benjamin was swept away from her by the surging crowd.

Anna looked about in a panic. Fighting had broken out in different parts of the courtyard. There was Benjamin, almost at the gate. More rebels had closed in. Someone's fist struck Benjamin's left cheek. Blood trickled from the wound.

Anna gasped. She pushed through the crowd. Someone

shoved her. She stumbled and fell against a pillar. The swelling crowd pulled Benjamin farther away. She looked for an opening in the throng. A soldier rushed ahead, waving his sword. Anna shrieked as the point pierced Benjamin's right side. The soldier, his eyes wide, withdrew his sword and let Benjamin sink to the ground. A bright red ribbon of blood flowed from Benjamin's wound and spread down his pure white tunic.

Anna screamed. The courtyard spun around her. The shouting buzzed in her ears. Her vision blurred, and she fell to the pavement.

When Anna opened her eyes again, she was in her own bed. Sunlight streamed through her window, bathing her in warmth. A dark shadow passed in front of the light. Judah was pressing a damp cloth to her forehead. She squeezed her eyes shut. The old man gently stroked her cheek.

"Anna. Anna."

She opened her eyes and started to shiver. Abi came near and laid a sheepskin blanket over her.

"Benjamin?" Anna tried to push herself upright. "My son," she murmured.

Judah placed his hands against her shoulders and gently forced her back on the pillow. "Rest, Anna."

She searched Judah's face. "Where is he?"

Judah shook his head. "Benjamin was badly wounded. The priests carried him to their chamber and summoned a physician."

"My son," Anna moaned. Tears trickled down both sides of her face and dropped onto the pillow. "He needs his father. He needs Eleazar. I must go to him. I should be at his side."

"No," Judah said, his voice firm. "Women are not permitted beyond the wall. You cannot enter the priests' quarters. Benjamin is in Yahweh's hands now."

Eleazar had chosen to spend the night under the stars. Alone. He couldn't bring himself to join Reuben and the two cursed ones inside the cave. Part of him still hoped he did not have the disease.

Now he awakened to a dew-soaked mantle and the sound of early birds chattering in the brush. Reuben emerged from the cave, stretched, and searched the sky.

"We have good weather for our journey," he told Eleazar. "Look at the horizon. Not a sign of red."

Eleazar followed his gaze to the east. "Nor is there a cloud," he said. "We'll be at the mercy of an angry sun."

Reuben nodded. "Better than rain and wind," he said, smiling.

Eleazar ate two fig cakes from his pack, and Reuben cut up a pomegranate. Then they bid farewell to the other two, and they departed.

"The village where we are going is on this side of Jericho," Reuben explained as they walked. "Beyond the village are the ruins of Joshua's victory as well as King Herod's winter palace. We won't be going to either of those places. At the first signs of the fertile valley, we'll leave the main road and go south toward the village situated in a valley few people know about.

Eleazar's interest was stirred. "Why the mystery?"

"Many lepers reside there—men, women, and, yes, even children. Most of them appear as healthy as anyone walking around in Jerusalem," Reuben assured him. "Don't be afraid of them. Keep your distance if you must, but I am certain you will soon be able to look beyond their afflictions and see what I see—people. Simply people like yourself who did nothing to bring this terrible fate upon themselves."

Eleazar thought about the sore on his arm, hidden beneath his sleeve but painfully real. "It seems none of us can escape."

Reuben nodded with understanding. "Those who do escape never forget how close they came to a living death. We must pray that you will be among the healed."

"Yes," Eleazar agreed, a ray of hope entering his heart.

Reuben turned to look at him. "Is someone waiting for you at home?"

Faces came before Eleazar, and he smiled. "My family," he said, his throat tightening. "My father is with us. And there is my wife, Anna, and my children—Mara, my eldest and married to a fine young man, Benjamin, my only son, Abi, our frail daughter, and little Martha, the joy of my life." As he spoke their names a surge of guilt pressed his heart.

"I fear I have neglected them far too long," he confessed. "I provided whatever they needed—a big house filled new furnishings, an abundance of food, the finest clothes, gold and jewels for my wife, and servants to help with the household duties. But—" He bowed his head. "I failed them, Reuben. Except for Martha, I made no bond with any of them. In truth, I never knew them, and I never gave them an opportunity to know me."

Reuben released a sigh. "Our choices in life sometimes bring sorrow," he said. "You have strayed from what is right, that is true, but it's not too late, Eleazar. Now that you've been brought low you can turn to Yahweh and ask His forgiveness. Yahweh alone can restore you to good health. He alone can send you back to your family."

Eleazar cast a sideways glance at Reuben. "How can you say such a thing? Yahweh should be turning His back on me. Why would He bless a miserable sinner like myself? I rejected my father's choice of a spouse for me and secretly met with the woman I wanted. I defiled our marriage bed. And I continued to shun the poor woman who has served me well all these years. Yahweh would be right to cut me down."

"No, my friend. As the Psalmist wrote, *The Lord is nigh unto them that are of a broken heart, and saves such as be of a contrite spirit.* I have never met a more broken and contrite man than you are at this moment."

Eleazar shook his head as he recalled the pain on his children's faces the moment he entered the house each evening.

"My older girls, Mara and Abi, fear me. I ruled them like a king, commanded their obedience, and now I've denied Abi a chance for happiness. The poor child wants to marry the son of my worst enemy. In spite of her pleas, I refused to sign the contract."

Eleazar wiped tears from his cheek and went on. "I neglected my son, Benjamin. I was angry that I couldn't cure his stammering. It's no wonder he chose to become a scribe rather than follow me in medicine. I didn't have to say a word. He saw my displeasure. And so, he ran to his grandfather for comfort and guidance."

"You have to stop punishing yourself, my friend," Reuben said with pity in his voice. "We all make mistakes. But we have a merciful God. You can lay your faults at His feet." He gazed into Eleazar's eyes and smiled. "You may be one of the fortunate ones. You may have time to repair your wrongs. The truth is, you don't have to wait for the Day of Atonement, you can repent *anytime.* You can repent *now.*"

Eleazar stopped walking. He looked at Reuben with unseeing eyes. "What do you mean? Are you talking about the Passover sacrifices? Do you think those unending slaughters can wipe away sins as great as mine?"

"No, Eleazar. I'm not talking about sacrifices or the killing of animals or any other kind of rite. I'm talking about something far greater." Reuben stared into Eleazar's eyes. "I'm talking about drawing near to Yahweh in repentance. The Baptist preached it."

Eleazar knew of the desert man who drew people to the Jordan a few years ago. He'd purposely stayed away from the lunatic.

"The man is dead, beheaded by an order of Herod."

"Yes, but his message lives on," Reuben said as they started walking again. "Think about King David. He also neglected his family, and he suffered for it."

Eleazar grunted. "I certainly don't consider myself equal with David. I failed my family, my wife most of all. I strayed from our marriage bed, pursued another woman, and then I left her to die at the hands of an angry husband. I didn't go to defend her, didn't speak on her behalf." Eleazar began to sob. "She died because of me. The light in her eyes went out because of me." His shoulders shook with his weeping. "My selfishness hurt both my lover and the woman I married."

He stared ahead at the growing patches of green and the appearance of palm trees on the horizon. More memories surfaced. Eleazar had created a river of confession. For the first time in his life he had found a willing ear. Unable to stop the flow, he spilled out the rest of his pain.

"My sins go deeper, Reuben."

Without speaking a word, the poor man nodded his approval for him to go on.

"In my desire for success, I also wounded a dear friend, a man named Thomas who had done me no harm." He bowed his head and shook it back and forth. "Thomas is dead now, too, and it was because of me." He looked at Reuben. "There is no end to the pain I have caused."

Reuben sighed long and hard. "David sinned in much the same way," he said. "He had many wives and concubines, including Bathsheba, who belonged to another. Then he arranged to have her husband killed. I do not condone such sin, of course, but just as David restored his faith in Yahweh, so can you. As long as you have the breath of life, Eleazar, there is hope."

"I want to believe that," he said with resolve. "If I'm allowed to go home—if this blemish heals, and I end my separation—I want to make things right with my family. I want to let Mara know her father has loved her since the day she was born. If it's not too late, I want to give Benjamin the father he's needed all along. And I want to give Abi my consent to marry the young man she loves."

Reuben patted him on his back. "Perhaps the Lord will restore you and give you time to do all of that and more."

"I don't deserve such kindness," he confessed, more to himself than to Reuben. "It's to my shame that our youngest daughter, Martha, is *my* daughter, but not Anna's. She was born to my lover." He looked at Reuben. "Listen to me and you will know what a kind and forgiving woman my Anna is. After Ruth was stoned to death, her husband rejected Martha. He cursed the child and threw her in the street like a piece of rubbish. Anna heard about his evil deed. Without saying a word to me, she went out to find my daughter. Who would do that? Who would care about a child that was born by her husband's lover?"

He wiped a tear from the corner of his eye. "Anna put aside her own pain and agreed to raise Martha."

Reuben exhaled a long breath. "You've had the right woman in your life all along, Eleazar. It's sad that you're only seeing her value now."

"I long to make peace with my wife. Even if I should die of this horrible disease, I need to let Anna know how much her loyalty meant to me. I need to beg her forgiveness."

Anna had recovered, though she still had a knot on her forehead, likely from striking the pavement when she fell. She felt strong enough to make another journey to the temple, this time with the two girls, Abi and Martha, running along at her side.

Weakened by the previous day's tumult, Judah remained behind. "It will do you no good to attempt a visit," he told Anna. "Benjamin is behind locked doors."

"I will take a sacrifice," she said with firmness. "Surely, Yahweh will see and approve."

A young male servant accompanied the women with a lamb draped over his shoulders. They separated from him near the women's court, with the servant moving ahead toward the sacrificial altar, and Anna and her daughters slipping behind the lattice wall on a spread of pavement reserved for the women.

With the girls standing on either side of her, Anna peered through the lattice and waited. Tears flowed down her cheeks. Quietly she prayed that her sacrifice would move Yahweh to heal her husband and her son. Others also had brought sacrifices. The days were leading up to the Passover. Sacrifices would continue all day and all night, filling the temple with the aroma of burning carcasses and echoing with the shrill cries of slaughtered animals.

The high priest, Joseph Caiaphas, considered to be the most powerful man in Israel, mounted the steps to the altar. He wore the same type of vestments used centuries before by Aaron and his sons. A breast piece and ephod, both of fine linen, with blue, red, and purple threads woven through, and underneath a pale blue robe with a fringed border. The ephod was decorated with gold rings and two glittering gemstones. More gold circled the hem of his outer robe, with a row of tiny bells that sounded with every step he took. A gold rosette graced the front of his turban. With his head held high, Caiaphas was the image of supreme power.

Anna eyed his self-righteous pomp with bitterness. Had it not been for the misfortune that had fallen on her home, she would have stayed away, for she doubted her small sacrifice would be seen amidst the thousands that came before and after it.

Caiaphas strode to the center of the court. Before him spread a sea of white robes, as devout priests prostrated themselves in front of the altar. At his command, several priests rose from the floor and took their places, assigned to them earlier in the day through the casting of lots. Three bore the difficult duty of slaughtering the sacrificial lambs. The others had charge of sprinkling the blood on the altar, trimming the lamps, and tending to the incense. They padded about the court barely making a sound with their bare feet.

Caiaphas raised the scroll he had selected and faced the congregation. In a booming voice, he read the words that told of Israel's deliverance from bondage and the ordinance of Pesach as established by Yahweh. He would repeat the ritual several times throughout the Week of Unleavened Bread.

When Caiaphas finished speaking, a young priest approached the slaughtering table and raised his knife above a struggling lamb. Anna's stomach tightened. The writhing animal looked like the one she had selected from her pen. She uttered another prayer for her son and her husband, then she lowered her eyes, unable to watch the slitting of the animal's throat.

From the time she was a little girl she had watched the same offering. Over and over again, year after year, animals were put to death on the altar, leaving a stain of blood that never washed away. She couldn't help but wonder if such sacrifices were ever enough to atone for all the sins of all the people.

"The animals don't suffer," her father had reassured her. "Slitting the throat is the kindest way to kill anything. It is quick. It is painless. And in the end, Yahweh smiles down on the sacrifice and on the one who offers it."

CHAPTER FORTY

The sun crept overhead and set the air on fire. Eleazar and Reuben stopped to rest beneath a cluster of palm trees. Placing their packs on the ground, they settled back against the trunks, where they would be sheltered from the harsh midday light. A spread of palm branches fanned out above them and cast ragged shadows all around.

Eleazar gazed out at the blinding white road still ahead of them. In the shimmering heat it quivered like a pool of water.

Eleazar dug into his pack and pulled out the rest of his food. He offered a handful of dates to Reuben along with one of the last two fig cakes. The young physician accepted the offered food and shared some bread and cheese from his own bag. Reuben then pulled a sheepskin from his pack and splashed water on his face and into his mouth. Eleazar did the same with the goat's horn he had filled at a stream near the Ophel Ridge.

Feeling refreshed, he looked at Reuben and smiled, amazed at how quickly they had become friends.

"My father was a lot like you, Reuben," Eleazar told him. "He served the poor, and he cared for the lepers. When I was thirteen, we visited the caves near the one where I met you. I have to confess, I didn't want to go there. I didn't share my father's passion for those people. One trip. That's all it took for me to reject my father's way of serving. A terrible thing happened while we were there. One of the lepers—a feeble, old woman—sprayed me with her vomit. For weeks afterward I feared I would come down with the disease."

Reuben listened with interest.

"I'm sorry to say, I looked down on those people," Eleazar lamented. "My heart was set on serving the rich and the powerful—not the forsaken ones. I had no use for the lepers *or* the poor." He smiled at the man. "Until yesterday, when I met you." His smile grew wider. "You have what my father had, Reuben. You love the helpless. You care for the unfortunate. It's a special gift. My father had it too. But I—" He bowed his head in shame. "I have never known the joy of practicing such charity."

Reuben took another drink of water. "Don't envy me, Eleazar. I'm a physician who visits the most despised and frightening groups of people. It's not something one plans to do. For some of us—myself especially—it's something I fell into. I like to believe it was a calling of God. But in reality, it happened because of a terrible misfortune."

Eleazar kept his eyes on Reuben, his interest aroused.

"My little girl had leprosy," Reuben said, sending a hot dagger into Eleazar's heart. "I've come to accept it, my friend," he quickly added, as though aware of the blow he had inflicted. "My wife died in childbirth. I raised Esther alone. She was seven years old when she first showed signs of the disease."

Eleazar thought of Martha. He felt like he couldn't breathe. "My youngest is almost seven," he said, his throat tightening.

"Esther was a precious child," Reuben continued thoughtfully. He picked up a twig and began to draw circles in the sand. "I had planned to remarry, to give my child a new mother. I met a woman who would have treated her well. Then Esther's hair started to fall out on the right side. A blemish appeared on her cheek. It began as tiny pink dots, but in a few weeks, they merged and spread. Her face had no feeling. Then she lost her vision in her right eye."

Reuben paused to wipe away a tear, then he drew more circles in the sand. "The Hassan at our synagogue in Galilee declared Esther unclean. He didn't even offer her the required seven days. Certain she was afflicted, he condemned my little girl to a life without hope." He stopped drawing and looked at Eleazar. "Of course, my betrothed canceled our wedding plans. And to my dismay, neighbors threatened to harm us if I kept Esther at home. They read the law to me and insisted I send her away."

Eleazar couldn't believe his ears. "But she was a child!"

"Yes, she was. But she had a frightening disease." Reuben blinked back a flood of tears. They spilled onto his cheeks and ran off his chin. "My friends feared for their *own* children, and rightfully so. I cannot judge them. But I felt like a failure. Here I was, a physician, and I couldn't save my wife from a difficult childbirth, nor could I rescue my daughter from a deadly disease."

Eleazar thought of his mother dying along with her infant. His father was a physician. He couldn't save her. Then Anna gave birth to frail little Abi. Eleazar had failed to help her. The sorrow he was feeling for his new friend mixed with a stab of guilt over his own failure.

They both sat in silence, weeping and brushing away tears until there were no more to shed. It was a long time before either of them spoke.

At last Eleazar drew a deep breath, mopped his face with the corner of his mantle, and asked the question that had been preying on his mind.

"Did you send her away?"

Reuben shook his head. "I couldn't put my daughter in the care of strangers. She was confused. Frightened. I did what any loving father would do. I went with her. I packed my belongings and took her to the village we'll be visiting today. The lepers welcomed us into their fold. They asked no questions. They accepted Esther and made us both feel welcome. When they found out I was a physician, they showered me with presents.

And though they had struggles of their own, they helped me care for my child. She died in my arms two years later."

Eleazar shook his head as more tears fell from his eyes.

"You lost her?"

Reuben nodded. "It was hopeless. I buried her there in the graveyard they built for their own lost souls."

"And so you stayed on with them?"

Reuben took a long, trembling breath. "How could I leave? These people had shown me kindness. As their physician I have been able to heal some of their milder illnesses, but not all, of course. I would love to find a cure for leprosy. Perhaps there isn't one. Though I've tried many different remedies, I've had no success." He leaned back and began to spin the stick in the air, as though writing a message. "So you see, Eleazar, I learned about the disease through a misfortune of my own. It is because of my little girl that I continue to serve the lepers."

Eleazar couldn't imagine how he would respond if a child should die in his arms. Though he'd witnessed many a death because of his work, he always had avoided the thought of losing one of his own children to death.

"Was her passing difficult for her?" he carefully asked.

Reuben broke the stick in half and tossed the pieces aside.

"If this is too difficult—" Eleazar offered.

Reuben merely stared off at the desert. "One night, Esther and I decided to lie outside on our mats, instead of sleeping in the comfort of our home. We were staring up at the heavens when she raised a tiny hand, pointed at the stars, and asked me if her mother was up there. I assured her she was, and that she was whole, and happy, and full of life. Then, my little girl said the strangest thing. She said she wanted to go there, to be with her mother, and to be whole again. I couldn't speak for a long time. Later, that same evening, after the entire camp had settled down, I lay there with my arms around Esther. In the stillness, I could feel those stars beckoning to my little girl, and I made the decision to let her go. That night, she fell peacefully asleep, and she never woke up again."

Hot tears flooded from Eleazar's eyes. This time, he didn't bother to wipe them away but allowed them to flow freely. His throat tightened until he thought he wouldn't be able to take another breath. His new friend had suffered much.

Eleazar sat in silence, pondering all that he had heard, unable to speak for the ache in his throat. He searched the heavens. The sun had moved to the west, and the air had cooled slightly.

"Let's move on," Reuben said, rising. "If we hurry, we can reach the village before dark."

Eleazar had a lot to think about as he walked farther from his home in Jerusalem. A change had come over him. He couldn't describe it, he only knew that he felt different about life, his family, his work, and even his dreams.

As they drew closer to the Jordan Valley, the air turned from arid to moist, and a gentle breeze came up.

Reuben pointed to the south, and together they left the smooth, paved highway and stepped onto a broken, overgrown path that seemed to lead nowhere. Suddenly, the aromatic scent of balsam filled the air. The humming of long-necked cranes and the warble of doves welcomed them to the river valley, and the dead wasteland immediately came to life. Stately palm trees welcomed them to a lush paradise, rich with dates and figs, blossoming shrubs, and gardens overflowing with leeks, cucumbers, melons, and stalks of beans and corn.

"We need to hurry," Reuben said, picking up his step. "The 14th of Nissan draws near. When the sun sets, the Passover will begin."

Several moments later, Eleazar caught sight of a watchtower and a half circle of small clay-built houses, their flat roofs covered with palm branches. Shadows moved about the center of the square carrying garden tools, as though finishing their day's work. A group of children tumbled down a nearby slope, shouting and waving sticks after a herd of sheep as they guided them into a stone enclosure. After forcing the animals inside, one of the taller boys placed a thorny branch across the opening. At the sight of Reuben and Eleazar, several smaller children screamed with joy and rushed toward them. Reuben patted their heads, laughed and talked with the older ones, and gently punched the arm of the tall boy.

At the sound of the children's screaming, several women spilled from their homes. They also crowded around Reuben and pressed him with questions.

"Do you have news from Jerusalem?"

"Did you speak with my relatives?"

"What has changed since the Romans arrived?"

Reuben smiled into their eager faces. "I'll answer all your questions during our evening meal."

The women eyed Eleazar with interest but didn't try to speak with him. They clung to Reuben, followed him into the square and dispersed into their own homes. Then several men approached.

"*Shalom,* Reuben."

"We're happy to have you back with us."

"Praise the Almighty. You've returned in safety."

"Come. Dine with us. The Passover meal is about to begin."

Eleazar looked about with amazement. Instead of eating in the privacy of their homes, these people had prepared a long table in the center of the square. There were no pillows on the ground for reclining. Their furnishings were raised, like those of the Greeks, and like the tables and chairs in Eleazar's home. Somehow, despite being sheltered in the valley, they had moved away from the traditions of their forefathers. Life went on for these people.

A teenage girl brought a pan of water and two towels. Reuben and Eleazar washed quickly and joined the others at the table. Eleazar studied the gathering. He counted 30 men, plus women and children. Most of them appeared normal and healthy. If they had leprosy, the signs of it were well hidden beneath their clothing.

A few women brought candles to the table, and with the setting of the sun, the Passover began with one of the older men speaking the customary prayer. As they dined on roast lamb, bitter herbs, and lentils, Reuben told the people how he had met Eleazar. They greeted him warmly. Then the young physician satisfied them with the news they'd been expecting.

"The Romans have overrun the city," Reuben began with an air of sadness. "The situation in Jerusalem grows more severe every day. Herod Antipas oppresses the people with more rules. The man fears treason. He's even killed members of his own family."

This news was greeted with murmurs and mumblings.

"The authorities have begun to punish insurrectionists with the Roman practice of crucifixion. It's a horrible way to die. They make a public display of prisoners by placing their crosses along the main road into the city for everyone to see. Be glad, my friends, that you are safe here in your little village, far from such misery."

Eleazar listened closely, mournful that he had been aware of what had been happening in Judea, but he had turned his face away. For a little while he had been consumed with keeping Marcus happy so he could spend time with Ruth. Then, after she was gone, he simply didn't care anymore. He didn't care what the Romans were doing. He didn't care if he never saw Marcus again, didn't care if his work suffered, didn't care if he lived or died.

But once he saw the spot on his arm, something happened inside him. Suddenly, he wanted to live. And now he had come to this place with Reuben, and he was learning about what mattered and what didn't.

He kept watching the people, listened to their talk, and began to see them in a different light.

He lifted a sliver of lamb to his lips. The man sitting next to him offered him a piece of unleavened bread. He hesitated at first, then he accepted it. Except for a few who had visible scars on their faces, most of them appeared whole, though Eleazar knew that the disease had touched them in some way. A man sitting across from him had several lumps on the back of his neck. A woman was missing one side of her nose. An old gentleman had only three fingers but was able to pass a platter of dried fruit to him. He took it, managed to smile, and thought about the prescribed cleansing he was going to have to endure.

Eleazar looked at the circle of homes, then he caught Reuben's attention and raised his eyebrows in an unspoken question.

The physician nodded with understanding. "Mine is the farthest one on the circle, the one with the red door. You'll stay with me tonight."

Eleazar pulled off another sliver of lamb and slid it into his mouth. Hungry from the long journey, he piled vegetables on his plate, added another piece of bread, and used it to sop up the juices from a bowl in the center of the table. He looked around at the many faces for someone with red hair and blue eyes. Achim wasn't among them.

When he finished eating he approached Reuben. "Where's Achim?"

The physician shook his head sadly. "You won't find him here." He pointed toward the hill. A row of caves stood out on the ridge above the sheep pen, looking much like the leper caves near Jerusalem.

"He's there," Reuben said.

Eleazar stared in confusion.

"It's where the badly crippled live." Reuben told him. "We have separated them for the sake of the children. And, it helps them too, because they can't move around like they used to. We feed them and bathe them and care for their wounds. They remain in their caves—and wait for the end."

"Is Achim alone?"

"Each of them has a private cave," Reuben explained. "The women take food to them, and the men attend to their bodily needs. Their situation is hopeless, Eleazar. When they go into those caves, they know they won't be coming back. We've placed a heavy stone near each opening. When the person who lives there dies, the body is anointed and the stone is rolled in place, sealing the cave for a tomb."

Eleazar thought of Achim in that horrible black hole, and he began to sob.

Reuben rested a comforting hand on his shoulder. "The villagers have named the ridge, *The Entrance to Heaven*," he said. "It's fitting, is it not?"

Eleazar stared at the row of caves, then he looked at Reuben, who offered him a tender smile. His heart ached for his friend. Once a happy, healthy man, Achim had become a prisoner of a horrible disease.

"When can we go to the caves, Reuben? I want to see my friend."

"We'll visit him in the morning. Darkness takes over quickly here in the valley. But, I must warn you, Eleazar, what you find there will be painful. The disease has ravished your friend terribly. And, I need to tell you, Achim may not recognize you."

"No, Reuben." Eleazar shook his head. "Not Achim. He will know me. I'm certain of it."

*I*n Jerusalem preparations had been completed for the Passover. Anna's servants had swept every corner of the house free of leaven. Anna and her daughters had purified the cooking vessels, the table, and all the bowls and eating utensils. A portion of lamb turned on a spit in the courtyard.

In keeping with tradition, Judah spread lamb's blood on the doorposts and said the customary prayer. Anna and Abi went about lighting candles and preparing the table. They set out platters of unleavened bread, the lamb, a lentil mash and other vegetables, bitter herbs, and a cruse of vinegar.

When it came time for the meal, Judah took Eleazar's place at the head of the table. Anna sat to his right and the two girls settled across from her. At the opposite end, Anna had set three places, each with a cup for wine and an empty plate. According to tradition, the center place was for Elijah, who was expected to come to the house and announce the arrival of the Messiah. Every home in Judea would have honored the prophet in such a manner.

On either side of Elijah were settings for Benjamin and Eleazar. Anna stared at those two vacant places and choked back a sob. She imagined her husband somewhere alone and hungry, enduring a bitter cold night in a cave or lying on the hard ground with only his mantle to keep him warm and a rock for a pillow.

As for Benjamin, she had yet to learn if he had survived the stabbing. She recalled his cry of pain, the anguish on his face, the way he dropped to the pavement.

Judah broke through her thoughts when he stood for the opening blessing. His hands shaking, he raised the first of four cups of wine and began the scripture remembrances about Israel's captivity in Egypt and the release on the very first Passover.

Anna lifted her cup, took a sip of wine, and gazed longingly at the vacant settings. If Eleazar and Benjamin had been present, they would have carried out the question and answer portion usually reserved for father and son. In their absence, Judah and little Martha adopted those duties, the old man's heavy growl nearly drowning the child's meek voice.

Suddenly, there was a knock at the door. Everyone froze. Anna couldn't imagine who would come to the house at such an hour. Most families, even those with members who were ailing, would have waited until after the Passover to come for medicines. It couldn't be Eleazar. His time of separation had not yet ended.

Abi hurried to see who it was. She swung the door open and released a strangled cry. Anna leaned to one side to get a better look. There stood Benjamin, alive and well.

She leaped to her feet, nearly knocking over her chair. She ran to her son, flung her arms around his neck, and wept tears of joy. He wrapped strong arms around her, assuring her that he was really there in the flesh.

Stepping back, she looked him over, confused. Where was his bloody shirt? Where was the bruise on his cheek?

Benjamin laughed aloud. "Yes, Mother, I'm healed. Look." He lifted his shirt. She stared in awe at the place on his side that had been pierced by the soldier's sword. No blood. No wound. Not even a scar.

At that moment, little Martha ran to her brother and lunged into his arms. He held her fast. Martha released a cry of delight.

Her big round eyes glistened. "My Benjamin is home. My Benjamin. My Benjamin. My Benjamin."

Anna kept shaking her head in awe. "I don't understand? What has happened?"

The boy laughed again. "It was the Healer, Mother." He craned his neck and looked past her at the Passover table. "I'm hungry."

Taking his arm, Anna led him to his place at the table. He settled there, a smile lighting up his face.

Instead of continuing the retelling of the Passover story, Judah lowered himself in his chair and invited Benjamin to partake of the meal. The boy lunged at the platter of meat, scooped a large helping of vegetables onto his plate, and held his cup toward Judah to be filled with wine. Between eager bites of his meal, Benjamin told the story of his miraculous healing.

"When the temple physician could do nothing for me, two of the priests carried me on a pallet and sought out the man from Galilee. I had no knowledge of it, although I do recall being jostled about, the walls of the city passing over me, and strangers gathering around my pallet. They found Jesus at the city gate as He was about to leave with His disciples."

"The next thing I knew, I was able to sit up. And my pain was gone. It was amazing, Mother. I remembered what happened in the temple court. I recalled the plunge of the dagger, the spray of blood, the agonizing pain. I touched my side and found no wound there. One of the priests called it a miracle. I rolled off the pallet and onto the ground at Jesus' feet, grateful to be alive."

Anna shook her head in wonder. "I don't understand. Are you saying it's true, that He really is the Messiah, the Deliverer we have been waiting for?"

Benjamin's face was shining. "I believe He is. Though I wanted to follow Him, the two priests invited me back to their chamber where they gave me these clothes." He spread his arms and showed off the clean tunic. "Then they sent me on my way, shouting praises to God."

Anna could hardly believe her son had come home and

without a mark on him. In her mind she had been planning his funeral. It all had seemed so hopeless. Now she was listening to an amazing account about his healing. She suddenly became aware that another change had taken place in her son.

"Benjamin. Do you realize you have not stammered once since you walked in this house? Not once. Could it be that this miracle worker also has healed your stammering?"

He nodded. "It's true, Mother. I am completely healed. All of me, including my tongue. Now do you believe Jesus is who He claims to be? Do you agree He truly *is* a healer, a great prophet, possibly even the Messiah?"

Happy tears spilled down Anna's cheeks. "I do, Benjamin. How could I believe otherwise after seeing such evidence? I am like the widow of Zarephath. Just as Elijah healed her son and restored him to her, so also has Jesus done for me."

Judah stood to his feet and raised his cup of wine. "It is like the scriptures say. *Then the eyes of the blind will be opened, And the ears of the deaf will be unstopped. Then the lame will leap like a deer, and the tongue of the dumb will shout for joy.*"

The old man pointed his cup at the place Anna had set for Eleazar. "Perhaps there is hope for my own son, as well," he said, his eyes glistening.

Darkness had settled on the Holy City. The shofar had sounded from the Temple, signaling the start of the Passover. Thirteen men had gathered in an upper room and were sharing a meal. One of them rose from the table and went around washing the others' feet, all the while telling them to follow His example by showing kindness to one another. Afterward, they dined together and spoke in soft voices between bites of food. Then, suddenly, He began to talk about a lost friendship and betrayal, leaving them confused and questioning.

Shortly after, a lone figure stood up and slipped from the room. He descended the outer stair to the street, hurried along the pavement, his eyes darting from one side to the other. His shifting shadow fell on this wall and that wall. Stumbling and tripping, he headed for the temple and the awaiting chief priests.

With the one man absent, the host stood and spoke about mansions and a place in his Father's kingdom, and He promised to return for them. He talked about a comforter who would come in His place. Then He sent up a lengthy prayer on behalf of His followers. As they always did, they listened and committed His words to memory.

Then, the Passover finished, the eleven joined Him in the chanting of Psalms. They followed Him out of the building and along the street toward the Mount of Olives, singing along the way, with little concern that the path they were on was the same one used for the scapegoat on the Day of Atonement.

Soon, they arrived at the Garden of Gethsemane. The man named Jesus took three of them aside and asked them to pray. Then He moved off by Himself, knelt in the shadows, and lifted His voice toward heaven.

*T*he leper community came alive with the rising of the sun. People flooded into the common court and gathered in a circle. An old man stood in the center with a scroll in his hand.

Eleazar drew close to Reuben. "Who is he?"

"His name is Uzai. The people anointed him as their priest, and rightfully so. Uzai is a wise man. He serves as counselor, mediator, and healer of lost souls. What's more, the scriptures roll off his tongue like he'd swallowed them whole."

Eleazar stood watching as Uzai unfurled the scroll and began to read from the Psalms. His eyes often strayed from the parchment, and he spent more time looking up to the heavens, but he never missed a word. By the time he finished, the entire assembly had settled into meditative silence. The people bowed their heads and moved their lips quietly in prayer.

Suddenly, from somewhere within the circle, another man began to sing the Hallel. Soon, everyone was singing the treasured Passover hymn. Eleazar shut his eyes and listened. From out of nowhere, the verses he had learned as a youth came sailing back to him. Without shame, he opened his eyes and blended his own voice with the others. He wondered if the God he had neglected nearly all his life would hear the praises that now poured from his broken heart.

When the singing ended, the men began to disperse. A few of them went to the animal pen and released the sheep and goats to the grassy hillside. Several entered a small cave and brought out hoes and sickles and pruning hooks. Others hurried to their homes and returned with carpenters' tools.

The women, too, busied themselves with the fetching of water from a central well. Some squatted in their doorways, pounding dried locusts into flour. Others took to spinning wool or fed the strands onto a giant loom.

Eleazar surveyed the neat circle of homes. He admired the simple yet well-kept mud and rock houses, the open windows, and the heavy doors. Patches of wildflowers tied the dwellings together, creating a sense of unity in the village.

Reuben came out of his house and stepped beside Eleazar. "Your thoughts?" he said.

Eleazar shrugged. "I'm amazed. These people—*your* people— seem to take much pride in their homes. They must know that the work they are doing won't last, that all of this is merely a stopping place on the road to death. Yet they work as though they have many tomorrows ahead of them."

"Yes," Reuben said, thoughtfully nodding. "They've tried to create as normal a life as possible. For their children's sake, of course, but also for their own. There is something healing within the lie that life will go on."

"I'm curious," Eleazar said, his eyes on the men in the garden. "They work hard, even on a holy day. What about the law?"

Reuben looked back at him, his eyes challenging. "In this place, you have to look beyond the law," he said. "We could demand they obey every jot and tittle. But the truth is, life is but a vapor for these people. They have to seize each moment. Sometimes, it means breaking the law so they can take care of their families for one more day. The Pharisees would frown on such an act."

Reuben's dark eyes challenged him. "So, tell me, Eleazar, which is more righteous? Following the law so others might see how holy you are? Or doing good on the Sabbath? In this humble place, the people have no other hope but what they can do for themselves. They have to take care of their own."

Eleazar thought about the self-righteous men of the Council. If they knew what was happening here they would bring judgment on them. He shook his head with distaste. Such was the group of leaders he had wanted to join.

He was still pondering this new revelation when a sweet melody interrupted his thoughts. Two young girls bearing water pitchers were walking toward him, singing, their voices blending in perfect unity. They hurried past, laughing and singing and looking like any two maidens who might be doing the same thing in Jerusalem. In this place, however, they had no good reason to laugh and sing. He watched after them, and his heart broke, for he knew that somewhere on their young bodies was an infection much like the one on his arm.

He turned to Reuben who was also watching with tears in his eyes. "They'll never marry, will they?" Eleazar said, his throat tight.

"No, but they have accepted the truth."

Eleazar thought about his own daughter, Abi, and how he had condemned her to a lonely, unmarried life, simply because of his hatred for Levi.

"What a fool I've been," he said now. "Why did it take a physical mark on my arm to make me aware of what's been happening inside of me? A terrible disease has been eating away at my heart from my youth. I've hurt the people who depend on me most, people who should have received my love and care, but I ignored their needs in favor of my own selfish desires. How can I expect Yahweh to take away this physical disease unless he first heals the leprosy that's been growing inside me?"

Reuben rested his hand on Eleazar's shoulder. "With Yahweh all things are possible, my friend."

He shook his head. "Yahweh sees all of this, but He allows it to continue. Doesn't He have the power to remove the disease from the earth? It all seems hopeless. My good friend, Achim, has suffered all these years. Now I'm about to see him again. What hope can I offer him when I have no hope for myself?"

"Perhaps you will find the opposite is true. Perhaps it will be Achim who gives you the hope you are lacking."

Reuben gestured toward the row of caves on the hill. "Would you like to see him now?"

All he could do was nod, for he was so troubled he couldn't speak.

Reuben went back to his house and returned with a leather scrip. Eleazar stood very still, staring at the row of caves, and he started to tremble.

"Let's go," Reuben said. He prodded Eleazar's arm. "It's the one on the far end."

They followed a narrow, winding path up the hillside. Sparse vegetation grew on either side of them. Sun-scorched grass protruded from the rocks. There was no shade here, yet, even in the warmth of the mid-morning sun, Eleazar felt a chill.

They mounted the ridge and drew closer to Achim's cave. Eleazar hesitated at the opening. Reuben eyed him with impatience.

"You came here for a reason," he said. "Don't you want to see your friend?"

Swallowing hard, Eleazar moved past the physician and stepped from bright sunlight into near darkness, from the fresh air into the odor of human waste. He looked around in the dimly lit cave, amazed at how the villagers had brought comfort to Achim's pitiful hovel. An oil lamp burned in the corner and cast its light on a small table. Pillows and blankets covered a sleeping mat that had been raised off the dampness of the ground.

Reuben took his arm and led him toward the mat. A sheepskin moved slowly up and down. Heavy breathing rose from beneath it. Hidden somewhere under all of that bedding was Achim.

Prepare yourself," Reuben whispered as he pulled back the sheepskin.

Achim moaned and turned toward them. Eleazar stepped back, a bitter acid tightening his throat. Achim's body had wasted away. The round-faced merchant was now skin and bones. His face and neck were covered with sores. His eyes, once two sparkling sapphires, had disappeared inside folds of skin, and his parched lips expelled an odor that turned his stomach. Gone was the high-spirited young man who breathed life into everyone who met him. This horrible creature couldn't be Achim.

Eleazar considered leaving. He could flee this place and go back to Jerusalem. He could hold onto the memories of their times together and forget what he saw in the cave.

But Reuben held his arm and pulled him closer to Achim's mat. "Achim. Wake up," Reuben said. "Wake up, Achim," he repeated, louder. "You have a visitor."

The frail form moved slightly. Eleazar held his breath.

Coughing and moaning, Achim struggled to push himself upright. He dropped back against the mat, his bones rattling like spoons falling into a drawer. Reuben grabbed a pillow and slipped it behind Achim's head.

"Your friend is here, Achim. He's come a long way to see you."

Achim's eyelids fluttered open, and for a moment two blue orbs sparked to life. Then the blue faded to a dull gray.

"He can't see you," Reuben whispered. "The disease has taken hold of his entire body, including his eyes."

Eleazar stepped closer. "Achim," he said softly. "It's me, Eleazar. Your old friend."

He searched Achim's face, but there was no response. Then Achim's lips parted into a weak smile."Eleazar?" His voice was faint.

"Yes, Achim. I've come to give you comfort, my friend."

Reuben reached into his pack and withdrew a wineskin. He uncapped the lid and the aroma of mint and rose water cut through the stench. He dripped some of the liquid onto Achim's lips.

"Eleazar?" Achim murmured, the rose water spilling from his mouth. "Where are you, my friend? Where?"

Achim reached out with his right hand. Eleazar pulled back. Then he thought about Reuben's bold rejection of the law of separation, and he grabbed Achim's outstretched hand and held it tight. At that moment he could think of nothing else but to comfort his friend.

"I've thought of you often, Achim. After I left you that day in the marketplace, I came back, as I'd promised. I brought medicine, but you had left. Why did you leave, Achim? Why didn't you wait for me?"

Achim smiled. "I'm afraid you were too late, Eleazar. He raised his left hand. There were no fingers, only an ugly stump. Eleazar turned his eyes away. They filled with tears.

Achim pulled his good hand out of Eleazar's hold. "As you can see, I had no hope—not then, and not now," he said. "Within weeks I developed more sores. I couldn't feel anything. One by one, the fingers of my left hand fell away." He gave a little shrug. "I must have injured them and didn't know until it was too late."

Eleazar let out a long sigh. "You have suffered much, my friend. No man should suffer as you have."

Achim shook his head and laughed weakly. "Don't you see, Eleazar? This is my rightful punishment. Lying here, day after day, has allowed me time to think about my past and how it could have been different. How it *should* have been different. I sought pleasure wherever I could find it, at home, on foreign soil, without any regard for the outcome. I hurt people. Women trusted me. I used them for my own pleasure. I ignored my friends. You included. I neglected my mother. I charged my customers far more for my wares than what they were worth."

Reuben leaned close. "Don't torture yourself with such thoughts, Achim. You mustn't think of this disease as a punishment. In the village are many others who have been afflicted. Men, women, and innocent children. Do you think leprosy is also a punishment for *them*?"

Achim tried to smile, his lips so parched they oozed drops of blood. For a brief moment, his blue eyes shone again, taking Eleazar back to their childhood. But just as quickly, Achim's smile faded and his eyes retreated behind a yellow cloud.

Eleazar rested a hand on Achim's shoulder. "My friend, think about all the people who found joy from having known you. Your customers didn't come to your stand simply to find a bargain. They could have fared better dealing with some of the other merchants. No, Achim. They came to hear your amazing stories of distant places. They came to share a bit of laughter, to forget the troubles of the day. And what of me? When I struggled to learn more about medicine, you gave me those wonderful scrolls. You were always thinking of others. *I'm* the one who should be pleading for mercy. *I'm* the one who deserves to be punished. Not you."

Tears ran down Achim's face. He opened his mouth to speak but no words came.

Eleazar blinked against the sting of his own tears. "I thought I saw you once, Achim, on the Jericho Road. Tell me, do you remember the time? Was it you?"

"It may have been."

"A shrouded figure passed close to me. I saw the blue of his eyes. They could have been your eyes."

Achim smiled softly. "It doesn't matter now, does it?" He took a deep breath. "My mother—is she well?"

Eleazar shifted nervously. "I'm sorry, Achim. She died three years ago, following a long illness. The medicine we used to bring her didn't seem to help anymore. She fell into a deep sleep that lasted for several days. Neighbors stopped at your house to care for her. She never woke up."

Achim's mouth twisted with grief. His sad eyes released another flow of tears. He wept for several minutes, fell into a coughing fit, then gasped for air. He was facing Eleazar, but it was as if he didn't see him. "And your family, Eleazar? Is Anna well? Do you have many children?"

"Yes. Anna is well. We have four children now. My daughter Mara was joined to Enos' oldest. My daughter Abi is going to marry Levi's son."

"What? Have you gone mad, Eleazar? You have always despised Levi, and now you want to join your families?"

"It's true," Eleazar said, a bit sheepishly. "I have yet to give my consent, but I have decided to do so. Call me mad if you will. I have to do this for my daughter. Abi pines day and night for Malachi. I want her to be happy."

Achim nodded with understanding. "And what of Ruth?"

The mention of his love's name brought a sharp pain to Eleazar's heart. He drew in a deep breath and told Achim about Ruth's bitter end, though it pained him greatly to speak of it again.

"We had a daughter. Her name is Martha. She lives with me now."

"What about Anna?"

"She made the decision and went out to find the girl."

"Anna." Achim said her name with reverence. "Didn't I tell you she was a prize?"

Eleazar smiled, though Achim couldn't see him. "Yes, my friend. I know that now."

Achim cocked his head. "You have prospered, Eleazar. I need to ask, did the Sanhedrin ever call for you?"

"Yes, only last week. I have yet—"

"Last week? And what are you doing here? Shouldn't you be answering their call?"

"There is time." He pondered whether to tell Achim about the sore on his arm. "Let's talk about you," he said. "What can I do to help?"

Achim snorted. "You must know there is no cure. The body dies a slow death, and there isn't a medicine on earth that can stop it. There's only one who can heal me now, and I fear he's too far away."

Eleazar was confused. "What are you saying, Achim?"

"The man Jesus from Galilee, the miracle worker."

"What?" There was that name again.

"Jesus alone can restore my body. More than that, as I've been told, He also can restore my soul."

"I know nothing of such a healer," Eleazar lied.

Achim shifted on his bed. "I can't believe you haven't heard of Him. It's said He travels to Jerusalem for the feasts, and while He's there He draws a large following." Achim's eyes grew wide and they almost turned blue again. "When you go back, I want you to seek Him for me. I've heard He can heal from afar. Ask Him to heal me, Eleazar. Plead with Him."

Eleazar frowned. "My friend, I'm afraid you've been deceived. No one can heal your soul, except Yahweh. That man from Galilee is no healer. *I'm* a healer. *I* trained for years to help the sick, and I can't heal leprosy, so how can *He*?"

Achim raised off his pillow. "I don't know, Eleazar, but it's the truth. He's a healer. I'm certain of it. He claims to be the Son of God. If that's true, He has the power."

"Blasphemy!" Eleazar shouted. "Blas—"

Achim reached for Eleazar's robe. Finding it, he seized the cloth and held onto it. "Find Him for me, Eleazar. Find the man called Jesus. Ask Him to heal me. He doesn't have to come here. He only needs to say the word, and I'll be healed."

Then, drained of strength, Achim dropped back on his pillow. He took shallow breaths for a while. Then he fell asleep. Eleazar stared at his friend, unable to move away. How had Achim allowed himself to be deceived in this way?

He stepped away from the bed.

Reuben stood nearby holding a cruse of water and a clean towel.

"I'm going to cleanse him," he said. "Perhaps you would rather wait outside."

Eleazar nodded and slowly backed away. He left the cave with Achim's anguished plea still swimming around in his head.

Anna could think of nothing else but to find the man who healed her son and thank him. More than that, she wanted to ask Him to help Eleazar. She hurried into the temple court and began asking people where to find the man called Jesus. Some responded with a frown. Others simply shook their heads and turned away.

Discouragement began to build up inside her. She was about to leave and go home when she saw Levi at the far end of the court. Though she detested the man, he had already told her he knew who Jesus was. She hurried to catch him, but he was walking fast, pulling a small goat on a cord, and he was about to pass through the wall of separation at the men's court.

Anna ran after him. "Levi! Wait."

He spun around, his black robe sweeping his ankles. He stared at her with cold eyes.

Anna stepped closer. "The Nazarene called Jesus, where can I find him?"

He raised one eyebrow. "What have you to do with *Him*, woman?"

"He–He healed my son. I want to thank him."

Levi grunted. "He's gone."

"Gone? Where?"

"To His judgment, I hope. They arrested Him last night. I only know He went before the high priest who sent Him to Pontius Pilate, who then sent Him to King Herod." Levi spoke with pleasure in his voice. "They passed Him from one to the other throughout the night. When it grew late, I retired at home, thankful that they had finally made Him pay for His deceit."

Anna shuddered, unable to speak. He left her standing there and passed through the gate to the sacrificial altar, dragging the small goat behind him.

Anna thought hard about Jesus' trials. The high priest. Pontius Pilate. King Herod. In the end, the decision would fall to Pilate.

She hurried to the governor's judgment hall. She reached the place called The Pavement where a crowd of people had gathered. A group of men shouted and shook angry fists in the air. Several women clung together, weeping. Voices yelled curses and blessings all at once.

Then the crowd turned away from the judgment hall and began to move as one, like a surge of tide, quickening its rush to the shore. Hoping to find Jesus in their midst she plunged into the throng. Then she saw Him. Stunned, she put her hand to her mouth. He was stumbling along the road ahead of the crowd. His back was scarred and bleeding. His shoulders bowed under the weight of a large, wooden beam. Roman soldiers cracked whips and goaded Him on with spears, driving Him toward the city gate. She knew where they were going. To the hill, Golgotha, the place of Roman executions.

Her heart sank within her. Was this the man who, only two days ago, stood in the temple court, confident, bold of speech, unmoved by His accusers? She looked around at the angry faces. Where were His followers now? What had become of the young men who eagerly listened to His words? What of the hundreds, or possibly thousands, He was said to have healed?

She stood back from the crowd and watched from a distance as Jesus limped on, and the crowd closed in behind Him. They exited through the Sheep Gate, the doorway to the temple where shepherds brought their sacrifices. Beyond was one of Judea's most heavily traveled roads and the rise of hill known as Calvary.

Anna swallowed hard. She had purposely stayed away from that place in recent weeks, for many executions were taking place there. The Romans had brought their worst form of punishment to Jerusalem. Angry tears stung her eyes. She remembered Levi's bitter accusations only a day before when she met him in his courtyard. What kind of threat had that humble man imposed upon Levi?

She had wanted desperately to thank Him and to seek His help for Eleazar. But He couldn't even help *himself*. Bowed low under the weight of failure, she turned away and started for home, an overwhelming sadness consuming her. She looked back only once. Her final hope was passing through the Sheep Gate to His death.

That evening, Eleazar and Reuben dined alone inside Reuben's tiny home. Reclining on pillows around a low table, they shared a lentil mash and roasted potatoes, some unleavened bread and wine. Eleazar was still troubled by Achim's request for him to find the healer named Jesus. He was not going to admit he may have misjudged the man. He only knew the *healer* had lured Ruth away from him, and now she was gone.

He needed to turn his mind to something else. He and Reuben worked in the same profession, but their labors had taken them in different directions. While he had remained true to the people of the Upper City, this man had turned to the hopeless. He looked across the table at his host, who was mopping up the last of his lentil mash. Perhaps he could learn from the younger physician.

He leaned toward Reuben. "After living with these people for so long, have you discovered a possible cure for their affliction, or perhaps a remedy that might prolong their lives?"

Reuben reached for a piece of unleavened bread. "A cure?" He grunted. "Though I have tested a number of herbs and powders, I have never been able to find anything that works. The disease is cruel." He tore the bread in half. "It attacks the body in two different ways—slowly for some, taking years to show up on the skin—and for the less fortunate, like a raging fire, consuming the body, much like it did to Achim. Those victims have little time to prepare."

"And they die from leprosy." Eleazar thought of Achim. Tears rushed to his eyes.

Reuben shook his head. "They don't actually die of leprosy, but the disease weakens a person's ability to feel. They injure themselves and lose fingers and toes. They fall prey to other diseases. Their open sores breed infection. Growths on various parts of the body keep them from normal activities."

Eleazar pushed his plate of mash aside and refused Reuben's offer of half his bread. He had little appetite over the last few days. He leaned back and sipped his wine, trusting it would promise him a better night's sleep than what he'd been having.

Reuben ate both pieces of bread and brushed the crumbs from his fingers. His eyes on Eleazar, he raised his cup of wine and gave him a nod.

"This must be difficult for you, Eleazar, seeing your friend near death, struggling with your own problem and wondering if you, too, will perish. I want to assure you, I have seen miracles. At least four of our people showed signs of healing in the last year. They were able to leave our village and return to their former lives. As for me, I continue to care for those who remain and have committed to simply relieving their pain." He shrugged. "I fear that's all I can do for now, Eleazar. These people have learned to trust me. I won't leave them."

"So there's little hope for me, and even less hope for Achim."

"Achim is dying. I can't believe that he's lasted this long. As for you, Eleazar, it's still uncertain whether you have the disease at all. In a few days you'll get your answer. If you're free of it, you can cleanse yourself, follow the statutes set down by the law, go back to your life in Jerusalem, and forget about us."

A stab of pain struck Eleazar's heart. He doubted he would ever forget this place, just like he hadn't forgotten Hilda and the people on the Ophel Ridge.

He studied Reuben with interest. This man had taken many risks to help the people of the village, yet he'd never gotten the disease.

"My friend," you dipped your bread in the same mash I ate. You are sharing your home with me. You come close to me and the people of the village, sometimes touching us. Tell me, *why?* Why put yourself in harm's way?"

Reuben laughed and shrugged his shoulders.

"Perhaps it's a death wish. Think about it, Eleazar. What would be better for me than to be reunited with my wife and my little Esther?"

Eleazar held up a hand and scowled at his friend. "You speak foolishness. You have a calling, Reuben. These people need you. Your presence has restored hope in their lives. Do you really want to deny them that?"

Reuben shook his head with sadness. "No, I don't." He brightened. "I'm going to keep searching and testing, and if I ever find a cure for this disease, what a wonderful blessing that will be—to them *and* to me."

Eleazar considered the diverse paths their lives had taken. He, in his selfishness, had pursued a career that promised him great wealth and status among his peers, while Reuben had given up everything to help the lowest of the low. Other differences now troubled him. Eleazar had pursued a woman outside of his marriage, and Reuben yearned for the wife he had lost. Eleazar had spent little time with his children, but Reuben was willing to die to be with his little girl. The two of them were so different, yet, here they were, drawn together in this distressing place, sharing food off the same plate, and uniting in friendship in a way he had never thought possible.

Eleazar sighed with still another realization. He was Judah's son, but this man had more of the old man's qualities than he had ever acquired. Over the last two days, he had learned far more than how to practice medicine among the lepers. He had learned what it meant to be a man of honor.

He looked into Reuben's eyes. "My time here will soon end. I must leave for Jerusalem in two days."

Reuben smiled. "And what will you do, my friend? You'll walk away from this village, from Achim, from me, from the lepers who live here, and you'll put it all behind you."

"No, Reuben, I won't forget," Eleazar insisted.

Yet, in his heart, he knew he would like nothing better than to get on with his life. Though he appreciated what the villagers had done with this place, he was eager to leave it. His examination with Mattathias could go two ways. It could set him free, or it could send him running back to the Jordan Valley.

Eleazar rose before anyone else in the village. He stepped into the clearing and stood for a long time in the semi-darkness. He looked at the slumbering houses and the slowly awakening garden, listened to the stirring of the sheep and goats in their pens. Then he turned his attention to the trail that led to Achim's cave, and heartache overtook him. Today would be their last visit. Today would be a time for farewells, for he needed to leave early in the morning to travel the long road back to the Holy City. He was planning to spend the night in the cave where he left his belongings and leave early the next morning in time for his reexamination.

Reuben came out of his house and stood beside Eleazar.

"I have prepared a warm herbal drink and some unleavened bread for Achim. Are you ready to return to the cave?"

"Not at the moment." Eleazar raised his hand against the sliver of sunlight on the horizon. "Yesterday's visit left me empty. I need to refresh my thoughts, to decide what I can say to my friend. I don't know how to help him, Reuben. I'm afraid I'll fall apart and make things worse." He waved the young physician off. "I'll follow shortly."

Reuben nodded and moved on without him. Eleazar watched him leave and realized he was going to miss him.

His thoughts turned to Achim. He'd left many things unsaid, things that had been on his heart but had not crossed his lips. He needed to tell him about his own affliction, but he was afraid the news would crush his friend's spirit. Or perhaps it would create an unbreakable bond between them, sealing their friendship forever.

Reuben was almost at the cave door. Eleazar took a step toward the hill when several children ran to his side, their high voices reaching him before their little hands did. Two of them grabbed hold of his cloak. They turned eager faces up at him. One young girl with a round face framed in black curls stood in front of him, blocking his path. She looked to be about Martha's age. She smiled shyly and held out a yellow flower. His heart melted.

"I'm Suzannah," she said, her dark eyes blinking against the rising sun. Except for a blemish on one side of her face, her skin was like alabaster. She thrust the flower toward him. "A gift for you."

He went down on one knee and accepted the flower. "Thank you, Suzannah. It's beautiful." He smiled and stroked her chin. Then he added, "And so are you."

Suzannah giggled. She wrapped her arms around his neck and planted a kiss on his cheek. Then, as quickly as she had come, she hurried off with the other children, laughing and looking back at him only once. Eleazar rose to his feet and watched her until she disappeared over the hill by the sheep pen.

Tears welled up in his eyes. How he wished he could heal that precious child. Perhaps he'd spent too much time making remedies for the rich to value the thankful smile of a poor little girl. Instead of filling Marcus' hands with opiates he should have been working night and day to find a cure for the people his father served. All of that training in Alexandria was worthless if he could not find a remedy for the worst disease in the world.

He tucked the flower inside a fold of his robe, and releasing a long sigh, he turned toward the caves. He made his way along the hillside but paused halfway up. For a moment he was thirteen years old again, and he was climbing a hill behind his father and their donkey Balaam. He was approaching the leper caves outside Jerusalem. He was about to encounter the hopelessly lost people, rejected from their homes because of an incurable illness. Like before, a chill ran through him. This time he wasn't going to visit deformed men and women who spilled from the caves in tattered cloaks, and Hilda, the old crone who spit in his face. This time he was going to visit a friend.

Eleazar found Achim propped up against a pile of pillows. He was laughing at something Reuben had said. It was a wonderful sight. Eleazar shook his head in awe as he watched the two of them exchanging stories. There was no doubt, he could learn much from this young physician. The man had raised no barriers. He humbled himself to the level of the person he was with, yet he also displayed the confidence of someone who had weathered difficult storms.

Eleazar acknowledged Reuben with a nod, then he knelt beside Achim's bed, reached out and patted his friend's one good hand.

"You appear to be in better spirits today."

Achim turned toward him. Though his brow creased with the pain he must have been feeling, he offered Eleazar a smile.

"I asked Reuben to hold back the medicine that makes me sleep," he told Eleazar. "I need to stay alert for our visit."

He fell into a coughing fit and struggled for a breath of air. Blood oozed from the corner of his mouth. Reuben quickly moved close with a clean cloth and mopped up the flow.

At that moment, Eleazar knew the truth. Achim didn't have much time. Though Reuben had warned him, he'd been afraid to admit it until now. Seeing his friend suffer that way, he silently prayed that Yahweh would take him quickly.

Achim caught his breath and rested against his pillow. He turned his face in the direction of Eleazar, but his eyes had clouded over and he was staring somewhere beyond him.

"Your visit has worked like a medicine for me," he said, grinning. "I can almost leap from my bed and dance around this hovel I call *home*. Then, *you'd* be the one trying to keep up with *me*."

They laughed together. For Eleazar it was a bitter-sweet moment. It felt good to be able to see Achim again. He'd been a true friend when they were children, always there at every turn of the road, in good times and bad times.

Achim fell into another coughing fit. He lurched forward and gasped for air, then, releasing a long sigh, he settled back on his pillow.

Eleazar and Reuben exchanged a glance. The young physician came close to Eleazar's ear. "Tell him," he whispered. "Tell him about your infection."

Eleazar inhaled deeply and nodded. Then he leaned toward Achim. "I'll be leaving soon, my friend. Tomorrow morning. But, first, I must confess something of great importance."

A crease lined Achim's brow, but he didn't speak.

Eleazar folded his hands and tried to remain strong. "You are not alone in your affliction, Achim."

Achim's eyebrows went up.

"I, too, have signs of the disease," Eleazar told him.

Achim didn't move, didn't even appear to breathe.

"A mark appeared on my arm only last week," Eleazar went on. "When I checked this morning, I saw that it had spread, a sign that it is not a simple infection."

Achim let out a groan. "No, my friend. This can't be. You have so much to live for."

"It seems I've been pierced by a double-edged sword. At last I've been considered for a seat in the Council, but I had to leave the city, and, instead of gaining a position of honor, I am a castaway."

"Please, say this isn't true. Are you telling me this is your week of separation?"

"Yes, Achim. Mattathias offered me privacy in the room at the temple, the one where you stayed. But I chose to go outside the city. Good fortune brought me to Reuben, and he brought me to you. Now I'm nearing the end of the seven days. Tomorrow morning, I'll go back to the city, and on the following day, I'll see Mattathias, and I will learn my fate."

Achim struggled to sit up. His lips quivered with the rise of tears. "Forget the priest, Eleazar. Find the Healer. Find Jesus and ask *him* to heal you."

Eleazar shook his head. "Achim—" he said, as if he'd caught his friend in a lie.

"It's true," Achim persisted. "He's your only hope, Eleazar."

"And what about you, Achim? Only yesterday you begged me to ask for healing for you."

His friend shook his head. "That was yesterday. Can't you see how I am? It's too late for me. This morning, I awoke to a new understanding. My time is short. Before you reach the city, I will have passed from this life into the next."

"Achim," Eleazar began to protest. "You don't have to—"

Achim raised his good hand.

"Don't be sad, Eleazar. I will be free of this torment, free of my sins, free to enter God's kingdom. For though I've never heard Jesus speak, others have repeated his words of hope to me. Reuben, of course, and Uzai. They both heard his wonderful promises. I have repented and I believe, Eleazar. Jesus *is* the deliverer, the anointed one of Israel. I believe in him, and I have peace."

Eleazar turned to Reuben and lowered his voice. "It's the disease, isn't it? The disease causes him to speak this nonsense."

"No, my friend." Reuben shook his head, the hint of a smile on his lips. "Achim speaks the truth. I have seen Jesus. Not long ago I made a journey to Galilee. I saw him feed more than 5,000 men, plus women and children. He started with only a few scraps of food. The man fits the prophecies, Eleazar. His place of birth—Bethlehem— as predicted by the prophet Micah.

His mother—a virgin—as prophesied by Isaiah. Then there's his ability to heal and to create a sense of calm wherever he goes. He's been gifted beyond any other man's ability. I believe Jesus is exactly who he claimed to be—the Son of God and Savior of the world."

Eleazar stood up, his heart pounding. "If what you say is true, then why doesn't he heal Achim?" Anger boiled within him. "If he's the Messiah, then he knows everything. Everyone's pain. Everyone's dream. Everyone's need. Why doesn't he heal my friend from afar, as Achim has said?"

Reuben shook his head. "You don't understand because—"

"Because you are a stubborn mule!" Achim's loud outburst cut into Reuben's words.

Eleazar looked with surprise at Achim. His friend continued to speak. "I never got the opportunity to approach the healer. No one spoke to him on my behalf. But I have heard his messages through others, and I have chosen to believe. Whether healing of the body or of the soul, both require faith. I have accepted my fate. I want to die, Eleazar. I want to leave this world of pain and suffering. But there is still hope for you, my friend. You can be cured of your illness, and more than that, you can be healed of your sins, if only you'll believe."

Raising himself off his pillow, Achim struggled to take a breath. "You think I've lost my mind, don't you? That this disease has confused me. Don't be a fool, Eleazar. My body may be afflicted, but my mind remains clear. I've tried to tell you about the only one who can help you. Jesus can restore both your body *and* your soul. Go back to the Holy City. Find him. For your sake, find him now. Though he makes his residence in Galilee, He faithfully attends the three festivals in Jerusalem. This is your hour, Eleazar. It's the Passover week. He'll be in the city, but he won't remain there long. So hurry. Fly like the wind. Go to Jerusalem and find him."

Drained of strength, Achim dropped back against his pillow. His breathing became shallow. His sudden weakness frightened

Eleazar. He reached out and placed a hand on Achim's shoulder. "You must rest, my friend. "Don't try to speak."

Achim shook his head. "No. I will speak. You must hear my words. I've made peace with Yahweh. I'm ready for the grave. I have leprosy, but I'm clean. Clean! The scriptures I learned as a youth have come back to comfort me. *Though my sins were as scarlet, he has washed them white as snow. Though they are red like crimson, they will be like wool.* I believe the words of Isaiah. I believe, Eleazar, I believe."

With those words barely off his lips, Achim coughed again, his head dropped to one side, and he was gone.

Following the law, Reuben summoned Uzai and the elders. They anointed Achim's body with myrrh and wrapped him in clean linen. One of the villagers, an older man, played a sorrowful tune on a lyre. The women stood outside the cave and wept softly. There was no marching or wailing or paid mourners. These people had attended so many funerals, they kept everything simple. A quiet grief prevailed over the camp for the rest of the day.

That evening, Eleazar stood with Reuben in the center of the courtyard. The villagers went to their own homes. A dark cloud of mourning had settled on the village.

"For a while, before he went to the cave, the children thought of Achim as a friendly grandfather," Reuben told him. "They loved him. Loved to hear his stories about distant lands. Achim made everyone laugh. He will be missed."

Eleazar wept more tears than he could have imagined. No sooner did he mop his face dry than more moisture spilled from his eyes.

"How do these people survive funeral after funeral?" he asked Reuben, his voice rough from all the crying he'd done.

"They've seen more death and dying in the last year than most people see in a lifetime," Reuben admitted. "Though they try to make their lives as normal as possible, when one of them dies, they're reminded of the fate they all must face. Of course, what troubles them most is the children." He shook his head and pinched tears from the inner corners of his eyes. "I don't know a single parent who doesn't want to die before their little ones do. All too often, the parents are left behind to mourn the loss of a child. After enduring such grief myself I don't wish it on anyone."

Staring off in the direction of Jerusalem, Eleazar set his jaw as he considered his own family. His daughters, Mara and Abi— he'd neglected them badly. His failure to understand Benjamin, his only son. Martha, the little one who had captured his heart. Anna, the faithful. He'd rejected her all these years, though she'd stood by him, despite his infidelity.

With overwhelming regret, he considered Judah. Why hadn't he listened to what his father was trying to tell him long ago? Perhaps, if he had received Judah's counsel, he would have made better decisions throughout his life.

"I suppose I should do as Achim said and locate the healer before I go to the priest." Eleazar surprised himself with that decision. "If what Achim said is true, I must at least try."

"Yes," Reuben agreed. "You must do it, Eleazar. Find him, and plead with him to heal you."

*T*he scratching of hyssop sweeping the ground outside Reuben's door drew Eleazar from his first restful sleep in more than a week. He stretched, raised himself from his bed, and stepped out in the morning sun. He found his host there, clearing the dust from his doorway.

Reuben tossed aside the branch of hyssop and greeted Eleazar with a smile.

"This will be a good day, my friend. I prayed for you during the night, and I fell asleep comforted. I am certain all will go well for you in Jerusalem."

Eleazar wanted to believe, but when he checked that morning the spot was still there. Had it diminished in size? Perhaps. He wouldn't know for certain until Mattathias pronounced judgment.

A quick wash at the central laver, a few bites of date bread, and several swallows of a sweet herbal drink offered by one of the ladies in the circle, and Eleazar was ready to leave. But first, he had to bid farewell to the people of the village. During the brief time he'd been with them, a sense of companionship had prevailed. These people had welcomed him into their fold. They had offered him kindness, had asked him no questions, had passed no judgment on him. The spirit that existed within this place was unlike anything he had known in Jerusalem. The most powerful men controlled the city's mood. They sat at the gate and looked with suspicious eyes on anyone who passed by. And to think he had desired to be one of them.

Now he had witnessed a different kind of community, and he preferred the humble manner of these people. While they suffered with the worst kind of physical disease, their hearts were pure. Those in the city had a different kind of sickness, unseen but eating away at their hearts.

Seeing Eleazar, the villagers broke away from their labors and began to flood into the courtyard. Several called out good wishes for a safe journey. A woman with a bent back handed him a sack of unleavened bread and a goatskin filled with fresh water. Several men came close and spoke words of blessing on him. Little Suzannah peered at him from behind her mother's skirt. Eleazar smiled and waved at her. She responded with a sweet grin that made him ache for his little Martha. In the same way, he would never forget Suzannah's innocent face and her dark, pleading eyes.

Though his departure was difficult, Eleazar turned away and set his eyes on the road to Jerusalem. The people continued to wave and sing out to him until he reached the edge of the valley. Reuben went a short distance with him and stopped walking short of the Jericho Road.

"Tomorrow marks the end of your seven days and the beginning of an uncertain future," Reuben said. "I will be thinking about you and will be hoping for good news. Somehow, get word back to us."

Eleazar stood facing Reuben. The two men smiled into each other's eyes, a message of deep friendship passing between them.

"I am tempted to remain with you and the villagers," Eleazar said with a chuckle. "It is the Sabbath, and I will be breaking one more law by walking this great distance."

Reuben smiled. "Sometimes, we must go beyond every jot and tittle and do the necessary thing."

"Yes, and the necessary thing is that I have to go back. I have to learn my judgment, no matter what it is."

He clasped Reuben's arm. Reuben did the same.

"Thank you for bringing me here and for making it possible for me to see my friend as he lay dying."

"It might give you pleasure to know that for the first time in months, Achim had a good day because of you. His final moments went far easier with his best friend at his side."

Reuben's face blurred as a flood of tears filled Eleazar's eyes. He shook his head in amazement. "I never cry," he said, embarrassed. He shrugged. "I suppose it was time I did."

Reuben stroked his back. "You must look ahead now, Eleazar. The Passover is over, and the week of Unleavened Bread has begun. Your examination has come at a time when our people celebrate Israel's release from bondage. I pray the Lord also will release *you* from the bondage you've been living under far too long."

With tears in his eyes, Reuben bestowed a final blessing on him. Eleazar felt humbled by the young man's unselfish spirit. Though he may never see Reuben again, he had made a lasting friendship, a needed comfort for the long journey ahead.

They parted near the Jericho Road, and Eleazar started off for the Holy City alone. With each step, he drew closer to his fate, closer to a decision by the temple priest, closer to the rest of his life. He would accept whatever judgment came, able now to admit he deserved the worst punishment because of all his transgressions. Yet there remained a sliver of hope that the Judge of all the earth would have mercy on him. The One who really held his life in His hands had seen everything he had ever done, had heard every vile word he had ever spoken, had even looked into his heart and watched his evil plans come to life. He could only hope that Yahweh's mercy would prevail over all of his sins.

Several hours later, Eleazar caught sight of the city of Jerusalem.

The distant wall glowed yellow and orange in the glow of the late afternoon sun. The path he traveled moved ever upward. The air was thick with the heat of the desert. A burst of hot wind stirred a cloud of dust. Eleazar coughed and kept walking. Though tired from his journey, he continued on, his eyes on the Holy City. A stream of gray smoke rose from the temple, a remnant of the many sacrifices that had taken place on the Passover. Eleazar had watched the sacrifices from the time he could walk, his fat little hand in his father's big paw. Perhaps, as Achim had insisted, such sacrifices could never satisfy an angry God. People needed something more to end their guilt forever.

The truth was, once the offerings had been made, everyone seemed to go about their daily business the way they always had, with no change in their selfish bargaining, their greed, or their deceitful words. They continued to sin, continued to hurt one another in business and at home.

Then what did they do? To atone, they offered more sacrifices. Hundreds of thousands of innocent animals slaughtered for man's sins. But what if that wasn't enough? What if Yahweh wanted something else—a change of heart perhaps, and a change of ways? What if the Almighty had a different plan? What if, as his friend had said, it had to do with the Galilean named Jesus? Achim had insisted that man was the Son of God, that he believed in him, though he had never met him face to face. Could it be that simple? Could it be people only had to believe?

Still pondering these things, Eleazar ascended the Ophel Ridge where he would spend the night.

Tomorrow, he would look for the man named Jesus and ask him to prove himself. Then he would know for certain if the Messiah had really come.

That evening, as the sun began its gradual descent in the west, Eleazar located the cave where he had spent his first night of separation. He found his belongings as he had left them, hidden in a corner of the cave. In the last week, moisture had settled there in the shadows, away from the warmth of the sun.

Now he sat on the ledge with Benjamin's scroll on his lap. He wanted to use the remaining daylight to read again the words of Isaiah. Faithful to his calling, Benjamin had copied the passage on a fresh parchment. Several mornings, Eleazar had caught sight of his son, bowed over the scroll, carefully printing each letter, and his fears had faded away. Benjamin had found his way in life. It was time Eleazar supported him.

He wiped the outside of the scroll with a corner of his mantle. Then he carefully unrolled the fragile sheet of papyrus and finished the passage he had started reading a week ago.

Suddenly he was a youth again, seated at the feet of Rabbi Heth. Prompted by the rabbi's sharp rod, he'd recited the verses aloud. Now he did so again—not because he was compelled to do so, but because he *wanted* to. He wanted to let the holy scriptures roll off his tongue, wanted to make them his own.

Raising his eyes toward the heavens, he began to speak.

Even the youths shall faint and be weary, and the young men shall utterly fall: But they that wait upon the Lord shall renew their strength, they shall mount up with wings as eagles; they shall run, and not be weary; and they shall walk, and not faint.

Wait upon the Lord? There was little time. The rising of the sun would mark the day of decision for Eleazar. Strength had to come now, tonight, while it could still grow inside him.

An invisible sword pierced Eleazar's heart. He bowed his head to his knees and wept in total abandon. Never before had so much guilt and shame come upon him. The last week had brought a cleansing of sorts. The unexplained spot on his arm and the possibility of final separation from his family and friends had left him fearful. Then there was the inevitable threat of suffering and death. The gates of hell had opened up to him, and all of his past came spilling out with the promise of eternal damnation.

He hoped that Achim and Reuben had been right, that a

rescuer had come to the Holy City, that he might be able to find Him, lay his sins at His feet, and beg for mercy.

Eleazar raised his head and stared out at the great expanse. The wasteland stretched to the nearby hills and beyond to the purple mountains of Moab. He could leave the cave and walk away, never to hear Mattathias' judgment. To the east, the Jericho Road beckoned him back to the leper village. To the west, another major highway led to Galilee. He could lose himself on any of those roads, never again say the word, "Unclean," and thus deceive everyone who came in contact with him.

But was that the answer? Didn't he have people waiting for him at home? Anna and the children? Judah? His neighbors? The sick who depended on him? For their sake he needed to continue. He had to go to the temple and see Mattathias, had to show him that the spot remained, and then receive whatever judgment the priest should pronounce. He had to do it for them.

With the setting of the sun another cold night descended on the hill. Eleazar shivered, partly from the chill but also from a fearful expectation of the fate that awaited him. He pulled a piece of flint from his bag, found a rock and a bunch of hyssop near the opening of the cave and created a small fire. He made a pillow of his leather scrip, wrapped himself in his mantle, and lay on the ground outside the cave near the blaze.

Sleep didn't come. Overhead, a blanket of stars had him thinking about Reuben's little daughter Esther and her wish to be with her mother. A heavy sigh escaped his lips. Tomorrow would bring answers. Either the end of life as he'd known it, or a new beginning.

Eleazar didn't know when he had fallen asleep. The words of Isaiah were still running around in his head, and there came a time when he simply drifted off.

He awakened with a sense of peace he could not explain. Except for his first and last evenings on the hill, he'd never felt separated from anything. He'd met so many wonderful people over the last week. Reuben, a faithful servant to the lepers, a man who showed little concern for his own safety but reached out to everyone with compassion. Then there were the lepers who welcomed him into their humble community. They fed him, talked with him, comforted him over the death of his friend. He thought about the young girls who would never marry, yet they laughed and sang and danced as if tomorrow wouldn't come. And little Suzannah, whose dark, innocent eyes had melted his heart.

He thought of Achim. His friend had spoken with such confidence about the Healer who claimed to have the power of God. Then with amazing peace Achim had crossed the threshold into the afterlife. Eleazar wanted that peace, wanted to believe what Achim believed.

From the pinnacle of the temple the blast of the shofar

signaled the start of a new day. The gates around the wall opened. Eleazar could go directly to Mattathias for his reexamination. But, as much as he needed an answer, he couldn't go without first trying to find the Healer.

He sat for a while on the ledge outside the cave and rested his back against the cool rock wall. Reaching inside his scrip, he pulled out the last of the unleavened bread provided by the villagers. He took small bites and ate slowly. When he finished, he brushed the crumbs from his beard, reached for the scroll of Isaiah and read again the last words of the passage: *Those who hope in the Lord will renew their strength. They will soar on wings like eagles; they will run and not grow weary, they will walk and not be faint.*

His hands trembling, he dropped the scroll on his lap. Then he pressed his palms against his eyes and shook violently with a sudden rush of tears.

Like a disobedient child brought before his father, he turned his tear-stained face toward heaven. "Lord, forgive me, for I'm a sinner of the worst kind. Release me from this disease that has plagued me all my life. Heal my heart and my soul. Then, if it be your will, heal also the spot on my arm. I beg you, restore me to my—"

"Father!" The shout came from the direction of the city gate. Over the rise of the hill came a familiar form. His son, Benjamin.

Eleazar quickly wiped the tears from his face and struggled to his feet.

"Don't come any closer." He raised his hand. "I have yet to be examined by the priest."

"I know, Father. I want to go with you to the temple. Mattathias told me I'd find you here."

Eleazar narrowed his eyes. Had he heard correctly?

"Say that again, Benjamin."

The boy laughed. "I said, Mattathias told me I'd find you here."

He frowned with puzzlement. "Your speech—"

Benjamin laughed again. "Yes, Father. It's a miracle. I've been healed, and I have much more to tell you."

Eleazar shook his head in amazement. He quickly gathered his belongings and joined his son on the path. "You have to tell me what happened," he said, his heartbeat quickening.

"While we walk," Benjamin promised. "We need to get to the temple."

He listened with eagerness as the boy talked about his injury in the temple, his near death experience, and the healing of his wounded body and his stammering tongue.

"It was Jesus," Benjamin said, his face aglow.

Eleazar gasped at the mention of the name. It was just as Achim said.

Benjamin picked up his step and continued his tale. "The priests brought me to him. I knew nothing until later when I arose from the pallet and found my clothes stained with blood. But, I had no wound, Father, not even a scar. The priests told me what had happened. They clothed me in a clean garment and sent me home."

Eleazar stared in wonder at his son. "So, you are completely healed?"

"Completely."

"I've heard about this Healer. His reputation has spread all the way to Jericho and possibly beyond."

He then told Benjamin about his trip to the leper village and his visit with Achim. As he spoke about his friend's death, tears filled his son's eyes. The boy lowered his face as though grieving the loss with him.

"Achim died peacefully," Eleazar assured him. "But before he passed, he spoke about this Healer from Galilee. He said I would find Him in the Holy City."

They passed through the city gate, and headed for the temple, but Eleazar stopped short of the broad steps.

"What is it, Father?"

"Before we go to see Mattathias, take me to see this Jesus. I want to meet him. I want to ask him to heal me."

Benjamin stepped back, his face clouded with sadness.

"What is it, my son?"

The boy sighed and shook his head. "Father, you're too late. Jesus—the Healer—has been crucified."

"Crucified?! The punishment of the Romans? But why? For what crime?"

"None that anyone could prove. His enemies brought two witnesses to speak against Him. They spoke lies. Pontius Pilate, the Roman governor, offered to punish Him and release Him. The chief priests wouldn't accept a mere beating—not for this one who had offended them so many times. They incited the Jews against Jesus. Instead of pleading for His freedom, they demanded the release of a murderous rebel named Barabbas. And they insisted that Jesus be crucified."

A terrible hopelessness washed over Eleazar.

"So if the Jewish authorities had charge of the punishment, He would have died by stoning or burning or strangulation," he said. "But they left it to the Romans to carry out their evil plan." He shook his head despondently. "They must have truly hated the man to send Him to the most humiliating, painful punishment of all."

Benjamin ran a hand through his hair and nodded. He appeared to be on the verge of more tears. "Perhaps they feared Him," he offered. "In the end, they brought Roman judgment on one of their own—a kind-hearted Jew from Galilee, a worker of miracles, and what's more—the Messiah." The boy said the last word with such reverence, Eleazar felt a surge of heat rush to his heart.

Of course, the weak Pharisees and temple officials would have protected their own names by sending Jesus to the Romans for punishment. They would wash their hands of the judgment.

"The Romans are barbarians," Eleazar said, his voice harsh. "They've been known to place people in a sack to be drowned in the river. They've fed their enemies to wild beasts and dragged them behind running horses. Crucifixion is one of many ways they torment their foes."

"Crucifixion is still the worst of them all," said Benjamin. "Such a punishment doesn't begin and end with the nails. For Jesus, it meant a brutal flogging using a cord with nails and sharp stones attached. He was badly scarred, Father." The boy began to weep. "After they humiliated and tortured him, they made him carry his own crossbar. The humiliation continued on the road to Calvary. He hung on the cross for six hours and died a horrible death. Suffocation. That's what happens to someone who can't raise himself up to take a breath of air."

Eleazar stopped walking and faced his son. "Where were His friends? His followers?"

Then a depressing thought struck him. "If the Healer couldn't save himself, then what hope would there have been for *me*?"

Benjamin wiped tears from his face. "I don't understand it either, Father, but I do know He healed me and many others. But it's not too late for you. I've heard that all it takes is for you to believe, to trust that, even from the grave, He can heal you. You don't have to stand before Him. You don't need Him to touch you. You can simply believe."

Eleazar shook his head, a wave of despondency rushing through him. "I don't know, Benjamin. It all seems so hopeless." He stood very still pondering his choices.

"I want to go to Golgatha to the place of crucifixion—to Calvary. I want to see for myself."

"He's no longer there, Father. He was buried almost immediately, because of the Sabbath."

"I must go there. Quickly now."

They turned away from the temple and started toward Golgotha.

"They placed his cross at the highest place on Calvary," Benjamin told him. "His followers requested His body shortly before the Feast of Unleavened Bread, and they buried Him in the grave of a wealthy Pharisee named Joseph from the town of Arimathea. That wealthy man surprised the authorities when he asked for Jesus' body. It seemed he no longer feared their judgment, but proudly declared himself a follower."

Eleazar raised his eyebrows. "A Pharisee? Taking such a risk?"

"Yes, Father. And he wasn't alone. Another Pharisee named Nicodemus brought spices to anoint Jesus' body. More people are starting to come out of hiding after his death."

They exited the city at the Gennath Gate. When they reached the hill they found only the upright posts where crucifixes once stood. The hillside was strewn with stones, strips of cord, and long nails, the only remnants of the cruel acts that had taken place there.

Eleazar stepped upon the barren mound. An overwhelming sadness flooded over him. Kneeling, he bowed his head and pressed his fingers into the soil where only a short time ago fresh blood had dripped. Despite being near a heavily traveled road with people hurrying past, he felt no shame as he wept freely. He rocked back and forth, pouring out his sorrow, when a metal object caught his eye. The rising sun cast a glimmer of light on an iron nail lying within his reach. He picked it up and stared at it. Dried blood stained its sides.

He'd witnessed enough crucifixions to know what had happened on that hill. He had an image of a Roman soldier, this nail in one hand and a hammer in the other. He imagined the man swinging the mallet with all his strength. He pictured the flesh separating and the blood spurting out. He heard the splitting of bone and the anguished cry of the afflicted one. Sobbing, he pressed the nail to his bosom and bent his forehead to the ground. People continued to pass by. Some slowed their step. He felt their stares, heard their mumbled comments. Nothing mattered now except that he might meet the Healer somewhere amidst the broken ground.

Benjamin knelt beside him. "Father," he said softly.

"How could this have happened?" Eleazar straightened and sent his plea to heaven.

"I don't know, Father. He had enemies. The traitor who turned Him in was one of his own people. Yet, even in death, Jesus forgave His enemies. He hung on the cross for six hours and spoke only words of kindness to His persecutors. Many disturbances happened then. At midday, a darkness fell over the earth. The moment He passed, a terrible earthquake struck. People stumbled about. Several were killed by falling rocks. The ground opened up. Young men leaped aside and saved themselves. Levi was there. He'd been standing near Jesus' cross, a wicked smile on his lips. Then the earth separated, he tripped over his own feet and fell into the hole, and the ground closed over him."

Eleazar looked at his son in disbelief. "Levi was killed that day?"

"Yes, Father. That evil man came there to witness Jesus' crucifixion and he met his own end."

Eleazar stood to his feet and brushed the sand off his robe. "I'm afraid it's also too late for me."

"Perhaps not. Only a week ago, when you left home, Grandfather showed me a portion of a scroll written by the prophet Isaiah. He told me to read it and to commit it to memory. It goes like this, *All we like sheep have gone astray; we have turned every one to his own way, and the Lord hath laid on him the iniquity of us all.*"

Struck by the prophet's words, Eleazar could only nod. "I am a sheep that has gone astray. I turned to my own way. I deserve punishment."

"There's more, Father. The passage goes on to say, *He was pierced for our transgressions, he was crushed for our iniquities; the punishment that brought us peace was upon him, and by his wounds we are healed.* Don't you see, Father? We are healed. Not only my physical wound and my voice, but my soul. Yours too, if you would accept the truth of his promise."

He stared at his son, amazed that so much wisdom should pour from a mouth that once stumbled over simple words.

"Grandfather said the scripture points to the Messiah," Benjamin went on. "Can you see how Jesus fulfilled the prophecy? Can you believe, as we do, that He was who he claimed to be, the Son of God, the Deliverer?"

Eleazar left his son standing there and walked to the top of the mound. He looked out over the barren wilderness, then he turned his eyes to the sky and spoke the words that would change his life forever. "I do believe. Save me, Yahweh, from my sins, from the deceit of Satan, even from myself. I believe Jesus was who He claimed to be. The Messiah. *My* Messiah."

Moved again to tears, he inhaled deeply. Then turning toward Benjamin, he said, "I need to tell you how sorry I am for having neglected you these many years. Sorry I have been so consumed with my own selfish plans that I ignored the needs of my family. Please, forgive me, Benjamin."

The youth smiled. "I already have, Father. Come on. Let's go to the priest for your examination. Your family awaits you."

They located Mattathias in the men's court. As soon as he saw Eleazar, he hurried toward them, his priestly robe swirling about his feet.

"Physician, you have returned at an appropriate time. I've completed my early duties, and I'm free to examine you. Now, show me your arm."

His fingers trembling, Eleazar grasped his sleeve, then hesitated. "Whatever happens, I want you to know, Mattathias, that I am at peace."

The old priest smiled with understanding. "Eleazar, lift your sleeve."

Eleazar obeyed, but he looked away, unable to set his eyes again on the ugly blemish. Mattathias bent close. Eleazar's heart quickened.

"Physician, what have you done?" Mattathias' amazement was obvious.

"What do you mean? I haven't done anything."

"You used no ointment? No balm? No special herbs?"

"No. Nothing. I haven't even *looked* at my arm today. I refrained from setting my eyes on it, afraid of what I might find."

"Well, you can look *now*, my friend. Because the spot is gone."

Mattathias' lips broke into a broad grin. "Praise be to Yahweh! Eleazar, you are healed."

He looked at his arm and found his skin to be smooth and brown. There was no wound, no white hairs, no mark at all where the blemish had once been.

Benjamin shouted with joy. "You're healed, Father! You're healed!"

Mattathias pulled a handkerchief from his robe and mopped his brow and his eyes, then blew his nose. The old priest laughed aloud.

"My friend," Mattathias said, his voice quivering. "I rarely see such a change. The mark is gone."

Eleazar pressed the area where the spot had been. He dug his nails into the skin and flinched from the sting. It was as if the wound had never been there at all.

The cloud that had been following him over the last week had been lifted. He looked around, and what had seemed dull and uninteresting now burst with color. The walls of the court took on a golden hue. The sky was bluer. The singing of birds became clearer.

"I was afflicted, and now I am healed," he said with assurance. "Yahweh heard my prayer. Like King David declared, *In my distress I called upon the Lord, and I cried unto my God. He heard my voice out of his temple, and my cry came before him, even unto his ears.*"

He turned toward Mattathias. "I need to go home. I want to hug my daughters. I want to tell my wife I love her. I want to apologize for giving her so many years of grief. I want to tell Abi she can marry Malachi. I want to toss my little Martha above my head. And, most of all, I want to tell Judah he was right all along."

Mattathias held up a hand and laughed. "You will go home, but first, the law requires you to bathe and shave your head. We must sacrifice two birds. We'll kill one over fresh water, and we'll dip the other in its blood. Afterward you may go home. And, in eight days, you must return to the temple with a sacrifice of two male lambs and one ewe, plus an offering of grain and oil." Mattathias grunted out another laugh. "I'm afraid your release carries many conditions. But it is the law."

"Yes, yes, I know," Eleazar said, his heart pounding. "I am healed."

CHAPTER FORTY-SEVEN
Two Months Later

*E*leazar had heard the reports. Over the last few weeks, Jesus' followers had spread the word. Despite all the stories the chief priests told to explain away the empty tomb, a growing group of believers had gone around the city proclaiming the truth. Jesus had risen from the grave.

At the time of the crucifixion, many of them, fearing for their own safety, had gone into hiding for a while, but now they had begun to emerge from their hiding places and were teaching the good news. They met in homes to pray and to break bread together, and they told all who would listen about the wonderful works of Jesus their Savior.

Word went out that the resurrected Healer had been appearing to hundreds. Though Eleazar had never witnessed such an event, he believed the stories. As the number of Jesus' followers grew, they came out in the open and moved their meetings to public forums, risking their very lives to preach the good news of salvation through the anointed one.

On a warm summer morning, Eleazar and his son, Benjamin, loaded up two donkeys with packs of food, medicine, and clothing. Anna approached them in the courtyard. Eleazar stepped toward her and kissed her warmly.

"Did I remember to tell you this morning that I love you?" he said, his voice soft.

Anna didn't speak. She merely shook her head as tears streamed from her eyes.

Old Judah stood in the doorway, a satisfied smile on his lips.

Then Abi and little Martha burst from the house and leaped into Eleazar's arms. He stroked their hair, planted kisses on their foreheads, wrapped his arms around them.

Abi pressed her face against his chest. "Thank you, Abba, for giving your consent. You have made me very happy."

Then he lifted Martha above his head, spun her around until she squealed, and then handed her to Anna. "Be a good girl," he said. "Take care of your mother."

Releasing a contented sigh, Eleazar gathered the reins of the two donkeys, kept one set and handed the other to Benjamin. Then Father and son left the courtyard together. The girls followed for a short distance, laughing and dancing on the path behind them. Their voices grew fainter as he and Benjamin proceeded down the hillside into the Lower City.

At length the two of them reached the Dung Gate. The heavy wooden doors swung open and let in a blast of fresh air. They stepped outside the city and paused on the ridge. Eleazar took a deep breath. Then he stepped up to his donkey and opened one of the packs. He reached inside and withdrew a straw doll—a gift for Suzannah. It's curls were made from yarn and a black line of thread created a smile on its face. It wore a garment of soft blue linen and a veil of white lace—Anna's handiwork. He smiled and gently returned the doll to the pack.

Before starting out, he turned to his son. "Are you in agreement?"

"What do you mean, Father?"

"I told you where I am going. You can turn back if you want."

"No, I'm not afraid. Not as long as I'm with you."

"All right then. Come." He waved his hand.

As they walked, Benjamin drew close to his father, a perplexed frown on his young face.

"I wondered about your decision, Father. You waited for years to be summoned by the Council. Now that they offered you a seat, why did you turn them down?"

Eleazar laughed. "Isn't it obvious, Benjamin? I have better things to do."

Then, facing east, he gave the donkey's rope a tug, and the two of them started off in the direction of Jericho.

Therefore if any man be in Christ,
he is a new creature:
old things are passed away;
behold, all things are become new.
1 Corinthians 5:17

Acknowledgements

As always, I thank my beta readers who gave me valuable feedback that helped to make this book better, including Paula Parker, Chuck and Delores Kight, and my daughter, Joanna Jones.

This manuscript remained in a drawer for 30 years and would never have been published if not for Mike Parker and Word-Crafts Press. Mike's editing skills have brought my work to a much higher level, and his words of encouragement keep me pressing on.

Thanks also go to cover designer, David Warren, a talented artist who has designed beautiful covers for all my books.

And, of course, I am eternally grateful to my Lord and Savior, Jesus Christ. Because of his gift of salvation I no longer have to live with a leprous heart, and I am free to extol His amazing virtues within the pages of my books. There is no doubt, he is the real star of *The Leper*.

Sources

All the Miracles of the Bible, by Herbert Lockyer, Zondervan Publixhing, 1965.

Ancient Israel, (Volume 1), by Roland DeVaux, McGraw-Hill, 1965.

Baker's Bible Atlas, by Charles F. Pfeiffer, Baker Book House, 1979.

Basic Judaism, by Milton Steinberg, Harcourt, Brace & World Inc. 1947.

Bible as History, The, by Werner Keller, Bantam Books, 1979.

Bible Almanac, The, by J.I. Packer, Merrill C. Tenney, & William White Jr. Thomas Nelson Publishers, 1980.

Chronological Charts of the Old Testament, by John H. Walton, Zondervan Publishing, 1981.

Chronological Charts of the New Testament, by H. Wayne House, Zondervan Publixhing, 1981.

Columbia Viking Desk Encyclopedia, The, Viking Press, 1968.

Eerdman's Handbook to the Bible, Ed. David & Pat Alexander, Wm. Eerdman's Publishing, 1973.

Encyclopedia of Bible Difficulties, by Gleason L. Archer, Zondervan Publishing, 1982.

Feasts of Israel, The, by Victor Buksbazen, The Friends of Israel, 1954.

Field Worker's Medical Manual, Summer Institute of Linguistics, 1978.

Finding Out about Bible Times, by Deborah Manley, Chariot Books, 1980.

540 Little Known Facts about the Bible, Ed. Robert Tuck, Doubleday & Company, 1980.

God and His People, by Harold Bassage, 1966.

Gospel in the Feasts of Israel, The, by Victor Buksbazen, The Friends of Israel, 1954.

Great People of the Bible and How They Lived, Reader's Digest Association Inc. 1971.

Handy Home Medical Advisor, The, by Morris Fishbein, M.D., Doubleday & Company, 1963.

In the Steps of the Master, by H.V. Morton, Dodd, Mead & Company, 1934.

Jerusalem, by Colin Thubron, Time-Life Books, 1976.

Jerusalem as Jesus Knew It, by John Wilkinson, Thames & Herdson Ltd. London, 1978.

Jewish Community, The, Volume 3, by Salo W. Baron, Jewish Publishers, 1942.

Jewish Holy Days, by Coulson Shepherd, Loizeaux Brothers Inc. 1983.

Jewish Theology, by Kaufmann Kohler, Macmillan, 1918.

Josephus, Complete Works of Flavius Josephus, Translated by William Whiston, Kregel Publications, 1981.

MacMillan Bible Atlas, by Yohanan Aharoni & Michael Ani-Yonah, Macmillan Publishers, 1977.

New Chronological Bible, The (KJV), Ed. R. Jerome Boone, World Publishers, 1980.

New Compact Bible Dictionary, The, Ed. T. Alton Bryant, Zondervan Publishing, 1977.

New Harper's Bible Dictionary, The, by Madeleine S. Miller & J. Lane Miller, Harper & Row Publishers, 1973.

New Marked Reference Bible, The (KJV), John C. Winston Company, 1980.

New Scofield Reference Bible, The (KJV), Ed. C.I. Scofield, Oxford University Press, 1967.

New Testament Survey, by Merrill C. Tenny, Eerdman's Publishing, 1961.

NIV Pictorial Bible, The, Zondervan Publishing, 1978.

Our Jewish Friends, by Louis Goldberg, ThD. Moody Bible Institute, 1982.

Philosophies of Judaism, by Julius Guttmann, Jewish Publishers, 1964.

Principles of the Jewish Faith, by Louis Jacobs, Vallentine Mitchell, London, 1964.

Promised Land, The, by M. Dubuit, O.P., and Raoul Blanchard, Hawthorn Books, 1966.

Ryrie Study Bible, The (NASV), Charles Caldwell Ryrie, Moody Press, 1978.

To Be a Jew, by Rabbi Hayim Halevy Donin, Basic Books Inc. 1972.

Traveler's Key to Jerusalem, The, by Martin Lev. Alfred A Knopf Publisher, 1989.

Treasures from Bible Times, by Alan Millard, Lion Publishing, 1985.

Understanding the Middle East, by Joe E. Pierce, Chares E. Tuttle Company, 1971.

Unger's Bible Handbook, by Merrill F. Unger, Th.D, Ph.D, Moody Press, 1979.

Victor Handbook of Bible Knowledge, The, by V. Gilbert Beers, Victor Books, 1981.

Village of the Outcasts, by Robert M. Wulff, Doubleday & Company, 1967.

Whycliffe Historical Geography of Bible Lands, by Charles F. Pfeiffer & Howard F. Vos, Moody Press, 1979.

About the Author

Pulitzer Prize nominee in the field of journalism, Marian Rizzo has won numerous awards, including the New York Times Chairman's Award and first place in the 2014 Amy Foundation Writing Awards. She worked for the Ocala Star-Banner newspaper for 30 years. She also has written articles for the *Gazette*, *Ocala Style Magazine*, and Billy Graham's *Decision Magazine*.

Several of Marian's novels have won awards at conferences and retreats. In 2018, her suspense novel, *Muldovah*, was a finalist in the Genesis competition at the American Christian Fiction Writers Conference.

Marian earned a bachelor's degree in Bible education from Luther Rice Seminary. She trained for jungle missions with New Tribes (now ETHNOS 360), and she served for two semesters at a Youth With A Mission training center in Southern Spain. Several years ago, she made a trip to the Holy Land, a visit that provided much of the backdrop for this novel.

Marian lives in Ocala, Florida, with her daughter, Vicki, who has Down Syndrome. Her other daughter, Joanna, has blessed her with three wonderful grandchildren.

Also Available from
WordCrafts Press

The Sisters of Lazarus Trilogy
by Paula K. Parker

Jesus * Judas
by Ralph E. Jarrells

Oh, to Grace
by Abby Rosser

The Black Series
Jennifer Odom

www.wordcrafts.net